SENTINEL

TITLES BY MARK GREANEY

THE GRAY MAN

ON TARGET

BALLISTIC

DEAD EYE

BACK BLAST

GUNMETAL GRAY

AGENT IN PLACE

MISSION CRITICAL

ONE MINUTE OUT

RELENTLESS

SIERRA SIX

BURNER

THE CHAOS AGENT

RED METAL

(with Lt. Col. H. Ripley Rawlings IV, USMC)

ARMORED

SENTINEL

SENTINEL

MARK GREANEY

BERKLEY

NEW YORK

BERKLEY
An imprint of Penguin Random House LLC
penguinrandomhouse.com

Library of Congress Cataloging-in-Publication Data

Names: Greaney, Mark, author.
Title: Sentinel / Mark Greaney.
Description: New York : Berkley, 2024. | Series: Armored ; vol 2 |
Identifiers: LCCN 2024005644 (print) | LCCN 2024005645 (ebook) |
ISBN 9780593436912 (hardcover) | ISBN 9780593436929 (ebook)
Subjects: LCGFT: Thrillers (Fiction) | Novels.
Classification: LCC PS3607.R4285 S46 2024 (print) | LCC PS3607.R4285
(ebook) | DDC 813/.6—dc23/eng/20240207
LC record available at https://lccn.loc.gov/2024005644
LC ebook record available at https://lccn.loc.gov/2024005645

Printed in the United States of America
1st Printing

Book design by George Towne
Interior art: Helicopter in the sky with lightning © Lafoto / Shutterstock

For my wonderful mother-in-law, Anne Gibson.

We love you, Mimi!

Only the thing for which you have struggled will last.

Nigerian proverb

CHARACTERS

JOSHUA "JOSH" DUFFY: Special Agent, Bureau of Diplomatic Security, U.S. Department of State

NICHOLE DUFFY: Foreign Service Officer, U.S. Department of State

AMANDA "MANDY" DUFFY: Age 8

HARRY "HUCK" DUFFY: Age 6

JAVIER "JAY" COSTA: Regional Security Officer, Bureau of Diplomatic Security, U.S. Department of State

CHAD LARSEN: Assistant Regional Security Officer, Bureau of Diplomatic Security, U.S. Department of State

BENJAMIN MANU: Foreign Service National Investigator, U.S. Embassy, Accra, Ghana

JENNIFER DUNNIGAN: U.S. Ambassador to Ghana

ROBERT GORSKI: Senior Operations Officer, Central Intelligence Agency

RICHARD MACE: Chief of Station, Ghana, Central Intelligence Agency

KANG SHIKUN: Senior Operations Officer, People's Republic of China, Ministry of State Security

HAJJ ZAHEDI: Colonel, Islamic Republic of Iran, Revolutionary Guard Quds Force

FRANCIS AMANOR: President of the Republic of Ghana

CONRAD "CONDOR" TREMAINE: Former South African National Defence Force Lieutenant Colonel, Director of African Operations—Sentinel Security Inc.

LEV BELOV: Former Russian military officer, former Wagner private military contractor, Sentinel mercenary

CORNELIUS (KRELIS): Sentinel mercenary—Netherlands

ISAAC OPOKU: Police officer, River Command—Volta River Authority

JUNIOR: Sentinel mercenary—South Africa

KWAME BOATANG: General, Ghana Armed Forces (GAF) Central Command

PROFESSOR MAMADOU ADDO: Leader of the Dragons of Western Togoland Restoration Front (Ghanaian rebel force)

JOHANNA ALDENBURG: High Representative of the European Union for Foreign Affairs and Security Policy

JULIAN DELISLE: Director of the high representative's protection detail, European Union

CHEN JIA: Senior Technical Contractor, People's Republic of China, Ministry of State Security

ABBREVIATIONS

AIC: Agent in Charge

ANP: Afghan National Police

APD: Ambassador's Protection Detail

ARSO: Assistant Regional Security Officer, Bureau of Diplomatic Security, U.S. Department of State

ARSO/I: Assistant Regional Security Officer for Investigations, Bureau of Diplomatic Security, U.S. Department of State

BNI: Bureau of National Intelligence, intelligence agency of Ghana

COS: Chief of Station, CIA

DS (OR DSS): Bureau of Diplomatic Security, U.S. Department of State

FSNI: Foreign Service National Investigator, U.S. Embassy, Ghana

FSO: Foreign Service Officer, U.S. Department of State

IRGC: Iranian Revolutionary Guard Corps

LBG: Local Body Guard, U.S. Embassy, Ghana

LGF: Local Guard Force, U.S. Embassy, Ghana

MSS: Ministry of State Security—Chinese intelligence arm

PRC: People's Republic of China

RSO: Regional Security Officer, U.S. Department of State

VRA: Volta River Authority—Ghanaian government-owned administrative body of the Akosombo Hydroelectric Dam

SENTINEL

PROLOGUE

THIRTY-FIVE YEARS AFTER ITS MAIDEN VOYAGE, THE *TOSCANA*
Empress still had never sailed anywhere within twenty-five hundred
nautical miles of its namesake of Tuscany, Italy; nor, for that matter,
had any of its crew. An offshore supply vessel based at the Port of Lagos,
Nigeria, the seventy-meter-long craft had been used for decades to
transport personnel, equipment, and provisions to Nigeria's thirteen
offshore oil rigs, all within a couple dozen miles of Lagos, but it had
never traveled beyond these familiar waters.

Until now. From the predawn mist, the rusty red-hulled vessel
glided into view of the coastline, 140 miles to the west of Lagos,
growing in size as it neared the bright lights of a modern shipping
terminal.

The West African nation of Togo is an impoverished place, ranking
143 on the world economic scale between Mauritania and Kyrgyzstan,
but the Port of Lomé on the southwestern edge of the nation was new
and modern, sparkling in the fog like a beacon towards the sea.

The Chinese had loaned Togo the money to construct this terminal, but the interest had been high for the locals; in exchange for
the funds to build the port, they'd given up nothing less than
their territorial integrity. Ostensibly the Togolese owned the land and

controlled access to the facility, but in truth the Chinese had the ultimate say on what, and who, made its way into the country by water.

They called it "debt-trap diplomacy." Loan a poor nation enough money to get itself into trouble, then control it with the compromise of debt.

The Chinese didn't invent this ploy, but they had perfected it in Africa.

A man on the dock watching the approaching supply ship adjusted his binoculars, then lowered them, taking a moment to look around his environs. Four men stood behind him, as still as stone. Twelve tractor-trailers, each with a local driver at the wheel, were parked in a row behind them, and a cluster of seven worn but powerful Land Rovers idled nearby, as well.

The man with the binoculars began approaching the water's edge, while the four behind him held their positions.

The *Toscana* sailed right into port, dockworkers who came in early this morning for the arrival tied it down at the bow and the stern, and within minutes the gangway lowered on creaking chains. As previously planned, the man climbed the steps onto the vessel, and after receiving directions from a crewman, he made his way across the deck, down a ramp, and into a massive cargo hold.

The lighting was poor but good enough for him to see exactly what he'd hoped to see.

His mercenaries.

Twenty or so in number, sitting on or standing around crates and duffels. More crates rose to the ceiling on the far side of the space. Sleeping bags had been rolled up, gear packed up smartly, but the hold smelled like food, sweat, and piss.

Mostly piss.

But the man was not fazed, because it was impossible to faze Kang Shikun.

According to his business card, Kang Shikun was the director of Shenzhao Star Global, a midsized private security company that protected Chinese-owned mining and construction concerns all across sub-Saharan Africa. There were hundreds of such firms on the continent because of China's interest in the development and extraction of resources from dozens of nations here.

But Kang's position with Shenzhao served merely as a front for his real work. For the past sixteen years Kang had been employed by the Ministry of State Security, China's all-encompassing foreign and domestic intelligence concern.

The four men traveling with him were MSS, as well. Body men. Former People's Liberation Army officers; intelligent men all, but men also good with guns, good with knives, good with intimidating looks.

Kang himself knew how to fight. Before becoming a spy he'd spent eight years as a member of Arrow, the elite Beijing Military Region Special Forces Unit.

And now Kang was the African expert that Chinese intelligence sent in to do the most difficult tasks, and his reputation as a tough, smart, and resourceful operative had grown into legend back at MSS.

Virtually all the mercenaries in front of him now wore beards, cargo pants, and either T-shirts or tank tops, or else they were bare-chested. The hold was stuffy and the nighttime temperature over eighty degrees. Some were Black, most were white, and Kang quickly scanned the crowd for signs of alcohol use. He searched for bleary eyes, empty bottles, cuts and bruises on their faces, the telltale signs of bar fights. He'd dealt with drunk mercs here in Africa in the past, and he demanded utter sobriety at all times from the people who worked under him.

This ensemble of hard men, to his pleasure, seemed completely switched on. Even in the poor light he could make out clear and serious faces, though the majority of them appeared completely un-impressed with his arrival.

These men were clearheaded, at least, but they didn't have the discipline that Kang had learned to expect and appreciate in his own men. Here in the cargo hold, backs were slumped; many mercenaries had kept their seats when he entered.

A man in back spit on the deck in front of him.

A show of disrespect, or it would have been if Kang didn't know this type of individual. They'd keep up their air of detached defiance, and they would do their jobs.

And that was all he needed out of them.

It took him a moment, but he finally recognized a face in the crowd. A strongly built bear of a man in his late forties, with a dark brown mustache and a goatee, and skin just slightly pocked from a childhood disease, stepped forward and extended a hand.

Kang shook it with a little bow. He said, "Hello, Tremaine. Nice to be working with you again."

The man did not smile back. With a strong South African accent, he said, "Let's hope this goes better than it did in Niger."

Kang considered his response before he spoke. Finally, he said, "Niger was a success, on paper, at least, but of course I understand why you might not see it that way."

"Three of my boys dead. Three more injured and sent home to their families with no ability to earn a good wage. I guess I missed the paper that described that as a success."

Kang said nothing, unfazed as always. He just eyed the larger man.

After a time the South African seemed to lighten up, if only just a shade. He turned to the men behind him. "Boys, you take orders from me. I take orders from him. It's as simple as that."

The men in the shadows looked on.

"How many?" Kang asked now.

"Twenty-one of us, myself included. The usual suspects."

Kang looked over the man's shoulder at the group arrayed there. With a nod, he said, "As we discussed, I'll need more. A lot more."

"You have an aircraft available for me?"

"As you requested. A Cessna Caravan. Local pilots, but good. Fueled and at your disposal."

Tremaine nodded. "I'll fly out tomorrow to talk to the Russians." His eyes drifted a moment. "They'll be looking for work; their last job didn't turn out so good for them." He again fixed his steely gaze on the man from China. "I reckon I can get us fifty more quality operators."

"Good." Kang looked past Tremaine now, past the other humans in the hold, and fixed his eyes on the crates and pallets behind them, stacked to the ceiling. "What did you bring?"

"Two hundred forty-six tons. Everything we talked about. Body armor, small arms, heavier weapons." He shrugged. "For the rebels . . . old stuff, but battle tested, bought in Nigeria from the underworld, stolen from a government cache in Port Harcourt. Four hundred eighty AKMs, seventy thousand rounds of 7.62, fifty-two PKMs. Twelve cases of pistols, nine-millimeter ammo, plus basic load. Webbing, walkie-talkies. We aren't equipping a proper army, but we'll kit your boys up to make an honest show of it."

The Chinese intelligence officer was pleased. "Very well. Your men will begin training the rebels immediately while you go and talk to your Russian friends."

"Didn't call 'em 'friends,' did I?"

"Is there a problem?"

Tremaine shrugged. "I've operated against them before. I won, they lost." He added, "Here's hopin' they aren't sore losers, yeah?"

"We need them."

"I can be charming." Tremaine deadpanned this, causing Kang to question whether the South African could be charming in the least.

From the back of the cargo hold a voice came. "We ain't just training troops, are we? We're gonna do some killing, as well, yeah?"

Kang pegged this accent as South African, just like Tremaine's. He stared the younger man down a moment before he replied. "You know what you need to know for now."

Tremaine looked back at his subordinate. "Nothing more out of you, Junior."

Junior still looked into the angry eyes of the Asian man as he answered his superior. "Yeah, boss. Sorry."

Kang held the gaze, but then he answered. "You will be doing quite a bit of killing. It is West Africa. Violence is a given. Even where we are going." He seemed to think a moment. "*Especially* where we are going."

When he said nothing more, the men all rose and began moving the crates with two-wheelers out of the cargo hold and up a ramp to the main deck.

AFTER AN HOUR AND A HALF THEY WERE LOADED UP, AND THEY began leaving the shiny new container port as the first glow of morning sun began to burn the fog.

Less than a mile up the blacktop road, Kang, Tremaine, and the first few trucks were joined by six pickup trucks full of men. Tremaine looked out at the vehicles, at the dark figures in the beds. He saw no weapons, which was good. A convoy of this size drew enough suspicion, even with the vehicles spread out with a kilometer of space between them.

Guns in the hands of the men visible would draw more.

They'd be armed, of course, but they kept their weapons out of view, and the South African respected this.

Tremaine himself carried a Beretta 92FS pistol on his hip. In his bag was a folding-stocked Vektor R5 battle rifle, just like the rest of the team.

A Dutchman who went by the nickname Krelis—his given name was Cornelius—sat next to the South African and leaned close in his ear. "You've got a history with this Chinaman?"

Tremaine nodded. "The guy looks like a history professor, but he's as cold a fucker as I've ever come across. He had us slot a roomful of bandits in Eritrea, all of them just boys. They'd stolen a couple of trucks, but the trucks had equipment he needed. He didn't know what the boys had seen, and he didn't trust the kids to keep their mouths shut. Must have been a dozen. We shut their mouths, we did. No comebacks."

Krelis looked up at the man sitting behind the passenger seat. "What happened in Niger?"

"What always happens to guys like us?"

"You were expendable."

"And Kang didn't have a problem expending us. Three dead out of eighteen; we survivors were paid well." He shrugged. "That's the job, isn't it?"

Krelis nodded.

"Kang is the best operations man in country for his government, and the Chinese are throwing money around this continent to make sure he gets his job done."

Krelis said, "When China throws its money my way, I grab it, salute, and do what it tells me."

"Do what *I* tell you," Tremaine said, a finger in the Dutchman's face. "We're here to kill, not to die. Stay out of a body bag, and then you can enjoy that Chinese money."

"An order I'm happy to obey, boss."

The truck rolled north out of town, disappearing into triple-canopy jungle just as the approaching dawn began to illuminate the blacktop road.

ONE

OVER ONE HUNDRED TWENTY CONTRACTORS EMPLOYED BY UNITED Defense Services Group, a private military corporation based in the United Kingdom, lived and worked here at Forward Operating Base Blackbird on the outskirts of Jalalabad, Afghanistan. Conditions weren't nearly as austere as some of the regular military FOBs in the area; the men at Blackbird enjoyed decent chow, a well-appointed outdoor gym, good Internet, and a team room with a massive projection TV, along with a collection of over three hundred DVDs.

And alcohol, under certain restrictions.

The big TV in the team room came alive at four p.m., and a crowd of men sat in front of it, all guys who were finished with their work and had no more missions scheduled for the rest of the day.

They'd cleaned their trucks, cleaned their weapons, and changed out of their gear, and now they lounged around the team room on cheap sofas or sat in camp chairs. A couple of the men smoked cigars. Beer or hard liquor was consumed by those who were officially off the clock, but others drank water and soda, knowing they could still be called out at any time on an in extremis op, even if no movement had been previously scheduled.

After a heated argument between the half dozen men who gave a shit, *Blade Runner* was chosen for the afternoon film, and the DVD was slipped into the machine.

A bearded man crossed the room in front of the crowd and pulled the blinds shut, removing a harsh glare from the screen, blocking out the scorching Middle Eastern summer's day outside.

The film began with an opening crawl of text that explained the Nexus phase of replicants created by Tyrell Corporation, but many of those in the large room continued their raucous conversations, to the displeasure of someone on a sofa at the front.

"Everybody shut the fuck up!"

"The movie hasn't even started yet, mate," a man with an Aussie accent shouted back.

"The hell it hasn't. Listen to that Vangelis score. *That's* what I'm here for!"

The chatter died down a little, but not much.

"Somebody turn off the damn light!" a different voice yelled out now, also from the front near the TV, and a young man in the back of the room got up from his padded nylon chair, walked barefoot to the light switch, and flipped off the overhead.

He returned to his seat, reached over to the drink fridge next to him, and pulled out a can of Red Bull. Taking a sip, he told himself he'd watch the show until Sean Young saved Harrison Ford by killing Leon, and then he'd go back to his hooch and call his girlfriend in Richmond, Virginia.

Out of all the men in the room, out of all the men working here at FOB Blackbird, in fact, Josh Duffy was the third youngest at twenty-six. But he was far from a newbie. After four years in the U.S. Army, he'd been hired as a high-threat civilian contractor providing security around the Middle East and North Africa, and now, after nearly eight uninterrupted years living in the sandbox, he was a seasoned veteran, despite his boyish looks.

The contractors in the room slowly simmered down as the film played, and Josh sat there alone sipping his drink. He wore a gray United Defense T-shirt and khaki cargo shorts, a light brown beard and mustache, and hair that hung almost to his neck.

His girlfriend liked his hair long, and in the nearly two months since he'd last seen her he'd been trying to grow it out for her approval upon his return to the States.

And that wasn't all he'd done that he hoped she'd approve of.

One of the contractors here at Blackbird used to work as a tattoo artist, and he'd inked a lot of the men around the team house. Josh had gone to him just a couple weeks earlier, and now on his left pectoral the young man wore a heart with the name "Nikki" across it, still slightly red and slightly raised.

He hadn't revealed this new addition to his body to his girlfriend yet; it was a major statement, after all, and not something to just whip out on a random FaceTime call.

But it wasn't like she didn't know how he felt. They'd gone engagement ring shopping in Europe on his last leave, and in Florence they found what she said was the perfect ring, if not for the high price tag.

Josh had applied some misdirection, agreeing that it was more than he could afford, but as soon as he put her on a plane back home to Virginia the next morning he raced back to the shop and bought the ring.

It *was* too expensive, in fact, but he didn't care. He'd give her the ring in three weeks on his next leave, and he was already working on his proposal.

He'd booked a table for two at the most romantic restaurant in Richmond—according to the Internet, anyway—and he'd spent time in his hooch over the past couple of weeks writing out what he wanted to say.

He was in the middle of reciting his proposal to himself while the movie played on, and only stopped when an African American sitting on a dirty vinyl couch just in front of him turned and said, "Yo, Duff, pass me a Miller Lite. Make sure it's cold."

Everybody here called Josh Duffy "Duff," and he doubted most people knew that it wasn't his real name.

Duff obliged the man's request, reaching into the fridge and pulling out a cold can of beer, then bringing it over.

"Thanks, kid."

"You bet."

Mike Gordon was Josh's team leader, but Duff had a tendency to do what people asked of him without complaint, even if they weren't his superiors.

Gordon cracked the can and brought it to his lips, but before he could take a sip, a booming voice with a South African accent yelled over the soundtrack of the movie.

"Got an in extremis to the airport! I need three volunteers to go with me."

Heads turned to a big man standing in the doorway. He was in his early forties, with a handlebar mustache, a camel-colored bush hat, and a lean, pitted, and tan face. He wore his armor loose over his body, the cummerbund of the load-bearing vest hanging down halfway to the floor.

"Not it!" a tall South African with dark curly hair said near the front of the room.

"Not it," Mike Gordon said, as well, and he started again to take a drink of his beer.

But the South African just said, "Caruth, Gordon, Duff. Let's go."

"You said you were looking for volunteers," Gordon complained.

"Yeah? Well, you just got volun*told*. Picking up a couple of VIPs and dropping them at Fenty."

Duff knew this big South African. His name was Tremaine; his call sign was Condor. A senior section leader for United Defense, before that a major in the South African army, he'd been contracting around North Africa and the Middle East for the past five years or so. Duff had only been with this company for six months after moving over from another private military corporation, but in that time he'd conducted dozens of ops with Condor both here at J-Bad and on another contract down in Syria.

Condor was competent and highly intelligent, in Josh's estimation, but he was too sure of himself, too reckless, too dismissive of opinions other than his own.

In short, he was like a lot of senior contractors Josh had worked with over the past several years.

Gordon, Duff knew, neither liked nor trusted Tremaine. He'd had run-ins with him before and thought the senior contractor was shady, prone to deceit.

Duff, for his part, stayed out of it. Tremaine was his superior . . . Duff did what Tremaine told him to do.

Mike Gordon put his beer down on the table next to him, then stood reluctantly. The tall, curly-haired South African, Caruth, rose in the front of the room, let out another annoyed grunt, and began walking towards the door. "It's bleedin' *Blade Runner*, Condor."

"Back in ninety mikes," Condor replied. "We're taking the Askar, leaving the FOB at sixteen thirty. Move your asses!"

The other two men recruited for this hasty operation continued bitching, but Josh just rose, followed the big South African out the door, and hurried back to his hooch to gear up for a run outside the wire.

LESS THAN TEN MINUTES LATER, JOSH DUFFY ARRIVED AT THE MO-
tor pool and made his way past the dozens of vehicles parked there, finally arriving at the Askar, a Turkish-made armored personnel

carrier. The sun beat down on him, made all the more brutal by his full load-out. He wore a flameproof tunic, Kühl cargo pants, body armor, a ball cap, Vasque boots, Oakley sunglasses, a chest rack full of M4 magazines, and a utility belt holding a Glock 9-millimeter with extra mags for the pistol.

He carried his primary weapon in one hand and a go-bag in the other. The rifle was a Heckler & Koch 416, painted a faded green, brown, and camel camouflage and equipped with a three-power scope, a white light, and a laser.

The go-bag was full of food and water to last him seventy-two hours in the field, plus extra ammo and additional medical supplies that didn't fit in the IFAK, the individual first-aid kit that he wore on his load-bearing vest.

Andy Caruth and Mike Gordon showed up a minute later, both dressed similarly to Duff, and then Condor stepped out of a prefab building next to the motor pool with an M249 light machine gun on his shoulder, carrying a sheaf of paperwork in one hand and a cardboard whiskey carton in the other.

He put both items in the front passenger seat, then turned back to the three men standing around.

"We'll run buttoned up. Intel reports roaming Taliban in technicals, but IEDs continue to be the main threat. Big Army got hit about a klick from the airport yesterday. Just some potshots, no casualties, but let's stay inside the armor till we're at our destination."

Caruth took the wheel, Tremaine rode shotgun, and Gordon and Duff sat in back, leaving the third row empty for the two VIPs the South African had mentioned.

As they rolled out past the razor wire, the Hesco barriers, and the bomb-sniffing dogs, Josh automatically switched into full-on security contractor mode. He didn't think about Nikki, he didn't think about wedding rings or his future, he thought about his mission.

And Josh's mission was his sector. He looked out the rear

passenger-side window, scanned buildings and rooftops, empty dirt- and rubble-covered fields, roadside kiosks and market stalls.

And he also checked the road itself. It was Condor's job in front of him to help Andy Caruth watch for roadside bombs, often disguised or simply buried, but Duff couldn't help but keep an eye out, as well.

He'd run over an IED once in Syria; no one had been seriously injured, but it had rattled him for days.

Duff much preferred an enemy he could see, an enemy he could kill.

J-Bad was a dangerous place, but Josh had been here for three months, and other than some indirect fire—mortars dropped on FOB Blackbird from a distance—he hadn't seen any real action here.

Each and every day he worked escort missions around the city, and bad shit had happened in town since he'd been here; it just hadn't happened to him.

Still, he remained completely focused, at least until ten minutes into the drive to the airport, when Condor abruptly changed the mission.

"Caruth, take the next right. We're going straight to Fenty."

FOB Fenty was the main U.S. military forward operating base in Jalalabad, a five-square-mile complex that had been here for over a decade.

Gordon spoke. "What about the airport?"

"Gents, we're on special assignment."

"What assignment?" Caruth asked.

Condor said, "The company has authorized me to pick up an allotment of rifles from weapons depot"—he looked down at the paperwork in his hand—"vault twelve. It's there on the west side of the FOB behind the pistol range."

"How many weapons?" Caruth asked.

"One-twenty AKs."

Gordon cocked his head now. "How we gonna fit one hundred twenty AKs in here with the VIPs?"

The South African sniffed, then said, "We aren't picking up at the airport. Just going to Fenty and then back."

"Then why'd you say—"

"This operation is clandestine, signed off on by the home office."

Duff and Gordon looked at each other. Neither of them was sure what was going on, but both of them had skeptical expressions on their faces.

Caruth asked, "What does United need the AKs for?"

"I mean," Gordon said, adding to Caruth's thought, "if they're AKs in a weapons depot at a U.S. FOB, they're probably the property of the U.S., confiscated from the enemy and then handed out to the ANP. Why would we be—"

Condor said, "United's starting a counternarcotics training center, off site from Blackbird. They're bringing in a cadre from our base in Kabul, hiring some ex-DEA guys, and pulling trainees out of the Afghan army. The U.S. is giving us guns for the center. It's a CIA operation, need-to-know type of deal, and you three now know all you need to know."

This explanation did not slow down the questions. Gordon asked, "How do we just go to a U.S. military base and pick up all these weps?"

"I sign for them. It's all set up." After a moment of silence he said, "Just watch."

Gordon looked to Duff and mouthed the word *Bullshit*.

Duff turned back to the window and continued watching for trouble, but he was starting to think that trouble was inside the vehicle.

THEY ARRIVED AT THE FRONT GATE OF THE FOB, SHOWED THEIR DOD contractor badges to get on base, then drove for several minutes more before arriving at a weapons storage facility with a sign out front that read Vault 12.

Caruth stayed behind the wheel while Condor led Gordon and Josh through the harsh sunlight and into a dark and cavernous building.

Duffy noticed that Condor was carrying the carton of whiskey with him.

They made it to a check-in desk, and here an Army warrant officer in his thirties stood. Duff saw that his name tape read "Thacker," and he seemed to be expecting Tremaine. "Condor, good to see you. How's everything over at Blackbird?"

The South African looked around. "About the same as here, I expect."

"Doubt that," the warrant officer said, looking at the carton in the United senior officer's hand. "You've got booze over there."

Condor opened the carton, pulled out a bottle of Booker's, and put it on the table. "You've got booze here, too, if you know where to look."

Thacker smiled. After a moment he seemed to remember his task; he snatched a clipboard off his desk along with a pen, made an X on the line he wanted Condor to sign on, then passed it forward.

Gordon took a step forward and looked over Tremaine's shoulder as he signed, then slipped back next to Duff before the South African turned around to address the pair behind him. "Duff, Gordon, load 'em up."

The rifles came ten to a crate, and each crate also held forty magazines, plus a sling and a cleaning kit for each weapon.

Duffy and Gordon carried the twelve crates back to the vehicle, one at a time.

As Gordon shut the rear he turned to Duffy. "If this was a CIA op, we'd be getting this shit from the Agency, not from an Afghan police stockpile. Either Condor, United, or both are up to something pretty fucking fishy."

"How do you know, boss?"

"Because he just signed his name as 'Eric Cartman.'"

Duff's eyebrows furrowed. "The kid from *South Park?*"

Gordon looked furious. "We're being roped into something illegal here, kid."

Duff shrugged. "I just do as I'm told, Gordo."

The two men went to the back doors and climbed into their seats.

They left the base soon after, and back on the road it was quiet in the vic, only the radio chatter of other United vehicles in convoys around the city. It was a quiet afternoon—so far, anyway—and the roads weren't too heavily trafficked.

Eventually, Gordon spoke up. "I mean . . . no way we're not doing something shady."

Caruth gave a vigorous nod as he drove.

Condor sighed. "What do you feckers want me to say? Regional command called me from Kabul this afternoon, told me to take one truck to Fenty to pick up a dozen cases of rifles, and that's what I just fecking did."

Gordon snapped back at him. "They tell you to sign your name as a fucking cartoon character and to drop off a hundred-dollar bottle of whiskey to the warrant officer at the front desk?"

Condor sniffed now. After several seconds he said, "As a matter of fact, they did."

Gordon shook his head, and Duff felt tension rising in the vehicle.

The lone African American in the truck said, "Just tell us, man. What have you roped us into?"

Now Condor turned around in his seat and put a finger up towards Gordon, but before he could say anything, Caruth called out from behind the wheel.

"Oi! Eyes out. Somethin's not right."

"What is it?" Condor asked as he lowered his hand and turned back around.

Duff spoke up because he registered it, as well. "It's too quiet, boss."

They passed through a market area, usually bustling, even this late in the afternoon.

Condor looked out his window. "Where the feck is everybody?"

Gordon himself got back on mission. He called out from next to Duff. "My sector's clear but . . . you're right, this is like twenty percent of the people you normally see here at this time."

"That means increased Taliban activity," Condor said. "Stay sharp," he barked, and then added, "Duff, up on the two-forty."

The M240 machine gun on the top turret would provide a good defense to any attack, and though they'd been most concerned about roadside bombs, now the intelligence they were picking up from the atmospherics in the street was that there might be enemy personnel in the area.

Duff unfastened his seat belt and reached up for the top hatch. Fully engaged on popping out of the roof and manning the machine gun, he didn't see what Gordon and Caruth had both missed on their side of the vic.

A portion of the curb that was whiter, newer-looking than the rest of the road, just a meter in length. A torn and empty burlap sack lay across it, an attempt to hide the curb or, more exactly, an attempt to hide the fact that this was no real curb.

The few kilograms of concrete molded into the side of the road housed a 120-millimeter artillery shell, and a man a kilometer away on a rooftop had been watching this stretch of road for over ten hours, willing the U.S. military to pass by. The desert-sand-colored Askar was not an American military vehicle, but from the bomber's distance it looked like one, and no matter who was in the vehicle, he was certain they weren't Taliban, and that was good enough for him.

Just as Josh grabbed hold of the hatch lever, the man command-detonated the device with his phone, and it went off just ten meters in front of and to the left of the armored personnel carrier.

Josh Duffy registered nothing. His world simply turned black.

TWO

DUFF OPENED HIS EYES AND FOUND HIMSELF ON HIS SIDE, HIS BODY armor hiked up to his nose, his right temple and right shoulder hurting like hell.

His jaw felt like he'd just taken a left hook from a heavyweight.

It was so dark at first that he thought it was nighttime, but quickly the choking fumes in his throat and lungs told him something else was going on.

A sudden loud banging sound, somewhere close, helped to bring him back to the present.

He felt around and quickly figured out he was in the back of an armored car that had flipped onto its right side.

Another bang, just ahead of him, sounded like something had slammed into the roof of the vehicle at high velocity.

There were three men in here with him; he couldn't see them but he remembered now.

Two rapid pounding sounds came next, bullet impacts on armor, and now the smoke began to clear.

Condor was in front of him, on his side and moving. Caruth was strapped in behind the wheel, arms and head hanging down, either unconscious or dead.

Duff heard a voice, just a foot or so away from him on his left. "Fuck me." Mike Gordon coughed, and Duff felt a splatter of either spit or blood on the side of his face.

He slowly sat up to help Gordon out of his seat.

Condor spoke up now after a raspy cough. "Sound off."

"Gordon's good," Mike said with a cough of his own.

"Duffy's okay."

Caruth was moving now. The South African shook his head and spoke weakly but with humor. "Andy C's in the house."

Suddenly, automatic gunfire raked the truck. Bullets pinged off the armor, snapped against the bulletproof glass of the windscreen.

Condor reached for his radio, but then a heavy machine gun somewhere out on the street laid down fire on the stricken vehicle.

Condor screamed to the men in back. "Back hatch! Back hatch! Bail, bail, bail!"

Duff climbed over the big crates of AK-47s, making his way to the rear of the truck. He flipped the lever to open the hatch, then fell out of the door and onto the street, pulling his rifle along with him.

All the gunfire seemed to be directed at the front of the fallen Askar, so Duff used the machine to shield his body as he posted security for the other men while they bailed.

Almost instantly he saw a technical roll into view from a side street; a man stood in the back of a white pickup behind a Russian-made machine gun. Duff went prone on the asphalt and opened fire. His first half dozen shots hit the vehicle itself or sailed high, but then he slammed a .223 round into the machine gunner's stomach, causing the bearded man to fold up and fall out of the bed of the vehicle. Turning his attention to the two men in the cab now, Duff fired until he saw blood splatters on the glass, and then the technical rolled slowly forward until it hit an empty food stall and stopped.

He felt someone kick his boot and looked back to see Gordon on one knee just behind him, covering to the west. Caruth crawled out of the back of the vehicle next, blood dripping out of his beard, and took up a position facing east.

The last man out of the ruined armored car was Conrad Tremaine, call sign Condor.

He stayed low, walking on his kneepads, until he had his M249 light machine gun out the back, and then he rose and peered around the side of the vehicle, just under the still-spinning back left tire, six feet in the air.

He started to raise his weapon, but after a moment, he pulled his head back around.

He shouted to the three men around him. "PK shooter is reloading! We're going to that wall! Move!"

Duff looked up and saw a long, low concrete wall around a parking lot in front of a two-story building under construction. It looked like it could have been a shopping center of some sort, and Duff assumed he and the others would try to use the structure for cover as they bounded on foot away from the kill zone. He rose and led the way to the wall, his rifle up, and as soon as he came around the side of the fallen APC he began firing short bursts in the direction of where they'd been taking fire.

He wasn't even trying to hit anything, that would have been too much to hope for at the moment; rather, he was simply trying to keep heads down while he and his mates got to cover.

In seconds he'd crossed the fifteen yards to the low concrete wall; he rolled over it, then crawled a few feet along the wall so he wouldn't pop up right where he'd gone over. He brought his weapon up and emptied the rest of his magazine at a group of armed men positioned on a rooftop across the street while the other three contractors tumbled over the wall next to him.

Tremaine rolled back to his kneepads, ducked down low, and then grabbed his radio. "J-Bad Op Center, J-Bad Op Center, this is Condor, we are in heavy contact from technicals and dismounts at this time, how copy?"

There was no response.

Duff looked behind him, already planning to begin bounding out of the area, and he realized Tremaine had put them in a bad spot. The building next to the parking lot had no doors on this side of it; it was just a flat concrete wall with a small lip about three meters high and a row of open windows above it.

With their weapons and body armor and packs, there was no way they were climbing that wall to access the windows, especially under fire.

Tremaine squeezed several bursts out of his M249, the most potent weapon the four contractors had in this fight. Enemy had positioned themselves for an ambush, and Duff could tell that the only reason he and the others were still alive was that whoever detonated the IED had done it about a second too early.

He turned to Tremaine now while Caruth and Gordon fired at targets across the street to the east and north. "Boss! We've got to move laterally off the X, go around the side of this structure on foot."

Tremaine did not acknowledge him, he just shouted again into his radio. "J-Bad Op Center, this is Condor. We are in contact, time now. How copy, over?"

A response came, but it was garbled, and just as Condor was about to ask for the op center to repeat last, the PK machine gun opened up again. Bullets slammed into the wall just on the other side of them. Duff raised his weapon and fired without looking, still hoping he could get the attackers to bug out if he sent enough lead their way.

Duff saw that Tremaine was spending significantly more time on the radio than on his gun.

The South African shouted over the fire from the other three weapons. "Repeat last! You have us geo'd? We need QRF. Facing at least ten oppo."

Duff reloaded his weapon a second time. "Condor, we gotta go!"

"Negative," he shouted, and all of the others stopped firing and looked at him.

Tremaine said, "We hold this ground till the QRF comes." He fired a long burst from his M249 at a rooftop across the street.

Duff knew this was exactly the opposite of the doctrine contractors used in times like this. They had to get away from the ambush, because in a city like J-Bad, more and more fighters would respond to the sound of gunfire.

The correct course of action was flight, and Duff couldn't understand why Tremaine wasn't ordering them to move.

"Boss, we—"

Heavy machine gun fire blew massive chunks out of the wall they hid behind, dumping rock and masonry and concrete onto the men as they hunkered down.

Tremaine finally made contact with the ops center and was told QRF was en route with an ETA of ten mikes, and he fired again over the wall. As he ducked back down, he said, "We're not leaving those weapons! We have to take control of this intersection!"

"We have to do fuckin' *what*?" Gordon screamed as he dropped the magazine from his HK and slammed a fresh one in the mag well.

The PK machine gun continued chewing up the wall; all four men crawled twenty feet or so and popped back up, then continued firing on men and a couple of gun trucks.

And behind the wall, the four contractors continued arguing. Duff said, "We've got to boogie!"

Tremaine shook his head. "My orders are to guard those guns with my life."

"Go for it. But not *my* fucking life," Caruth shouted now.

The Taliban machine gunner walked the rounds down so that

they were now pulverizing the wall at the exact spot where the men had moved.

Tremaine moved again, then looked over the wall quickly. Once back out of the line of fire, he said, "There's an unmanned MG on a technical to our right!"

Duff knew about the unmanned Russian-made PK machine gun because he'd just killed the man who'd been operating it, as well as the pair in the cab.

Duff said, "What about it?"

"Go get on that PK, kid."

Gordon fired three rounds, then ducked back down. He shouted now, "No fucking way! Duff, you do *not* go out there."

All four men moved again, and seconds later the wall where they'd been taking cover completely failed, and bullets whizzed through the parking lot where the men had just been kneeling.

Duff raised his weapon at another part of the wall, then laid down an obscene amount of fire. After expending an entire mag, he knelt back down. "Condor, we can go around the side of this building and be a block away from all this shit in thirty seconds."

"I gave you a direct order, Duff! Get on that feckin' MG!"

Duff poked his head over the wall again and saw that the truck was about twenty-five yards away. It would have been suicide to run for it if not for the Askar lying on its side in the middle of the road. Duff thought the armored truck would block the enemy's view of him for about seventy-five percent of his run to the technical.

Gordon said, "Tremaine! We have to get out of here!"

Tremaine grabbed Duff by the shoulder strap of his body armor and shook him. "Kid, I'm not going to tell you again!"

Duff unslung his rifle and took off his pack. Leaving both there on the ground, he rose into a squat and then began moving along the low wall for another ten yards. Once there, he rolled over the top of it, landed on the street on the other side, and then began sprinting as fast as he could.

The machine gun on the other side of the armor kept booming at a cyclic rate, but Duff didn't feel that the fire was being directed at him until he passed the tipped-over Askar with the crates of AK-47s lying behind it.

As soon as he did so, asphalt blasted into the air in front of him, an AK chattered, and Duff knew at least one Taliban rifleman had seen him.

He kept running, the armor weighing him down, both his arms pumping furiously and, after a spray of rounds snapped right over-head, he climbed into the open bed of the truck, rolling onto his side. He scrambled behind the PK, pulled the bolt back to charge it even though the dead Taliban had already done so, then looked through the iron sights for the enemy.

The road ahead of him was nothing if not a target-rich environment.

He opened fire on the street, took out the enemy technical just as it blasted through another section of wall where his three coworkers had positioned themselves, then began walking his fire along a line of men at a wall on the opposite side of the street.

When the men scattered, he began raking bullets across a rooftop full of men.

He took some return fire, and something slammed into his chest plate, but he kept dumping big machine gun rounds in short, measured bursts.

He heard Tremaine's M249 working the area, as well, but he didn't hear either Gordon's or Caruth's weapons in the fight.

Forty-five seconds after manning the PK, thirty seconds after knocking out the other machine gun up the street, the Taliban force bugged out. Duff emptied the last of a two-hundred-round box-fed magazine at a fleeing truck, missing it low, and then he knelt to the bed, grabbed another ammo can, and began switching it out as fast as he could.

As he did so he shifted his focus over to the wall for an instant, just long enough to see Condor standing there, his M249 up to his shoulder, covering Duff's reload.

Once he racked a fresh round into the smoking-hot gun, Duff himself began looking for more targets, but only until he heard Mike Gordon yelling for him.

"Duff! Duff! On the double!"

Duff leapt off the gun truck and sprinted back across the road, passing the Askar and heading over to the ruined wall. Once there, he realized he didn't have to roll over the top as before; he could simply jump over some low cinder blocks, because there was a gaping hole in the wall carved out by the enemy machine gun.

Once he was on the parking lot side, he stopped in his tracks.

There was blood everywhere.

Andy Caruth lay on his back; Gordon had gotten his armor off him, revealing a gunshot wound to the upper chest, almost in his underarm area. The man's broken sunglasses were on the ground next to him, his eyes glassy and unfixed, and though he moved his mouth some, Duff couldn't hear a word he was saying.

Duff had more trauma training than Gordon, so he immediately took over the man's care. When Gordon didn't move away from the injured man, Duff said, "Gordo! Cover!"

Gordon nodded, almost imperceptibly, then lifted his rifle and began scanning the market ahead of him.

Immediately Duff went into action, pulling his IFAK out and removing a chest seal.

Tremaine continued to pull security; Duff could hear the sounds of approaching APCs and he knew the quick reaction force was on the way, but Duff had had as much medical training as anyone who would be on the QRF, so he was just going to have to try to save Andy Caruth on his own.

For the next five minutes, now protected by an eighteen-man QRF in three armored gun trucks, Duff worked on Caruth, putting an airway in his nose, doing what he could to control the bleeding. He'd been shot through a lung, the bullet had exited his back, and even with two chest seals and a thick roll of bandaging, he continued to bleed.

And then the bleeding abruptly stopped.

Duff's hands, his arms, and even his right cheek were smeared red by the time he sat back, wiped sweat off his brow with his forearm, and looked up to Gordon. "He's gone."

Duff looked around for Tremaine, then saw he wasn't even there. He found him in the middle of the road, working with more men to retrieve the crates of Kalashnikovs from the IED site and load them into the QRF's trucks.

Gordon called out to him. "He's dead, Tremaine."

The South African sighed in frustration, then walked back over to the two other men. Duff rose from where he'd been kneeling, then scooped up his rifle and his pack, putting them back on his body.

Tremaine turned back to one of the men by the QRF trucks. "Bobby, we need a bag."

"Yeah, boss."

A black body bag was pulled from the back of the vehicle and brought over, while Duff just looked on. The adrenaline was leaving his body now; he felt exhaustion, depression.

And then he felt rage. After several seconds standing there, covered in Caruth's blood, he said, "Andy's death is on you, Tremaine."

"Fuck you, kid. We weren't leaving all that equipment for the enemy."

Duff stormed up to the South African, his rage getting the better of him, and balled his fist. The older man threw a punch, but Duff ducked it, came back up, and threw his own punch.

Condor took a glancing blow to the side of his head, but with his next swing he dropped the younger, smaller, and less experienced man to the ground with a hook to his kidneys.

The South African stood over him now; Duff heaved and spit into the grit on the road. He tried to roll onto his side to get back up, but he found he couldn't move a muscle.

Right next to him on the ground, Andy Caruth's body was unceremoniously rolled into the body bag facedown and zipped up.

Tremaine had another body bag—Duff didn't know where it came from—and he opened it up, still standing over the prostrate American.

Duff lay frozen while Tremaine put him inside. He wanted to scream, but no sound came; his heart pounded in terror, but he could do nothing to stop it.

The zipper slowly shut over his face, over his eyes, and then all was dark.

THE MAN IN THE BATHROOM SAT ON THE TOILET WEARING TRACK pants and a sweat-soaked threadbare T-shirt that read "Army." His chest heaved up and down, and he wiped his eyes with the back of his forearm.

Though he breathed heavily, he did so quietly, biting the inside of his mouth to focus his thoughts and to push away the panic that threatened to overtake him.

It was just a nightmare, this he knew, but it was *always* just a nightmare, and that never seemed to make it any better.

And, if he was being honest with himself, it was *not* just a nightmare. The event *had* happened, though some of the details were different than what his conscious brain remembered; nobody put him in a body bag, for example, but the gist was the same.

Josh Duffy rose from the toilet, pulling himself up by the sink, then leaned against the sink's edge and wiped sweat from his clean-shaven face with a towel hanging nearby. He washed his face with cold water and dried it again. Staring into the mirror, he saw the twitch in his upper lip that often came in moments of high stress, and then he told himself that it would go away.

Just like it always did, it would go away.

And just like it always did, it would come back.

Maybe not the same twitch, the same nightmare, the same country, the same weapons, or the same outcome.

But the combat he'd experienced in his life seemed like it was always there to relive, hanging out just under the surface of his consciousness.

He hadn't dreamed of this particular event in Jalalabad in many months, maybe longer. The shootout had happened nearly ten years earlier, and in that time Duff had experienced quite a few other traumas that had taken J-Bad's place in his nightmares.

And not all of the trauma he'd experienced was contained solely in his brain. He flipped off the bathroom light before opening the door, then hooked his left underarm over a crutch and began moving into his darkened bedroom.

Josh Duffy moved nimbly across the floor, silent as a cat, even though he was missing his left leg below his knee, and even though the panic attack he'd just dealt with had made him want to crawl out of his skin screaming bloody murder.

But he made it back to his side of the bed quietly, sat down slowly and gently, then leaned his crutch against the nightstand and looked at the clock.

Three twelve a.m.

He sighed.

Carefully, he lay back in bed, covered himself with the blankets, and stared out the window in front of him. Biting the inside of his mouth again, he took a few calming breaths, then closed his eyes.

Every. Fucking. Night, he said to himself, over and over.

THREE

THUMPING AFROBEATS MUSIC PLAYED OUT OF SPEAKERS HANGING from trees, and locals drank and laughed and danced on the dirt-floored courtyard in front of a small thatched-roof structure that was nearly as dark as the jungle that encroached on it from three sides.

The gravel out in front of the roadside bar crunched under the weight of a dirty gray Land Cruiser as it pulled up and parked on the far side of the path, just off the riverbank and next to rows of scooters and motorcycles.

Five men climbed out of the vehicle and began walking through the crowd, and although the music kept pumping, the patrons of the bar immediately began to quiet down as heads turned.

The new arrivals weren't regulars. And they weren't locals, either.

All five of the white men wore beards, and one was bald; they ranged in age from late twenties to late forties, and the patrons of the bar didn't spend any time pondering who they were. This establishment lay just off a rural road on the Ubangi River, outside the city of Bangui in the Central African Republic, and every single person in the bustling courtyard was instantly certain of three things about the new arrivals.

They were Russian, they were mercenaries, and they were trouble.

The men strolled into the darkened covered area, a bar on a low concrete slab with a thatched roof above it, and sat down at a plastic table. A wary waitress crept over, her boss watching her from behind the bar while she took their orders, and within minutes she returned with their drinks.

By the time the men were served, the entire place had all but cleared out of locals, save for a stalwart few who were not intimidated and a couple more who were either too drunk to notice or too drunk to care.

A single fan hanging from the thatched ceiling only served to stir the warm night air around the five as they drank, illuminated only by a couple of small neon signs across the space and the glow from a strand of Christmas lights hanging from a wooden support beam. Fat flies buzzed all around, ignoring the gently swirling night air, and the chanted lyrics of a thumping hit by Fireboy DML had been turned down by the staff in hopes the foreigners wouldn't complain about the racket.

But the men did not complain, they just downed bottles of "33" Export beers and shots of Wa Na Wa vodka, and they kept to themselves.

Gruppa Vagnera, or the Wagner Group, was a private military corporation controlled by the Russian government that had fought in Syria and Ukraine, but its forces throughout Africa were simply known as Afrikanskiy Korpus, or Africa Corps. Here on the continent, the Russian organization operated like a mafia organization, but one of its many specialties was providing private security for weak leaders in exchange for lucrative natural resource rights.

The Russians had run timber, gold and diamond mines, and alcohol production and distribution all over Western and Central Africa, but when Wagner's leader's aircraft was blown out of the Moscow sky with him in it late one afternoon a year earlier, the organization immediately fractured, and the Kremlin began projecting its direct authority on the heretofore semiautonomous Russian contractors on the continent.

For that reason, the five in the bar here were no longer Wagner Africa Corps employees. They'd instead taken various security gigs on the continent, straight merc work, most recently here in the war-torn Central African Republic and across the border in the DRC.

And there were hundreds more Russians just like them around: here, in South Africa, in Nigeria, in Niger, in Ethiopia.

Some Wagner contractors had returned home, but most had not, because home meant the war in Ukraine, and the war meant stepping into a meat grinder. It also meant the previously well-paid soldiers of fortune would earn an enlisted soldier's wage in exchange for their deaths, a small fraction of what they were paid for fighting other people's battles down here in Africa.

These men felt abandoned by their company, by their country, by their people. They burned through their local money in bars and started fights, channeling the aggression that had been a key component of their jobs into their bleak civilian lives.

They were a powder keg waiting for a spark, and that spark arrived shortly before midnight.

A sudden gust of warm night air scattered the flies from the table a moment, and then the five Russians put their drinks down, because a lone white man approached through the nearly empty courtyard, stepping around the trees and tables on his way to the raised thatched-roof bar.

The stranger was athletically built, six feet tall, maybe fifty. He had wrinkles on his forehead and crow's-feet around his eyes, and he possessed a lean face pockmarked with some childhood ailment that even his dark goatee could not completely hide.

He wore a sweat-stained light blue linen shirt with epaulets, khaki cargo pants, and Merrell boots. Central casting for a Western security man in Africa, the men all realized, and over his shoulder hung a well-used Arc'teryx backpack.

The man seated at the head of the table watched him approach. The Russian had a bald head and a bushy beard, and he spoke softly in his native tongue, just audible to the others around him under the music. "Anybody know this asshole?"

The chorus from the men was unanimous. "Nyet."

A pistol hammer clicked under the far side of the table.

"Steady, Oleg," the man at the head of the table said.

The stranger stopped directly in front of him now. "Lev Belov? I'm told you speak English."

Belov's eyes narrowed. After a moment he said, "Who told you that?"

"Can you and I go somewhere to talk in private?"

"Hand your pack to one of my associates and lift your shirt."

The man in blue did as instructed; he wasn't carrying a firearm, and nothing in the bag aroused suspicion.

Satisfied, Belov nodded, motioned to the bartender, and ordered a beer and another bottle of vodka, and then he waved to the one empty seat at the little wooden table.

"Buy us a round of drinks?"

"Of course, but my business is with you. We can go discuss—"

"Sit down. These men don't speak five words of English between them."

The bearded stranger didn't seem pleased, but he did comply, taking an open plastic chair next to Belov.

Two bottles, a beer and a vodka, were placed in front of the new man by a waitress who immediately disappeared; rounds of the Wa Na Wa were poured for everyone and then downed without a corresponding toast.

Mistrustful eyes flitted around the table.

But the new man appeared relaxed, Lev Belov noticed. After he put his glass down, the stranger used his left hand to hold the beer while he reached out to the man at the head of the table with his right. "Conrad Tremaine."

Belov shook the man's hand. "You're South African?"

"From Pretoria."

One of the men at the table said something in Russian, asking Belov what the man was talking about, and Belov told him to shut up and to drink his beer. Finally, after pouring himself another shot, Belov said, "What do you want with me?"

"I want to hire you. Others, as well."

Belov sniffed out a laugh. "To do what?"

"You and your men are fighters, but if you only wanted to fight you would be back home by now, dying in a ditch in Ukraine. You're still here, which tells me you're looking for what comes next."

Belov didn't disagree with any of this. He just sat silently until the South African continued.

"My friend . . . *I'm* what comes next."

"Who says we need work?"

"You're in exile. Wagner has been folded into Russia's Ministry of Defense. Yeah, there are Africa Corps guys still out here, but they work for Moscow, they're paid shit Moscow wages, and they wake each morning hoping Moscow doesn't call them home to fight their neighbors.

"You and hundreds like you left the organization but stayed on the continent. You're working shit security contracts while the gold and timber and diamond extraction moves right on by you on its way back to Russia."

"You working alone?" Belov asked.

"No. I'm with Sentinel Security."

Belov just shrugged. "Sentinel. Never heard of you."

"You know us by our old name. Armored Saint."

The Russian's eyes narrowed now, a new tension in an already tense atmosphere. "Armored Saint was in Congo."

"Yes." Tremaine nodded. "I was there. Till the end."

Belov nodded. "So was I." After a moment he added, "On the other side."

"Sorry that didn't turn out so good for you guys," Tremaine replied. Off a look from the other man, he added, "That was a year ago, mate."

Belov's eyes narrowed even more. "You killed my friends a year ago."

"And you killed mine. But look around you. Surprise, surprise, Belov, the world keeps turning without them."

The other Russians had remained silent only because they didn't speak English, but Belov bristled at this. He was about to let this bastard know that he hadn't forgotten his friends, but then the bastard said something that instantly changed things.

"This employment contract will be for a maximum of seven months, six in training. I need you and I need a lot more men, and you will be paid a finder's fee for each quality shooter you bring me." He added, "By Christmas you'll be a very rich man."

Belov turned away from Tremaine and spoke Russian once again, this time to the man on the opposite end of the table. "It's okay, Oleg."

The audible sound of a pistol's hammer being decocked from under the table was not lost on Tremaine; Belov could tell it in the man's face when he looked back to him, but the South African made no mention of the fact that there had been a gun pointed at his balls.

"How many men are you looking for?" Belov asked now.

Tremaine remained cool. "I have twenty. South Africans, Nigerians, Germans, Dutch, a Chilean . . . I'd like fifty more. Can you get me that many?"

Belov whistled. "That's a massive crew. What's the job?"

"Direct action," the South African said without hesitation. "After the training, that is. Real spec ops work. Three- to five-man fire teams. Various weapons systems, various objectives. Blitzkrieg speed."

"Where?"

"Here in Africa. We'll be in Togo until the action, and for that we'll go over the border."

"Into Burkina Faso or into Benin?" Belov knew both of these border nations were exceedingly unstable.

"Into neither. Into Ghana."

"*Ghana?* Why there?"

Tremaine did not respond.

Belov looked off into the black jungle rimming the bar. "You won't tell me the reason, fine. Just tell me this: are we working for the government of the target nation or the opposition of the target nation?"

"That's another question I can't answer yet."

Belov raised an eyebrow, then sipped his beer. "When?"

"The planning's already begun. I need you and your boys now."

"What's the rate?"

"Five thousand euros a week per man . . . beginning once they're hired. That will shift to fifteen thousand a week once the operation begins. A completion bonus at the end, seventy-five thousand more."

"Benefits?"

"A death payout to the family of fifty thousand."

When the Russian didn't speak, Tremaine said, "A good wage for a half year's work, mostly planning and training. An excellent wage for an operation that should only require a week or two at most. And then a bloody ransom for when it's over. Don't try and negotiate with me. I know this is a dream opportunity for you and your people."

Belov sat in silence a moment. It was clear the man from Pretoria was annoyed by the delay, but the Russian just eyed him up and down as he drank his vodka.

"Well?" Tremaine finally prodded.

Finally the Russian said, "My people, my former employer, we have a reputation in Africa. We're the new colonialists. We're the invaders. The devils.

"But you white South Africans have done more killing on this continent than we ever will. Your mercenary outfits. You've got laws against them on the books, but you register your companies offshore so you can keep on doing your dirty work."

Tremaine didn't speak; he just sipped his beer, his eyes looking over the sweaty bottle at the Russian in front of him.

"Where is Sentinel registered?" Belov asked.

"Manila" came the reply, and Belov laughed.

"I told you."

Tremaine put his bottle down. "You think I traveled all the way to this shit hole for a lecture from an ex-Wagnerite?"

"No. I think you came all the way to this shit hole to get a crew of Russians who can help you with something dark and dirty. I can see it in your dead eyes, Mr. Tremaine. You are here because you are preparing your next slaughter, and you would like my help."

Tremaine did not blink at the accusation. "Have I wasted my time and yours?"

Putting his bottle back on the table, the Russian said, "You have not. We will take the work. I will find the men." He looked to the others here with them. "Two of these guys. Not the other two. Their door-kicking days are behind them, they just haven't accepted it yet."

Tremaine reached into his backpack under the still-mistrustful eyes of the other men. He first pulled out a wad of bills and threw them on the table, payment for his round of booze, and then he retrieved a small folded paper and handed it over to Belov.

The Russian took it and looked it over. "Signal number?" Tremaine nodded and handed over a blank sheet and a pen, and Belov wrote his own encrypted Signal phone number on it.

Tremaine said, "Wire info, too."

Belov jotted down the number of an account in Cyprus, folded the sheet, then handed it back. The men shook hands again while the others looked on.

The South African rose, and the Russian followed him up. Tremaine said, "I'll wire you some travel money tonight. Once you get me the first five men, I'll pay your wage, and theirs, for the first two months. It is in all of our interests to keep this a friendly relationship."

With a nod to the others, Tremaine turned away and began walking back into the courtyard and towards the front of the building.

The Russian sat back down, looked to the four men at the table, and spoke in Russian. "That man came alone. Unarmed. Big balls."

"What did he want?" Oleg said, and Belov just looked at him. After a moment he said, "Oleg, Vlad. Your drinks are on me." After a pause, he added, "Now . . . fuck off."

After an awkward silence, the two men stood and walked out into the night.

The two remaining Russians scooted closer to their leader. One of them said, "Who was that?"

"Tremaine. I've heard of him, but I didn't let on. A year and a half ago he was our mortal enemy down in the Congo. Now . . . now he's hiring us." Lev Belov added, "We're going to do some killing, boys."

"For who? For him?" the other man asked.

Belov shook his head. "That South African . . . he's one of us. A merc in the dirt. There will be someone else calling all the shots." The Russian sighed. "There's *always* someone else."

"Where are we off to?"

"Training in Togo. Action over the border in Ghana."

The man's response was the same as Belov's had been. "Ghana?"

Belov held his hands up, indicating he had no clue. But he said, "It's in the middle of the coup belt of Africa, even if it's not known as unstable. We're either going to go support a coup, or we're going to go defend against one by hunting rebels." The men hefted shot glasses, downed one more vodka, and then rose. Looking around the darkened bar, Lev Belov sighed and said, "In the end . . . who really cares?"

FOUR

ALEXANDRIA, VIRGINIA, LIES ON THE BANKS OF THE POTOMAC RIVER, just south of Washington, D.C., but this little cul-de-sac well west of the water felt a thousand miles away from the hustle and bustle of the nation's capital.

Tree-lined and quiet, Candlelight Court was the epitome of the burbs.

Just after seven a.m. on a frigid January morning the only movement inside 3802 Candlelight came from a woman opening the freezer in the kitchen, retrieving a box of Eggo waffles, and dropping two in the toaster. She then moved to a cabinet, pulled out a pair of white cups with the eagle emblem of the U.S. State Department on the side, and added creamer from the fridge to them both.

Nichole Duffy was an attractive thirty-five-year-old blonde, and she wore a dark blue pencil skirt with a white blouse, low heels, and eyeglasses. Already wide awake after a run and a cold shower, she'd even staged her purse, her heavy coat, and her shoulder bag by the door the night before.

A creature of habit, Nichole was a highly disciplined individual, and she knew her efficiency would be helpful this morning because she had others to lead.

After pouring coffee into both cups and taking a long draw from one of them, she pulled bowls of hot oatmeal out of a microwave, then made her way to a drawer and grabbed a fistful of forks and spoons.

She moved with pace, but methodically, not frantically. After all, she did some version of this most every morning.

A man in a dark suit came down the carpeted stairs and stepped into the family room, checking the knot of his burgundy tie in the mirror on the wall. Satisfied, he looked over to the steaming mug of coffee still on the counter and began advancing on it.

"Morning, babe," he said, a little tiredness in his voice, contrasting with his wife's more alert response.

She glanced his way as she pulled a plastic bottle of syrup from the pantry. "Any nightmares last night?"

"You look gorgeous today."

She looked at him and chuckled. "Thanks. I must have wandered into some good lighting. Any nightmares?"

"Not that I remember," he said, and he averted his gaze to pick up his coffee.

She turned away after a moment herself, then went back to what she was doing.

She knew Josh had been up during the night; she'd reached out for him in the dark and felt nothing but sweat-drenched sheets. His PTSD was unrelenting, and it aggravated her when he tried to keep it all bottled in.

"What's your schedule?" he asked just before taking his first sip.

Nichole shook off a moment of melancholy. This wasn't the time for a deep discussion about her husband's mental health. "Dropping the kids," she said. "Then I have to be at Foggy Bottom at eight thirty. Mandy and Huck will stay at aftercare till I grab them at six."

Both Josh and Nichole worked for the U.S. Department of State, she as a junior political officer, and he as a special agent in the

Bureau of Diplomatic Security. But their offices were miles apart. She worked in D.C. proper, while he had a little desk at DS's Washington field office in Dunn Loring, Virginia.

He smiled at her now, waking up with the introduction of caffeine into his bloodstream. "Today's the day, isn't it?"

Looking out the window over the sink into the cul-de-sac, she said, "Yeah. It's ridiculous. I've spent two years waiting for a foreign posting, and now that I'm about to learn where they're sending me, I'm nervous as hell."

"It's *not* ridiculous. This is a pretty momentous thing." He moved closer to her. "You've proven yourself with everything you've done. They'll send you somewhere interesting, don't worry."

"Hopefully not too interesting," she replied.

He put his hand on her shoulder. "Wherever they send you, we'll *all* go, together."

"That's the best part," she said, and then she took plates down from the cabinet.

"You driving today or taking the Metro?" he asked.

"Driving. It'll shave eleven minutes off the Blue Line commute, and I don't love the parking at Van Dorn station, anyway."

"Okay," he said. "I'll take the Toyota."

Nichole cocked her head in surprise. "Why aren't *you* taking the Metro?"

"Have to be in Dupont Circle at eight sharp."

"What's in Dupont Circle?"

"Got a text last night. A Dutch EU official is here for meetings with members of Congress and some other foreign dignitaries at the Washington Hilton. They want a four-person team on her, and with all the other dips in town, they needed an extra body."

Nichole had been stirring milk into a bowl of oatmeal, but she stopped and looked up at him. With only the slightest hint of worry in her voice, she said, "Any specific threats?"

To this, Josh was adamant. "Not at all. Typical detail for something like this. I'm the junior, so I'll probably get tasked with standing
outside the shitter when she takes a bathroom break."

"What's a shitter?"

The question did not come from Nichole; rather, it came from a
high-pitched voice on the staircase behind them.

They both turned towards the new participant in the conversation. Mandy Duffy, age eight, wore purple leggings and a jean jacket;
her sandy blond hair was in pigtails and she looked ready for school,
exhibiting all the efficiency of her mom.

Nichole looked back to her husband. "Great, Josh."

"Shit," he mumbled.

She rolled her eyes now. "Stop talking, please," she said, and then
she turned to her daughter. "It's nothing, sugar. Your dad's speaking
French again." She gave a little wince. "But . . . but don't say that word
in school, okay?"

"Shitter? Or shit?"

"Neither," Nichole blurted out. "And don't say them at home,
either."

"I'm not a kid, Mom. I know what those words mean."

"You *are* a kid, so don't say them, please."

Mandy looked like she was going to carry this further, and then
the toaster popped behind her mom.

Her attention shifted, Mandy shouted, "Eggos!" and then skipped
to the kitchen table.

"Eggos!" Duff echoed.

Nichole said, "You wish. Oatmeal." She handed him his bowl.

Josh then stepped over to the stairs. Calling up, he said, "Huck?"

A six-year-old boy with a sandy brown bedhead came down seconds later. He was barefoot, but his school clothes were on, at least,
and when he saw the Eggo on a plate at his seat, he rubbed his eyes
and ambled forward.

Soon all four sat, the adults with their oats, the kids with their waffles. Mandy said the blessing—she insisted on saying the blessing both at breakfast and at dinner, and Huck seemed fine letting her do so.

Mandy then looked to her mom. "Tonight you're going to tell us what country we're moving to?"

"That's right, sweetheart."

The little girl sighed. "I don't want to move."

Nichole and Josh flashed a glance at each other, and he put a hand on his daughter's shoulder. "I know, sweetie. But it's the job. I promise you, wherever we go, you are going to make lots of new friends and have lots of new experiences, and you're going to love it."

Nichole raised an eyebrow. It wasn't beyond the realm of possibility that they'd be sent to some developing nation where the kids couldn't travel outside a bubble of American diplomatic families.

But Josh was trying to keep Mandy from having a meltdown, and Nichole appreciated the attempt.

To the surprise of both of them, their young son said, "I want to go to Africa."

"Africa, Huck? That's new."

"I want to see a monkey."

"A monkey?" Nichole smiled now. "They have those in South America and Asia, too."

"Really?" he said, excitedly. "Why don't we have monkeys here?"

"I've got two of them right in front of me," Josh said.

Huck laughed, and Mandy grinned with a mouth full of waffle.

Nichole added, "And I've got three." After a moment she took a sip of her coffee, then looked over the mug at her husband. "Got to be honest. I'm a little annoyed."

Without missing a beat, Josh said, "Again? Or still?"

She laughed a little; Josh often made her laugh when she didn't want to, but finally she turned serious. "I don't love that they've got you on a protection detail today, just out of the blue like that. I like it better when you're sitting at your desk doing visa fraud investigations."

"I'll be doing that the rest of the week. This is a staffing issue. We just walk some Dutch EU diplomat through her day. There will be a lot of muckety-mucks with security at the hotel, so as long as we don't all step on each other's toes, we'll be fine."

Nichole looked incredulous.

"It's no big deal. It's not like the old days."

After holding his gaze a moment, she looked back down to her food. Softly, she said, "Thank God for that."

Josh said nothing in reply, and Nichole noticed this. "You sleep okay?"

He had not.

"I did."

Her eyes narrowed; she was evaluating him, trying to peer into his brain to feel what he was feeling. Eventually she said, "The fact that they don't use you to work protection much . . . as far as you're concerned, is that a good thing or a bad thing?"

Josh shrugged as he dipped a spoon into his bowl. "It's just a thing."

Nichole was going to dig deeper, but Mandy changed the subject. "Daddy, can we do karate after dinner tonight?"

Josh had been showing Mandy and Huck self-defense techniques out of a concern that everyone in the world could possibly be a danger to his kids. Nichole knew where his paranoia came from, that was no mystery, but she still didn't love that her husband was teaching the children how to fight.

He said, "As soon as we load the dishwasher after dinner, I'll show you and Huck how to do a wrist lock. You can drop anyone to the ground with this move, and it's really easy."

"Have you ever done that on a bad guy?" Huck asked.

Josh thought a moment. He'd never wristlocked an opponent in the real world, but he'd always wanted to. He decided not to say that at the breakfast table. Normally in his past life he'd just shoot people in the face, but he wasn't going to bring that up, either.

Before he could answer, his wife said, "Your dad's a lover, not a fighter." Raising an eyebrow, she said, "Right?"

"That's right," Josh replied, and then he winced a little and scooted back from the table. He stood and put his left foot on his chair, then lifted his trouser leg and made an adjustment to his sock. Doing so exposed, just for a moment, a high-tech-looking black prosthesis.

He began quickly rubbing his left hamstring.

"Cramping?" Nichole asked, and Josh nodded, concentrating on his massage.

Josh had lost his left leg below the knee while working as a civilian military contractor in Beirut six years earlier, long before joining State, and he was now on his fourth prosthesis, this one a super light and strong carbon fiber model that he'd grown so accustomed to he almost never took it off except to bathe and sleep.

Nichole watched him reposition his upper leg on the chair. "You okay?"

He nodded. "I just need to get it recalibrated. It's been too long. Still . . . I ran four miles yesterday. Hamstring's a little sore, but it's the good kind of sore."

"What's a good kind of sore?" Huck asked.

"The kind you get from exercise," Josh replied to his son. "Not the kind you get from banging your nose." Josh used the back of his oatmeal-covered spoon to gently bop his son on the nose.

Huck grinned and wiped his face, his blue eyes still sleepy. "That didn't hurt."

"Because you're tough," Josh said. With a wink to Nichole, he said, "Just like your mom. She's a fighter, not a lover."

Nichole didn't love the joke. "Josh!"

"Just kidding. Some people are so cool, Huck . . . that they can be both."

Huck said, "I'm a fighter."

And Mandy jumped on the bandwagon. "I'm a fighter, too."

Nichole looked at the kids' plates. Huck was done with his waffle, but Mandy hadn't finished her breakfast. "I need you to be an eater right now." Then, to both kids she said, "Ten minutes—coats, hats, and in your case, Huck, *shoes* on. Let's go."

"Yes, ma'am," Josh said. She was talking to the kids, not him, but Nichole ran the mornings around here, and Josh had learned to follow orders in the U.S. Army, so when an officer, even a former officer, even his wife, gave an order, he saw it as his duty to comply.

EXACTLY TEN MINUTES LATER THE KIDS WERE LOADED INTO THE minivan, a five-year-old gray Pacifica the Duffys had bought with money earned from a security contract Josh had worked in Mexico. Nichole kissed her husband, then climbed behind the wheel.

"Be safe today, Josh."

"It's D.C., babe. *You* be safe."

"That's fair," she replied.

The Pacifica disappeared up the cul-de-sac, and then Josh climbed into the family's eight-year-old Camry. He drove out of his neighborhood, then north on the Richmond Highway towards the city, the speakers blasting out a self-development audiobook his wife had recommended to him. The narrator talked about leadership and setting goals, and Josh made his way through the heavy traffic while listening, albeit somewhat distractedly.

Nichole loved personal development books, and she wanted Josh to love them just as much.

He did not, but he *did* love her, so he listened.

He'd met Nichole in Syria. At the time, she was a captain in the U.S. Army, the commander of an Apache gunship, and he was a young security contractor working in the war-torn region. When her helicopter was shot down in enemy territory, he alone came to her aid. Though she was injured in the crash, the two of them fought their way out of danger.

Nichole was an officer, the daughter of a general, and a born leader. Josh, in contrast, was a "sled dog," a "gun monkey," an enlisted infantryman who left service after four years and then became a private security contractor.

They could not possibly have been more different.

But after he visited her in the hospital in Germany while on leave from Syria, something sparked between the two of them, and within weeks of her crash the two of them had fallen in love.

Nichole fully recovered from her injuries in time, but she decided to leave the Army, much to her father's displeasure. Marrying Josh only added to the retired general's discontent. Soon they had Mandy. At the time, Josh was making big money doing high-threat work, nearly always abroad, while Nichole was back at home in Virginia, transitioning from Army life to motherhood.

Life was hectic but good; Nichole became pregnant with their second child, but before his birth, Josh was gravely wounded in Lebanon.

He lost his leg, Harry was born, and Nichole worked tirelessly, caring for three. The money stopped coming in and the bills kept piling up. She began cleaning homes and offices overnight out of desperation, and eventually Josh recovered enough to secure a job as a mall cop in Northern Virginia.

Depressed and nearly destitute, he finally agreed to a high-paying but ultra-high-threat contract in Mexico, serving for the first time in his long career as a team leader.

He and his team went through a gauntlet of danger in the Sierra Madre mountains, and he was only able to bring two of his men home alive.

This weighed heavy on him. Even now, three years later, he dreamed about it, just as he'd dreamed about Beirut before that, and Jalalabad before that. He had full-on PTSD, his wife told him over and over, but Josh minimized his struggles as much as he could.

Nichole worried about him; this he knew. Hence the endless self-help books and audiobooks. Positive thinking and discipline, assertiveness, leadership, and management. She told him he needed to have a growth mind-set; he needed to move on from the mountains of Mexico and his other experiences with combat, to put the pain and doubt behind him and develop himself.

His loving wife had his best interests in mind, of this Josh Duffy had no doubt, but this morning, like most mornings, he found himself just wanting to listen to some classic rock on his way to work instead of some hard-charging ex–Navy SEAL telling him that he needed to get off his lazy ass every morning and make his fucking bed.

He flipped on his satellite radio and began listening to the four-minute guitar duel at the end of "Free Bird" as he took the Arland D. Williams Jr. Memorial Bridge over the Potomac and into the District.

After all he and his family had been through, this was a damn good life, Josh told himself as he passed the Lincoln Memorial on his right. The State Department jobs for him and his wife had been absolute godsends. Nichole got hired as a Foreign Service Officer first, not long after the attention the couple received in the media from what happened in Mexico had died down. She'd worked as a political officer for the past two and a half years in the Foggy Bottom neighborhood of D.C., and she was known as an exceedingly smart and diligent employee, even in her short time there.

Josh's path had not been as smooth as his wife's, because the nature of the DS job and the nature of his leg injury meant he had to undergo arduous physicals and eventually receive special dispensation because of his amputation. But he'd worked hard, he'd made it through months and months of training, and now he spent the vast majority of his time at a desk in Virginia trying to track down visa and passport fraudsters.

But not for much longer. Josh and the kids would go to whatever country Nichole was sent to, and hopefully Josh would find an opening for himself with DS's Regional Security Office there at the embassy and travel with her as a tandem spouse. State was good about moving spouses and families together, and even if there were no job openings he was qualified for at the embassy, DS would allow him to take a leave of absence without pay to follow her, and this was something that factored in highly to their decision to both apply for jobs at the department.

They'd move as a family, so Josh was eagerly awaiting news of where Nichole would be sent.

They both knew their first foreign assignment would be somewhere in the developing world; virtually nobody at State was sent to London or Paris or Rome their first time out, but they also knew that the Regional Security Office at the embassy would make it a safe environment for the children, and this was more important to them than any personal or professional ambition.

Wherever they ended up, Josh knew two things to be true. One, Nichole was going to soar up the ranks at the embassy; she was a natural at her job, an overachiever with a brilliant mind. And two, Josh would never experience the intensity of true combat again, like he'd done so many times in his past.

Diplomatic security was serious work, but it wasn't running and gunning in wild cartel combat in the mountains of Mexico.

And that was fine with him.

As Josh drove along Twenty-Third Street NW, he looked out at the frigid January morning, and he was glad today's work would be indoors. He was armed with a SIG Sauer P320 Full-Size pistol tucked in a holster at his three-o'clock position and hidden by his suit coat and his black wool three-quarter-length coat. He also carried handcuffs and pepper spray on him, a pair of extra magazines, a folding knife, and a small flashlight.

But Josh Duffy's most important pieces of gear were his affable, intentional, and competent nature, as well as the earpiece in his left ear and the radio on his belt that would keep him in contact with the rest of the detail.

Today would be easy. The high representative of the European Union for Foreign Affairs and Security Policy wasn't a protectee that anyone was too worried about, especially since she would be spending her day in a location cordoned off by dozens of members of law enforcement.

Still, it beat sitting at his desk trying to find people who had lied on their visa apps to get into the United States.

He tried to tell himself he didn't miss the excitement, but though events in his past gave him regularly recurring nightmares and occasional panic attacks, something told him he was just wired for the exhilaration of high-threat protection.

But as he'd told his wife, that was his old life, and his new life, while not pumping him full of the same amount of adrenaline, was stable, and stable was good.

The last notes of Boston's "More Than a Feeling" faded away as he parked his Camry in front of the Dupont Circle Hotel.

FIVE

JOSH MET THE REST OF HIS TEAM IN THE LOBBY. HIS AGENT IN charge for the detail today was a senior DS employee named Chuck Ames. Josh had first met Ames at the DS training facility in Blackstone, Virginia, when he was a trainee. Ames had been a good instructor, and the few times they'd worked together since had run very smoothly.

Also with Ames was Pete White, a member of Josh's training class.

The fourth DS special agent on today's detail was introduced as Stephanie Millibrew, and after a quick introduction and a comment from her about seeing him on TV "back after that Mexico thing," the four of them headed inside.

Duffy, Ames, Millibrew, and White collected the EU diplomat at the door to her hotel suite. Johanna Aldenburg was a tall fifty-four-year-old Dutch woman with red hair and designer eyeglasses, and Josh was pleased to see that she and the five members of her staff were ready to go. The American agents formed a diamond around Aldenburg and escorted her downstairs to a trio of armored black Chevy Suburbans while her staff trailed behind.

Josh took the left rear seat in the lead vehicle, with two other agents, but only after their protectee and the AIC were locked into the armored middle Suburban, referred to as the limo.

They took off, and in his earpiece Josh heard Ames confer with a member of the advance team of DS agents already at the Hilton. "Keith, at the drop in five."

"Five minutes, understood."

Five minutes later he climbed out of the SUV and took up a position behind Aldenburg, and while doing so Josh couldn't help but flash a glance to his left. It was here, at a side door to the hotel, where Ronald Reagan had been shot by John Hinckley in 1981. The location looked different from the video footage Josh remembered watching; a portico had been built in front of the door to shield it from the street, but the rest of the scene appeared largely unchanged.

It was the Secret Service that got Reagan off the X and out of danger, not the Diplomatic Security Service, but both agencies were tasked with watching over people with targets on their backs.

The Dutch diplomat made it safely inside the hotel, and Josh trailed in the formation around her as they headed to a ballroom for their first meeting.

AT TWO THIRTY P.M. HE SHIFTED HIS WEIGHT OFF HIS LEFT LEG. HIS hamstring was still giving him issues, and he leaned on his right leg to shake it out. He'd done six hours on duty already, mostly static like this, and both his legs as well as his low back made him aware of it.

He was positioned outside a small conference room with White and Millibrew, while Aldenburg was inside talking to a pair of senators. U.S. Capitol Police stood in the corridor as well, along with various aides who milled about, entering and exiting other conference rooms with such regularity that Josh had committed dozens of faces to memory.

Understanding patterns and establishing who belonged in an area where he was working security were key, plus it kept him focused and awake.

AIC Ames remained inside with the EU official, and just after Josh looked at his watch, he heard him broadcast on the net in a soft voice. "They're wrapping up."

A minute later, the door next to Josh opened, and Aldenburg exited with the agent in charge.

Ames tapped his radio's talk button, addressing the agent standing outside the vehicles in front of the hotel.

"Keith, pick up in five."

"Five minutes, roger."

Aldenburg told Ames she needed a bathroom break before heading back to her hotel, so Duffy and Millibrew escorted her to the women's room. As Ames updated Keith on the delay, Stephanie went into the bathroom to check it, gave the all clear, then stood on the other side of the door from Josh as the foreign minister stepped inside.

Ames waited just across the hall from them, his eyes on the exit.

When Aldenburg reemerged three minutes later, she was holding a phone to her ear, and her previously calm expression had morphed into one of concern. She pulled the phone away to address Chuck Ames. "I'm terribly sorry, but I need to ask you to make a detour on the way back to the hotel."

Josh groaned inwardly. They'd wrapped earlier than he'd expected, so he'd allowed himself to entertain the possibility that he'd be able to make it home in time to get a stretch or a workout in before dinner.

But with an unscheduled movement, he saw that possibility quickly fading away.

Ames asked, "Where do you need to go, ma'am?"

The woman looked a little agitated, possibly annoyed. "The Turkish ambassador's residence. Out in front of it, actually. My daughter is a senior at Georgetown, and she and some fellow students have joined a rally there. I need to go by and speak with her. It's not the kind of publicity I need, as I'm sure you can imagine. I'll need five, ten minutes, and then we can be on our way."

Josh wasn't in charge, but he didn't like the idea of taking his protectee to some sort of a protest he knew absolutely nothing about.

Still, DS was trained to accommodate their protectees' requests when possible, and he assumed Ames would find a way to comply.

After a moment the AIC said, "How about we send a car to pick her up, bring her right to your suite? Probably better all around, from a security—"

She shook her head. "Ria won't leave her friends till the protest is over. I'll have to go to her. This won't take any time, I assure you."

Ames thought another moment. Before he spoke, Aldenburg said, "Do you have children, Special Agent?"

"Four, actually."

"Then you, of all people, get it. She has a mind of her own, and I need to go stress to her that she also has a responsibility to her mother."

Ames nodded. "All right, ma'am, I just need a couple of minutes to set this up."

"Thank you very much."

Duffy found himself glad he wasn't in charge today; this sounded like it was going to be a headache to organize.

They all went out to the vehicles and Aldenburg climbed into the limo, and then while Duffy stood outside in the sunny but frigid afternoon, the three Suburbans idled while Ames made some calls on his phone. He spoke with Aldenburg again and had her air drop a picture of her daughter to him so he could share it with his agents.

Finally, Ames moved back over to Duffy and the three other close-protection agents, and he conferred with his team.

"Okay, this is a movement in the blind, so eyes sharp. I just talked with DC Metro PD; everything's stable at the rally—for now, anyway—though there are some counterprotesters arriving that they will need to keep their eyes on. We'll adopt a lower profile for the move. We'll keep the vics spread out a little so we don't blow in there looking like a motorcade. We park on Massachusetts, on the other side of the circle from the residence. I sent a picture of Ria Aldenburg to DC Metro, and they are going to find her in the crowd and bring her to us."

He added, "At no time will the high representative leave the limo."

Duffy nodded. "Understood. You want to send the pic to us so we know who we're looking for if Metro can't find her?"

Ames pulled out his phone. "Doing it now."

Special Agent Stephanie Millibrew and the other two agents nodded their assent, and soon the three vehicles left the Hilton for the short drive west to Embassy Row.

AS THEY ROLLED THROUGH THE HEAVY AFTERNOON TRAFFIC, JOSH looked at his cell phone, studying the picture of Ria Aldenburg sent over by Ames.

He tried to imagine the girl in the image, who was wearing a tank top and shorts and sitting in a sunny outdoor café, as she would now look: no doubt dressed in a big winter coat, as the outside temperature hovered in the midthirties.

Millibrew spoke to the others in the vehicle around her. "Short blond hair, twenty-one, somewhere in the middle of a rally." She whistled softly. "This should be fun."

Duffy said, "If the cops bring her to us, we can load her up and get some distance off the X."

Sheridan Circle is a small grassy park with a large statue of Civil War general Philip Sheridan riding a horse in the center, surrounded on all sides by stately mansions. Tree-lined Massachusetts Avenue runs northwest to southeast, and Twenty-Third Street NW branches off to the south.

The three Suburbans of the high representative's detail arrived there in no time, though the vehicles had to pick their way through traffic before parking behind a row of police cars and motorcycles on the north side of the circle.

The residence of the Turkish ambassador sits on the south side of the circle, next to the Latvian embassy, and as soon as Duffy's lead vehicle stopped on Massachusetts, he scanned the area.

AIC Ames came over his earpiece at the same time. "DC Metro says the counterprotest is on 23rd Northwest, and it's grown in size in the past five minutes. Police have them barricaded back from Sheridan Circle, but we definitely need to keep our eyes on them."

Josh saw a large cluster of counterprotesters waving Turkish flags in the street on the other side of the circle; they were tucked tightly together and held back by barricades and several motorcycle police. Between him and them, the rally on the grass in the circle had formed on the southern edge, close to the residence and on the far side from Josh of the Civil War statue. He estimated the protest to be maybe seventy-five in number. Some held signs, one spoke into a megaphone, and many shook their fists in the air.

Josh could tell that a lot of the protesters were young, in their twenties, and he wondered which one was Ria.

The counterprotesters were harder to count, as they were farther away and bunched more closely together.

Soon Ames came over the net again. "The police are now saying they don't have the manpower to bring her to us; they're focusing on keeping the two groups apart. Millibrew, you're up. Duffy, you support."

"Got it," Stephanie Millibrew said into her mic. "I'll go find her, bring her back."

Josh and Stephanie climbed out of the Suburban and walked around to the side of the protest. There was chanting and shouting, fury in the tone, and Josh realized the fury was coming from both sides.

Together they stood there a moment, just taking in the scene, until Duffy spotted someone in the crowd holding a red sign over her head. "Got her. Red sign, yellow ski jacket, black jeans, and white boots."

Millibrew looked a moment more, then spoke into her mic. "Eyes on."

Special Agent Millibrew began walking towards the EU official's daughter, and Josh trailed behind her.

But they'd only taken a couple of steps before Ames came back over the net. "All hold. Stand by."

The female agent turned and looked to Duffy with an expression of mild confusion. He began scanning the scene more carefully, not understanding the reason for Ames's hold.

Quickly, however, the AIC came back through the agent's earpieces. "Metro says something's happening in front of the ambo's residence."

Duff didn't have a direct line of sight on the driveway from where he stood, so he quickly moved a few feet to his right to see around the rally. Soon he could make out a few sleek black SUVs parked in the drive, and a large cluster of men in dark suits standing around them.

One man leaned into the back of a limousine, as if he were conferring with someone there.

Soon the man looked back up over the roof of the car towards the protests, then back down to the limousine.

Ames said, "Metro advises the Turkish president is in that limo."

Josh Duffy heard the transmission, but his focus remained on the man, obviously a Turkish security agent, talking to someone in the limo. The man rose back up and began speaking into a cuff mic, and by his body language, Josh anticipated trouble.

The Turkish security officer shouted commands to the men close around him, pointing towards the protest across the little street.

And then the dark-suited individuals began to move.

Josh Duffy broadcast on the net quickly. "Got eyes on ten to twelve Turkish protective detail leaving the residence and moving across the street towards the rally." He added, "Looks like they're about to go hands on with the protesters."

As soon as he said that, the men in black fanned out and broke into a run. Behind them, the police barricade holding the Turkish counterprotesters came flying down as another dozen or so men there surged forward, then ran towards the circle.

To Josh's right, the door of the middle Suburban opened and Johanna Aldenburg began to emerge.

Duff could hear Ames calling to her from the vehicle. "Ma'am! Wait till—"

"I have to get to Ria!"

Ames made it out of the Suburban right behind her, and he took the EU official by the arm, stopping her advance. He looked up to Josh. "Duff! Get the daughter!"

Josh sprinted off past the police motorcycles, running onto the grass on the northwest side of Sheridan Circle, making a beeline towards Ria Aldenburg. His arms and legs pumped furiously, his prosthesis not slowing him down at all as he advanced on what was turning into utter chaos before his eyes.

A full-on brawl had kicked off on the south side of the circle, spilling into Massachusetts Avenue in front of the residence.

Men in black suits began ripping signs out of protesters' hands, kicking and punching, knocking college students and others to the ground, then kicking them again.

Duffy saw other men, all in civilian attire, as they joined in.

These people had not come from the counterprotest, so he determined that they must be Turkish government security or intelligence operatives who had embedded inside the rally.

There were probably two dozen DC Metro cops around, and they were doing their best to stop the rest of the counterprotesters from making it to the circle, but within seconds Josh had completed the calculus in his head. The Turks were more numerous, more aggressive, more motivated.

They were going to pulverize these protesters.

Josh wore a suit similar to what the Turkish security guys were wearing, so as he passed a pair of cops waving their nightsticks in front of them, he shouted, "DS! Move!" They stepped out of his way, turning their attention to a tall bearded security man heel-stomping a college-aged male with a ponytail, as if grinding the young man into the dirt.

Josh ran on past this scene, his focus totally on Ria, who had been pushed to the ground under another protester as people around her were mercilessly beaten by the Turks.

He was less than one hundred feet away from her, but his path was blocked by a fit twentysomething counterprotester in a white T-shirt, completely incongruous with the frigid January afternoon. The Turk threw a wild punch at an older man with a bullhorn in his hand, knocking the man down to the grass with a blow to the left side of his head. Josh's mission didn't include breaking up this fight, only pulling the Dutch woman out of the middle of it, but as the young counterprotester turned to him with a balled fist, Josh waylaid the man with a shoulder to the chest, sending him flying out of the way.

As he ran on, he reached under his coat to his hip, pulled a canister of pepper spray, and drew it out in front of him, and then he ducked under a burly Turkish protective agent trying to tackle him.

Rising back up, Josh spun around, aimed the spray in the man's direction, and sent a stream across his chest and up into his face.

Josh turned away and ran on. In his earpiece he heard Millibrew.

"Duffy, I'm fifty feet behind you! Keep them off her till I get there and I'll pull her out! You cover us back to the vic."

"Roger!"

A muscular Turk in a brown coat fired a jab at Josh as he passed, striking the forearm the American had raised to protect his face, and instantly after, Josh closed on the man and grabbed him in a bear hug. Lifting the attacker into the air, he fell back with him, but spun around and landed hard on the man, who grunted violently as the wind was knocked out of him.

The American climbed back up and ran on.

Josh knew that certain members of the Turkish president's detail were authorized to carry handguns, even here in the District, so he was hypervigilant, checking the hands of everyone he saw. If one of these guys pulled a weapon, he'd have no choice but to use deadly force, as his protectee was probably still outside the armored vehicle behind him and therefore in any potential line of fire.

And through all the chaos, Josh Duffy retained the presence of mind to marvel that this bullshit was going down right in the middle of Washington, D.C.

SIX

RIA ALDENBURG SHOOK HER HEAD TO CLEAR IT, THEN CLIMBED BACK up to her knees, her mind still not quite processing that she'd been shoved to the ground along with a friend of hers. All around her men punched and shouted, police swung batons, college students and anti–Turkish government protesters kicked and shoved, ran and chased, bodies slammed into the ground, and splatters of blood soared through the air in arcs as fists met faces.

Ria rose all the way up now, thought about running, thought about grabbing a fellow rallygoer still on the ground and helping him up, but before she could decide on a course of action, a large man in a black suit came charging at her from the sidewalk, just five meters away. She looked into the man's eyes and saw a seething fury, and she realized he held a squat black object in his right hand and was in the process of raising it over his head.

She knew she was this man's target, and he would be on her in an instant.

Ria put her hands up in front of her, a futile gesture, she had no doubt.

The big man darkened the sun as he loomed over her, and she

began to close her eyes, not accepting her fate but too paralyzed with fear to prevent it.

The man swung his arm down, swinging the object he held with it.

And then . . . he was gone, and the sunlight returned.

A figure had flown through the air on Ria's right. A man in a suit, his body parallel with the grass beneath her. He'd collided with her attacker, sending the approaching man sideways to his right.

Both men hit the ground and rolled, and then the brown-haired man in the suit began fighting the darker-haired Turkish security officer for the item clutched in his hand.

The new arrival took hold of the object, then swung it violently in a backhand across the Turk's left temple.

The big security man for the president of Turkey instantly fell to the ground and went limp on his back in the grass.

Ria didn't have time to focus on her protector because she was suddenly grabbed from behind and spun around. A woman's voice in her ear shouted, "Miss Aldenburg! Come with me, we're getting out of here!"

Ria and the woman holding her began running around the statue of General Sheridan in the middle of the circle, and the young girl's mind was even more confused about what the fuck had just happened.

JOSH DUFFY DROPPED THE LEATHER SAP ONTO THE UNCONSCIOUS body of the man he'd just taken it from, and then he shoved away two people who had pushed against him from behind. One was a DC Metro motorcycle officer, and the other a Turkish counterprotester in a jean jacket, but Josh was only concerned about getting the young Dutch woman into the armored vehicle and keeping any attackers off her and his fellow agent.

He took off behind Millibrew and Aldenburg, but as he neared the statue he identified a new threat. To the right of the two women Josh saw another Turkish security officer climb back up to his feet, having been knocked down by a cop who had now turned his attention to a counterprotester mercilessly kicking a college-aged boy in the fetal position.

As the man rose, Josh saw a rage on the Turk's face that instantly told him the man had lost all control of his emotions, and there was no telling what he'd do next.

Josh was twenty feet from him as the security officer reached under his coat to his right hip.

Fuck, he thought. *Dude's going for his gun.*

Josh put his hand on the grip of his own pistol, but he did not draw; instead he kept running at the man, used his left hand to grab the man's wrist as the Turk pulled his pistol free of its holster, then slammed into him, sending him back.

The gun made its way into Josh's hand as the man fell onto his back, but as soon as the Turk hit the grass he did an acrobatic back roll, made his way back to his feet, and then charged.

Josh tucked the Turk's firearm into his waistband under his coat, then dropped his pepper spray, because he knew that it wouldn't stop this guy.

The Turk took a wild swing; Josh pivoted away on his prosthesis, then spun around and landed a spinning back fist against the side of the man's face.

The strike wouldn't have been much if the Turk hadn't had his own momentum working against him, but the impact stunned him, and he stumbled, then fell face first onto the steps up to the Sheridan statue.

Josh again broke into a run.

He looked up to see that Stephanie had control of Ria Aldenburg; the young woman looked back in his direction, and he could tell she'd taken a hard blow to her left cheek. It was dark and swollen, but at least she and Millibrew were still on their feet and closing in on the limo.

Duff started after them but only made it a single step before he was clutched from behind in a powerful bear hug, arresting his forward progress.

From the size of the man, he realized it was the same guy as before, and his fury was apparently more powerful than Josh's punches.

But the man made a tactical mistake by holding him too close. Josh slammed his head back, shattering the Turk's nose and causing him to loosen his grip. Spinning around, he punched the man once with his right fist, directly in the attacker's bloody broken nose, and now the Turk fell to the ground screaming.

The American was moving again instantly.

He made it to the north side of the statue now, just fifty feet or so from the lead Suburban. He saw Stephanie put Ria inside it; the EU minister was already in the limo with the door shut now, no doubt pulled there by Ames.

Now Josh only had to get back to his SUV and then all three Suburbans would get the hell out of this mess.

But then it happened. A protester knocked to the cold ground by an attacker rolled in front of him; Josh tried to leap over the body, but his carbon fiber left foot caught the raised leg of the innocent man.

Duff went down hard, chest first, slamming into the grass just beyond the prostrate rallygoer.

He began to climb back to his knees, but he sensed movement on his right.

He turned just in time to see a black dress shoe moving in a blur towards his face.

And then the lights went out.

JOSH DUFFY SAT UPRIGHT IN A HOSPITAL BED; HIS WINTER COAT, HIS suit coat, and his tie had been removed, and he wore a thick bandage on his head.

He repositioned the ice pack behind his neck; he felt the effects of the morphine drip, but still his head throbbed, and his forehead stung under the thick bandaging there.

The door opened and Chuck Ames entered, followed by Special Agent Millibrew.

"How you feeling, slugger?" Ames asked.

"Slugger? Did I punch somebody?"

"Yeah, you wailed a tune on three or four guys. I'm sure your hands will start hurting soon enough."

Josh touched the bandages on his forehead now. "They're fine for now, but it feels like I punched somebody out with my head."

Millibrew looked at the bandage. "Eleven stitches, the doc says."

"No big deal," Duff replied. "A little embarrassing, though."

Ames looked over the bandaging now, as well as the scratches on the other parts of his face. "They say anything about whiplash?"

"More than I wanted to hear. It's a given. No concussion, but they said however bad my neck feels right now, tomorrow morning is when the fun *really* starts." He shrugged; it was painful to do so. "Not the worst thing that's ever happened to me."

Ames said, "That's a pretty high bar, though, I'm sorry to say. You did one hell of a job out there. I wish I'd been there to help you, but—"

"But Ria wasn't the principal, and you had to protect Aldenburg. I know that, Chuck."

"Good."

He looked around. "What about the pistol I took off the—"

"We've got it, along with your piece and your gear. Two cops came up behind the guy who kicked you and tuned him up with their night-sticks, dropped him right next to you. I guess the Turks will get their gun back eventually."

Josh just leaned back into the ice on his neck. "Gotta love diplomatic immunity. They won't even get a slap on the wrist."

"Wouldn't be so sure. Eleven protesters injured," Stephanie said. "Two seriously."

Duff noticed Millibrew staring at him, a look of bewilderment in her eyes.

"What?"

She said, "Everything that happened to you in Syria, in Lebanon. In Mexico. I have to ask . . . does this kind of shit just follow you around wherever you go?"

Josh laughed a little. "In my experience, usually when guns are pulled, guns are used. I'd say this turned out pretty low-key."

"Thanks to you," Ames said. "If you'd shot that Turkish agent when he drew on you, you'd have been within your rights, but you'd have created one hell of an international incident that nobody wanted."

Stephanie added, "And you might have kicked off a bloodbath in that park."

After a few minutes the two DS agents left, and five minutes after they'd gone Josh heard an authoritative female voice out in the hall, demanding to know what room Special Agent Duffy was in.

Here we go, he thought.

The door opened and Nichole Duffy raced in, a look of concern on her face. "What the hell, Josh?" She embraced him carefully. "How do you feel?"

"Like some guy used my head as a soccer ball."

"I heard." She looked over his bandage, then kissed him on the lips. Tightening the muscles in his face to kiss her back pulled on his stitches and hurt. Nichole said, "This is where you say, 'You should see the other guy.'"

Josh closed his eyes and smiled, and that hurt as well. "I wish *I* saw the other guy. All I saw was his foot about an inch from my face."

"My God." She shook her head in amazement. "They told me you took down three of them before you got knocked out."

"Really? Badass." He fought through the pain of another shrug. "I honestly don't remember."

She leaned closer, holding his hand. "I'm proud of you, but I *really* wish when you left for work every morning I had a high confidence that you were going to come home uninjured."

"Makes two of us, Nik."

"How do you feel . . . otherwise?"

"Otherwise?"

She shrugged. He knew what she was talking about, but he hoped she'd let it go.

She did not. "The panic attacks. The nightmares. The PTSD. Are you feeling . . . okay after what happened today?"

Duff smiled. "Maybe it's the morphine, but I'd say I feel pretty damn good at the moment." And then a new thought popped into his drug-clouded brain. "Wait, have you gotten your posting yet?"

She didn't seem as though she wanted to change the subject, but after a moment she nodded. "I have."

With a little smirk he said, "*Please* tell me we aren't getting posted to Istanbul."

She laughed. "Nope." After a pause, she said, "If I could be sent anywhere in the world that you wanted, where would that be?"

Josh wasn't sure of the answer she was looking for. Sure, Paris or Luxembourg or Berlin would be amazing, but Josh was most inter-ested in his wife being sent someplace where there was also a need for a new Diplomatic Security agent. Otherwise, he'd have to take a leave of absence from DS to follow her and try to find some other mundane job at the embassy he could do while she worked a Foreign Service Officer position.

He said, "There are about five openings for DS at places where there were FSO openings, so honestly, I hope they are sending you somewhere I can be useful, too."

She squeezed his hand with a grin on her face. "They did. We're going to Ghana, Africa. There's a political officer position there for me and a DS opening for you there, too. You'd be a lock to get it, especially after those hijinks you pulled today."

Josh had known they could be sent anywhere, and he'd spent the last year looking over various postings, wondering where they might go. He knew a little about Ghana, enough to know it had the most stable democracy in all of West Africa. He also knew it was a big installation, with over one hundred fifty Americans at the embassy, and a local staff several times that size.

Nichole said, "I checked. Really great schools, and residential housing looks nice." She squeezed his hand again. "I have to leave in three months."

Josh thought a moment. "I've got six months till I can go."

She said, "Yeah, we have some logistics to work out, but we'll get it all arranged." She kissed him again. "Promise me you're not going to get into any more fracases here while I'm gone."

He promised, and they embraced again; it hurt him to do so, but he laughed as he grunted with the pain of her squeeze around his neck.

"Here's to getting out of D.C. and getting into someplace safer."

"Like sub-Saharan Africa," she said with a smile.

SEVEN

JOSH DUFFY STOOD IN THE AFTERNOON HEAT, PERSPIRATION ON HIS forehead, painfully aware that there were dozens of sets of eyes on him.

He felt like a gazelle being watched over by a pack of lions.

He tried to push the anxiety away, to concentrate on what he was doing with all his effort, because he knew the pressure was on, and he had to get this right.

He loomed over the large charcoal grill, ignoring the heat, sweat draining into his eyes now as he flipped the hamburgers as fast as he could.

He'd only been able to fit twenty-four patties over the heat, which meant he had another two dozen waiting in the wings.

And time was short, because the kids were hungry, to say nothing of the parents.

Nearly two dozen children, including both of his, splashed in the swimming pool at the center of the lush courtyard of a three-story apartment building. Parents and other embassy staff sat around at picnic tables, drinking beer and wine and hard seltzers, laughing and talking, most people keeping at least one eye on their kids while they enjoyed themselves.

The Iris Gardens was an apartment complex in the Cantonments neighborhood of Accra, the capital of Ghana, less than a quarter mile away from the rear wall of the U.S. embassy compound.

The Iris Gardens looked a lot like a higher-end garden apartment complex in Florida, except for a few differences. For starters, two armed local guards sat in a hardened shack at the front gate, eight-foot-high fences rimmed the perimeter, security cameras captured all angles of the exterior of the facility, and the ground-floor windows had steel bars across them.

A police car patrolled regularly, as well.

Twenty-six embassy families lived here at the Iris Gardens, and most of them were in attendance today at the weekly Sunday afternoon cookout.

Ambassador Jennifer Dunnigan often made an appearance though she didn't live here, but she was back in Washington till Monday. The deputy chief of mission was in attendance with his family, as was the political chief, while the gunnery sergeant in charge of the seven-man Marine Security Guard force at the embassy stood by the pool monitoring his three-year-old twins as they played.

All the DS agents in Accra at the moment were here; a couple of single guys from CIA had dropped by, as had several local Ghanaian embassy employees, including the Foreign Service National Investigator for Diplomatic Security, a forty-three-year-old ex–local police captain named Benjamin Manu.

Josh wore swim trunks, a U.S. Army T-shirt, a Casio G-Shock watch, and wraparound Oakleys. His sandy brown hair was cut military short, though this had been his own decision and nothing mandated by DS.

In his swim trunks his prosthesis was exposed to everyone here at the cookout, and this was something he wouldn't have dared to do on his last contracting job. Here, in contrast, everyone knew about his injury, and no one really cared.

Josh also had the benefit of not being the only agent in the Bureau of Diplomatic Security with a prosthetic leg.

The amputation made life tougher, for sure. He'd have to fly to Italy or Germany in a month or two to see a doctor to get the leg recalibrated again, but he'd already decided he'd turn that outing into a short family trip to salvage something positive from what otherwise would have been an annoying negative.

He and Nichole had decided they had enough money for a few days in an Airbnb outside the city center, as long as they took the metro and ate at budget restaurants or at street stands. Maybe they'd take the kids to a couple of parks to play and, if they could swing it, a museum, and although the towns around the medical facilities in Landstuhl, Germany, and Sigonella in Sicily weren't exciting like Paris or Milan or Munich, they would still have a great time.

Josh threw cheese on the burgers, tossed the next round of buns on the toaster rack, then took a quick moment to look across the pool at Nichole. She was deep in conversation with an African American Foreign Service Officer; Josh had been introduced to so many people in the week he'd been in country he couldn't remember the woman's name. Nikki had a hard seltzer in her hand, and her sunglasses were up on her blond hair; he caught her flashing her eyes towards the pool to check on Huck, who was punching a beach ball back and forth in the air with some older boys.

Josh took it all in and thought that this might have been the most perfect moment in his life.

A Hispanic-looking man in his late forties, a couple inches shorter than Josh and wearing a Hawaiian shirt, khakis, and flip-flops, stepped up to him. "I need a sitrep on the smash burgers, Duff."

"Cheese is melting now. I'll have enough for the kids in about two minutes. Another ten minutes for the rest of us."

Diplomatic Security Regional Security Officer Jay Costa shouted to a muscular man in his twenties standing shirtless next to the pool, tattoos on his upper arms, chest, and back, and his hair even shorter than Josh's. "Hey, Gunny! Rally the kids and get their butts in their seats; the new guy's grilling skills are about ready for inspection."

The gunnery sergeant immediately got to work emptying the pool of dependents, and the kids made their way to their towels and then, eventually, to their parents at the picnic tables, waiting to be served.

DS Special Agent Chad Larsen and his fourteen-year-old son Kyle stepped up to the big grill, ready to help. Larsen was blond-haired and bearded, his son nearly his height of five-ten, and together with Costa and Benjamin Manu, they began dressing the cheeseburgers with pickles and ketchup and delivering them to the tables while Josh slapped another twenty-four patties down on the heat.

TWENTY MINUTES LATER HE TOOK A LOAD OFF AND SAT IN FRONT OF a paper plate with a hamburger, potato salad, and a bottle of Club Lager, a local brew he'd already come to love in his short time here. Virtually every one of the fifty or so embassy personnel or dependents had already consumed their meals, and Josh breathed a sigh of relief that he hadn't screwed up, because he'd never cooked for so many people in his life.

Nichole was across from him; like most of the others she'd already finished her lunch, and now she sat with Huck on her knee, a plastic cup of ice water in front of her.

Mandy ran up to her and whispered into her ear, but Duff could easily hear her. "Mom, is that lady pregnant?"

Nichole and Josh both looked around. On the far side of the pool a woman leaned over a garbage can, holding her stomach, and her face looked white as a sheet.

"No, sweetie, I think she just ate something that didn't agree with her."

Mandy kept watching her a moment, then was distracted when

two other kids ran over and asked her if she wanted to see a lizard. Together all three ran off across the courtyard.

The woman looked like she was having dry heaves, and Nichole started to get up to go check on her, but Jay Costa spoke up from the next table over. "I'll check her out, get her to the doctor if she needs it." He climbed out of his seat and jogged over to the woman. They talked a moment, and then he helped her inside her apartment.

Josh watched the entire scene in silence, but when she was gone, he said, "I *really* hope that wasn't my cooking."

Nichole laughed. "No. That's Kathy from Commerce. She went up north a few days ago, caught a stomach bug. I heard her telling someone she was sure it wasn't malaria, but she also said the mosquitoes were biting, so . . . who knows?"

Josh said, "Why did Mandy ask if she was pregnant?"

"I told her that I was sick a lot when I was pregnant with her and said that I threw up some. Now every time some woman has a stomachache she asks me if she's pregnant."

Josh laughed. "As long as she doesn't do it in front of the woman."

"Believe me," Nichole said, "that has been stressed to her."

The cookout broke up around three; families went back to their units, while Josh, Nichole, and a dozen other adults stayed behind to clean up.

A HALF HOUR LATER, JOSH AND NICHOLE MADE THEIR WAY BACK TO their second-floor unit, then sat on their balcony looking out over the courtyard. Beyond the perimeter walls of the Iris Gardens, the traffic was light this Sunday afternoon, aided greatly by the fact that this was a quiet residential neighborhood.

Josh cracked open another beer as he looked out over the little stretch of the city that he could see from his balcony.

His kids loved their school, their new friends, and their young nanny, Portia. His wife was challenged and engaged in her job as a political officer here in the nation of over thirty million, and so far Josh got along great with his cohorts in the embassy's Diplomatic Security Office.

Nichole put her arm around him.

He said, "And to think, four years ago we had nothing."

Nichole shook her head now. "Don't say that. We had each other. We had Mandy and Huck." She thought a moment. "We had our spaghetti nights."

Josh sipped. "Yeah. I just mean . . . this feels nice."

His wife nodded and said, "It's nice now, but in a few days you and I will be damn busy."

He nodded at this. "Will be nice to get out of the capital and see the countryside, though."

"We won't see much," she said. "This is going to be a whirlwind trip. My eyes will be on my iPad keeping things on track, and your eyes will be on Ambassador Dunnigan's ass."

"I'm not going to have my eyes on—"

"You told me yourself your position in her security detail is the rear of the diamond. Where does the rear of the diamond stand?"

Nichole had made this joke before about his security work. Regularly, in fact.

Josh played along. "I stand behind the principal."

"Where you can look at her butt."

"I'm a trained professional, babe."

"Sure, dude." After a moment in silence, Nichole turned to him. He could see the sudden seriousness on her face. "You're keeping something from me. You were up last night again. Three a.m."

He looked back out to the street. "Sorry, didn't think I woke you."

"That's not the issue, and you know it."

Josh took another swig of beer. "I know."

"You're having the nightmares still."

Defensively, he said, "Sometimes. Not that often."

"Is it Mexico?"

Josh looked off, out over the complex, past the front gate and the guards there, and into the haze over the city in the warm afternoon. "They're just dreams."

"Are you going to be ready to travel this week? We're talking about real security work."

"I'm fine with that. One hundred percent."

She looked at him with a worried gaze. Finally, she said, "I still think you need to get some help with this."

"We've been through this a hundred times, Nik. Some shrink diagnoses me with anything more than PTSD, they say I'm depressed or whatever, then my career is toast. I promise you, it's getting better, it's not affecting my work, and it's just stupid nightmares."

"You're right," Nichole conceded. "We *have* been through this a hundred times." With a sigh, she added, "And still . . . nothing ever seems to change."

She kissed him, rose, and went back into the apartment.

HAJJ ZAHEDI FELT UNCLEAN FOR WHAT HE WAS ABOUT TO DO, which was an unusual sensation for him, because he'd been a ruthless killer all of his adult life and didn't spend much time battling moral discomfort.

But tonight was different. It felt wrong to be walking into this West African hotel nightclub, filled with infidels, alcohol, and debauchery, but he was at least pleased to see that the space was expansive and dark, and a three-piece band sat on a low riser in the corner playing soft Western music that would serve to drown out his delicate conversation to come.

Scanning around the support columns in the room, he found the man he was looking for sitting at a table in the back corner by velvet curtains.

The tables nearby had several occupants: Black men in local attire or business suits, and Asian men in suits, as well. A couple of Zahedi's own men were here, sitting at the bar and doing a fair job of fitting into the foreign environment.

Zahedi himself wore a gray sharkskin suit he'd had tailored in Milan a year before and only brought out for special occasions, such as tonight. He needed to fit in as a traveling businessman here in Sierra Leone, and this meant he could hardly wear his military uniform, his combat gear, or even the long white robes he liked to don on those few occasions when he was back home in Tehran.

He made his way past the groups of men; to his pleasure he was ignored by his own pair of security officers as they sipped tea and watched the band, and more pleasure that the four Black men barely glanced his way, but he felt a little displeasure in the fact that three white men sitting in casual attire looked him up and down warily.

These infidels showed no respect, but Zahedi had expected nothing more, and he knew he just had to deal with them.

Colonel Hajj Zahedi was a field commander in Unit 400, an action arm of the Iranian Revolutionary Guard's Quds Force. He'd been here in Africa, on and off, for over two years, and in that time he'd had a few meetings like this one tonight.

Working with infidels was simply part of his job.

As was working with Sunnis, and that was the reason he was here. The Iranians were Shia. The Muslims of West Africa were, with only a very few exceptions, Sunni, but the Iranians had been liaising with various extremist groups on the continent for some time.

The man at the corner table stood as he arrived and gave a slight bow. The Asian was some five years younger than Hajj Zahedi, and there was an intensity and a vibrance in his eyes that Zahedi remembered from the last time they'd met, years ago in Mali.

"Mr. Kang," the Iranian said as he shook the smaller man's hand, and then they sat down as the little band began playing something new. A saxophone over a synthesizer, with a woman singing and playing an acoustic guitar; the song was soft and melodic, but Zahedi didn't recognize it.

Kang drank white wine. A teapot and cup were also on the table; the Iranian assumed it had been ordered for him, but he turned around and motioned to a bartender to come to him.

Kang sat in silence while the man approached, and when he arrived, Zahedi spoke to him in fluent English.

"Double Knob Creek. Neat."

The bartender nodded. "On the way, sir."

Turning back to the Chinese man, Zahedi saw the incredulous look. Kang said, "I thought you could not partake in—"

"I'm in cover. Makes no sense for me to be drinking tea." He leaned forward a little more. "Don't assume things."

"I won't. It has been some time since we've seen each other. I had forgotten the lengths to which you go to maintain your cover. I must say I respect this greatly."

Zahedi wasn't here for the compliments. "Why are we in Freetown, in a cursed hotel? This meeting could have happened anywhere." He added, "What is wrong with you?"

Kang answered with the utmost calm. "My nation is aware of all Western intelligence operatives in Sierra Leone. We find Freetown a safe place to do business, even if our business is two thousand kilometers away, as it is in this case." When Zahedi didn't seem convinced, Kang said, "This hotel is Chinese owned. We control the cameras, the access, the clientele. And most of the people in this room work for me, in some capacity."

Zahedi nodded; now it all made sense. He glanced around, looking for his damnable alcohol. A pair of young and attractive women made eye contact from the bar. They were prostitutes, Zahedi realized quickly, and he looked away.

He was absolutely surrounded by debauchery.

Debauchery in the form of his glass of bourbon arrived; he made eye contact with Kang as he took a healthy sip.

May Allah forgive him.

Kang said, "Your forces? They are ready?"

Zahedi nodded. "They will all be in country by Wednesday. Nigerians, mostly. Sunnis, of course, but they do our bidding when we support them well, pay off their commanders, promise them either plunder or paradise."

"Two hundred men?"

"I said one to two hundred," Zahedi clarified. "The true number is closer to one hundred. But the quantity isn't as important as the fervency."

Kang did not hide his displeasure. Skeptically, he said, "Tell me about their fervency."

"Jama'at Nusrat Al-Islam Wal-Muslimin. Experienced. Ruthless."

Kang knew JNIM were the Group for the Support of Islam and Muslims. They'd formed in 2017 when four smaller West African extremist groups joined forces, following the Al Qaeda role model.

"And you are certain you have control of them?" he asked.

"I give them weapons, training, support. Of course I control them. Without the backing of my nation they would still be in the slums of Lagos or Abuja, in the dusty Sahel outside the villages of Burkina Faso." Zahedi smiled. "They will sow the discord we both seek inside Ghana."

"How will you move them?" Kang asked.

"We will bring them south and west. I had considered transporting them through Togo and then by sea, but the overland routes have been scouted and are safe."

Kang nodded, pleased.

The Chinese intelligence officer said, "My mercenary leader will have his own force, already in country and spread around the key areas we've identified. When the local rebels begin moving on the capital, he and his shock troops will make them appear to be a much more formidable group than they actually are."

"Your South African knows nothing about me, correct?"

"As we have agreed. The involvement of your proxy force will come as a surprise, but he won't know you are working for me and, by that point in the operation, he will be committed to moving forward. Everyone will help one another when the time comes, whether or not everyone would be agreeable to working with one another in advance."

Zahedi nodded. "Your nation and my nation do not work well together, especially here in Africa. Our aims are not the same. We want to destabilize, to cause Islam to flourish in the region and Western influence to recede.

"You people . . . you are all businessmen. No ideology other than money. Gold. Diamonds. Oil."

Kang said, "Only regime change in Ghana will stabilize business for us in that nation. And if this business model works for us, as I am sure it will, then I assure you we would like to replicate this. Your pockets of influence will grow across the continent, and together we can push the West away, and my nation's influence will grow, as well."

Zahedi took another drink. He wouldn't allow himself to realize that he liked the feel of the hard liquor going down his throat; he just told himself he was suffering for his work. Finally he said, "I understand the relationship, and I will provide you with what we have agreed upon."

He rose from the table, turned, and left the bar, ignoring the music and the security men looking his way as he did so.

EIGHT

JOSH DUFFY SAT IN HIS CUBICLE IN THE CHANCERY OF THE U.S. EM-
bassy in Accra, Ghana, and scrolled through images of doorknobs on
his computer.

He wasn't in the market for a doorknob himself; rather, he was
trying to find digital locks to upgrade the ones at another nearby
apartment complex that the State Department wanted to begin using
to house employees.

Part of Josh's portfolio here was to keep the residences of the U.S.
embassy staff up to the right security protocols. This meant every
time a new local landlord offered an apartment building or condo
facility, Josh had to check it for suitability and bring in local contractors to upgrade it if necessary.

Walls, cameras, locks, bars on windows, secure access to entrances
and common areas . . . it was all subject to precise specifications laid
out by DS.

He was new here, on the job just a week, but he'd already been
given a lot to do. He'd been put in charge of the Residential Security
Program, hence his search for doorknobs, but he also supported the
assistant regional security officer for investigations, which meant he
spent a large chunk of each day, when he wasn't looking at locking

mechanisms or checking in on the guard forces at all residential compounds where Americans worked, looking into potential acts of visa fraud committed by Ghanaians trying to come to the United States.

The U.S. embassy in Ghana had one hundred fifty or so Americans working in it, but some six hundred fifty locals worked here, as well. This was one of the larger embassies in Africa, and it was a busy place for DS, but that wasn't due to any insurgent threat like what could be encountered in some nations, or a hostile local government like in others.

No, here the biggest challenge to the security of the embassy and those who worked there came in the form of EDPs. Emotionally disturbed persons were a daily occurrence around the perimeter of the compound, people outside the fence of the embassy who wanted in, many of whom were under the impression that America was their enemy.

These were small threats that usually the LGF, or Local Guard Force, took care of before the EDP made it within the walls of the compound itself, but here in the chancery, the center of the embassy and the building where the ambo herself worked, Josh and the rest of the DS staff were always vigilant, prepared on the off chance that the shit might someday hit the fan.

Behind where he sat at his desk looking at doorknobs, just in front of the bulletproof window, a wooden stand held his green body armor with the emblem for the Bureau of Diplomatic Security stitched in, a rack of rifle magazines, and a utility belt from which a Glock 19 in a retention holster hung. On the top of the stand a helmet rested, and night vision goggles were mounted on them.

The name tape on the chest rig of the body armor read "Duffy," and a pair of black Pelican cases also stenciled with his name sat right beside it.

His rifle was in the armory down in Marine Post One at the front of the chancery, a bulletproof box of a room manned by a Marine guard 24/7, watching security cameras and staying in contact with the Marine Security Guards who lived here on the compound.

While an attack on the embassy here in Accra was considered highly unlikely, there was something else on Josh's plate that did, in fact, look like actual security work. A joint delegation from the European Union—including Johanna Aldenburg, the diplomat whose daughter he'd rescued in Washington six months earlier—would be arriving in two days, and then she, her entourage and security team, Ghanaian president Francis Amanor and his contingent, as well as U.S. ambassador Dunnigan and her team, would be shuttling to six locations around the country via helicopters on a thirty-six-hour press tour.

The EU and the United States had partnered on several new infrastructure and development initiatives here in Ghana, and this was seen as both a fact-finding trip for the EU's chief diplomat and an opportunity to publicize to the rest of Africa just what the West could do for them in exchange for good relations.

It was no secret that China had garnered major influence on the continent in the past decade or so, loaning money and building bridges, ports, and highways, all as part of Beijing's Belt and Road Initiative. The United States and Europe had been all but squeezed out in that time, but an economic crisis in China had offered an opening to the West that the EU and Americans had been quick to capitalize on.

Josh knew that the trip through the country on board French military helicopters would be interesting, and he was also excited by the fact that the U.S. ambassador had asked Nichole to join her for the journey.

As he clicked out of a web page and made some notes on a pad about checking the locking mechanism in his own residence, he heard the door up the hall open with a click, and then the voice of the Diplomatic Security Office management assistant. "Hey, Nichole," she said.

"Morning, Olga."

He looked at his G-Shock watch and realized it was time for a meeting about the upcoming mission.

While Josh worked in a decent-sized cubicle, a larger office was just across from him. RSO Jay Costa, the top DS agent at the embassy, stepped out of it just as Josh's wife made it down the hall to her husband, and the three of them went to a conference room across the second-floor atrium of the chancery building.

Here they met Benjamin Manu, the Ghanaian Foreign Service National Investigator who worked for State, as well as Assistant Regional Security Officer Chad Larsen. The fourth DS special agent had gone on a temporary-duty assignment to Morocco, but she'd be back before the trip to watch over the embassy while Manu would serve as another member of the ambassador's protection detail.

The DS contingent and Nichole sat down in a conference room with several embassy staffers, everyone going on the trip except the ambo herself. Four Foreign Service Officers including Nichole—Josh could only remember a couple of their names—plus four Local Body Guard agents on the ambassador's protection detail. These Ghanaians, like Benjamin Manu, were former cops and worked here at the embassy after strict vetting and training in the United States, and all four had sworn to guard the ambassador with their lives.

Costa ran the security portion of the meeting. "Today is Monday," he began. "Wednesday, the high representative of the European Union for Foreign Affairs and Security Policy, Johanna Aldenburg, will arrive around two p.m. There will be a reception for her and her staff, for us, and for the Ghanaians at the French embassy at seven p.m. The ambo will attend, so me, Duff, and Chad will serve as her detail for the event.

"The next morning is when the fun starts. Six stops in thirty-six hours, all over the nation. The only way to do this is by air, so the French are bringing in three Airbus H225M Caracals for the trip, one for the EU, one for President Amanor and his group, and one for us. Each bird seats twenty-four, and there are fifty in total, including security and traveling press, so we won't have to worry about space.

"Day one is the coastal harbor in Takoradi, then we go up to Kumasi to a new medical clinic, then Tamale to cut the ribbon on the EU/US-funded industrial park there. We've coordinated with local police; we'll have armored transpo and mobile SWAT teams at all three stops. Day two will be Yendi for another drop-in to learn about the security situation up by the border; that will entail a short motorcade for the entourage to the tribal chieftain's home, supported by Ghanaian army troops. Next, we fly back down south for the short press opportunity to announce the joint redevelopment program at the Akosombo Dam. That one is just a twenty-five-minute stop, wheels down to wheels up, and we'll land at the facility so there's no need for a motorcade. We'll be supported there by River Command police, as well as local cops from Akosombo town nearby.

"The last stop is back here in Accra at Jubilee House, the president's residence, for a get-together, and then we return to the embassy."

Jay said, "To sum it up, we'll leave Accra from the airport at eight a.m. on Thursday and return at four p.m. on Friday, and then the EU high rep will board her aircraft back to Belgium by seven."

He added, "It's a tight timeline with a lot of moving parts to it, but we're ready."

A Foreign Service Officer named Karen Chamberlin spoke next about the protocol, who they would be meeting with, where everyone was to stand at the events, even the length of each speech planned. There were questions and clarifications, of course, but after an hour the meeting broke up. Josh walked his wife back to her office on the second floor of the chancery, and as he did so he leaned closer to her and spoke softly, lest anyone else hear.

"It's one . . . big . . . two-day . . . photo op."

Nichole sighed. "It's optics, babe. The press coverage of this prestigious joint Ghanaian, American, and European delegation going out into the countryside to talk to the officials and to herald new investments in the country will mean something to the people here. We have to show them we are partners who are committed to these projects."

"I'll just be glad when it's over."

Nichole stopped in the hall and looked at her husband. "You guys at DS have had meetings with CIA about the mission, right?"

"Jay did."

"What did they say about the threats?"

"Jay says they basically told us to keep an eye open, and we should be totally fine."

She chuckled at this. "Well, *that's* super helpful."

"Yeah. Seriously, though, Jay thinks our biggest threat will be EDPs at the sites and at the hotel in Tamale, and no terroristic threat to speak of."

Nichole started walking again, and her husband followed. "So you have to work during the party at the French residence?"

"Unfortunately," Josh said. "You're going, right?"

"Yeah. I'll ask Portia if she can stay late."

Josh smiled. Addressing his wife, he said, "Dude. We have a fucking nanny."

She laughed. "I know. I feel like an elitist asshole."

"You've scrubbed your share of toilets. You don't have an elitist bone in your body."

They kissed, she went back to her office, and Josh went back to his computer to look at more doorknobs.

NINE

MISTY GREEN HILLS OVERLOOKED THE VILLAGE OF KADJEBI, A TINY border settlement in Ghana's east, just west of the nation of Togo.

The rising jungle terrain outside town was filled with the sound of birdcalls at nine in the morning, even with the rain, but the songs were disrupted by the rumble of a burgundy Toyota Hilux truck that rolled out of the town, then up a steep and winding graveled road, finally reaching a canopy of trees and then continuing higher, splashing through the brown muck as it picked its way up the hill.

Chinese intelligence officer Kang Shikun and South African mercenary Conrad Tremaine were the only two occupants of the Hilux, with Tremaine behind the wheel. They'd driven in from over the border the night before, leaving their mercs and their rebels behind, and they'd brought no weapons with them at all.

If anyone in the Ghanaian police or military had questioned Kang, he would have been able to claim credibly that he was there working for his front company, Shenzhao Star Global, heading to visit a diamond mine to bid on a security contract, and Tremaine was his employee.

But no one stopped them at the border, and no one stopped them in the village.

Eventually, however, someone *did* stop them. Twenty minutes east of Kadjebi they turned a corner on the climb, then saw a group of three men in civilian clothing standing in the road. There were no weapons visible, but Tremaine slowed down nonetheless when one of the men motioned for him to do so.

They were all three young, fit but thin, and their eyes were neither mistrustful nor malevolent, only intense, as if excited.

Tremaine gauged the look, as he assumed Kang did next to him. These guys weren't soldiers. They'd probably lived rough lives, but they'd never seen combat, never watched their friends die in their arms or felt the bowel-loosening horror that came from indirect fire seeking out their hiding space in a shallow ditch.

No, these kids were just playing war.

He wondered what he always wondered when he encountered the untested. He wondered what they'd do when the fighting started.

Coming to a stop and then rolling down the window, Conrad Tremaine didn't wait for the sentries to ask him about his business.

"The professor is expecting us."

One of the kids looked at both men in the vehicle, then gave a nod. In English, he said, "Park over there. Get out. Leave weapons in the car."

"No weapons, my friend," Tremaine said, and then he did as the boy asked. Soon he and Kang walked back over to the three men, who by now had been joined by two more who'd appeared from the trees along the side of the road. Each of the men had an AK around his neck, but they looked just as fresh and unspoiled as the first group Kang and Tremaine had spoken to.

The South African and the Chinese were quickly patted down, and Tremaine saw this as a good sign, because the last time they'd come here to meet with the rebel leader, his people had been too poorly trained to realize that it might be a good idea to check the strangers to make certain they weren't here to kill or capture their leader.

The frisk was competent enough, and when the check was complete, Kang and Tremaine followed an armed rebel as he walked along a rocky trail for several minutes, passing other forces, virtually all in their teens and early twenties. Eventually they arrived at a picturesque waterfall, a slim chute of spray falling some thirty meters into a crystal clear pool no larger than a tennis court.

A narrow stream ran from the pool, twisting on its way down the hill, which was especially steep here.

A cluster of tents and tarp-roof structures were arrayed along the base of the cliff, everything an olive drab that matched the surrounding flora and made it invisible from the air.

The sentry nodded to a pair of men standing outside one of the tents, their AKs on their backs and their posture relaxed like kids lined up at a high school lunch line, and one of them waved the two foreigners inside the open flap and into the darkness there.

The temperature outside was already above eighty, but it was cool here in the tent. An operations center of some sort had been arrayed in the middle of the low-lit space on a cluster of camp tables. Laptop computers, cell phones, even old FM radio sets were attended by a group of men in plain clothes.

The men looked up from their work for a moment; one motioned to a back corner, and here a small man sat on a cot, his legs crossed in front of him. He wore a brightly colored dashiki shirt, red and blue and green and gold, untucked, with a wide embroidered V-shaped collar and long sleeves.

The small man stood, and without smiling he shook the two newcomers' hands.

"It is good to see you, Professor Addo," Kang said.

"You, as well." He looked up at the much taller white man. His eyes narrowed. "Condor."

"Professor."

Addo said, "Let's go outside and talk, then we will come back inside and relax a moment."

Tremaine wasn't here to relax, but he followed the other men as they left the tent and walked outside, then over towards the waterfall. A couple of armed sentries stood around, but the trio left them behind, then moved towards the rocky cliff face, so close to the cascading water that the mist blew on them, cooling them instantly.

Here they could not be heard by others, nor by any listening devices if any intelligence agency was aware of the group's presence here, which, from Kang's checking of his sources in Accra and back in Beijing, seemed highly unlikely.

When the rebel leader stopped, Tremaine looked him over, not for the first time.

Professor Mamadou Addo stood five feet, seven inches, and he carried himself with an urbane air that belied his relatively young age. Thirty-five years old, he'd received a doctorate in public studies at Accra University before working for a time with the government in Ghana's Western Togoland region.

A radical from birth due to political activism on the part of both parents, Dr. Addo joined the Togoland resistance while teaching at the University of Lomé. From the beginning he found the resistance unorganized and inefficient, and he set his sights on professionalizing the organization.

By the age of twenty-nine he was their leader.

He spent two years doing hard labor in prison after an attack at a radio station led to a government roundup of the usual suspects, and when he was released, he immediately traveled into Togo so that the Ghanaians could not arrest him again.

He broke off from the organization he'd been a part of and eventually formed the Dragons of Western Togoland Restoration Front. They slipped back into Ghana and had a few skirmishes with police in the Volta region, but a warrant went out for his arrest, and he fled once again back over the porous border into Togo.

He'd been out of Ghana for nearly two years, spending his time on social media and on radio that bled into Ghana, espousing his beliefs that the Western Togoland rebellion was growing in power despite the devils in Accra who were oppressing the people of the region.

He claimed, over and over, that between four and five thousand young men had been trained and armed and were ready to fight, but in truth the number had been in the low dozens.

At least until Kang had come to him a year earlier and begun supporting him with money and equipment, propaganda and cyber warfare.

And then Kang brought Tremaine in, referring to him only by his call sign, Condor.

Now, with Addo's power of persuasion, the Chinese money, and Sentinel's training, Professor Addo commanded four companies of troops, well over four hundred men in all.

He looked around nervously now before speaking, making sure there were no spy drones or enemy infiltrators. Tremaine found this silly but said nothing.

The professor finally addressed them in a hushed tone. "I have spoken to my chief lieutenants in the camp back in Sadomé. They say all training is complete. Weapons are cleaned and ready. The men are fed and rested, trucks and vans are loaded, and they are prepared."

Tremaine confirmed this. "Four hundred forty-eight well-trained fighters, Professor. You will move into position on Thursday to begin final preparations along with my mercenaries."

Kang said, "Professor, you must remember. You have to keep your forces hidden until six a.m. Saturday morning."

"Yes, I know. You are afraid of endangering the Western diplomats who will be traveling around the nation."

Tremaine shook his head. "It's not fear. It's expedience. The wider world must not know this is happening until it has already happened."

Kang nodded. "The EU representative leaves Ghana Friday evening. Saturday morning, there will be no stopping us."

Addo said, "I have some concerns."

"Tell me, please," Kang urged in a calm manner.

"The Ghanaian military, of course, or parts of it. I am not worried about Northern Command. They are on the border keeping the Islamists up in Burkina Faso. Our movement from the river to the capital will take hours, not days, and by then it will be too late for them to intervene.

"I am not too worried about Southern Command. They have good equipment and numbers, but their garrisons are completely unprepared for an attack, and according to the intelligence you have shown me, many of their soldiers would support our rebellion."

Kang nodded. "There will be token resistance, but the majority of Southern Command will be on your side, Professor."

"I do, however, remain concerned about Central Command, in Kumasi. General Boatang is popular, and his forces are well equipped and trained. He can travel from Kumasi to Accra faster than I can travel from Western Togoland to Accra. If he gets any early word of our movement, his troops could ruin everything."

Kang said, "Leave Central Command to me. I have a plan."

"As you have said. A plan that you will not reveal."

"All will become apparent soon enough."

Addo wiped mist from the waterfall off his face with the back of his hand. "I will require the support of the people in the south."

"And you will have it," Kang said. "My nation has arranged everything."

Tremaine broke in now. "Boatang will be tied up when you take the capital. After you take the capital—"

"After you take the capital," Kang interrupted back, "my nation will negotiate with him. He will fall under your rule."

"How can you be so sure?"

"There are some . . . compromises. Information my nation has on the general and his extracurricular activities. You have my assurance he will be happy to comply and to serve you faithfully."

Addo just looked back with mistrustful eyes, Tremaine saw, but he noted something else in those eyes. Just like the boy rebels at the checkpoint, there was an energy in them. An energy that came from ambition.

The professor *wanted* this nation, *wanted* his rebel force to take the capital, *wanted* his rule to be accepted by the world at large.

Addo's logic took second place to Addo's unquenchable lust for power.

Tremaine moved the conversation along, lest Addo spend too much time talking over the minutiae. "We expect to achieve our objectives by nightfall Sunday. The president and his cabinet will be deposed, they will flee the country, and they will be permanently exiled by sympathetic military forces in Southern Command.

"By the time the capital opens for business on Monday, the world will learn of the new leadership of Ghana."

Kang said, "A fait accompli, Professor. You will be filmed speaking in Black Star Square, the Gulf of Guinea in the background, and my people will spread your speech, flood the news with positive stories about you and negative stories about the deposed government."

Addo's eyes lingered mistrustfully at the much larger South African now. Finally, he said, "I don't know why we need you here, Condor. Of course I appreciate the training your men have provided my men these past several months. But now that it is time for my people to act, having you nearby, associated with my cause . . . I don't see how the risk is worth it."

Kang began to speak but Tremaine beat him to it. "That's understandable, Professor. You have never been in combat. But trust me, once the shooting starts, you will know *exactly* why I am here."

Addo just glared at the bigger man a moment. There was a smugness in the professor that Tremaine wanted to beat out of him, but the big South African just stood there, his clothes dampening in the waterfall mist as he waited on the rebel leader to come to his point.

Professor Addo finally spoke again. "When this is over, I want you and your men gone."

Tremaine smiled. "We will leave the moment you are in power. Not before, not after."

Addo let it go. To Kang he said, "The social media campaign you initiated to foment the will of the people has been a great success."

The Chinese intelligence officer nodded. "Beijing is committed to your objectives. Their resources will be helpful, especially when you come to power."

"And . . . and what does Beijing require in return?"

Kang raised an eyebrow and hesitated, but he finally replied. "I have told you already. Once you sit in Jubilee House, emissaries from Beijing will come to ask you to improve relations with us."

Addo smiled. "*You* are an emissary of Beijing. I am asking you now. What do you want?"

"As I have told you before, I do not have that answer. When you take power, I will be long gone. The diplomats will be better suited to deal with you than I am."

"One question I have," Addo said. "What if you install me, what if your plan works exactly as described, and then I refuse to give China the resources and access it has worked so hard to acquire? What then?"

"Is that a possibility?"

Addo shrugged. "I am a professor. We deal in hypotheticals."

"Well, that is a question best left to the diplomats."

"I don't want diplomatic speak."

Kang looked across at the waterfall, then slowly back to Addo. "If you do not uphold your end of this bargain, I imagine I will be sent back by my government."

"To do what?"

"To do what I am ordered to do." He paused, then said, "Whatever that may be."

Addo nodded slowly. "I know this to be true. I only wanted to see if you would be transparent with me."

The three men stood in silence a moment, and then, for the first time in the conversation, Professor Mamadou Addo grinned, his teeth shockingly white. He said, "You put me in Jubilee House, Mr. Kang, and the palace door will always be open to China."

AFTER TEA AND CONVERSATION WITH THE PROFESSOR BACK IN THE tent, Tremaine and Kang returned to their Hilux, and the South African began motoring back through the jungle, down the hill towards the town of Kadjebi.

They were a few kilometers past the last Dragon checkpoint when the South African finally spoke. "That bastard has no bloody idea what he's in for."

"He does not," Kang agreed. "And that is just the way we want it."

"You know," Tremaine said, "I've been thinking. There's one thing that would make this coup of yours a lock, a sure thing."

Kang chuckled a little. "Oh yes? Tell me, what have I missed?"

"If President Amanor was assassinated, then there would be no countercoup. I've looked into the politics of this nation. It's fractured. Amanor is the only one with any real pull on the people."

"How do you propose to kill him before he knows the coup is under way?"

Tremaine said, "You move up the attack. Kill him Friday afternoon at Akosombo Dam, then start your coup. I'm one hell of a sniper. I'd take the shot myself if the price were right."

Kang shook his head vehemently. "We need that dam to be in our control before we show our hand. We *must* have that leverage. There are seventy-one Sentinel men in Ghana now, almost four hundred fifty rebels either here or just over the border. The plan is set. The time is set."

"Okay, Kang. You're the boss."

They drove on. Kang Shikun sat in silence, but his mind was active. Just like Professor Addo, Conrad Tremaine did not know the entire plan, either, and that was just the way Kang wanted it.

Kang was the chess master, and his pawns would be used and they would be sacrificed, because that was simply how the game was played.

TEN

THE FRENCH AMBASSADOR'S RESIDENCE IN ACCRA, GHANA, WAS A
beautiful white colonial building in the center of a leafy walled-off
parklike landscape, sandwiched between the U.S. and French embassies in Accra's Cantonments district.

The French embassy grounds were arguably even more secure
than the American embassy next door, since the State Department
had decided that the U.S. embassy property would not have razor
wire rimming the top of its encircling fence. It was a bad look for
America, or so they'd decided back in Foggy Bottom. The French,
however, had no such qualms. Though the French residence and embassy were beautiful and as ornate as anything anywhere in the huge
metropolis of Accra, from the outside it looked like a third-world
maximum-security prison.

Yet even though the building was surrounded by an unwelcoming
fence, the resplendent residence inside was known for its lavish but
tasteful parties.

Tonight's reception for the chief diplomat of the European Union
had been in the planning stages for months, and the planners were
well versed in throwing summertime soirees, so well versed that they
knew to account for the fact that this event would fall during the

rainy season. Plan A had been to host the ninety or so guests out by the pool, under the trees and stars, but the evening was muggy and misty with the promise of rain that could come at any time, so the party had been efficiently moved inside, into the vestibule, the living room, and a long, wide gallery in the seventy-year-old two-story structure.

The French had entertained over one hundred guests at a time in this space in the past, so they knew tonight's event would fit nicely indoors.

The French ambassador had insisted on hosting the EU diplomatic contingent when they came to town. They'd invited local government officials as well as the Americans, and they'd pulled out all the stops. High-quality champagne from Épernay, exquisite Sancerre from the Loire Valley, pinot noir from choice vineyards in Bordeaux. The food was Ghanaian-infused French hors d'oeuvres crafted by local chefs in partnership with the full-time chef here at the embassy. Even the music was from a well-known Ghanaian DJ who kept the tunes pumping in the background as the residence began filling with partygoers at seven p.m.

Nichole Duffy had come alone, but she had no problem working the room, ambling from conversation to conversation with other FSOs and French diplomats while the party got started. She wore a dark burgundy gown, her hair up and her heels high yet manageable. Tomorrow she would fly up north with the delegation, and dress would be casual for the travel. Tonight, on the other hand, was one of only a few opportunities for her to wear one of the three nice dresses she owned, all bought around Washington, D.C., after receiving last-minute work-related invites to posh parties there since joining the Foreign Service.

She nursed a glass of white wine, telling herself she had to stay sharp because tonight was work as well as play, but even as she chatted with French diplomatic counterparts and Ghanaian officials, her eyes continued flitting towards the vestibule and the front door, because she eagerly anticipated her husband's appearance with the U.S. ambassador, who had yet to arrive.

Just then the door opened and Jay Costa, the regional security officer, stepped into the room just ahead of Jennifer Dunnigan, the U.S. ambassador to Ghana. Jay would be in charge of the ambo's security tonight, Nichole knew, and her husband and one other special agent would be here to support him.

Jennifer Dunnigan was a fifty-five-year-old career diplomat who'd most recently served as the deputy chief of mission in Peru. African American and tall at five foot nine, she had bright eyes and an easy smile. She was known here in Ghana as being a good listener and a tireless supporter of good relations between the United States and the West African nation.

Next to Dunnigan was Manfred House, Nichole's boss as the State Department's political chief of the embassy, and standing next to him was Chad Larsen, the assistant regional security officer and Josh's slightly younger coworker.

The other ARSO, the new guy here at Accra station, trailed behind the small entourage, and Nichole smiled a little as she saw her husband in his dark suit, the coat open so he could access his firearm, if necessary, and his brown eyes flashing left and right, just like the other two security men.

Nichole couldn't deny it. It was kind of a turn-on to watch Josh work. It wasn't something she'd ever experienced when he was a civilian contractor, except for about ten minutes the first time they met, and she'd never been around the few times he'd done protection work in D.C. with Diplomatic Security.

The only time she'd really ever seen him doing any kind of work at all was in that year or so he was employed as a security officer at Tysons Galleria, after his leg injury and before he'd taken the contracting job in Mexico that nearly killed him but ultimately turned his life around. She'd meet him at the mall for lunch some days, and they'd sit on a bench in the parking lot or somewhere in the food court and eat sandwiches brought from home, but at the time Josh had been so utterly depressed about his injury and his financial situation that those lunches had hardly been occasions to remember.

But tonight, Josh was fully in his element. Nichole Duffy had had this week on her calendar for months for several reasons, but one of the main ones was she knew she was going to get to see Josh on the job, doing the work he loved.

As the American ambassador began shaking hands with a contingent of French embassy officials in the vestibule, Nichole moved next to a statue in the gallery and looked on, her glass in hand. Josh stood thirty feet away from her, his hands clasped in front of him as he scanned around the area, and in no time at all his eyes locked on hers.

She gave him an exaggerated wink, like a drunk girl in a bar making an awkward pass, and he smiled sheepishly and looked away, rolling his eyes.

Nichole loved embarrassing him, almost as much as he loved embarrassing her, but right now she had him at a disadvantage and she knew it.

Soon Dunnigan stepped deeper into the residence, her three-person security team remaining vigilant but not overly so, as the real security work wouldn't start till the next day.

Soon enough, the ambassador entered the galley, took a glass of champagne from the tray of a passing server, and entered into conversation with the French ambassador, a sixty-two-year-old with bushy gray hair, a wide smile, and a booming laugh.

Nichole accepted a cheese canapé offered by a server and popped it into her mouth, then grabbed a second when the man turned and began heading in the other direction. The ambassador was just a few feet away now, so close that Josh positioned himself against the gallery wall, just next to his wife.

"How's it going?" she asked, taking a sip of her wine.

"It's going," he replied, still watching over the room. "You look amazing."

"You're not supposed to have your eyes on me," she joked.

"Why not? Everyone else does."

"'Cause you're working, Special Agent." She smiled, fighting the urge to grab her husband and drag him into a coatroom.

The ambassador told a story to her French counterpart, and a few feet away Josh spoke softly to Nichole. "How's the wine?"

"It's outstanding, sorry to say."

Josh wouldn't be drinking tonight, Nichole knew.

The ambo finished her conversation with the French ambassador and then noticed Nichole standing there. She stepped closer; both women complimented each other on their dresses, and then Jennifer Dunnigan said, "I'm sorry your husband had to work tonight. I don't think there's a safer place on the continent right now than the French embassy in Ghana, but the protection order is over my head."

Nichole tipped her wine to the ambo. "No problem at all. It's funny to see him all serious and in detail mode. He's not quite so stiff at home. All those years as a contractor's wife, I definitely never saw him at work."

To this Josh said, "First time I met you, I was working."

Nichole smiled. "Okay, that's true."

"Where are the kids? With the nanny?"

"Yes, Portia has both of them and Chad Larsen's son, so she's got her hands full tonight. They're having a pizza party at our house, and I told her I'd be home no later than nine." Nichole looked down to the Apple Watch on her wrist. "I'll duck out of here shortly before, unless you need me for anything."

Dunnigan shook her head. "I'll need you over in Takoradi, in Kumasi, up in Tamale, and in Akosombo, but tonight, consider yourself off the clock. Have a little fun."

The ambo was greeted by a Ghanaian official, directing her attention away for a moment, and Nichole grabbed a small skewer of grilled shrimp from a passing tray and took a bite while Josh stood next to her, keeping his eyes on the ambo.

Nichole gave a soft moan, luxuriating in the flavor of the hors d'oeuvre. She said, "Oh my God, have you tried the shrimp?"

She was teasing him, and he just sighed.

"I'm sorry, babe," she said after another bite. "I'll drop a few into my purse for you for later." She stood next to him, looking out at the room. "Seems like a well-behaved bunch."

"Except for the lady who won't leave me alone to do my job." Then he shrugged. "She's hot, though. I'll give her that."

She said, "I don't even know why you guys have to cover her inside the French embassy."

His eyes remained on his ambassador. Costa was on the other side of her, and Larsen to his right, both doing the same.

Josh said, "We didn't clear this guest list, the French did."

"You don't think anyone is going to try anything, do you?"

"Trust me, Nik. The minute you start thinking you've got nothing to worry about is exactly when you've got *everything* to worry about. I always assume we're two seconds away from trouble."

Of course she understood. She'd once been flying in her Apache in Syria, setting up a rocket attack on an enemy miles away, when, from out of nowhere, she'd been knocked out of the sky.

"Complacency kills," she muttered.

"You get me, babe."

The front door opened and a new security team entered; they looked especially switched on and intense, and soon he saw why. Behind them, Johanna Aldenburg, high representative of the European Union for Foreign Affairs and Security Policy, entered, wearing a cream-colored dress and designer eyeglasses.

Aldenburg took a glass of champagne, then made her way over to the French ambassador to Ghana.

"Think she'll recognize you?" Nichole asked.

"No way. I never saw her again after that thing in Embassy Row. She sent us that nice letter and a fruit basket, though. Or one of her people did."

Ambassador Dunnigan stepped up to Aldenburg and the French ambo, and they all spoke for several minutes, but finally the Dutch woman's eyes flashed up to the security man standing along the wall next to the beautiful woman in burgundy, and Josh realized quickly that he'd been wrong, she *did* recognize him.

Aldenburg crossed the space quickly, a look of both surprise and pleasure on her face. "Mr. Duffy?"

"Very nice to see you again, ma'am."

"This is quite the surprise. What are the chances I'd run into you here?"

"I've read about how much traveling you do, so I guess the chances were pretty good. I've only been here in Accra a couple of weeks. May I introduce my wife, Nichole?"

Aldenburg and Nichole shook hands.

"An honor to meet you," Nichole said.

Josh said, "Nichole is a political officer."

"A family affair. How nice." Josh kept scanning the party while Aldenburg addressed his wife. "May I just tell you that your husband very well might have saved the life of my daughter. My own life, as well, as I was doing my best to get out there and help, and I'm not exactly much of a fighter."

"That is who he is, ma'am. He saved me once, as well, as a matter of fact."

The diplomat clearly took this as nothing more than a sweet metaphor, though Nichole had meant it quite literally.

"That's wonderful. Will you be coming along on the mission tomorrow?"

"We both are," Nichole confirmed.

"It should be a whirlwind." She looked at Josh. "Here's hoping it's an easier outing than the last time you were on my detail. Of course, you're on Ambassador Dunnigan's detail now."

Josh looked around at the EU security men, all standing close by. "Looks like you've got a solid crew."

At this, she turned and motioned to a man close to her. He was in his thirties; his hair was dark and combed back, he wore a gray suit and a red tie, and Josh had already ID'd him as the agent in charge of her European Union security detail. "Julian Delisle, meet Joshua Duffy. I told you about what happened with Ria in Washington. Joshua was the one who fought his way in and fought his way back out with my daughter."

While shaking Delisle's hand, Josh said, "My memory is a little fuzzy, but I think I only fought my way *most* of the way out."

All of them laughed at this; Aldenburg gave another handshake to Josh and to Nichole, and soon she turned and began speaking with Ambassador Dunnigan and the Ghanaian foreign minister.

Josh began following them as they strolled into the living room, and Nichole called out to him. "I'm going to make another pass at the food table. I saw an éclair with my name on it."

"Can't wait to hear all about it."

ELEVEN

FIVE MINUTES LATER JOSH STOOD BY AN OPEN PATIO DOOR; RAIN
poured outside but the noise was all but drowned out by the conversation and the music coming from speakers around the living room.
Ambassador Dunnigan sat on a sofa ten feet away, chatting with an
EU diplomat and the Ghanaian minister for the interior. Jay Costa
was closer to the ambo; it was his job as the bodyman to get her up
and out if the need arose. Chad was close to the entrance of the
room, so Josh was here protecting the back patio access in case they
needed to evacuate back to the motorcade parked outside.

Josh eyed the rest of Aldenburg's eight-person security team from
the EU, sprinkled around the room just as he, Jay, and Chad were.
All but one were male, and all wore suits and ties. They appeared to
be in their thirties and forties, carried themselves like soldiers, and
looked like they knew what they were doing. They all remained well
positioned but unobtrusive, and Josh respected that.

He saw a man in his fifties stroll into the room wearing a blue
blazer and gray slacks. A glass of red wine in his hand, he appeared
no different than a dozen others here at the party, meaning he
wouldn't have earned more than a single glance from Josh if not for
one thing.

The guy was looking right at him.

Josh thought the new arrival might have been eyeing the patio behind him, but instead he walked directly to Josh, turned around, and began looking back into the crowded rooms in front of him, as if he were mimicking the DS special agent's pose.

Josh fired a quick glance to the man on his right. "Evening," he said.

"Evening. I'd shake your hand, but I know you're working." He spoke with an American accent; he sounded like he might have been from Chicago.

The man didn't look familiar, but Josh hadn't met half of the Americans at the embassy yet. "Something I can do for you?"

"You're Josh Duffy."

"I am."

"Bob Gorski. Pleased to meet you."

"Mr. Gorski." Duff glanced his way again, looking the man over quickly. His first thought was he was CIA. In his contracting days in the Middle East and North Africa, Josh had become adept at determining the agencies that Americans worked for. That said, a lot of people he pegged as Agency personnel turned out to be defense attachés or DEA agents, so he knew better than to make too hasty a conclusion.

Gorski said, "I read all about your exploits in Mexico a couple of years ago. Gotta say, you impressed the hell out of me."

Josh moved a step to his left when someone in front of him partially blocked his view of the American ambassador. Gorski followed, and Josh said, "A lot of what was written was wrong."

Gorski chuckled and took a swig of his wine. "That's a given. Anyway, despite inevitably fucking up some details, I believe the gist of what I read about what you went through over there. You showed a hell of a lot of guts, intelligence, and resolve. My mom used to tell me, 'Bobby, you've got pluck.' Well, kid, *you've* got pluck."

Josh smiled politely, looking ahead. "Thank you."

"I'm OGA, in case you hadn't guessed." OGA was "other governmental agency," a low-profile way of saying "CIA" when you didn't want to say "CIA" out loud.

"Had a suspicion," Josh admitted. He noticed Costa looking his way now, then looking at Gorski and making a face of annoyance, as if he knew the man and didn't think much of him.

To Gorski, Josh said, "Haven't seen you around. You're not Accra station, are you?"

"No, no. I'm just visiting. Heard you were here, so I just wanted to drop in and say hi."

Josh was confused by this. "You came to this party at the French ambo's house to meet me?"

"I did." Then he shrugged. "And the caviar. You've got to try the toast points. I used to be stationed in Russia. It's better there, but the French can definitely pull it off, I've got to say."

"Are you trying to recruit me?"

Gorski laughed and tipped back more of his wine, and Josh began to wonder if the man might be a little drunk. "No. But having said that, if you ever want to make the leap over to the intelligence side, I'd steer you towards the appropriate people."

"Thanks, but I'm good. My wife and I are trying to build the right life for our kids, and we get to do that at State . . . I bet your job makes that sort of thing tough."

"Thrice divorced, no children, fifty-two. Not exactly the right guy to sell a family man on following in my footsteps." He laughed good-naturedly. "Still . . . it's nice to know there's another good egg around here, even if you aren't working for us."

Josh moved a little as Dunnigan rose and began mingling around the room, and Gorski walked along next to him, grabbing a glass of white wine now from a tray on the bar.

"So, again—" Josh said, but Gorski broke in before he could repeat his question as to why Gorski had come to speak with him.

"I hear you'll be going along with the ambo, the president, and the
high rep on the development mission tomorrow."

"I guess I won't ask where you heard that, seeing who you
work for."

"Yeah, the details aren't public knowledge for security reasons,
but honestly, that hardly took any cloak-and-dagger work." Gorski
took one sip of the white, then put it down on the bar and grabbed a
fresh pinot noir from a tray there. He said, "I wonder if I could ask a
little favor."

"A favor?"

"Yeah. I'm hearing some rumblings in the bush."

Josh turned to him now. "Rumblings?"

"Yeah."

"In the . . . in the *bush*?"

"That's right. Ghana is quiet, for now, but the rest of West Africa
is a shit show. Coups in Burkina Faso, Mali, Benin, and Niger; it's not
looking good for Togo. On top of that, there's Islamic extremists all
the fuck over the place."

Josh's brow furrowed. "Up north, yeah. Over in Nigeria, sure. But
not here in Ghana."

Gorski shrugged. "There are a lot of factors coming together we
need to keep an eye on. The economy is in the shitter, the politics
over in the east, on the other side of the Volta River, foreign influence, foreign money. I just thought you could let me know if you saw
or heard anything . . . interesting."

"Are you talking about possible unrest here in the country? A danger to the delegation?"

Gorski shook his head. "We've got absolutely nothing indicating
any uprising in the short term. The rebels don't have weapons, makes

it tough to force anyone's hand in Africa with nothing more than a machete."

"That's how they did it in Rwanda," Josh replied, still watching the ambo and those around her.

Gorski shook his head. "No, they did it in Rwanda by having tens of thousands of committed *killers* with machetes. Here? If there's two hundred fifty military-aged males out there in the east who want to make trouble for Ghana I'd eat my hat, and again, they're all but unarmed."

Gorski grabbed another caviar toast point off a passing tray. "But the problem isn't really the rebels. It's the Chinese."

Josh kept his attention on his duties, but he was most definitely interested in what the CIA officer had to say.

"How so?"

"They're pissed about the new port we're building, the dam we're refurbing, the schools, the industrial park. Hell, all the infrastructure the EU and the U.S. are supporting here. They don't like us nudging our way back into partnerships, and they don't like President Amanor in Jubilee House making nice with the West at the expense of Chinese access to the gold and diamond mines here. Beijing doesn't have the money to blow to counter us dollar for yuan, but I can't help but wonder if it might be in their interests to make some trouble. We've seen and heard inciting things, in print and on the radio. Just low-level bitching about Accra. About President Amanor and his cabinet. Stuff on social media, too, way too sophisticated to come out of the jungles of fucking Togo.

"Professor Addo and his radio show are pumping up the anger at Accra, but we think all this hype is being produced in Beijing." Gorski downed a healthy sip of his pinot noir and said, "It's exactly the same shit we used to do in Central America, everywhere else."

By "we," Josh took that to mean the CIA.

"What are you asking me to do?"

"Like I said. Just let me know if you see or hear anything."

"I'm just an ARSO. I've been in country like . . . eleven days. I'm not . . . I'm not *whatever* it is you are asking me to be."

"I'm just asking you to be another set of eyes. You'd be scanning for threats even if I didn't ask you to. I'm suggesting you pull out your Iridium sat phone and give me a ring if you see something, *anything*, that might be of interest to an old Africa hand who's tracking Chinese involvement in the area."

Josh didn't get it. "There are five American dips heading out on this movement, including the ambo. There's two other DS agents who are way senior to me, there's our Foreign Service National Investigator and our Local Body Guard force of four knowledgeable ex-cops. Why come to *me* for help?"

Gorski seemed to consider this, then said, "Because I figure you know what trouble looks like better than most."

Josh raised an eyebrow, but he kept his attention on Dunnigan as she chatted with partygoers. Finally, he said, "You've got a card?"

"No, but I've got your sat number. I'll send you a message so you have mine."

Josh nodded, though he didn't know how the CIA had the number to his satellite phone.

Gorski said, "One more thing. In all your years as a merc, did you ever—"

"I wasn't a mercenary. I was a private military contractor."

"Right. Okay, in all your years as a private military contractor, did you ever run into a guy named Conrad Tremaine?"

Duff's eyes widened. He stopped scanning the room and turned to face Gorski. "South African?"

"Yeah."

Josh nodded slowly, his eyes suddenly unfixed. "Yeah. I worked under him for a while when I contracted for United Defense."

Gorski seemed to know this already. "You were working for United when you lost your leg in Lebanon, right?"

Duff sighed. This guy knew everything somehow. He said, "Yeah, but I knew Tremaine before, when I was in Afghanistan. He made quite an impression."

"Positive or negative?"

"*Definitely* negative. *He's* a merc. Always was. He's a piece of shit. Got fired for working with some guys in big Army to steal a consignment of rifles. Tried to rope me and a few other Joes in with him, got a guy killed in the process."

"Damn," Gorski said softly.

Duff shook his head to clear it of the memories. "Tremaine lost his contract, but I heard he found another gig soon after."

Gorski nodded at this. "He now works for a company called Sentinel."

"Never heard of them."

"You *have*. When Armored Saint, the company that fucked you over in Mexico, went bankrupt, the principals and a lot of the contractors joined up with former United Defense employees, and they re-formed under the name Sentinel Security."

Josh knew none of this; he'd been too focused on his future to pay attention to things that he was sure were firmly in the past. He wasn't a contractor anymore, and never would be again.

"Why are you asking me about Tremaine?" For the first time since he'd entered the French ambassador's residence, his full attention was directed at something other than his duties here protecting Dunnigan.

The CIA man stepped closer. "He was photographed by an agent of mine at a grass landing strip in Togo two and a half weeks ago. We don't know what he was doing there, but where he goes, trouble often follows. If you don't know already, Togo's border with Ghana . . . how should I put it?"

"Does not exist," Duff said.

"That's *exactly* how I should put it."

Josh just nodded. Slowly he looked back to the ambo.

Gorski said, "Anyway, if you run into any mercs out there on your little junket into the bush, if you hear rumblings of China or tall tales of armed rebels or South African hired guns . . . or if you just want to talk . . . give me a ring."

Gorski patted Josh on the shoulder, put his half-empty wineglass down on a side table next to a sofa, and headed for the front door.

WHEN AMBASSADOR DUNNIGAN STEPPED INTO THE LADIES' ROOM ten minutes later, Jay Costa shouldered up to Duff outside the door. "I see you met Crazy Bob."

Josh turned to his boss. "Why do you call him crazy?"

"He's been in Africa for twenty years, all the hell over. Was station chief in Mogadishu, Deputy Chief in Angola. Now he's kind of a roving shit-starter. Tied to Africa desk at Langley and not to a station on the continent. He's always out there chasing worst-case scenarios, making trouble at whatever embassy he shows up in." Costa laughed. "Langley loves him for some reason. He's got friends on the Seventh Floor, I guess, but Dunnigan and the other ambos on the continent won't give him the time of day."

Josh said, "He mentioned a South African contractor I used to know. Said he was seen recently just over the border in Togo."

Costa squeezed Duff's forearm and widened his eyes like he was having a heart attack. "A mercenary was seen in Africa? Stop the fucking presses." The older man shrugged with a little laugh. "It's always like that with Gorski. He 'connects' a few dots that don't really connect, and then he says all hell's about to break loose. He called it right a couple of times over the years, a blind squirrel finds a nut, but he's been wrong a lot more than he's been right.

"Look," Costa added, "we got our briefing from Accra station about this movement tomorrow, and they are the in-country experts."

He added, "Don't let Crazy Bob's conspiracies waste space in your brain."

Josh, Chad Larsen, and Jay Costa followed Dunnigan into the gallery a minute later, and here Josh saw his wife speaking with her boss and some of the other political officers.

He decided right then and there he wasn't going to tell Nikki about his conversation with the CIA man. There was nothing to worry about, and he didn't want to burden her, because she had a lot on her plate for this trip already.

He himself put most of what "Crazy Bob" said out of his mind, but he couldn't stop thinking about Tremaine.

Gorski had been right about one thing, of this Josh was sure. Where Tremaine goes, trouble follows.

Whatever the hell Condor was doing, Josh hoped like hell that the son of a bitch would stay over the border in Togo and do it there.

TWELVE

KANG SHIKUN ENTERED THE RESTAURANT AT TEN P.M., ALONE, wearing a blue blazer and brown slacks. He carried nothing in his hands, and he had no weapon stowed; even his mobile phone and his satellite phone were locked in the glove compartment of the Land Rover he'd parked in front of the establishment.

This place was called Sapphire Valley: a sprawling, parklike wedding, party, and recreational venue on the outskirts of Kumasi, Ghana's second city. It was owned by Chinese interests and also contained a restaurant and bar on its expansive grounds.

There were a lot of Chinese in Kumasi these days, even with heightened trade tensions between Beijing and Accra, so he didn't feel out of place as he made his way past a wedding reception full of well-dressed and well-to-do locals and through the gardens, then finally into the back room of the restaurant.

He knew his way around here, and he knew the protocol. Two local men in casual attire met him just inside the doorway; he raised his arms and they frisked him. They weren't looking for guns or knives or bombs, Kang knew; they were looking for recording devices, hence their search was disrespectfully thorough.

But the Shenzhao Star Global executive from Beijing remained, as always, composed and relaxed.

He was waved through by the men, who then stepped outside and shut the door behind him.

Kang was not alone. The sole other person in the room was in his fifties, with a proud head of black hair that grayed at the temples, a broad chest, and a posture that gave away the fact that he was military, even though he wore an authentic hand-embroidered black, gold, and red dashiki shirt, casual drawstring pants, and leather sandals.

He offered no smile to the man from Beijing, but he did extend a hand and gave a strong shake.

Kang said one word as a greeting. "General."

Brigadier General Kwame Boatang was the leader of the nation's Central Command, one of three commands that divided the nation. Northern Command saw the most action; there were extremist elements in Burkina Faso that made their way down over the border and had been causing significant trouble for the Ghanaian military there. Southern Command was in the capital, and although it was considered the showpiece of the military, Kang had determined major weaknesses in their structure, their positioning throughout the city, their readiness, and, perhaps most importantly for his aims, their resolve.

But Central Command was, by Beijing's estimation, solid. It wasn't the biggest, the flashiest, or the most battle-hardened of the three commands, but it was the most effectively led, it had the most resolute troops, and, with its recent acquisition of infantry fighting vehicles given to the Ghana Armed Forces by the European Union, it was the most mobile of the three commands in the nation.

Boatang's force did have one flaw, but Kang saw it as an asset and not a liability.

Corruption in its leadership.

Organized crime elements from China were pervasive all over

Africa; they sought minerals, gems, cheap human capital, and oil, and one of the mainland Triads had gotten to Boatang five years earlier, offering him an under-the-table stake in a gold mine in nearby Bibiani if only he'd look the other way while they extorted from businesses in the center of the nation and conducted organized gambling and prostitution.

Boatang accepted the bribe with little thought at the time. After all, his job wasn't policing the central part of the nation, it was the constant preparation to repel any attacks from a foreign aggressor.

But the police in Kumasi had been similarly corrupted by the Triads, and soon Boatang saw that what the Chinese had bought from him was his promise to look the other way as they operated as they wished in his territory.

The gold mine in Bibiani produced riches for the general, riches the Chinese helped him bank offshore in the Seychelles, and as his accounts grew, the fifty-five-year-old career military man had been satisfied with the relationship overall.

Until nine months ago.

It was then he'd learned that Accra was looking into his dealings with the Triads; for the next few months he'd stayed occupied speaking to investigators, protesting his innocence to his superiors in the capital, and fearing that his world would soon come crashing down.

And then, six months ago, the small mysterious man from Shenzhao Star Global showed up.

Boatang was called to a meeting here at Sapphire Valley, where he usually met with the 24K, the Triad arm who bribed him, so he assumed it would be a normal meeting with the normal participants. That meant he'd expected another one of the big tough Asian mobsters who he'd been dealing with for years to walk into the room, but instead a smaller man in a business suit greeted him with a handshake and a smile, and then he ordered a glass of chardonnay from a waiter.

Boatang could tell immediately that this individual was no Triad. Kang was more urbane, more thoughtful, more strategically minded, more big-picture-thinking.

It didn't take him long to figure out that this man was a spy.

In that first conversation, Kang gave Boatang intricate details into the investigation against him, things that could have only been known if there were recording devices in the investigators' offices.

But more importantly, he also proposed a way out for the popular general.

Kang had said, in a soft tone that Boatang would learn to always expect, "They have you dead to rights. There is only one way to keep yourself out of prison."

Boatang's voice gave a hint of his desperation. "What is that?"

"You need to control the investigators. You need to control the courts."

The general had given a rumbling but unsure laugh. "How can I control the courts?"

"Simple. You become president."

General Boatang was a man of great ambition, and as surprised as he had been to hear this suggestion out of the spy from Beijing, he didn't send him on his way, because he wanted to know more.

And over the course of several more meetings the plan had been laid out, and the plan had been agreed to.

And now, a half year later, the plan was days away from going into motion.

Tonight they spent the first half hour of the meeting discussing pleasantries, politics, gossip. Kang did the vast majority of the talking. Calmly, with complete self-assuredness. Boatang, for his part, appeared nervous as he ignored his food and sipped scotch.

Boatang was tense tonight, excited by his prospects but nervous about what was to come. "This is very dangerous for me personally. I should not have worked with your people from the beginning, Kang."

"You did not work with *my* people. You worked with 24K. The most notorious Triad in the world. I was thousands of miles from here when that all took place. If you are having second thoughts of our plan, General, don't blame them on me. *I* am the one who is offering you a way out."

Boatang had grown mistrustful of the spy, just as he had grown more desperate to find a way out of his perilous legal situation.

He said, "You tell me you will put me in power. How many other people have you told you are going to put them in power?"

Kang laughed at this. "Only one. I told the professor that he would be ensconced in Jubilee House by Sunday night."

Kwame Boatang flashed a little smile finally, the first of the evening. He said, "If Addo really *is* a professor, then I'm very glad my kids didn't study under him. The man is a fool."

Kang shrugged. "You know academics. The plan I gave him is as intricate as anything he might read in a history book, and he believes what he reads. So why should he doubt me?"

"Why should I *believe* you?"

"Because you are the linchpin. You are the only man with the military power to take the capital, the charisma to lead the nation, and the intelligence to develop a better working relationship with my country, sending the West on their way."

This had all been decided, it had all been agreed to, but Boatang knew that tonight would be the last chance he had to voice his concerns. "Let me see if I have this right. Addo's rebels, they will cut power to Accra by controlling the dam, placing mines in it so the army cannot respond. Then they will begin attacking police stations and military checkpoints on the way to the capital. Once there, they will effectively tie up Southern Command, with help from soldiers of fortune you've brought into the country, until I arrive with my mechanized forces. My troops will rout the rebels, your mercenaries will slip away, and I will be left standing in the capital, victorious."

Kang said, "President Amanor and General Tetteh from Southern Command leave late Friday evening for meetings in Brussels. They'll be in Europe when their nation is attacked. My people will have footage of them lunching at a Michelin-starred restaurant. It's from an earlier visit, but it will make them look hopelessly out of touch, weak and floundering in response to the attack from Western Togoland, the power outage, and a few other tricks I have planned. My social media campaign will be ready to go for when power is restored, and you will be presented to the nation as the new way forward.

"Parliament will call for an election, you will win, and you will be sitting in Jubilee House within three months of today."

Boatang hadn't touched his meal, but he downed the remainder of the scotch that had been sitting in front of him the entire time Kang had been eating. Then he stood and said, "This had better work, Kang. For both of our sakes."

Kang shrugged. "It will work. But it will work for *your* sake, not for mine. I will leave Ghana when this is over, move on. You are the one who stands to gain with success, and lose with failure."

Kang Shikun could see the same look in the general's eyes as he'd seen in the eyes of the young rebel commander. A lust for power that for so long had been out of his grasp.

The Chinese operative could tell he had played the correct chess pieces for this match.

They shook hands. Boatang said, "Will I see you again?"

Kang shook his head. "In person, never. I'll be out of Accra by the time the smoke clears, but I'll be supporting you in the shadows until you attain the presidency. Then you will forget about me."

The Ghanaian general nodded. "I truly hope so."

MINUTES LATER THE INTELLIGENCE OPERATIVE WAS BACK BEHIND the wheel of his black Land Rover, heading for the airport. He'd hop a quick flight to Accra, then be picked up by his people and taken to his operating base in the hills to the north of the capital, from where he would watch his coup take place.

As he drove, he allowed himself a moment to think over what was about to happen.

His plot, he would freely admit, was an utterly cynical one. First, arm and poorly train rebels, promise them they had Chinese and mercenary support for an attack on the capital, and popular and military support, as well, and then use Ghanaian troops in China's back pocket to eradicate the rebels and seize power with "legitimacy."

And Kang would also employ Islamic extremists to both tie up the armed forces in the north of the country and sow panic and chaos in the south.

Just like with Conrad Tremaine, the general didn't know about the jihadis, because Kang knew neither man would willingly work with them, but Kang's relationship with Iran had given him an opportunity to create the bedlam and confusion in the capital he needed to ensure his plan's success.

Boatang's people would destroy the small extremist cells when they got there, but by then the jihadis would have the public utterly terrified and beyond disdainful of the government.

For all this to happen, for it all to work as planned, Kang Shikun knew that several things had to be true.

One, Tremaine's men needed to be a true force multiplier. The seventy mercenaries were a much more potent force than the four hundred forty-eight rebels, and by moving Sentinel around the country in small teams, they could make it appear as if the rebel army was materializing from all directions, perhaps even rising up out of the local citizenry.

Another thing that had to happen was for all communications in the country to be disrupted, at least for the first several hours of the coup. This would allow Kang's chess pieces to move to the most advantageous locations on the chessboard, so that when comms were restored, the coup would be a fait accompli.

Tremaine's people would deal with mobile and landline infrastructure, but Kang had his own Chinese technical specialists here to help jam satellite communications, television, Internet, and cable.

Kang Shikun had been involved in three other coups in the past four years, but Ghana was different. A stable democracy, a better infrastructure than the other countries Kang had worked in.

But while Ghana presented more challenges, it also presented more opportunities. Ninety gold mines dotted the nation; it was the second largest producer of gold on the continent. Several diamond mines had shown promise, as well.

The nation's warming relationship with the West was also a black mark on China's expansion efforts in Africa.

Bringing Ghana back into the fold, installing leadership in Accra that truly appreciated China's development efforts and business relationships, would go a long way to showing the other nations on the continent that resistance, in the end, was futile.

If Ghana went full partnership with China, the thinking in Beijing went, everyone else would, too.

But it was crucial for Kang to keep Beijing's involvement a secret in this. His Chinese technicians were ostensibly private contractors, just as he was, here in the nation to improve the country's communications system. The mercenaries were principally Russian, and Kang planned to exploit this fact when the time was right to do so.

The Dragons of Western Togoland would take the blame for the coup, and if word of foreign involvement *did* get out, well then Kang had fifty Russians, all former military, whom he could implicate, putting the focus on Moscow and not on Beijing.

He had the rebel, Addo; he had the general, Boatang; he had the Iranian, Zahedi; and he had the South African mercenary, Tremaine.

Kang Shikun's job was nothing less than "acquiring" Africa for

China. He wasn't the only one doing this; China had emissaries of all sorts, commercial and diplomatic. But Kang was the one sent in to seize territory by irregular warfare, to prop up helpful leaders and depose unhelpful ones.

And Ghana was by far the biggest target he'd ever had in his sights.

THIRTEEN

ISAAC OPOKU OPENED HIS EYES AND STARED UP AT THE SLOWLY
spinning fan above him, just visible in the low light. After a few seconds he pulled his pillow over his head and pressed it hard against
both his ears.

And then, after realizing his efforts were futile, he gave up and
tossed it onto the floor in frustration.

The baby's cries were just too damn loud for him to drown
them out.

He sat up slowly, rubbed his exhausted eyes, and glanced to the
clock on the nightstand next to him.

Six twenty-four a.m.

He pressed his eyes shut again as he sat there, willing himself to
wake up.

The baby had had him up during the night, he couldn't remember
what time that was, exactly, and he was absolutely wasted right now,
but that wasn't the worst part. No, the worst part was that he knew
he wouldn't have anyone he could complain to about his situation
because his wife had been up then, as well, and from the sounds
coming out of the family room of the little house here in the small
town of Atimpoku, she was most definitely up now.

Their son had arrived four months ago, and neither Isaac nor his wife had had a good night of sleep since then.

He wondered how many cries he'd slept through. Had she and the baby been up other times without him?

Opoku was thirty-one years old, just under six feet tall, and fit. His hair was short and his boyish face clean-shaven, but with his sinewy muscles he carried the appearance of someone who was well accustomed to physical labor.

Not that he felt particularly strong right now. He staggered out of bed in his boxers and a T-shirt that said "Super Dad" in bold red lettering across the front, and then he continued shaking the cobwebs from his mind as he headed into the family room, where he found his wife of two years, just beginning to nurse his infant son on the couch in front of the TV.

"Maa chi." *Good morning*, he said, speaking Twi, the language of the Akan people of southern and central Ghana.

Abina Opoku looked up and replied herself in Twi. "Sorry he woke you."

Isaac wiped the sleep from his eyes. "It's fine. I'll just go in early; it will be a busy day at work, anyway."

"I made some rice water; it's in the pot on the stove."

Opoku smiled a tired smile. "Let me get dressed first, and I'll join Kofi for breakfast."

A few minutes later he came back out of the bedroom wearing a dark green-and-brown camouflage uniform with a badge on the shoulder that read "VRA-RIVCOM." A Browning Hi-Power 9-millimeter pistol hung in a leather holster from his hip, a pair of extra magazines jutted from pouches on his utility belt, and a maroon beret had been stuffed under the epaulet on his right shoulder.

Abina was still feeding their son, so Isaac went into the tiny kitchen, grabbed a bowl from a shelf, and used a ladle to scoop the hot rice water into it. It was a simple breakfast, just as its name implied. Rice with extra water, making for a souplike consistency, flavored with milk and loads of sugar, just the way Isaac liked it. He grabbed a cup of Milo, a chocolate malt powder his wife blended with boiling water and left on the counter for him while she held her son in her other arm.

Sergeant Isaac Opoku sat next to his young family while Abina finished breastfeeding Kofi; the TV was on and the local news reported the story of the EU chief diplomat in the capital, making a speech at the airport the afternoon before about the West increasing its investments all across Ghana. She announced how excited she was to be visiting points around the nation to mark the beginning of a new era of cooperation and assistance from the EU and the United States.

Both Isaac and his wife were well aware of the EU lady's travel here in Ghana, even though the times and locations of her visits were not public knowledge.

"When does she arrive at the dam?" Abina asked.

"Tomorrow at two p.m."

"Maybe you'll be on TV. Your parents will love that."

Isaac smiled a little. "Woman, if I'm on TV, I'll be standing far in the background. You won't even know it's me."

"Still . . . who of us has been on television? Try to get them to take your picture."

"There will be thirty local police at the dam for the speech. Plus twenty-four of us from RIVCOM. Plus the fifty people from the helicopters." He thought a moment. "Plus the VRA plant operators. No one would see me."

Abina gave a tired smile as she stood from the sofa. She said, "Just start dancing or something. The photographers will have to take a picture of that!"

To this Opoku laughed a booming laugh, and as Abina put Kofi back in his crib, he finished his rice water and Milo, then took his dishes to the sink. "I *am* a good dancer."

"You could be famous," she said, continuing the joke. "Then you won't have to be a cop anymore."

Opoku said, "My dad was a cop. His dad was a cop. My sister is a cop. I'm always going to be a cop."

Abina gave a tired laugh. "Well . . . Kofi's *not* going to be a cop. He's going to be a doctor."

"Yes," Opoku said. "As soon as he retires from football, he will go right away to medical school."

It was a long-standing joke between the pair. Isaac had wanted to be a professional soccer player, but that dream died in his teenage years when he discovered he wasn't particularly talented. He'd instead followed his father's footsteps into the military, then followed them further into police work, but his special forces training in the army had helped him qualify for RIVCOM, an elite police unit that protected the hydroelectric dam and other critical infrastructure on the Volta River.

Isaac went back into the bedroom, and ten minutes later he came back out with a black canvas backpack and a motorcycle helmet on his head. He kissed his wife and now-sleeping baby, then went into the tiny carport of their tiny house and climbed onto his 250cc Honda dirt bike.

He fired up the twelve-year-old machine and rode out onto the road in front of his house, and soon he was out of the village, heading north towards his station at the dam.

TRAFFIC WAS EXCEPTIONALLY BAD THIS MORNING, BUT SHIFT change wasn't till nine, so this was early for him to be heading into work, right in the heart of the rush hour. And though the motorcycle gave him the luxury of slipping between gridlocked cars, eventually he found himself unable to advance any farther.

A traffic circle ahead was a daily obstacle for him; vehicles poured in from four streets, and there were no lanes marked, so sometimes the cars and trucks and motorbikes were five abreast, those on the left trying to nudge right to make a turn, those on the right giving no quarter to them as they themselves attempted to wind around to their own exit lane.

Still ten meters from the circle, he ran out of room, and he pulled up to a stop behind a green Hyundai Starex twelve-passenger van, putting his polished combat boots down on the ground and taking his hands off the clutch lever and the throttle to relax his arms.

He didn't pay any attention to the van in front of him at first; these vehicles were ubiquitous outside the capital, usually ferrying villagers from town to town. But when he realized it was belching a constant plume of gray smog right up into his face, the green van *did* catch his attention.

The traffic circle ahead tightened up even more; they weren't going anywhere for a moment, and not wanting to idle back here with the smog blowing in his eyes, Isaac pulled up on the left, walking his bike with his feet, squeezing between the green Starex and a white pickup waiting out the traffic next to it.

He looked into the green twelve-seater and saw ten men inside; he counted by subtracting the two open seats from the maximum number of occupants, and from the flash glance he gave the group he determined they were all young, in their teens or twenties. He looked into the pickup on his left and saw an older man talking animatedly on his cell phone, and then he turned his attention back to the traffic circle just ahead. It was gridlocked and tight; cars and trucks honked, and motorcycles tried to pick their way through to no avail.

Shit. He was going to be here a minute.

Lazily he glanced back into the passenger van next to him, his shoulder nearly touching it because he was wedged in between the two vehicles. The person on the other side of the second-row window just stared back at him, but not at his face. No, the young Black man was looking at the badge on his shoulder.

Glancing around at the others inside, he saw them all looking him up and down, taking notice of his uniform, his pistol, the helmet, the pack on his back.

Most Ghanaians that Opoku knew barely paid attention to the police. This group of men seemed exactly the opposite. As if they were more than curious about who he was, how he dressed and acted.

This piqued Isaac's own curiosity. Eight years in special forces and four years in an elite police unit made him size up people and situations automatically and with a suspicious eye.

He leaned back a little, not trying to hide the fact that he was looking into the van, and this paid dividends. Sitting in the back seat on the right, mostly hidden by all the men around him, was another person. He was larger; he wore a baseball cap and sunglasses and a khaki-colored balaclava that covered virtually his entire face, including his nose and his forehead.

Isaac couldn't see the man's features, the man's age, even the man's race.

He saw sweat dripping from the faces of the young Black men in the vehicle; several of the windows were open, and this told him either the driver wasn't running the van's AC or else it didn't work.

Why was this one man completely covered up?

Isaac could think of only one answer.

The man was white, or Asian, and he didn't want anyone knowing it.

He would be tall and broad for an Asian, Isaac determined, so he thought the man was likely white.

Opoku looked at him more closely. The man stared straight ahead, unlike those around him who couldn't help but look the way of the peering cop.

Just then the Hyundai lurched a little, fighting its way forward into the traffic circle.

The pickup began to move, as well, but Isaac hesitated, staying where he was so he could fall in behind the Starex.

Once he was behind it, he shifted to the right and moved forward with the van but at a slightly faster pace, so when both he and the Hyundai entered the circle and stopped in traffic again, he was half-way up on the right-hand side, perfectly level with the man wearing the face covering and sunglasses.

As before, the man didn't turn his way at first, but when Opoku knocked on the window, after all the other men swung their heads in surprise, the covered figure slowly rotated to look at the officer.

Isaac motioned for the man to pull down his mask.

The man did not.

The window was cracked open several centimeters at the bottom. Isaac looked at the man and spoke to him in English. "Good morning. Let me see your face, brother. Just a security check."

The man leaned forward towards the glass now.

Responding in English with an accent Isaac couldn't identify, the man said, "You're RIVCOM. We don't have to stop for you here."

"I can get an Akosombo police official and have you—"

A truck in front of the Hyundai found an opening in the circle and moved out of the way, and the man in the mask turned back in the direction of the driver at the front of the vehicle. "Go," he said, an authority in his accented voice that made Isaac think he was either military or ex-military.

He stayed there motionless on his bike, but once the Hyundai moved ahead, he quickly reached into a breast pocket, took out a small notepad and a pen, and jotted down the tag number.

Behind him a few vehicles honked, but no one close enough to see his uniform did, because, unlike the masked foreigner, they wouldn't dare defy a police officer, regardless of whether he had jurisdiction on this road.

TWENTY MINUTES LATER ISAAC OPOKU PARKED HIS HONDA OUTSIDE a two-story white cinder-block building with a sign out front that read "Volta River Authority—River Command Police." The building was right on top of the Akosombo Dam, with Lake Volta behind it and the Volta River in front of it, some thirty-four stories below. He fist-bumped a friend of his as the man left the building, and he stepped in, out of the morning sun and into the cool environs of a simple and drab office space.

It was just eight, but there was a lot of activity, mostly people cleaning around the building, though Isaac seriously doubted the joint delegation arriving tomorrow would have any interest in touring the drab police station.

No, everyone knew that the entire event here, to be held down at the power house at the bottom of the dam next to the switchyard, would last only twenty minutes or so, and then the dignitaries would leave.

And that was fine with Isaac.

He moved past his friends and coworkers without engaging anyone in conversation. He put his pack and his helmet in his locker and headed to the armory room door, where he punched a code in a lock. He opened the door and accessed his weapon, an M4 with an Aimpoint optic on the rail and a single thirty-round magazine in the mag well.

Checking it over quickly to make sure his coworker from the last shift had left the weapon in the same condition that Isaac himself had left it in after the shift before, he put it back in its locker and walked back through the halls, finally stopping at a door with a sign on it that said "Superintendent Baka."

Isaac rapped gently with his knuckles, but he didn't wait before going in.

Switching back and forth between English and Twi, he said, "Morning, boss. Etty sen?" *How are you?*

A portly officer in his fifties sat behind a desk covered in papers. He was hunched over a computer terminal, and he appeared annoyed by the intrusion.

The superintendent replied to him in Twi. "Can't you see I'm busy? We've got a lot to do today to prepare for the delegation tomorrow."

"Kafra." *Sorry,* Isaac replied.

The older man waved Opoku to a wooden chair in front of his desk and said, "The football pitch on the western side of the dam above the power house will be the landing zone for the helicopters. We'll need to rope that off today, rope off the trail through the trees down to the building. We'll position one squad there with the dignitaries when they come, plus we'll have three trucks, six men each, guarding the helicopters, the entrance to the switchyard, and the entrance to the dam itself."

Opoku shrugged. "That sounds manageable."

"Does it? Well, there will be armed security with the delegation, and Akosombo police haven't even told me how many cops they're sending, what vehicles they'll have, anything. It's going to be a congested mess, I can tell you that already. I'm about to head to town to walk in on the commander and make him give me his plan so our forces can be coordinated."

Isaac nodded, but his mind was on something else.

The superintendent saw this. "What do you need?"

"I saw a group of men in a passenger van on the way to work. I can't be sure, but I think they were up to something."

"Something on the river? Something at the dam or the hydro plant?"

"No . . . I mean . . . I . . . I don't know. This was on Tema-Jasikan Road, at the circle."

"So . . . kilometers away from our jurisdiction."

"I followed them a while, and they crossed at the bridge, disappeared."

The superintendent didn't look like he gave a damn. He reached for his cup of tea. "What about these guys?"

"Nine men, including the driver. All looked local but young. No one over twenty-three. And a tenth man, I think he was white."

"You *think*?" The superintendent shrugged. "It's not against the law to be a white man in Ghana, Opoku."

"No, sir. But he didn't fit in with the others. Not at all."

The commander waved a hand. "A missionary. Came here to fix all the problems of our youth." It was said dismissively.

"Definitely not a missionary," Opoku countered. "Missionaries don't cover their faces with masks and sunglasses and hats, they don't hide their race. They don't roll off into the bush with nine military-age males."

"I don't have time for this, Sergeant. What do you want me to do? Get in my car and drive around rounding up the whites?"

"Of course not, sir."

Baka sighed. "You get their tag number?"

"I did." Opoku held up his little notepad.

The older man rubbed sweat from his face and reached out for the number. "I'll check it out after I go to Akosombo town."

Isaac had suspicions his boss would do no such thing. He just said, "No worries, sir. You have to get everything sorted out for tomorrow. I'll call Accra and find out who owns the vehicle, see if it's registered to someone nearby. I'll let you know if there's anything to worry about."

The superintendent stood. "We have a *lot* to worry about. A bunch of different groups, all armed and all thinking they are in charge, are going to be walking all over my dam tomorrow, and I don't like it."

"Yes, boss." Isaac himself stood and headed for the door. He turned back around. "If I find out this van is registered to someone here in the area, you okay with me taking a couple of corporals and going for a quick look?"

Before the older man could reply, Isaac said, "Tomorrow is a big day. Those could have been protesters, bandits, whatever. If there is anything at all going on around here that could disrupt it, I think it's better we know now."

The superintendent waved Isaac out the door. "Only if it's close to the dam. No more than fifteen minutes. I need you here getting ready for tomorrow. We have trucks to wash, boots to shine, guns to clean."

"Yes, sir," Isaac said, and then he left to go to his desk to call the central police HQ in the capital.

FOURTEEN

JOSH DUFFY'S OAKLEY HOLBROOK SHADES PROTECTED HIS EYES from the tarmac's glare in the bright morning. He gazed fifty meters away at the trio of Airbus H225M Caracals, their rotors already spinning, and then swiveled his head slowly to his left and right. Around him here at Kotoka International Airport were a collection of stationary Chevy Suburbans, Ford Escalades, Mercedes Sprinter vans, and other conveyances, as well as thirty or so armed security officers, plus a large accompaniment of airport police.

All the VIPs for the trip—Johanna Aldenburg, the European Union's high representative for foreign affairs and security policy; Jennifer Dunnigan, the U.S. ambassador to Ghana; and Francis Amanor, the president of Ghana—remained in their vehicles, waiting for the all clear from DS Regional Security Officer Jay Costa, the Ghanaian president's chief of security, and Julian Delisle, the agent in charge of Aldenburg's security.

While the EU and American security men wore loose-fitting short-sleeve shirts and khakis or cargo pants, President Amanor's security team wore military uniforms. These were men from the President's Own Guard Regiment, which was, in actuality, a battalion of elite army troops entrusted with protecting the chief executive of the nation.

Most of the support staff of the three VIPs were busy loading bags into the rear of the helicopters while Duffy waited by the door to Dunnigan's armored Suburban, and as he scanned, he saw his wife working with the other American Foreign Service Officers, filling the lead helo with luggage.

At exactly eight a.m., Costa, the head of the President's Own Guard Regiment, and Julian Delisle gave the all clear, the doors to the armored SUVs opened, and the three principals stepped out into the morning heat. Josh; Benjamin Manu, the Ghanaian Foreign Service National Investigator for the embassy; Costa; and Larsen formed a diamond around Dunnigan. The other security moved with their protectees, as well, and soon everyone converged on the tarmac.

President Amanor was a bald-headed man in his late seventies, small in stature but surprisingly energetic considering his age. His eight-man security team from the President's Own Guard Regiment of the Ghana Armed Forces, all armed with handguns, stayed close to him as he picked his way through the crowd. His voice boomed as he greeted the ambassador and the high representative, and he took time to say hello to all their attendees, as well.

All except the security officers, that is, but Josh wasn't offended. He knew that blending into the surroundings was part of his job, so he didn't need any attention from the president.

They began moving for the helos, and Josh took his place in the rear of the diamond around the ambo, carrying his Glock 19 on his hip, same as the other two DS agents, the police representative, and the four-member U.S. embassy Local Body Guard protection team, four ex-cops hired and vetted by the embassy for close-protection work. Eight pistols wasn't a lot of firepower, but a pair of pickup trucks, each with five airport police armed with submachine guns standing around them, also watched over the foreigners on their short walk to the aircraft.

The airport police had been vetted by the State Department, but Josh still scanned their faces and their body language, checking them over for any cue that they were nervous or amped up.

They looked attentive but bored, and that was just how Josh wanted them to look.

He also watched the media entourage traveling with the group as they made their way forward. There was a reporter and a photographer from EuroMedia; another pair from GhanaSat, a national broadcaster; a two-person team from BBC; and a couple of freelancers.

All these people had been cleared by Costa and his staff over the past several weeks; Josh himself had been one of those who inspected their equipment and searched their bags back in the terminal, and all seemed in order.

Still, Josh kept a careful eye on them, as was his way, while they approached the helicopters.

Josh had learned from his briefings over the past several days that these French army helos had been involved in a training rotation in the Ivory Coast and then flown over here with military pilots for the diplomatic mission to Ghana.

None of the aircraft were armed, which Duffy did not love, but Costa had explained that the EU high rep's people made the decision that they didn't want to fly across Africa on a diplomatic mission with miniguns hanging off the side of their transport.

So the big weapons had been removed to improve the optics for the trip. Josh had known quite a few people who'd been killed in the furtherance of good optics, and though he didn't think for a moment he was going to need belt-fed MGs on these Airbus H225Ms, he would have found a little comfort in having them in case the need arose.

Each aircraft had room for twenty-four passengers, and since there were only fifteen in the EU helo, fifteen in the president's helo, and twenty in the American's helo, not including the flight crews, there would be plenty of space.

Not that Josh and the other DS guys would have plenty of space. No, in his helicopter Josh knew that the ambassador, the four Foreign Service Officers, and the eight members of the press with them would have the bulk of the space at the front of the cabin, while the security men would be packed in bench seating at the rear.

Soon Dunnigan, Aldenburg, and Amanor each stepped up and into a different helicopter. Josh had seen Nichole board the first Caracal when he was still forty yards away, and when he climbed in, he saw that she and the three other FSOs were already buckled into seats near the front of the aircraft.

He gave his wife the same silly exaggerated wink she'd given him at the party the evening before, she laughed, then he strapped in at the rear starboard side window, just next to Larsen and Manu and facing the four members of the U.S. embassy's Local Body Guard force.

The aircraft soon fought its way into the air, flying west towards Takoradi, just ahead of the other two Caracals.

The sprawling capital city slid by below them, a panorama of contrasts. The Gulf of Guinea to the south shone blue; the streets and buildings below the helicopters were almost uniformly redbrick, brown, and white; and green spaces pocked the urban landscape. The traffic ran thick on the dusty roads.

As the Caracals gained altitude, Josh put his headset on so he could communicate with others on the aircraft. As soon as he did so, Chad Larsen spoke to him. "Might as well get comfortable. Not a damn thing we can do for anybody till we land."

Josh knew this to be true. He'd spent a lot of time in helicopters on security gigs in the Middle East and North Africa, and there wasn't much security he could provide in a tin can a thousand feet in the air.

AT TWELVE TWENTY P.M. THE THREE HELOS CIRCLED OVER THE AIR-field in Kumasi. Police on the ground were ready in trucks, with armored vehicles parked in a row for the protectees. Delisle came over the radio from Aldenburg's helo and announced that he'd ordered the pilots to land.

They'd already pulled off the first event of the day, the port in Takoradi, and everything had gone smoothly. The president had made a quick speech, followed by the EU high representative, and then finally the U.S. ambassador. Everyone posed for pictures, and forty-four minutes after wheels down, they were wheels up again.

Kumasi, on the other hand, would be a bigger event. It was the second-largest city in the nation; they had to land at the airport some four miles from their destination and then move to the area in one large motorcade.

But Josh and the others were ready. He climbed out of the Airbus copter when it came to rest and took up his position before Dunnigan stepped out.

They escorted the ambassador to her vehicle, and he shut her, Nichole, and the three other American FSOs in before jogging to the lead vehicle, a Toyota 4Runner.

The fifty-person entourage moved out with a police escort, and three hours later they returned. Their visit to the opening of a medical clinic in Kumasi had also gone off without a hitch, even though only the administrators of the facility and the local police had been made aware of the stopover beforehand.

This element of surprise was a key component in protective movements. Complete surprise wasn't an option, of course. Key people at each of the six stops of this two-day mission had to be aware in advance, plus local law enforcement was required to augment the security in each location, but Josh was glad that this big loud delegation had made it into and back out of the nation's second-largest city without any complications.

Josh spent a few minutes in the rear of the helo expecting the rotor above him to begin spooling up at any moment, and to pass the time he watched his wife at the front of the aircraft. She was hard at work on her cell phone, no doubt communicating with the embassy in Accra about the next stop on the journey, scheduled to be all the way up in the north of the country in the town of Tamale. She was in her element, completely focused on her task, no doubt exactly how she'd been years ago when she served as an officer in the U.S. Army.

He beamed with pride watching her.

Eventually, however, he started to hear word on his radio from Costa saying he was talking to the EU security contingent, and the lead pilots had advised them that heavy weather was building up north that might impact their next stop.

He pulled up the weather on his phone and confirmed this. A massive thunderstorm, apparently unexpected by meteorologists, had formed just west and south of Tamale, and it appeared to be moving slowly to the east.

Costa spoke over the net a few minutes later. "Okay, we're going to hold here a bit. Aldenburg's people are looking at the other stops on the trip to see if we can knock something else off the list down here and go up to Tamale in the morning instead."

An hour passed; the security officers let the media, the Foreign Service Officers, and other lower-ranking government officials get out of the helos and stretch their legs, but the three protectees were kept buttoned up in the aircraft and surrounded by their protective details.

Duff stood watch outside Caracal 1, his hands clasped in front of him and his Oakleys masking his constantly shifting eyes.

Nichole knew not to bother her husband while he was working, but she pulled out her cell phone, stood near him, and called Mandy and Huck back at Iris Gardens, the walled apartment complex where they lived.

She put the phone on speaker so that Josh could hear the conversation. Even though they'd only left the kids early this morning, this was the first time both of them had been away, so just these several hours felt like a lifetime to the parents.

The kids, however, seemed to be just fine. After they had come home from school Portia had taken them to get ice cream. A girl Mandy's age named Shyla who lived in the complex and whose parents were in the CIA had come over and they were drawing pictures in the kitchen, while Huck sat nearby playing with a toy truck and watching cartoons.

Josh smiled listening to the kids recount their activities; the stability in his life still felt amazing to him, and he wondered if he'd ever get used to things going this well, because for several years of his life, so many things had gone so terribly wrong.

Finally, word came down through Costa that Julian Delisle had just told him that the helicopters would be taking off immediately, but instead of flying up north for their next scheduled stop, they'd fly an hour and a half to the southeast, to the Akosombo Dam.

Once they were done with the brief event there, they would then either fly up to Tamale if the weather had cleared, or else they'd come back to Kumasi, where a pre-vetted hotel had already been approved for such a situation.

The drop-in at the dam had originally been scheduled for two p.m. the next day; it was farther away than some of the other stops on the mission, but the weather was good along the route, and Akosombo had a couple of other things going for it that none of the other sites did.

First, the helicopters' landing zone was right there at the dam where the ribbon cutting and speech by Aldenburg would take place, so there was no need to quickly arrange a motorcade from an airport or some other remote landing site.

Also, the dam had its own police force of twenty-four officers already on site, so they wouldn't have to coordinate with local law enforcement about the rescheduling. All they had to do was contact officials at the Volta River Authority and let them know that tomorrow's appearance by the dignitaries would instead take place in about ninety minutes.

No doubt the officials at the dam would be forced to scramble to get ready on the rushed timeline, Josh surmised, but he also knew they would suck it up and comply, considering the president of their nation would be among the dignitaries.

Costa explained that it would be six p.m. before they landed, and once on the ground they'd have to rush to catch the fading light to get the three speeches planned on video.

Personally, Josh didn't love this change in plans. This wasn't exactly an "in the blind" movement—they had advanced the location and planned for the stop—but if they had traveled to Akosombo at the originally arranged time, he knew there would have been a larger police presence there.

When the decision came down from the EU helo, Josh saw Nichole talking to the ambo about it at the front of the aircraft. At one point his wife looked to him in the back and gave a shrug that indicated both that she knew Josh wouldn't be happy about deviating from the schedule and that there wasn't a damn thing she could do about it.

He just rolled his eyes, and they both smiled.

The rotors above them began to spin at four thirty p.m.

AT FIVE P.M., A BLACK RIVCOM KING-CAB PICKUP TRUCK PULLED OFF a dirt road and onto a dusty gravel driveway. A padlocked gate kept the vehicle from going any farther, so it stopped and four men in camouflaged uniforms climbed out, then looked around.

Sergeant Isaac Opoku of the Volta River Authority's River Command, along with three young RIVCOM corporals he'd "rescued" from mopping the floors of the police station, climbed up and over the low gate and back down onto the drive on the other side.

A sign over the gate said "Akwamu-Ajena Mining Co. Authorized Personnel Only."

Isaac looked at the GPS on his phone and realized he'd stopped at the back gate of the property, not the front gate, but he decided to just enter here and not drive around to the front.

Isaac held the highest rank in this group of four, but it also appeared to him that he was the only one of the group who cared about what was going on inside this property. The others checked their phones for service, bit their nails, and Corporal Konadu, the youngest officer in all of RIVCOM, quickly stepped over to some brush to take a piss before they all began walking up the hill towards their destination.

All four of the men wore their Browning pistols on their hips, but none of them, Sergeant Opoku included, had brought their rifles, because none of them, Sergeant Opoku included, expected any real trouble. They were just here to have a look around and talk to the manager about the men Opoku had encountered on the road.

The Hyundai passenger van he'd seen earlier in the day had been registered to a company that owned one piece of property in the region, this limestone mine on the eastern side of the Volta River, some twenty minutes' drive from the Akosombo Dam.

As soon as he saw that the vehicle was attached to a company that owned a mine in the area, he talked his boss into letting him take a few guys to go check it out at the end of his shift.

As Opoku walked, he thought about the young men and the stranger with them he'd seen earlier. He assumed they must work here at the mine in some capacity, but still, something didn't sit well with him. Ghana was full of mines and miners—the extraction of natural resources was the main source of wealth in the nation—but for some reason he couldn't put a finger on, those boys didn't look to him like they worked in a limestone mine. Also, the mysterious guy they were with could have been some sort of foreign contractor or security man who worked for the mining company. But if so, why the mask, and why the reluctance to speak to the police?

Isaac didn't have any jurisdiction here on the road just outside the village of Akwamu-Ajena, as this wasn't a VRA facility, but he didn't need jurisdiction for what he had planned. He wasn't here to make an arrest; he was here to look around and ask around. He hoped he could allay his concerns, maybe return to his superintendent with a little intelligence about the situation that would make tomorrow afternoon's event go off with less worry.

The walk to the limestone quarry was longer than he'd expected; the rocky driveway through the jungle rose and then turned, and then he saw he was probably another one hundred meters away from a big white building that must have been some sort of warehouse or storage facility. The jungle continued on his left along the drive, and up ahead and to the right on the winding road he saw other buildings in the distance, and he imagined that the chalky limestone pit would be somewhere beyond a row of vehicles parked there.

Young Corporal Konadu complained softly behind him about the mosquitoes, while Corporals Gyasi and Kwabena trailed a few meters behind, bored and annoyed about this excursion.

Isaac took his radio off his utility belt and called in to the RIVCOM communications room; he told the woman on duty there that they were on scene. He stayed close to the jungle on the left side of the drive as he advanced on the warehouse, the other men right behind him. They walked with quiet footfalls, scanned the area around them, and eventually made their way right up to the corrugated metal wall of the big structure.

Across the driveway on the right, past a row of vehicles not thirty meters away, was the edge of a massive quarry pit. Construction equipment sat parked there, as well, and it seemed like the mine was closed for some reason, as there were no noises other than the jungle sounds behind them.

He began to turn his attention back to the warehouse, but then he noticed the green Hyundai Starex van he'd encountered on the road earlier in the day. It was parked right next to two other passenger vans, all covered in dust.

The windows of the warehouse were completely covered in chalky white limestone dust as well, so Isaac began to walk around the right to the side of the building where he expected the entrance to be.

Just before he rounded the turn, however, he heard voices. Men speaking to one another in Ewe, a language common to the south-eastern part of Ghana and some neighboring nations, though it wasn't Isaac's native tongue.

Isaac himself could speak Ewe, although he only did so at the market or in certain shops owned by native speakers, as everyone he worked with spoke Twi as well as English.

He leaned around the corner and saw that the large sliding warehouse bay doors were closed, and he and the others began walking past the first bay door towards a small pedestrian entrance, hoping to find someone working here today.

They were halfway to the small door when the large one on their left began sliding up; it sounded like it was being operated manually by a chain, and all four cops peered into the darkness as the metal door rose.

When it was finally up, Isaac Opoku couldn't believe what he was seeing.

Right there in front of them, four king-cab pickup trucks sat parked, their doors open and their tailgates down.

Two were painted white, and they had the emblem for the Volta River Authority on the doors.

The other two were painted black, and they had a very familiar symbol and an abbreviation painted on the front doors, as well.

"VRA-RIVCOM."

The two black Toyota pickups were identical, or mostly identical, to the truck Isaac and his men had arrived in.

Around the vehicles, a dozen or more men stood, all wearing civilian clothing, though many were shirtless in the heat. Most appeared to be unpacking crates next to the trucks, but others held weapons in their hands.

One individual held several long rifles in his arms as if he were carrying firewood.

Most were young, they appeared local, and Isaac wondered if some of them had been in the Hyundai earlier when he'd tried to stop them. A few others were older, heavier, but they appeared to be local, as well.

None of the men pointed weapons his way; the rifles he saw didn't even appear to be loaded, as there were no magazines protruding from them.

But all of the men stopped what they were doing and looked towards the four new arrivals.

Isaac didn't know what to say at first, but after clearing his throat, he spoke in Ewe, trying to sound authoritative. "What is going on here?"

A man stepped around from behind one of the pickups. He was bare-chested, wearing khaki pants, and he was white with a bald head and a beard.

He held a pistol in his right hand, already raised out in front of him. He pointed it at Isaac, but he spoke angrily and in English to the Black men standing around him. "I told you bastards to maintain security at the entrance!"

Isaac recognized the voice. It was the man in the mask he'd encountered in the Hyundai earlier. Now that he'd said a few more words, the RIVCOM sergeant thought he detected a Russian accent.

To Isaac and his corporals, the white man said, "Raise your hands."

Trying to draw his weapon while a pistol was pointed at his chest was insanity, Isaac knew, so his only option was surrender. Softly, he said, "Men . . . do as he says. Slowly." He himself began raising his hands.

Corporals Kwabena and Gyasi did as instructed, but to Isaac's horror, young Corporal Konadu reached down to his hip for his gun.

FIFTEEN

THE RUSSIAN SHIFTED AIM QUICKLY, FIRED A SINGLE SHOT, AND HIT the corporal square in the chest.

Konadu's pistol fell from his hand and he tumbled down to the gravel. Kwabena knelt to grab him by the shoulder, but then he spun down to the dusty earth as well after a second gunshot, also fired by the Russian.

Isaac ducked low and pulled his Browning, fired at the Russian without aiming, then began shooting wildly all around the scene in front of him as he grabbed Corporal Gyasi and pulled him along, back around the side of the warehouse near the three passenger vans.

More shots kicked off, still from the Russian, and Isaac saw the window of one of the Hyundais right in front of him shatter. He dove to the ground, pulling Gyasi back behind the first of the vans.

Bullets kicked up dust and bits of rock around them. Opoku and Gyasi had concealment behind the vehicle but no real cover here; the bullets just tore through the body of the vehicle and streaked past their heads.

Isaac shouted to the corporal over the incredible noise as glass shattered above them. "Get behind the rear axle!" Isaac rolled to his left, positioning himself behind the front axle, hopefully making it harder for bullets to punch through and hit him.

Looking under the vehicle and back at the warehouse, he saw his other two men lying on their backs. Konadu appeared dead, but Kwabena was still moving. The young man tried to raise his pistol, but a shot cracked from inside the warehouse and then he fell back.

Isaac couldn't believe this was happening.

He rested the grip of his pistol under the vehicle, pointing it towards the darkened space twenty meters ahead of him. His heart pounded and sweat dripped into his eyes, making it hard to see the front sight of his gun, which, even though the weapon was supported on the ground, was still moving up and down rapidly with his near-frantic breathing.

He saw movement inside the warehouse and prepared to fire at it, but then he realized what he was looking at.

A young Black man in a green T-shirt and shorts held a machine gun. It looked like a Russian-built RPK, but Isaac didn't focus on it long enough to make certain.

Before he could squeeze off a shot the man opened fire, and the Hyundai that Isaac lay behind began shredding to pieces right above him as dozens of bullets ripped through it.

Isaac knew that if pulling a gun on a man with a pistol was folly, facing a machine gun armed with only a pistol was nigh on insanity.

More men in the garage had armed themselves and loaded their weapons, and flashes of gunfire came from several points within the warehouse.

Gyasi had made it to the back wheel for cover, but he leaned down to shoot under the Hyundai and immediately took a machine gun round in the forehead, splattering blood back against the van behind him and killing him instantly.

Isaac knew he'd be dead himself in seconds if he didn't find some cover.

He climbed to his feet and sprinted in a crouch, first behind the second van, and then behind the third. The gunfire continued, so he raced behind a front-end loader that was parked not far from the edge of the limestone quarry.

Instead of stopping there, he kept running, as fast as his feet would take him. He felt a tug and a sting on the right side of his waist, but he didn't break stride, he just raced on to the edge of the quarry.

Leaping into the air, he felt the snaps of more bullets whizzing close by, and they continued until he fell below the edge of the quarry and hit the steeply angled side, then began tumbling down the embankment.

Rolling and rolling, kicking up dust and debris as he dropped down, he felt his radio come off his belt and his pistol fly from his hand.

He landed hard on a ledge and thought his fall was done, but the momentum of his body sent him over the side of this precipice, and he began sliding and falling again.

He came to rest a second time in a narrow chasm. He had no idea if he'd fallen twenty-five meters or one hundred twenty-five; all he knew was that his entire body hurt, a dozen men were trying to kill him, and he was unarmed.

He had just begun pushing up to his knees when an avalanche of small stones and sand-like rocks cascaded down on him, forcing him to cover his head.

He felt a hard thump on his back as something fell on him, and he immediately recognized it for what it was. Digging around in the newly settled debris, he pulled his Browning Hi-Power out of the bits of rock and limestone chalk, ejected the fifteen-round magazine, and pulled another from its pouch on his utility belt.

Reloading the pistol, he slid the mostly expended magazine into his back pocket, and then he looked up.

He'd slid and tumbled down to a ledge here in the massive quarry, but from where he was now he couldn't see the edge of the pit above him or the vehicles he'd passed as he jumped, as there was a pronounced lip about twenty-five meters above him blocking his view. This was the ledge he'd landed on in the middle of his fall, so he assumed he'd slid down about fifty meters in all.

He heard noises high above; a few rocks rained down as if someone up near the ledge had disrupted the stones there and caused a small avalanche.

Looking around now to get his bearings, he realized quickly that the only way the enemy could get down here was to either foolishly leap down the embankment, risking breaking their necks, or else use a wooden staircase built along the rock wall thirty meters off Isaac's left shoulder.

He leveled his pistol, which was caked with white limestone like the rest of him and his belongings, and then he ran low in that direction. As he moved he felt the sting in the right side of his waist, but he didn't slow to look at the injury there, fearing what he might find.

When he was ten meters away from the stairs, an easy shot with his handgun, he found cover between a parked dump truck and the rock wall, and he went down to his knees.

Still aiming ahead, he waited, fully expecting that men with heavy weapons would be coming down here after him at any moment.

Only now did he look down to his injury. His wound was small, but the blood contrasted sharply with the white chalk all over him. Touching his torn tunic, he winced with pain, but he realized the bullet had merely grazed him, passing in and out just below the surface of the skin. It would hurt, and it would get infected if it wasn't treated, but he wasn't about to bleed to death.

As Isaac tried to catch his breath, concentrating the majority of his attention on the staircase and the ramp nearby, he realized his cell phone was in the truck and his radio was somewhere lost above him.

He had no way to communicate with RIVCOM, and no way to tell them that a group of killers had four phony VRA vehicles.

Isaac was no investigator, but he had no doubt that the men he'd just come upon were planning something for the delegation's arrival tomorrow at two, and he was glad he had nearly a day to warn his people about the danger.

KANG SHIKUN SAT AT HIS DESK IN HIS RENTED EIGHT-BEDROOM mansion on a street called Ankama Close high in the Aburi Hills, looking over the latest intelligence reports about the disposition of Northern Command forces up in Tamale.

Aburi Hills was a sanctuary for the wealthy here in Ghana: palatial estates, exclusive resorts, and restaurants with entrées that cost more than a week's wages for those in the flatlands below who were lucky enough to even have a job.

His four bodyguards were positioned around the walled three-acre property, and another pair of Chinese security officers manned a simple security room, looking at the cameras at the gates and at the garden, as well as all entrances into the large home.

He finished what he was doing, then stood in front of his desk to clear his mind with tai chi meditation. As he moved slowly but expertly through the poses, he found himself unable to relax.

Not because he was worried.

No, because he was excited.

Kang Shikun understood the landscape well enough to know that he had already won.

He'd created an unsolvable equation for an opponent who was wholly unaware of what was about to happen.

Instead of the meditation, he began thinking about his strategy, and this comforted him more than his tai chi ever could.

Kang was pleased at where he found himself. Still thirty-six hours before the operation began, and all his chess pieces were positioned on the board in the most advantageous locations, with his opponent's pieces still in their starting position, because Kang's opponent didn't even know he was about to play the game.

He had twenty Chinese intelligence technicians, twelve of them here at the home in Aburi Hills, and eight more at a remote staging area near the Volta Dam.

He had a force of four hundred forty-eight rebels to the northeast, seventy-one mercenaries in the east and south of the nation, and Iranian Quds Force colonel Hajj Zahedi's group of terrorists, roughly one hundred strong, already hiding out in the capital city and waiting for Saturday morning.

Kang shifted into a new pose, shook the smile from his face, and told himself to concentrate on the tai chi and not the coming action, but just then his sat phone rang on the table in front of him.

He let his arms hang and he stood up fully, walked to the phone, and tapped the button to initiate the call on speaker.

"Yes?"

Conrad Tremaine's voice came through the line, loud and agitated. "The fucking Dragons have been compromised!"

Kang picked up the phone and turned off the speaker function, then brought it to his ear. "What? Where?"

"Two squads painting trucks at the limestone quarry near the dam. My lead Russian there just called me, said a group of VRA police snuck up on them when they had weapons out in the open. There was an exchange of fire, three cops are dead, but a fourth made it into the quarry and they can't get to him."

Kang took a calming breath. "The equipment? Our men?"

"The Russian was nicked, but he's fine. One of the Dragons was injured, as well. Don't know how bad. The weapons and the trucks are still in our possession."

Kang thought it through, but as he was doing so the South African spoke up. "Look, the delegation is in country, but they should be most of the way to Tamale in the north by now, hundreds of miles from Akosombo. If we attack the dam immediately, the delegation will just go back to the capital. The ambassador will squirrel away in her embassy, and the high representative will jump on her jet and get the feck out of here. They aren't going to come to the dam at two p.m. tomorrow if the country is in the middle of a bloody coup d'état."

Kang said nothing, so Tremaine finished his thought. "I'm saying . . . forget about Saturday morning. We need to start the operation! Now! *Right* now!"

Kang had the same thought, but he was more careful, more measured than the fiery mercenary. "How long until the Dragons are in position to attack the dam?"

"I've already told my Russian to get his people and weapons out of that location. They'll be on the road in minutes. It's twenty minutes to the dam. Two more squads, each with a Russian embedded with them, are at the safe house on the other side of the river, even closer to the dam. I'm saying I can have thirty-two Dragons and three Russian contractors hit the dam in under a half hour."

"Is that enough?"

"There's twenty-four RIVCOM officers per shift. With all the subterfuge we have planned, we have more than enough firepower to take over the dam and plant the explosives. Once that's done, it won't matter how many people we have there, because no one will try to take the dam back."

"Where are you?"

"My plan was to be there at the dam for the attack, but I'm a half hour south of Akosombo with three of my men. I'm on the way up there. Say the word and we'll attack now, but your people have to knock out the comms so we maintain the element of surprise."

Kang's technicians, all working here in the living room and in bedrooms repurposed as office space in the villa above Accra, would be tasked with conducting cyberattacks on the telecommunications and cable Internet infrastructure up around the Akosombo Dam. Everything was ready, Kang knew, but no one expected to be doing this for another day and a half, so he wasn't sure how long it would take his team to act.

But he realized he had no other alternative. He had worked meticulously on a plan, and the timeline was now out the window. He knew he had to initiate, and he also knew that if Tremaine could get nearly forty gunmen to attack the dam in minutes, surely Kang could get his small force of computer warriors to do their job here in even less time.

The other issue he had to consider was the jamming of the satellite signal in and around the dam during the attack, because it was likely the Volta River Authority would have sat phones to use in emergencies.

Kang had a plan for this, as well.

A small team of Sentinel men protected a group of five Chinese technicians and their equipment in a farmhouse just southwest of the dam. In the back of a tractor-trailer there, techs had a dozen meterwide drones, each with a satellite jammer on board.

The technology was called "jamming the downlink." Once the drones flew into the sky above the dam, all satellite signals in the area would be lost.

With a half dozen units spread out on both sides of the river and several hundred meters in the air, an area over fifty kilometers square would be affected.

With resolve in his voice, the Chinese spy said, "We are only going to have the element of surprise for a few moments more. Tell your people to execute now. Communication will be disrupted as soon as possible."

Kang added, "Good luck."

"Don't need luck, my friend." The South African disconnected the call, and Kang immediately dialed the number of a Chinese technician near the dam, ordering him to begin satellite disruption operations.

He then rushed out of his office; looking out into the big living room with the sunken floor, he ignored the floor-to-ceiling windows with the hazy view of the flat city and the ocean beyond, and instead he called out to a woman sitting at a makeshift computer workstation at the kitchen island. "You!"

The woman launched to her feet, a startled look in her eyes. "Xiansheng?" *Sir?*

Chen Jia was twenty-eight years old, with long black hair, and she wore an oversized gray sweatshirt with the emblem for Nanyang Technological University in Singapore.

Kang didn't know all the contracted employees here with him, but he knew that this woman was from Beijing and served as one of the lead intel techs here.

He said, "Tell everyone in the house. We execute now! Right now!"

"Yes, sir," Jia said, and she swung back to the three laptops in front of her. Putting her fingers on one of the keyboards, she said, "All interruption operations will begin immediately, sir."

Kang knew he'd have no way to communicate with anyone around the dam once the entire operation was in play, and once the dam was in the hands of the rebels, power would be cut to the majority of the nation.

But not to this building. He had a Skylink satellite Internet receiver here that allowed him to communicate with Beijing. He also had generators around the property, robust and fueled with diesel, with more drums waiting behind the property to give complete power to the house for ten days, if necessary.

But Kang didn't think it would be necessary. Once the dam was taken and the power to the city shut down, once the Dragons made it into Accra, once Sentinel made the rebels appear to be an existential threat to the government, once the jihadis sowed chaos, then General Boatang in Kumasi would sweep down the N6 highway, eradicate the hapless rebels and extremists, and be on his way to taking power, and then Professor Addo and the other fools from Western Togoland would lose their lives for their culpability.

Kang smiled, unrattled by this change in schedule because he knew he was ready.

SIXTEEN

ISAAC OPOKU HAD BANDAGED HIS WAIST AS BEST HE COULD, USING a dressing he pulled from the tiny medical pouch he kept on his utility belt. His entire body was sore and getting sorer, but he was reasonably certain nothing was broken, nor had he suffered a concussion, which he found astonishing considering what he'd just been through.

But his focus did not remain on his poor physical condition for long, because soon he heard several trucks race by above him, as if leaving down the long gravel back drive.

He didn't know if these were the trucks painted in the VRA livery, or if they were the passenger vans he'd seen, but in either case he couldn't understand why they just left him behind, letting him go.

Did they think he was dead? It would be a reasonable assumption, he determined, considering the fact that he'd been shot and then fell down a steep slope into a rock mine.

Then it occurred to him. They left him behind because they had somewhere else to go.

By showing up here right now, he'd caused this unknown group to flee. He hoped like hell it would stop them from enacting whatever their plan was for tomorrow, because the only other alternative he could see would be for them to try to enact their plan right now.

Either way, Isaac knew he needed to alert the superintendent as to what was going on.

He rose on still-shaky legs, then headed for the wooden stairs and the long climb out of the quarry.

IT TOOK FIVE MINUTES OF ARDUOUS AND PAINFUL WORK TO GET TO the top of the stairs, and once there, he moved carefully, watching for any enemy left behind.

The vans were still there, but the trucks painted in the VRA and RIVCOM colors were gone.

The bodies of his three officers lay where they fell; he checked them all for a pulse but found none.

Five minutes later he'd made his way back down the rear drive to his truck. His tires had been slashed, but when he looked in the console he was glad to see that his cell phone was still there.

With a hand shaking from the stress his mind and body had incurred in these last twenty minutes, Isaac dialed a number, then waited.

Soon, a familiar voice answered.

"Superintendent Baka."

"Sir! It's Opoku! Officers down! We encountered unknown enemy, armed. Twelve, maybe fifteen, maybe more."

"Calm down!" the superintendent screamed back over the phone, though suddenly he was no calmer than Isaac. "What are you talking about? Where . . . where *are* you?"

"The limestone mine outside of Akwamu-Ajena."

"What happened?"

"Gyasi, Konadu, and Kwabena are all dead. The enemy has AKs! RPGs. Machine guns. Shit I haven't seen since the army."

"But . . ." The superintendent was poleaxed by this. "But," he stammered again, "the Togoland rebels don't have any of that."

"Well, *whoever* these bastards are, they look like they're planning something at the dam."

"Why do you think they are planning—"

"Because they had trucks painted to look like VRA equipment!"

The superintendent did not reply.

"Boss?"

After waiting a few seconds for a response, Isaac said, "Sir? Do you read me?"

But he heard nothing on the other end of the line.

He hung up the call to dial another number at the station, but as he began punching it in, he saw that he had no cell signal.

Sergeant Opoku had no idea why he'd lost communication with the police station, but he put his phone in his pocket, looked down the road in the direction of the dam to the south, and then began jogging, doing his best to ignore the growing pain in his torso from the gunshot and the aching just about everywhere else on his body from the long tumbling fall.

The dam was ten kilometers away, so he kept his eyes open for traffic, planning to commandeer the next passing car or bike.

SUPERINTENDENT JOSEPH BAKA HUNG UP HIS DESK PHONE WHEN he became disconnected with Opoku's cell, then reached for his own cell phone. Immediately, he saw it had no service.

Just then, he heard a low rumbling to the east, towards Akosombo town. It was an explosion, that much was certain, but it seemed to be a fair distance away.

Quickly he reached for the walkie-talkie on his desk, but as he did so, a new, more immediate sound echoed throughout the building.

Gunfire, fully automatic, close. The power flickered and then went out, cutting the light in Superintendent Baka's office by three fourths.

The big man rose behind his desk, shocked and confused about what his sergeant had reported and what he was hearing and seeing now.

More explosions emanated from outside the building, and distant gunfire grew; it sounded like it was coming from both the power house down by the river at the base of the dam and next door at the administration building, and only now did he understand the scale and scope of this.

The entire hydroelectric facility was under attack.

Another burst of gunfire came from inside the police station itself, then another, and the superintendent pulled the Browning Hi-Power off his hip and ran for the door to his office. He looked out into the hall to see a pair of men in camouflaged RIVCOM uniforms racing his way from the stairwell; he didn't focus on them at first but rather spun to check the opposite direction. As he faced away from the approaching men, something occurred to him.

Both men wore maroon berets.

Indoors.

Something no RIVCOM officer would ever do.

And the guns? Were those AK-47s? His men carried M4s.

He spun back around, swinging the pistol, as well, but he'd only just raised the weapon towards the first impostor when he was shot in the stomach with a single round from one of the men's AKs.

The superintendent lurched back into his office, and his weapon fell from his hands as he pressed down on his abdominal wound.

He lowered slowly to the ground, then rolled onto his back.

The two men in the hall each fired another round into his body as they passed, then headed down the hall, ready to either take prisoners or kill anyone who posed a threat.

LEV BELOV LOOKED DOWN AT THE WOUND IN HIS THIGH, BANDAGED but only perfunctorily. As he watched, blood seeped through the white gauze and tape and down onto the passenger seat of the pickup painted to look like a VRA vehicle. He ignored the pain, opened the door of the vehicle the instant the driver put it in park, and then stepped out into the parking lot in front of the power house at the bottom of the dam.

All around him, at the administration building and police station on top of the dam, as well as down here at the power house and switch-yard by the river, the fighters he'd trained for the past four months were finally getting their first real glimpse of combat. He knew that the men's limited skill set would be adequate for today's needs; the cops here wouldn't have been expecting six truckloads of men, four from the eastern side and two from the western side, to attack, and the fact that all the vehicles the Dragons and Sentinel men had arrived in were painted to look like VRA equipment only made this task easier.

He heard the sounds around him and knew that the plan he and Tremaine had drawn up for the attack on the hydro facility was being executed effectively, albeit a day and a half early.

He heard the boom as rebels took down a massive radio tower with a single brick of explosives, and soon the automatic fire on the top of the dam at the police station by the admin building seemed to die down, and he felt certain they were moments away from having full control of the facility.

Belov had two other Russian Sentinel men with him today, and they pulled up in another truck and climbed out.

Vadik and Gresha walked around to the bed of their truck, hoisted out two heavy satchels each, and put them on their shoulders, carrying their rifles on their backs.

They headed for the power house, which was already under rebel control.

Belov reached back into his Toyota, pulled out his sat phone, and looked at the signal.

There was nothing showing, confirming that a half dozen satellite downlink jamming drones hovered in the sunny sky.

Reports began to come over his walkie-talkie now. The admin building had fallen, the police station had fallen, the front guard-house on the road south of the power house had fallen.

The radio towers were down, and Internet and landline phone service had been shut off, almost certainly from the cyberattacks Tremaine had promised him the Chinese would carry out.

Casualties were significant on Belov's side; the Dragons reported five dead, three at the station and two more at the front gate, and three more lay wounded, but with the use of the RIVCOM uniforms and mocked-up vehicles, Belov was proud to see that his Dragons of Western Togoland had managed to take complete control of the Akosombo hydroelectric facility in under eight minutes.

He headed for the door of the building, already guarded by one of his men in a RIVCOM uniform.

Vadik and Gresha caught up to him. "You okay, boss?" Gresha asked. These two men had not been at the limestone quarry where the vehicles were being painted and where Belov caught the bullet to the leg.

"Fine. Lucky cop put a bullet through me. I'll live."

He opened the door and the three Russians entered the lobby of the building. They'd watched YouTube videos showing the facility, so they knew their way to the main control room, here on the ground floor above the massive generator gallery.

In the control room they found a squad of eight Dragons holding a dozen power house operators at gunpoint, all standing at their workstations with their hands in the air. Other than a single dead RIVCOM cop in the lobby, there were no signs of fighting here, and Belov was happy to see that the people who were able to control the dam and the power it produced were still alive, because he didn't have a clue how any of this shit worked.

He walked into the center of the room, ignoring the sting in his right leg where the RIVCOM cop had tagged him, and then he addressed the VRA employees. "Who is in charge?"

No one spoke.

He pulled his Beretta pistol from his hip and pointed it at a woman who stood to his right, just in front of her cubicle. She cried out when he pressed the gun to her temple, began sobbing as he spoke again.

"Who is—"

"*I* am in charge!" A voice came from the front of the room. A man stood there next to a computerized map of the Republic of Ghana, his hands in the air like everyone else here.

He had gray hair and thick glasses, and appeared, also like everyone else here, to be both stunned and terrified.

Belov lowered the pistol and began walking forward with a wince. Eventually he made his way up to the man. "What's your name?"

"Martin Mensah. I am the deputy plant operator here."

"Just the man I'm looking for, then. I want you to shut down the power grid. Now."

Mensah still held his hands in the air. They shook as he spoke. "Which grid?"

"The entire country. All power transfer from this facility will stop. Now."

"You mean shut . . . shut it down?"

Belov motioned to the lady in front of her cubicle. "Do I need to put my gun to that poor woman's head again?"

The Ghanaian shook his head. "No . . . no. I'll do it."

Mensah turned around, facing a large table with several older-looking computer monitors as well as analog switches and dials. He looked back to the Russian and spoke meekly, but there was gravity in his words. "If we do this, in minutes all the power will cease in the entire nation. Only facilities that have generators will continue to function."

"I know that."

"Hospitals, airports. They will only have generator power for a few hours. The rest of the nation, other than some private homes, has no generators. If you do this . . . it will cause chaos."

"Your country has power outages all the time. I'm sure you'll manage."

"Rolling blackouts are very different than a complete loss of—"

Belov lifted his pistol to Mensah's face. "Do it!"

The deputy plant operator nodded slowly, faced the table, and flipped a series of switches, then conferred with a woman standing nearby. In seconds she sat and began tapping keys on her keyboard, crying as she did so.

On the map in front of them, glowing white lines showing the map of the nation's power grid began to turn off, one after another.

As the flow of power ceased from the dam, the nation was effectively shut down.

Belov watched it all with interest. Finally, when all the lights were off, he said, "Well done."

"What . . . what now?" Mensah asked.

Belov didn't answer the Ghanaian; instead he turned to Vadik and Gresha, standing back at the entrance to the room. Mensah looked at the massive packs on their backs and in their arms.

Belov followed the deputy plant manager's eyes. "We are going to mine your dam. We will only destroy it as a last resort. We need the power to stay off for a period of time, but if the government tries to take this facility back, we'll shut the power off the hard way."

Mensah looked around at his coworkers, then back to the white man in the combat gear with the pistol in his hand. "I . . . I don't understand. You're . . . you're *not* here to kill the president?"

The Russian made a face of confusion. With a snorted laugh he said, "Kill the president? If we wanted to kill the president, we would come tomorrow when—"

Belov stopped speaking, because he registered something on the deputy plant operator's face.

Belov turned to the young Dragons in the room with him. They looked as confused as he was.

To Mensah, he said, "What are you talking about?"

Mensah said nothing.

The Russian raised his weapon yet again. "What is going on?"

Almost apologetically, Mensah said, "The joint delegation, it's on its way here. Now."

Belov was gobsmacked. "You're . . . you are lying."

"When they see that you've taken over the dam, they won't land, and they will return to Accra to alert the army. You might have defeated our police, but you won't defeat—"

Belov cocked his head. He believed the man now. "When do they get here?"

The man looked at him with confusion but said nothing.

The Russian pushed the barrel of his pistol into the man's forehead. "*When*, damn you!"

"In about . . ." He looked down to his wristwatch; his entire arm shook. "In about twenty minutes."

Belov shouted back in surprise. "Why?"

The deputy plant operator just said, "They had to change their schedule due to a storm up north."

"Shit," Belov said, and then he ordered the Dragons in the room to watch over the technicians while he ran for the door, pulling his walkie-talkie from his belt. As he stepped back outside he pressed the talk button. "Condor, Bear. Condor, this is Bear. Do you read?"

SEVENTEEN

THE THREE GRAY AIRBUS CARACALS FROM THE FRENCH ARMY FLEW five thousand feet over the flat plains, the villages, and the dense jungle of south-central Ghana, still some twenty minutes away from the Akosombo Dam landing zone.

Gray skies hid the fading sun behind them, but up ahead the clouds were broken, and conditions looked good.

Josh watched from the back as Nichole spoke on her headset to the ambassador at the front of the cabin, and slowly, as he looked on, he could discern an intensity in the conversation, an expression on her face that she was concerned about something. The FSOs and the ambo were on a different channel from the one DS was using, so he couldn't hear her.

But just when Josh thought about switching channels to listen in on her conversation, Jay Costa's voice came over his headset. Jay sat up with the ambo and had been able to hear the conversation she was having. He said, "Be advised. I'm learning we've lost communication with personnel at the hydro dam. We're looking into it now, but looks like service is down. Tried them on the sat but are having trouble with the signal. Must be interference from the helicopter."

Josh rogered up along with Chad and Benjamin Manu, and they

sat there another minute waiting for an update from Costa, while Nichole continued talking animatedly with Jennifer Dunnigan.

Finally, Costa came back on the net. "Still no comms at Akosombo for some reason. The EU thinks it's probably just a power outage in the area, and the Ghanaian president's staff agrees. They want to continue to the dam; we'll do an overfly to make sure everything is okay down there, but Aldenburg says the whole point of the trip to Akosombo is to announce the upgrade and refurbishment of the dam, so there are some good optics involved in making a stop there while the power is down."

Josh spoke up now. "Understood, Jay, but losing commo with the people at our destination could be a lot of things other than a power outage."

"I hear you. The president's detail will try to pick up somebody with the dam police there on FM radio when we have line of sight. We're continuing."

"Understood."

This third stop of the day was turning into an interesting one, Josh thought, and he hoped like hell it didn't get even more interesting.

CONRAD TREMAINE WAS STILL FIVE MILES SOUTH OF THE DAM, ON the western side of the Volta, racing along in a black Toyota Tacoma king cab. With him were three other mercenaries: Krelis from Holland; Junior, his fellow South African; and Baginski, from Poland.

The covered bed of the pickup was filled to the brim with rifles, a light machine gun, ammunition, an RPG-7 launcher, and a 60-millimeter mortar. The men carried their personal weapons on them; Baginski also had a short-barreled rifle on the floorboard in front of him, and they were fully engaged in the operation now, which meant they would stop for no one, including the police.

The only communications that worked in this area, already in the zone jammed by the drones, were radios, so the men in the truck listened to their powerful 10-watt walkie-talkies as the Russian mercenaries attached to the Dragon platoon broadcast their mission's successes to Tremaine, one at a time, reporting casualties along the way.

For his part, Tremaine was damn glad the delegation would be all the way up in Tamale when they learned comms were broken in the southeastern portion of the country and that electricity to the nation had been shut down.

But he found it a pity that the president would survive this coup. Tremaine had nothing against Amanor, but he'd been around enough African coups to know that leaving a former leader in place, even an embattled one, could be dangerous.

He'd suggested to Kang that a decapitation of the government might ensure in those first few weeks after the operation that no countercoup could rise up and reclaim power, but Kang had pushed back on this. He thought attempting to kill the president would only alert the wider world to the fact that the rebels had sophisticated outside help.

No, Kang had insisted, Amanor needed to be pushed out of power after failing to protect his country from rebels and power outages, not overtly overthrown and killed.

Tremaine strongly disagreed, however. He wished there were some way the rebels could be blamed for killing Amanor without it looking like they had to work too diligently to kill him, but he'd been unable to come up with a scheme that seemed feasible. By the time the rebels got anywhere near the president, he would certainly be under the protection of the President's Own Guard Regiment and totally safe from an assassin's bullet.

Suddenly, the men's walkie-talkies squawked throughout the pickup. "Condor, this is Bear. Do you read?"

Belov was Bear; all Sentinel operators had code names on the mission, though Tremaine only remembered the senior ones.

He drove with one hand, broadcasting with the other. "Go for Condor."

"Listen carefully. The president, the EU delegation, the Americans, they are on their way to the dam now! Approximately twenty minutes out."

Tremaine's heart skipped a beat. "Wait. Repeat your last?"

Belov repeated it, and finished with "Do we leave, or do we stay?"

Tremaine looked to Krelis sitting next to him; the younger Dutchman's mouth hung open.

Softly, and with utter confusion, Tremaine said, "They are supposed to come tomorrow."

Belov answered by saying, "They changed the itinerary. Something to do with the weather."

Kang and his people had been following the weather for the day of the planned attack Saturday, of this Tremaine was certain, but they hadn't been following the weather up north for Thursday afternoon. With all the things the brilliant Chinese intelligence officer had accounted for, he hadn't considered beginning his operation a day and a half early, and this was already causing unforeseen consequences.

Tremaine couldn't believe the scale of this clusterfuck, and he was in the jamming zone now, so the only ways he could communicate with Kang in Accra would be to take several minutes to contact his mercenaries with the Chinese technical team, then have them shut down the jamming, which would threaten the operation at the dam, or else turn around and drive ten minutes in the opposite direction to get out of the jamming zone.

But if he did that, he would be out of range with Belov.

No, whatever happened now, Tremaine knew that *he* was the man in charge.

Belov said, "Comms are down here at the dam. Maybe the helicopters won't land if they can't make contact with anyone here."

Tremaine shouted, his voice booming in the cab of the truck. "They already *did* make contact, otherwise the people at the dam wouldn't know they were on the way. Maybe they'll fly over to check it out if they can't establish comms again, but you can't just assume they'll go home just because they lost contact."

Belov transmitted again. "We haven't even set the explosives in the turbines yet. To do it right will take time. My two guys have to take an access panel off, then climb down to the weakest point and attach them, then program the detonation codes. They're going to need a half hour, at least. Maybe we should just go."

Tremaine thought it over. "You can't leave now, the entire operation will be ruined."

"Yeah? Well, it's going to be ruined when fifty people land here in helicopters."

The Sentinel commander kept driving, but he sped up. After several seconds, he said, "You stay. Continue what you're doing, planting the explosives. But get all the captives you have hidden and under guard, and clean up any signs of combat that could be visible from the air."

"Then what?"

"All your rebels are wearing either RIVCOM uniforms or VRA badges, correct?"

"Except for myself and my two Sentinel men."

"Make sure the rebels use the real RIVCOM's weapons. Hide the AKs and field the police M4s, the pistols, the chest rigs. The security people will notice if cops are carrying rebel gear."

"I know that," Belov snapped back.

"Then put the people where the helicopters can see them. Let the helos land, let the entourage come to the switchyard and the power house as planned for their media stop. They're only supposed to be on the ground for twenty-five minutes."

Before Belov could ask a follow-up question, Tremaine said, "Get the other Sentinel men to work on setting the charges, but tell the dam employees that they have to act normal, to convince the delegation that everything is fine for the entire time they are on the ground, or you and your men will kill everyone."

Belov said, "I'm not being paid enough for this."

"What's the alternative? You run now, you don't get *any* more money because the op is dead."

Now the Russian cussed into the phone. Tremaine didn't speak Russian, but he knew the word "Suka." *Bitch*. Finally, Belov said, "All right. I'll tell the deputy plant manager to deal with the delegation or I'll personally murder all his staff."

"Last thing, Bear." Tremaine thought a moment. "This is a hasty op, you didn't have time to prepare. Is there anything on your person, or with the other Sentinel men, that can relate back to me, Sentinel, or the Chinese?"

Belov was the leader of the fifty Russians on this operation, and other than Tremaine himself, he was the only one to carry a tablet computer that contained all the radio codes, waypoints, code names, and geographic coordinates for the operation.

Belov said, "I've got my tablet computer. I wasn't going to leave it at the compromised safe house, was I?"

Tremaine pounded his hand on the steering wheel as he drove. "That device cannot be captured, do you understand?"

Belov answered back defensively. "Of course I know that."

"You shouldn't have brought it to the dam."

"I didn't exactly have time to find other accommodations for it, Condor. It has a five-watt radio in it. I'll program the detonation codes into it and use it if we need to blow the dam."

The South African was furious, but he knew he had to let it go.

Finally, he said, "If you find yourself about to be overrun, you need to strap a grenade to that tablet, you understand me?"

"I'm not getting overrun, Condor. Bear out." Belov ended his transmission, presumably to ready his forces and his captives to try to fool the approaching helicopters.

The Sentinel chief kept racing along the highway, panic welling in him about the tablet computer in the Russian's possession and the damage it could cause, but soon something else came to him.

He turned to Krelis. "This fuckup, this change in the entire plan. Maybe we can use it as an opportunity."

"Meaning what, boss?"

"Kang wants the Dragons to take the fall for the whole operation so that his general can take over, yeah?"

Krelis nodded. "Yeah."

"Well, what if the Dragons assassinate the president of Ghana. Right here and now? Seems like it might make things a hell of a lot easier down the road if Amanor wasn't around fighting for power."

Krelis looked at his boss like he was crazy. "That wasn't Kang's plan."

"Yeah, well, Kang isn't here, and this is a better plan, isn't it?"

"Is it?"

"Look, bro, we can have that fecker in our sights in about twenty minutes. The Dragons there could do the job, but they'd probably just muck it up, and it makes more sense to me to have the Dragons stay in cover so the entire entourage doesn't engage. We make this look like an outside hit."

"The minute the president is shot, those Dragons are going to make it pretty fucking obvious they aren't real cops."

Tremaine nodded. "It's going to be a hell of a party down there, that's for sure." He looked to Krelis and saw the man's unease. "We're overthrowing a democratic nation here, we aren't playing patty-cake. If we lose all thirty-five rebels at the dam because I shoot the president and decapitate the government, then that's a bloody damn good return on investment as far as I'm concerned."

"What's Kang going to say?"

"I'll tell him the Dragons did it."

"Yeah, well, Professor Addo is going to tell him they didn't."

"Addo's not at the dam, he's still hiding in the bush, getting ready for his move on Accra. He doesn't even have comms with his men. He won't be able to tell Kang anything. And when I finally see Kang down in the capital, he's going to be glad President Amanor is no longer a problem and won't be able to stand for the election, and he won't question the hows and whys."

Krelis didn't seem so sure, but he said, "So . . . how do we kill the president? RPG when his helo takes off?"

Tremaine shook his head. "I've got a Dragunov in the trunk."

The Russian Dragunov SVD sniper rifle fired a 7.62×54-millimeter round and had an effective range of eight hundred meters.

Krelis thought a moment, then said, "If you do it, do it from across the river. Three hundred fifty meters or so. Easy day."

Just then the Adomi Bridge came into view. A couple miles south of the dam, the massive steel suspension bridge was the only way to cross the Volta on this stretch of the river.

Tremaine headed for the bridge, mentally preparing himself for the biggest operation of his life, but his fear was not that he might fail.

His fear was, instead, that his people at the dam might scare off the helicopters before they even landed.

JOSH DUFFY SAT BY THE REAR PORTAL ON THE PORT SIDE OF THE lead Caracal. His wife remained far ahead of him; she had been working furiously on her iPad for the past several minutes, probably, he assumed, making last-minute changes to the remarks the U.S. ambassador would be making at the dam.

He looked out the glass, saw something in the distance, then clicked his mic. "Jay? Can you look out the port-side window? Your nine o'clock."

A razor-thin plume of black smoke rose over the town of Akosombo.

After a moment, Costa replied, "Yeah, I see it. Let me see if I can figure out what's over there."

After a minute he came back on the radio. "Nobody seems to know what is down there that might be burning, but they aren't too worried about it. They want to continue to the dam."

Josh just said, "Roger that."

Soon the three helos flew over Lake Volta, the largest artificial reservoir on planet Earth, heading south to the hydroelectric facility. Once they came to the north side of the dam, they slowed their speed, then passed above the massive structure at an altitude of two hundred meters.

The lake was high; the dam spillways were open and water gushed down the steep concrete structure on the southeastern side, churning the river below white with foam. It was a gargantuan, impressive sight, and Josh caught himself looking at it in awe for a moment before scanning the area out his port-side window again, hunting for any danger below.

Costa spoke into the radio. "Benjamin, I'm passing binos to you. Check out the area and tell me if it looks okay."

Duff knew that since they'd been unable to establish communications with the people on the ground, they'd want to make sure they didn't see anything amiss before landing the helos. Even though the Airbus helicopters weren't armed, they could just rocket out of the area at the first sign of trouble while in the air, but that would change once they landed.

Even without the binoculars, Duff could see men in camouflaged uniforms on the top of the dam, along with marked vehicles.

Benjamin Manu looked out the portal through the binos that Costa passed to him. After several seconds he said, "RIVCOM trucks and officers on the dam and down at the power house, and I see a VRA truck with some civilians in it at the switchyard. RIVCOM guarding the front gate."

"How many RIVCOM cops do you see?"

"A lot. Twenty, maybe more."

"Good," Costa replied, then said, "Stand by." Several seconds later he transmitted again. "Okay, just got word the president's helo has made FM comms with the VRA down there. They confirm all power coming from the dam is down, they're working to restore it." After a pause, he said, "Uh . . . we're going to land behind the power house, as planned. The stage is set up in front of the switchyard. The people at the power house will stay inside working, but we'll have twenty RIVCOM men and the deputy plant operator joining us for the speeches. Another dozen or so RIVCOM controlling access to the facility."

The helicopter banked to starboard and headed for the landing zone.

ON THE GROUND, RUSSIAN SENTINEL OFFICER LEV BELOV STOOD IN the control room of the power house, looming over deputy plant operator Martin Mensah, who perspired so much now that his Coke-bottle glasses had steamed up.

Belov spoke to him slowly, emphatically. "It's all up to you, man. You have to convince those people that everything is fine here, that everyone is working on the issue so they can get the power going. If you fail . . . if they suspect something is wrong and pull out their guns, then we have over thirty men here ready to start shooting something."

Mensah clearly understood his assignment. He pulled a handkerchief from his slacks and rubbed his forehead, then nodded. "The delegation won't come in here?" he asked.

"They are supposed to stand on that riser out there with the dam in the background, talk into cameras for less than twenty minutes, and then leave." Belov put a finger in the man's chest. "And that is what is going to happen, or you and your staff in here will be among the first to die."

The middle-aged Ghanaian nodded again, wiped his forehead again. "Yes. Just don't hurt anyone and I will do what I have to do."

The two other Russians stood nearby, each with a pack on their backs, a rifle across the magazine rack and body armor on their chests, and a second military-style gray pack at their feet. While Mensah stood there, Belov walked over to them quickly, unzipped a pouch in the center of his chest rig, and pulled out a ruggedized black tablet computer. He turned it on quickly and began speaking to the men in Russian.

"Quickly, give me the detonation codes off your devices."

Gresha read off a long number as Belov typed it in, and then Vadik did the same. Belov closed the computer, placed it back in his chest rig, then said, "Once you set the devices, make sure you turn on their transceivers. When you do, I'll be able to det the explosives with my tablet if ordered to do so."

Now Belov motioned to the eight Dragons with him in the room. "Four of you will escort Mr. Mensah out to greet the delegation. If he says anything to give us away, kill him immediately."

Back to Mensah, Belov now smiled. "All on your shoulders, my friend," he said, and then he followed the two other Russians towards the stairs down below.

EIGHTEEN

ALL THREE FRENCH AIRBUS HELICOPTERS HOVERED OVER A DUSTY grass-covered soccer field just to the west of a thick copse of trees. It was just a hundred-meter walk down a path through the trees to the power house, at the bottom of the dam and alongside the swiftly flowing river.

As the helos landed, Josh caught a glimpse of the front gate of the entire facility. It was a couple hundred yards to the south and he could see a manned guard shack and a RIVCOM vehicle parked next to it, and the fact that this area was closed off to the public eased his mind considerably.

After the Caracals settled onto the dusty field, one in front of the other, everyone waited inside till the rotors spooled down. Once the door to their helo was opened, Josh, Chad, and Benjamin climbed out, followed by Jay and all four of the embassy's Local Body Guard protection detail. The LBG men put on their sunglasses and moved into position near the door to enshroud the ambo along with the DS men and Ben Manu.

It was just after six p.m.; the sun was low in the west, and it looked to Josh like it would set in a half hour or so.

Josh eyeballed the trees down the hill in front of him. A paved pathway intersected the copse, and beyond the trees he could see the Volta River in the distance. To the north was the dam and the lake, high above his position; to the south, about a mile distant, the river turned sharply to the west, surrounded by jungle on all sides.

A large cluster of hills loomed over the far side of the river, much higher than the top of the dam and covered in dense foliage, but Josh could make out antennas on the top of the hill, as if there was some sort of structure there.

Scanning up the road in the direction of the dam, he saw a pair of pickup trucks with men in dark camo and purple berets rolling towards the landing zone. Duff had never worked with RIVCOM before, as they were part of the Volta River Authority and nowhere near Accra, where Josh had been since his arrival in country, but Ben eyed the men a moment and then waved.

The men waved back, and then the vehicles stopped on the road next to the soccer field and the cops dismounted.

Duff, Larsen, Manu, and Costa escorted Dunnigan out, surrounded by the LBG protection detail, while the security teams for President Amanor and EU High Representative Aldenburg did the same.

The press that had flown in with the entourage scrambled to get in front of the principals as everyone began walking behind the RIV-COM men, who led the way on foot down the path through the jungle towards the power house and switchyard on the riverbank.

Duff found himself in the fray behind Dunnigan and realized he was walking along right next to Nichole. His wife carried a backpack over her shoulder and cradled her iPad, but he didn't avert his eyes to focus on her. Instead he looked over the road, the trees, even the skies above. He was one hundred percent in work mode now, as she had been in the helicopter.

Amanor, Aldenburg, and Dunnigan chatted as they moved down the trail; they were so close together that their security teams were intermingled. Nichole knew enough about Josh's job to give him some space, so she stepped away from the scrum, although some of the other European staffers and Ghanaian officials remained in the way of the security men, and the media presence made the situation even that much more complicated.

Josh had a good view through the entourage to the switchyard, a several-acre housing of transformers, switches, and breakers that energized or deenergized power on transmission circuits leaving the hydroelectric plant. He looked for signs of movement, and soon he saw some RIVCOM men standing next to their vehicle at a small equipment shack. They watched the procession, their American-made M4 rifles hanging off their chests.

At the front of the power house, a low riser had been set up with a lectern displaying the symbol for the Volta River Authority; it was positioned so that the backdrop would include the dam and the roiling river water, and the three principals climbed up onto it with two members of each security detail.

Chad and Jay climbed the riser with Dunnigan, while Benjamin went to the left side of the little stage, and Josh stayed by the steps on the right side.

Jay and Chad stood behind the ambo; Julian and the female EU security staffer stood behind Aldenburg, and two large Ghanaians, the agent in charge and deputy agent in charge from the President's Own Guard Regiment, stood behind President Amanor. Everyone had handguns but no one was too concerned because of all the RIVCOM men encircling the parking lot, their rifles at the ready.

The sun had dipped down even lower in the west; someone in the press contingent said light was going to be an issue if they didn't start immediately, but as far as Josh was concerned, the river and concrete of the dam were perfectly lit for the photo opportunity to come, even better than it would have been the following afternoon.

Jay spoke into his mic and it came through Josh's earpiece.

"Everybody scan sectors. Duff, the riverbank and jungle on the other side is yours; Ben, the switchyard; Chad, the dam. LBG, keep your heads on swivels."

Josh's job was to stand to the right of the riser near the three steps up, ready to pick up the rear of the diamond coverage after Dunnigan left the stage. He found his position, faced the river as instructed, and peered into the dense jungle rising on the hill on the other bank.

The door to the power house behind Duffy opened, and a man in a coat and tie stepped out along with a pair of RIVCOM police. They came to the riser, Josh looked them over, and then Nichole stepped up to the man.

"Good afternoon." She checked her iPad quickly. "Are you Mr. Mensah?"

The man nodded and they shook hands. He looked nervous, Josh noted, but he chalked it up to the fact that this plant employee was about to meet the president of his nation.

Nichole escorted him up the riser, and he greeted the three dignitaries.

Mensah spoke softly, but Josh was close enough to hear. As cameras rolled, he said, "I apologize that we do not have a better reception prepared for you. We are having a problem with the turbine controls, and we just received word of your visit a few minutes before we lost power."

Amanor's booming voice contrasted with that of the mild-mannered deputy plant operator. "I am the one who must apologize, Mr. Mensah. We're truly sorry about our unfortunate timing. I think we can manage here with our event, so you and your people can continue to do your difficult work. We know the power is the most important thing, so I encourage you to put all your efforts into fixing the issue as quickly as possible."

Amanor seemed to be playing to the various press outlets

recording this exchange. He said, "This illustrates how important and beneficial to Ghana it will be for the EU and the U.S. to begin modernization efforts here at the Akosombo Hydroelectric Facility."

Mensah just nodded, and Duff thought the man looked greatly relieved. He said, "Thank you. Now, if you will excuse me, Mr. President, Madam Ambassador, Madam High Representative, I must get back to the control room."

With a second handshake with the three principals, Mensah left the stage as Jennifer Dunnigan began her brief remarks at the lectern.

Mensah passed by Josh at the bottom of the stairs, and the DS special agent registered beads of sweat visible at the man's temples. Josh thought he must have some sort of extreme social anxiety, but no red flags were raised by this. In his career he'd seen military officers sweat while talking to senior officers, embassy staff shake in the presence of higher-ranking diplomats, even military contractors protecting celebrities show their nerves around their principals.

But as the two RIVCOM men began returning with the deputy plant operator to the power house, Josh took a moment to look over the cops. It was a common practice with all security forces: size up the equipment, the bearing, the demeanor of those around.

The RIVCOM men wore camo uniforms with the VRA RIVCOM patch on their shoulders, M4 rifles, Browning pistols, radios, and maroon berets. They appeared surprisingly young, early twenties, and very serious, again, Josh assumed, because of the presence of the president of their nation.

Josh had just finished his evaluation of the men and started to turn around to look out over the river when he looked back, this time more carefully.

Something was off.

He only caught a brief glimpse of the front of the man on Mensah's left, but it appeared to him the man was missing a magazine from the rig on his chest. The farthest left pouch seemed to be empty, and Josh found this both odd and unprofessional.

Having any magazine pouches empty was strange, but the front left pouch was the closest one to where a right-handed shooter reloads, meaning it's chosen first if a right-handed shooter needs another magazine in a gunfight.

And both the orientation of the other two magazines and the setup of the cop's rifle told him that this young police officer was, indeed, right-handed.

Not to be carrying a magazine there meant that if the shit hit the fan, this cop would have to reach farther to reload, slowing down the time it took him to get back into the fight.

Soon the three men walked back into the power house, and looking around, Josh couldn't see any more RIVCOM men close enough to him to evaluate the same way.

Benjamin Manu was on the other side of the three little steps up the riser, facing back towards the power house.

Josh caught his attention, then beckoned him over. Manu came close as Dunnigan finished her comments for the cameras, and Johanna Aldenburg stepped up to the lectern, shadowed closely by Julian Delisle and the female EU security officer.

Manu shouldered up to Josh, then leaned in.

Josh continued looking across the river as he spoke to the Ghanaian employee of the Bureau of Diplomatic Security. "These RIVCOM guys. They look right to you?"

Manu said, "Yes, although it is very strange that Superintendent Baka isn't here. He'd have nothing to do with fixing the power outage. He should be present."

"You worried?"

Manu shrugged. "I'll ask someone about him before we go. Maybe he's out sick today."

Josh nodded and said, "One of the men was missing a mag on his chest rig."

The Ghanaian police advisor for the embassy gave a little sigh. "These guys are so young. They're supposed to be elite, but . . . they aren't paid very much."

"Let's keep an eye on them," Josh whispered. Manu nodded, went back to his position, and resumed scanning his sector.

Just forty feet from Josh, Johanna Aldenburg spoke into the cameras. "The ingenuity, the creativity, the resourcefulness and resilience of this nation are all something to be admired, and something we in Europe want to learn from."

Josh tuned her out when he heard voices behind the riser. He looked there and saw three of the president's guards conferring over something in hushed whispers. He couldn't tell what they were talking about but imagined it must be important.

With nothing else to do he turned again to the front, looked over Manu's shoulder, and went back to scanning the hillside on the other side of the river, but still he wondered what the president's security guys were so agitated about.

CONRAD TREMAINE PULLED HIS RUSSIAN-MADE DRAGUNOV RIFLE from its canvas sheath, then hoisted his backpack and his shooting mat and left the Toyota behind on the rocky hill road, pushing himself deep into the dense jungle.

It took him a minute of navigating the brush before he saw the river below, then the switchyard, the power house, and the riser in front of it. The dam was on Tremaine's right, and he scanned it quickly, made sure he saw no threats there.

He went fully prone on his mat, pushed his pack in front of him, and rested the Russian rifle on top of it.

As he looked back to the power house, his laser rangefinder told him he was three hundred thirty-one meters from the lectern on the riser, so he dialed this distance into his scope and leveled the rifle, then aimed at the EU high representative. The sixteen-power magnification afforded him the ability to see the woman's face relatively clearly from this distance, and when he put the optic's chevron on her chest, he knew the Ghanaian president would present an even easier shot for him to make.

But he couldn't see the president from here. Amanor was seated, security officers stood on either side of him, and the South African across the river had no shot, at least not until the man rose to give his speech to the cameras.

Tremaine swiveled the weapon a little to the left and right to take in the entire entourage. Security officers stood around the two seated principals on the riser, more stood directly behind it, and here he saw some of the president's detail talking to one another, not even looking at their charge. He scanned right and saw the various junior diplomats and government officials behind the riser, standing there, no doubt, to make this photo op appear bigger than it was, when, in fact, there was no crowd from the facility in attendance at all.

Tremaine was happy to see that the Dragons of Western Togoland, all dressed as RIVCOM soldiers with the exception of four dressed as VRA technicians standing by the switchyard, were all staying off to the sides, none closer than twenty-five meters away from the security people. He knew that any real close scrutiny or questioning of the men would reveal that they weren't police and had never before set foot inside the gates of this facility, and he hoped like hell none of that happened before he took his shot, because his entire plan could unravel very easily if the delegation realized they were surrounded by rebel infiltrators.

None of these Dragons had any idea he'd be targeting the president, and Tremaine had no idea what their reaction would be when he did. He knew the protective details would pull guns, and he imagined the poorly trained Dragons would spook, and then all hell would break loose. He didn't think there was much chance the U.S. ambassador or EU high rep would get out of this unscathed, but he thought this would only benefit Kang's plan. If high-level Westerners were killed at the hands of the Dragons of Western Togoland when Kang's General Boatang took power by eradicating said rebels, then he would enjoy more support from the West because he was the one who achieved retribution for the deaths of their diplomats.

Tremaine smiled a little. The Chinaman wasn't the only bloke on this continent who could think strategically.

Shifting his view to the right side of the riser now, he clocked a couple more security men: one white and facing his way, and one Black, facing away towards the power house. They might have been here with the Americans or the EU, he couldn't tell; they weren't part of the president's detail, he was certain of that much.

He looked over the man facing him and eyed him intently, as if their eyes were locked on each other. And then, just for an instant, Tremaine got the feeling the man looked familiar.

As he was about to focus even more on him, however, Johanna Aldenburg stepped away from the lectern, and President Amanor rose from his chair and walked forward, presenting himself to the rifle hidden in the jungle.

The bald-headed man put his hands on the lectern; his pair of security men on the stage moved to positions just behind him, but neither of them impeded Tremaine's line of sight on the man's left temple. As Amanor began speaking, the Sentinel mercenary thumbed off the safety, took a deep breath, and then slowly let it out.

Then he took in another breath, pausing a moment to consider this move of his. Killing the president of the most democratic nation in West Africa would put a target on his back for the rest of his life if word somehow got out. He told himself he could no longer get drunk in bars or talk of his past exploits with friends, because that was the only way he could imagine this would ever come to light. Krelis, Junior, and Baginski wouldn't snitch; they'd been with him for years. The Russians and the Dragons wouldn't know, and his other mercs weren't around.

Tremaine was about to do something big, but something he'd have to keep secret for the rest of his life.

But he told himself that was fine. He *wanted* this trophy, wanted the knowledge that he'd personally decapitated a government, personally initiated a coup d'état.

And he wanted the extra quarter million euros he'd get for ensuring that the coup was a success.

And really, how could it fail if the president was dead?

Tremaine had to work to control his breathing now; the excitement threatened to get the best of him. But finally, some twenty seconds or so after Amanor arrived at the lectern, Conrad Tremaine took another slow breath and put his finger on the trigger of his sniper rifle.

JOSH DUFFY DID HIS BEST TO KEEP HIS FOCUS ON HIS SECTOR, BUT he found it difficult to do so because now the security men from the president's detail had begun slowly fanning out behind the riser. Any sort of repositioning while their leader was making remarks seemed bizarre, and he flashed his eyes up to Jay on the riser and saw him taking a quick glance back over his shoulder to check on the commotion, as well.

Behind the riser and right next to the men, however, he saw that Nichole and the three other American FSOs seemed completely unaware; they were concentrating on the president and his comments, and Josh told himself he needed to focus on his job and let the Ghanaians deal with whatever it was they were dealing with.

But just as he turned his eyes back to the other side of the river he caught a quick flash of light, halfway up the massive hill there, deep in the jungle. He furrowed his brow, looked again, but saw nothing. It had been brief, little more than a sparkle in the fading light, but he saw no metal, no water, no glass—nothing that could have made such a flash.

It was just green brush and grasses, darker green trees, and long black shadows brought on by the low sun.

Still, even though it had been nothing more than a flicker, his heart began to pound, and an alarm somewhere deep inside him went off.

He looked to Costa on the riser, then back to the jungle.

Bells clanging in his brain, he unclasped his hands.

And then it happened again. In the same area as before, a gleam of light in the waning moments of sunshine. There and gone.

It would have meant nothing to most, but Josh Duffy had lived in this world for a long time, and he knew what he'd seen.

Without hesitation he shouted at the top of his lungs as he moved, racing up the stairs and onto the riser. "Sniper!"

NINETEEN

ALL HEADS SWIVELED TO DUFF AS HE LEAPT UP. HE WAS HEADING for the ambo, but he was glad to see Amanor's agent in charge diving forward to cover the president, and Julian in motion going towards Aldenburg.

Jay Costa swung his body in front of Dunnigan, who was seated in her chair, and the EU AIC grabbed Aldenburg by the arm and heaved her to her feet as he covered her.

Amanor's agent in charge tackled the president from behind at the lectern, and as soon as he did so, he lurched forward, just ten feet from Josh Duffy.

The crack of a rifle pounded the air, then echoed off the dam and boomed again.

Costa had Dunnigan spun around and they were already moving down from the back of the meter-high riser, but Josh shouted into his mic to the RSO from fifteen feet away.

"Into the power house!"

"Negative," Costa answered back. "LZ!"

Josh was in the middle of the stage now, racing towards Dunnigan and Costa and the rest of the crowd. He saw Nichole stumbling away with the others when a second shot rang out from behind. A presidential security man next to him pitched forward, falling into the crowd of diplomats and other officials on the concrete.

Josh was too far away from the ambassador to cover her body, plus that was Jay's job. His job, he knew, was to stand his ground and neutralize the threat. His gun appeared in his hand, he spun back to the river, and he raised his weapon.

Eliminating a sniper concealed several hundred yards away with a pistol was virtually impossible, and Duff knew this, so he planned on just squeezing off shots to suppress the threat as best he could.

But before he fired the first round at the jungled hillside across the water, he heard a bullet's crack come from near the power house on his left. Before he could even react to the sound, Benjamin Manu shouted into his mic. "Contact, right!"

Instantaneously, a volley of gunshots boomed off to Duff's right and he swiveled his pistol there, only to see that the RIVCOM police and dam VRA operations personnel who'd been standing there were now aiming weapons at the delegation.

He extended his Glock at a target, aimed at a shooter, and fired. The man lowered his rifle and ran behind a pickup, and Josh was reasonably certain he'd hit him, though obviously not bad enough to fully shut him down.

Costa yelled into his mic now. "Alamo! Alamo!" This was the code to get the principal into the hardpoint at the location. Here, the hardpoint had been established as the ground floor of a large stairwell inside the power house. The president and the EU contingents, Josh had also been briefed, would use the stairwell on the opposite side of the building's lobby as a hardpoint.

But Josh wouldn't be going, not immediately, anyway, and neither would Ben or the LBG men. Chad and Jay would rush Dunnigan to the Alamo, while Duff and the others would do their best to engage the threats that seemed to be growing exponentially. Duff and the others were tasked with making *themselves* targets so that their protectees could get away.

Behind him nearly forty people, including his wife, scrambled for cover. He, in contrast, was the only living person still standing on the big riser, in full view of an unknown number of enemy, including a sniper who could drop him at will.

A bullet's overpressure bit into the air just inches from his head, coming from the switchyard, and he fired his pistol at the half dozen men standing or crouched there, thirty yards away.

CONRAD TREMAINE CRAWLED BACKWARDS THROUGH THE BITING brush as fast as he could, dragging the rifle and the backpack on the mat as he went, desperate to get out of the area to flee the chaos he'd just initiated.

He knew what had happened as soon as it happened. The sky had been gray earlier, but the clouds had broken in the west, and sunlight had then reflected off the front lens of his rifle scope.

Someone saw the flash and recognized it for what it was. He'd fired, but not before the president's AIC had dived in the way, taking a bullet in his back for his protectee.

Tremaine's second shot had missed the president, as well, hitting another of his burly security men, and then the Dragons dressed as VRA employees and cops began shooting, either because the security forces fired on them first, or else they just opened up on the delegation's security forces because they didn't know what the hell was going on.

"Feckin hell!" he shouted as he backed up farther into the jungle, the sounds of combat echoing all around him, and then he rose from his prone position, scooped up his weapon and his mat, and turned and began running for the truck.

Once in the Toyota, he looked at Krelis behind the wheel. "Get us off the hill!"

"What's happening?" the Dutchman asked as he floored it, the tires spinning on the gravel before digging in and propelling the vehicle forward.

Tremaine wiped sweat from his brow and stowed his Dragunov between his knees, the still-hot barrel pointing up. "Well, I didn't get Amanor, but there is good news. As far as anyone will ever know, the Dragons of Western Togoland just started this coup off with one hell of a bloody bang."

RIVCOM SERGEANT ISAAC OPOKU HAD SPENT THE PAST FIFTEEN minutes racing up a gravel road on a Kawasaki motorcycle he'd appropriated from a passing teenager not far from the limestone quarry, and now he was just a minute or so away from the eastern side of the dam. He thought he heard a popping sound coming from the engine, so he took his hand off the throttle and shifted the bike into neutral, and doing so allowed him to immediately recognize the distant reports of gunfire.

He could tell that the shooting emanated from the dam, and his heart sank. He had been the one who stirred up the hornet's nest, and now the hornets were stinging his friends and colleagues.

No! he thought. This was all his fault.

He opened the throttle, knowing full well that his one pistol wouldn't make much difference in the midst of the battle he heard raging, but also knowing he had a job to do. He'd already lost three colleagues today, and whatever the consequences, he was determined to expend his last breath trying to save the others.

He thought briefly of his son, Kofi, of his wife, Abina, and of his promise to her that this job at RIVCOM he'd taken four years earlier would be safer than the work he'd done for the Army's Northern Command.

He'd been in scrapes in the military up north, but he'd never heard any gunfight like the one just a kilometer or so to the south of him now.

He forced fear and family out of his mind. Isaac Opoku told himself he would fight off this threat to his friends or else he would die trying.

DUFF FELT ROUNDS WHIPPING PAST HIS HEAD AS A FULLY AUTO-matic weapon went cyclic. Another burst pocked the concrete lot in front of him between the riser and the building. The lectern on his right took a hit and crashed to its side, but Duff just kept firing at targets, men running in all directions and shooting at the same time. He dumped five rounds, eight rounds, twelve rounds.

As near as he could tell, everyone in a RIVCOM uniform was an enemy combatant.

He heard more shooting behind him, the loud report of more rifles. He finally dropped to his knees, bewildered that he hadn't been hit, and he unloaded the rest of his fifteen-round magazine at the men at the switchyard, and then went flat on the riser to reload again.

More bullets zinged by; much of it was outgoing fire. It sounded to him like the LBG guys were behind the riser shooting in both directions, as well as possibly some of the president's men and EU security personnel.

Duff wasn't alone, but he was the most exposed, and he knew that no matter how many people he had out here fighting with him, they were all surrounded and outgunned by the men in the RIVCOM uniforms.

Josh Duffy had been surrounded and outgunned before, and he

knew his only hope was to lay down an obscene amount of fire, to drop enough of the enemy into the dirt in the hopes that the rest of them would panic and break contact.

He rolled onto his side and aimed towards the river now, where he saw a pair of men in RIVCOM uniforms trying to flank to the east. He felt certain the sniper in the jungle had bugged out, otherwise there was no way Duff would still be alive here, alone on the big riser and in plain view of the hillside, so he dismissed the other side of the river and began dumping 9-millimeter hollow-points at the pair running along the edge of the parking lot on the near bank.

His earpiece came alive as he fired; he could tell it was the RSO, but he couldn't make out what Costa was saying.

So Josh just kept shooting, hoping like hell to at least get these two guys in his view out of the fight, either by dropping them or by sending them down the riverbank to cover.

Ben Manu spoke through his earpiece now, then Chad Larsen, but again, Duff couldn't make out the words through all his outgoing fire.

Soon both RIVCOM men by the river had disappeared, so he rolled to his right, over and over and over, crawled across the top of the dead agent in charge from the President's Own Guard Regiment, and then fell off the back of the riser, dropping a meter down and landing on the concrete on his left side.

Both incoming and outgoing gunfire continued blasting the air. He was in decent cover here, but chunks of concrete still blew into his face, and a sharp edge sliced his forehead. He ignored the pain, the blood dripping into his eye, and he rolled up to his knees, ejected the empty magazine in his smoking-hot Glock 19, and reloaded with his last mag.

While he was doing this Costa's voice came through again, and this time Duff was able to hear the transmission. "We're in the Alamo, all fall back on us. Bounding fire!"

Duff saw enemy forty yards or so away on his left, crouched behind trucks and some parked storage containers there, and he saw more men in the direction of the river, moving laterally, not firing at the moment. He scanned to the switchyard and saw several dead enemy, but there was still movement behind one of the VRA trucks.

Ben Manu and two LBG men remained between the riser and the switchyard, and though they were shooting their pistols from the prone position, they were more exposed than Duff.

He shouted to them.

"Move!"

The three Ghanaian men rose and began racing back to the power house. Manu had a pronounced limp, which slowed him behind the others. Duff fired suppressing rounds, first at the switchyard, then back to the left, then over at the river. He wasn't hitting anyone with this crazy fire, of this he was pretty certain, but screaming bullets might possibly keep heads down, and he figured that was the best he could do for now.

The problem was, Duff knew, that he was running out of ammo, and while suppressive fire might not require much in the way of accuracy, it was *extremely* demanding on one's ammunition.

He aimed in on a plainclothed man with a yellow hard hat and badge on his shirt on the left; this joker held an AK-47, different from the M4s wielded by the RIVCOM guys. Duff fired his Glock three times, and the man slammed against the truck and fell to the ground.

Duff's pistol locked open on an empty mag.

Just then, Manu's voice came through Duff's earpiece.

"Duff! Move!"

"Moving!" he shouted, then ran back for the power house, his empty gun in his right hand.

Manu and two LBG men were on their knees in the open doorway, shooting to Duff's left and right. A man from the EU security detail was with them, standing and firing towards the switchyard over

Manu's head. Duff ran on, passing at least ten dead and wounded in the parking lot, some male, some female, and he held his breath as he looked them over, hoping with all his soul that Nichole wasn't among them.

She was not, and he left the wounded where they lay because his job was to stay alive to protect the ambo.

Duff finally raced through the open door, came crashing into the darkened lobby of the facility, then fell onto the floor.

As soon as he did so, the man from the EU shut the door and locked it.

The room was lit only by emergency lights high in the corners, giving an eerie vibe, with long shadows drawn by the people inside and deep dark corners, impenetrably black.

"We've got wounded out there on the parking lot!" a British woman's voice called from a doorway across the lobby. Josh thought it might have been one of the crew from Sky News.

To this, Julian Delisle shouted from a doorway on the other side of the open lobby. "We don't have the firepower to go back for them yet. There's two dozen enemy, at least, and they have rifles. We hunker down inside this building while we compose a plan. That door stays shut!"

Almost immediately, more gunshots cracked, and the windows at the front of the lobby shattered and the blinds covering them tore. Josh climbed to his feet, ran towards the Alamo, and made his way through the door. Here he found a large stairwell area, with Ambassador Dunnigan sitting on the stairs, a near-catatonic look on her blood-speckled face, and two other FSOs, a man named Scott Clarke and a woman named Arletta James, huddled around her. Chad Larsen stood behind the ambo, higher on the stairs and covering the second floor with his pistol, and Jay Costa remained at the doorway, his weapon aimed through the lobby and towards the front door.

Neither of the other DS men appeared to be injured.

Josh's head spun frantically as he searched for Nichole, and then his heart stopped.

He saw a woman's feet, wearing low heels, protruding from the recess under the stairs.

Duff had no idea what shoes his wife had been wearing; he rarely noticed such things, much to her displeasure. He ran there, turned into the dimly lit recess, and opened his eyes wide to take in what little light he could find.

Foreign Service Officer Karen Chamberlin lay on her back, her head in the lap of Nichole Duffy. Nichole held pressure on a wound over the woman's right breast, and she looked up at her husband in horror.

Chamberlin was still alive, but Duff knew that the expression on his wife's face meant the poor woman stood no chance.

Duff knelt down quickly and embraced his wife. "Are you hit?"

She shook her head. She wasn't in shock, he could tell, but she was nonetheless overwhelmed by the events of the past ninety seconds or so. "You?" she asked, her eyes just slightly unfixed.

"I'm fine."

She looked up at him suddenly. "Why would the dam police attack us?"

Josh rose and spoke loud enough for others to hear. "They aren't dam police. Their tactics . . . they're a mess. Just a bunch of assholes with guns. I don't even think those guys expected the assassination attempt. The shot came from across the water, and the enemy around us responded to it even slower than we did."

Manu sat on the ground, his back against the wall, obviously in pain. His face perspired; an LBG man named Malike tore open the Foreign Service National Investigator's pants and used fabric to tie over a gunshot wound through his right quadricep.

But through wincing pain, Manu said, "Josh is right. The presidential detail were talking to each other in Twi, saying they didn't recognize any of the cops and wondering, like me, where the superintendent was. When the sniper fired, the President's Own Guard Regiment opened fire on the men in RIVCOM uniforms. I don't think the enemy was looking to fight us until our side started shooting."

Dunnigan spoke up now. "But . . . but they were bad guys. Right?"

Duff nodded. "They were bad guys. Rebels of some kind, here to take over the dam, would be my guess."

The gunfire through the windows had stopped—for now, anyway—and Duff wondered if the enemy, whoever the fuck they were, were preparing to attack. He walked through the low light back over to Costa, who was on the radio with someone on another channel. He finished his conversation and turned to Duff. "We've got two LBG dead, Tano and Yooku. Amanor and Aldenburg, along with all their people still alive, are sheltered in the stairwell on the other side of the lobby."

He added, "Julian sent the three helos away; they can come back and get us when the LZ cools off, whenever the fuck that might be, but he couldn't leave the birds on the ground a hundred yards away from a firefight."

Larsen continued covering up the stairs, his gun still pointing up to the landing. "Can the helos make contact with Accra?"

"So far no one is coming up on the net or sat phones. Somebody might have knocked down radio towers and jammed the sats."

"Jammed the sats?" Larsen said. "Rebels don't jam satellite transmissions. What the fuck is going on?"

Duff spoke up now. "Gunfire has stopped. I can check and see if the enemy bugged out, try to get any wounded back in here."

Costa shook his head. "EU will do that. I need you for something else."

Duff raised his weapon, its slide locked open. "I'm Winchester, boss."

Costa pulled a G19 magazine from his belt and handed it over, still aiming at the closed front door to the parking lot. He said, "Down the hallway to the left of the reception desk is a control room, usually about a dozen or so operators working in there, including the guy who greeted us. If the enemy took this place by force, which I assume they did, they might be holding hostages in there." Looking to Duff, he said, "I need you to take some guys and clear them out, and that means CQB against an unknown number of armed enemy, around noncombatants. You up for that?"

This sounded like a suicide run to Duff, but he understood the order. "Roger that."

Costa radioed Julian across the lobby and told him what the plan was, and the EU security chief said, "I'll send a man over to you to assist."

Costa turned back to Duff. "Take Malike, too. Good luck."

Malike was a fit thirty-five-year-old Local Body Guard who took his job incredibly seriously. Duff had only met the man in passing before today; he wasn't friendly or chatty, but he was professional, and Duff had no doubt Malike would be a good man to have on his shoulder for whatever was about to happen.

Seconds later, a silver-haired bodyguard in a blood- and sweat-stained white polo shirt came across the lobby, stopping behind the reception desk where he scooped something up, and then continued forward at a run. He held a SIG Sauer pistol in his hands, and he nodded to Costa. In a Scandinavian accent he said, "I'm Anderson."

"You hurt?" Duff asked.

The man looked down at his shirt. In a grave tone he said, "That's not me. That's Edina, a Hungarian development officer." Softly now, he said, "She was twenty-seven."

Duff knew they didn't have the luxury of processing grief at the moment; they had to stay on mission.

He got into Anderson's face. "Are you able?"

Now the middle-aged man nodded with complete resolution. "I'm waiting on you."

"Let's go," Duff said, and he led the way out of the doorway with Malike and Anderson, heading down the darkened hallway.

TWENTY

SERGEANT ISAAC OPOKU RAN ACROSS THE TOP OF THE DAM AS FAST as his legs would take him, his Browning pistol swinging with his frantic movements. The heavy shooting had stopped down below, for now, anyway, but he didn't know if the shooters there would be coming up here, or if there were already more enemy up here with him.

He'd dumped the bike in the jungle at the eastern edge of the dam so he could arrive more quietly, but this meant a quarter-mile run over open ground, and considering the fact that every joint, every bone, every muscle in his body ached from his fall into the limestone quarry and his high-speed journey on the bumpy road, the run was pure torture.

The only place he didn't really feel pain at the moment was where he'd been shot above his right hip, and he didn't know if that was good news or bad.

He saw no one, friend or foe, as he raced all the way across the top of the dam to the administration building, where he stopped and leaned his shoulder against the western wall, keeping out of view of the windows here. He decided to bypass this building and head next door to the police station, in the hopes that some of his compatriots would still be in there.

He broke into a reluctant run again, then went around the back of the admin building, and as he passed the doorway here, he looked inside a window.

There, standing alone at the end of a corridor, was a RIVCOM man, his rifle slung over his shoulder. He seemed to be guarding a door, but the man was too far away for Isaac to identify.

He breathed a sigh of relief and reached to open the door, but as he put his hand on the latch, he stopped himself and looked in.

The officer down the hall was wearing his maroon beret on his head.

There was only one cop here at RIVCOM who would ever possibly do anything that stupid, and that was Corporal Kwabena.

And Opoku knew that Kwabena was ten kilometers away, lying dead in the limestone dust.

Isaac quickly backed away from the door, turned, and began running again towards the police station.

So the enemy didn't just mock up vehicles to look like VRA personnel. No, they had uniforms, and the fact that the rifle around the man's neck appeared to be one of the RIVCOM standard-issue M4s told Isaac that they'd managed to get into the armory and take their actual weapons.

A minute later he was moving slowly and methodically through the police station, his Browning pistol out in front of him. Blood on his hands from his many cuts and scrapes slicked the grip of his weapon, and sweat poured into his eyes, but he kept working, "slicing the pie" to each room, moving laterally a few inches at a time when he got to a door so that he would only expose himself to the parts of the space he could cover with his weapon.

He went up a staircase to the second floor, made it to the door to the kitchen, and then opened the door, keeping the majority of his body behind the wall as he did so.

Two men in RIVCOM uniforms stood there; neither had their

berets on but both had their hands on their rifles, while over a dozen more sat lined up on the floor, their heads down.

One of the guards looked Isaac's way, focused on him a moment, and then said something in Ewe.

"What's going on?" the man asked. Isaac didn't recognize him; he knew all twenty-four men on his shift, as well as all the men on the other shift, so he fired his pistol, hitting the man square in the torso just above the magazine rack on his chest. He fired again for good measure, then switched aim to the other target, who was in the process of raising his AK up in his direction.

Isaac fired three more times, hitting the man in the pelvis, the stomach, and the head as he fell.

He now focused on the hostages on the ground. They looked up; they were cops from his shift, he recognized each and every one of them, and he ran towards them. Seeing that their hands were zip-tied behind their backs, he pulled his small folding knife from his pocket.

Cutting the zip off the first man, he handed the knife to the newly free RIVCOM officer, grabbed one of the M4s lying there by a dead enemy, and swung it towards the door in case anyone came in, responding to his gunfire.

The other RIVCOM man began cutting his mates free. The third man grabbed the other rifle off the floor and shouldered up to Sergeant Opoku.

"Where is Baka?" Isaac asked.

"The superintendent is dead. I saw him fall."

"Damn."

"And they've got our guns."

"Where are *their* guns?" Isaac asked.

"Don't know. They had AKs when they hit us. One I saw had an RPK. Any idea who they are?"

Opoku said, "They speak Ewe."

"Yeah," the man said. "They're West Togoland rebels? They actually exist?"

"Maybe," Isaac said. "I saw about fifteen or twenty."

The officer shook his head. "I saw the trucks approaching from both sides. There were thirty or forty men, had to be. And they've got white men helping them."

Isaac knew this already, of course. He just said, "Russians."

Now the officer looked to him. "Did they kill the president?"

"The president? The president of *what*?"

"Of Ghana." The young officer explained the early arrival of the joint delegation to Isaac's astonishment and horror. He seethed inside, still thinking this was somehow all his fault by stirring up the hornet's nest. He said, "Is Amanor dead?"

Another man in the room said, "We don't know. I heard the helicopters land and then leave about twenty minutes later. We lost five of our guys in the initial fight, but they looked like us; they came in so fast, we didn't know what was happening."

Isaac thought for a moment. "Well, we do now. Before we do anything, I want everyone to take off your tunics. I don't care if you have an undershirt on or not, I don't want you wearing a full uniform out there. The enemy has our camo, our weapons. We have to stand apart from them or we're going to start shooting each other." The men began doing this, and when the first two were down to their white tank tops, they took the rifles from Opoku and the other officer so Isaac and the other man could do the same.

While the rest of them were still getting their tunics off, Isaac said, "Let's get to the armory first. They must have left their rifles there when they pulled ours, so maybe we can use them. Once we have enough guns, Sergeant Ofori, take three men and clear the admin building. Expect hostages. Get them downstairs and out the exit at the motor pool, then link back with us. All the shooting has been going on at the power house, so we're heading there."

Ofori was a tall man about Opoku's age, and he nodded readily.

Isaac saw that he had fifteen men with him now, minus Ofori and the three he chose to take with him after they found more weapons.

Isaac took the M4 back from the corporal who held it, then led the way out into the hall towards the armory.

JOSH DUFFY KNELT TO PUSH THE DOOR LATCH THAT WOULD GET HIM into the control room, staying below the window in the door so that any enemy inside wouldn't see him.

Behind him, Anderson from the EU and Malike from the U.S. embassy's Local Body Guard team waited with their weapons up.

Duff had organized this hasty room-clearing operation with whispers and gestures. He'd open the door and cover anything in the ten o'clock to two o'clock position while prone, Anderson would burst in to the left side of the room and Malike would go right, covering nine o'clock and three o'clock respectively.

If the enemy knew what they were doing, which though not evident so far could also not be ruled out, then they would put men in the far corners on either side so that they would both have an angle on anyone breaching from the hall, while remaining out of each other's crossfire.

Duff had more territory to cover, of course, but he'd also be safer. As dangerous as opening the door was, falling flat on the floor to engage threats made him a smaller target.

After a quick look back to the others to make sure they were ready to go, he tried the latch and found it locked.

Fuck, he thought.

He began to rise up; he knew very little about picking locks, and he wasn't a criminal or a spy, so he planned on retreating so he could call Jay to see if he had any ideas.

But Anderson put a hand on his shoulder. Softly in his ear he said, "Switch with me. I got a set of keys from behind the reception desk. Might take a minute, but I'll get us in."

Duff did so; he took the left wall and rose as Anderson knelt down. The man pulled a ring of at least a dozen keys and a dozen more key cards, then began looking them over while examining the lock on the door latch, trying to find which one might fit.

His first try didn't work, but his second slipped right into the lock. He glanced back over to Duff and nodded, and then he placed his pistol on the floor in front of him, turned the key with one hand, and opened the latch with the other. Once it was cracked open, he hefted his SIG pistol and shoved the door open with force, dropping down into the room on his chest.

Duff and Malike raced in on either side of him, and Duff heard a gunshot from his side before he even cleared the doorway.

He swung in and saw a man in a uniform with an AK-47 at his shoulder, and the weapon was pointed directly at him. Duff fired, then dove to his right, into the room, firing twice before crashing into the ground on his right arm.

The shooter in his corner got off one more round before he caught one of Duff's hollow-points in the side of his neck. Blood shot across the white wall behind him, and he fell to the ground, clutching his throat.

Duff shot him again while gunfire behind him barked.

He scanned his entire sector of the room while on his side and saw several civilians crouched on the ground or folded under their desks, but no more opposition, so he rolled in the opposite direction.

In the far right corner another man in a RIVCOM uniform had slumped down in a seated position, a crimson stain behind his head. There were no more targets here, either, only terrified dam employees, so Duff sat up and checked on his two partners.

Anderson lay facedown in the doorway, clearly dead. He'd been shot through the left side of his head by the man Duff had then dispatched.

The EU security officer had taken Duff's position and, through no fault of his own, paid the ultimate price.

Duff knew it could just as easily have been him, and he felt panic welling up inside him. He stifled it down when he looked at Malike, and saw that the Ghanaian had blood pouring from his left hand and onto the floor. The LBG man shook his arm, and more blood splattered down.

Duff climbed to his feet, balanced himself awkwardly on his prosthesis as he did so, then rushed to him, all but forgetting about his panic, though his gun remained up and aimed at the civilians. "You good?"

"Hit my forearm. I'll live."

Duff turned to face the room. "Any more enemy here?"

One man rose, his hands in the air. Duff immediately recognized him as the assistant plant operator who had greeted them outside. "None here, sir, but there are more in the building."

Duff spoke into his mic. "Jay, we're clear in here. Bring the principals in quickly, we might have more problems."

Costa burst into the room, the ambassador just behind him and both Larsen and Manu just behind her. Nichole, Scott Clarke, and Arletta James followed, and Josh saw that Karen Chamberlin, the wounded Foreign Service Officer, was not with them.

He knew his wife would not have left Karen if she were still alive.

The group from the EU entered moments later, and the president, the surviving government employees, and the surviving men of the President's Own Guard Regiment just after that. Julian saw his dead coworker on the floor, and Costa realized that Malike had been injured. He pointed to a control room worker, a woman in a dress, still squatting in the corner. "You have a first-aid kit?"

"Yes. Yes, we do."

"We need it. Is there a washroom?"

A man next to her pointed to a door. He turned to his three agents still standing. "Get the high representative in that room."

Johanna Aldenburg was escorted past the control room personnel and put in the bathroom, and seconds later, the seven surviving members of President Amanor's detail brought him in, as well.

Five members of the press were here, and Duff assumed that meant they'd lost three in the initial gunfight.

The control room technician produced a first-aid kit from a box on the wall, and the lone non-injured LBG man, a burly fifty-one-year-old named Kaku, took it and brought it over to Malike, who was now seated on the floor, holding his bloody arm.

Costa rushed up to Mensah now. "Any other ways into this room other than the one we came from?"

"Stairwell down. There, next to the bathroom door."

"That it?"

"If you go back into the hall there's an elevator, and on the other side of the lobby are more stairs and a freight elevator, but from here, you can only get into the main part of the dam by taking the stairs down to the generator gallery."

"How many entrances to the building in all?"

Mensah thought, but just a moment. "Ten, twelve maybe, including the subterranean levels."

"Son of a bitch," Larsen muttered. "We've got to lock this room down. We can't cover the entire building."

Julian ordered two of his men to stay at the hallway door and two more to go to the stairwell.

Now Costa looked back to Mensah. "Tell me everything, as fast as possible."

"There's only time to tell you one thing, man. Three Russians are here, and they are planting bombs."

"*Russians?* They came with the others?"

"Yeah."

Costa looked to Duff and said one word. "Wagner."

Duff nodded.

"Where are they planting the bombs?"

Mensah looked like he might have a heart attack. Sweat poured from him, and his movements and words were rushed. "Downstairs. They are doing it right now."

"Okay, calm down. Where are they?"

Mensah thought a moment. "Below us is the generator gallery, and below that the turbine gallery. There are elevators up to the top of the dam, other levels with equipment and piping and electrical relay systems." He shook his head. "They were speaking to each other in Russian, looking at a tablet computer, and the one in charge said something about the turbines and needing to program detonators."

"You speak Russian?" Costa asked.

"No, but they said 'turbina,' 'programa,' and 'deetonators.' Not exactly a secret code."

Duff muttered softly now. "Oh shit." He looked to Nichole for support but saw her hurriedly bandaging the upper thigh of a wounded male government official from the EU diplomatic group.

Costa needed more information. "What happens if they blow up bombs down there?"

"The amount of explosives they have? They had four satchels, but I don't know if they all carried bombs; one looked different than the others. Each of the other three looked like they could have been twenty kilos or so. Sixty kilos, it's not enough to blow the dam, I don't think, but I'm not a structural engineer."

He thought a moment. "I guess, depending on if they know what they are doing, if someone told them *exactly* where to put them at the base of the turbines, they could damage the flow from the penstock, filling the chambers with water. If that happens, then the dam wall could burst, killing tens of thousands downriver."

With a distant stare he said, "And it could remove power from our nation's circuits for a year or more, killing tens of thousands more."

The president could hear all of this from the open bathroom door. He began conferring with some of his aides.

"What kind of bombs?" Julian asked now.

"What kind of bombs? I have no idea. They have three of the rebels with them; they told them they needed to come guard them while they prepare and plant the explosives, that's all I know."

"How long ago?"

"Right before I heard the helicopters."

Costa looked at his watch. "Twenty minutes. Fuck. How long does it take to plant—"

He stopped talking, clearly, Duff reasoned, because he knew Mensah would have no answer to his question.

Now the RSO turned to Duff. "Those bombs are a danger for the ambo, so that makes them a priority. We've got to clear those guys out."

Duff hefted the AK-47 rifle from the floor. "I don't know how to dismantle a bomb."

"If you can't stop them before they plant them, you better damn well get your hands on whatever they're using to detonate them."

Ben Manu sat in a chair, stanching the blood coming from his thigh with his own hand while the U.S. embassy's LBG man Kaku pulled more dressings from the first-aid kit. Manu said, "You know how to use that AK, Josh?"

In his career as a contractor, Josh Duffy had probably fired the AK-47 and other variants of this rifle more than all the other guns he'd ever fired in his life put together, including the M4, which he'd carried in the army. He just nodded. "I know my way around one, yeah."

Duff raised the Kalashnikov, examined the sights, pulled the bolt back a bit and looked inside, then dropped the magazine. Reseating it, he went over to the dead rebel and took two more mags from his chest.

Julian said, "I'm sorry. I've got all my team covering this room, and I've got to stay with the high rep. I can't spare you anyone."

Kaku drew a fresh Browning pistol from the hip of one of the dead guards. "I'll go."

Manu and Malike both rose, but Costa ordered them to sit back down. "You two aren't fully bandaged yet, and you're still losing blood. Get yourselves patched up, *then* you can get back in this fight."

Duff had the feeling he was about to go with only Kaku, and so did his wife. Nichole heard what was going on, and she rushed over. Squaring off to Jay Costa, she said, "You can't possibly expect—"

A booming voice interrupted her. President Francis Amanor stepped out of the bathroom, despite his security men's attempts to hold him back. He moved over to Costa, but he needn't have bothered. Two steps from the bathroom he was audible throughout the room.

"I have six men left. How many do you need?"

Duff answered before Jay did. "Two."

The president nodded, peeled two of his men off him, and sent them forward. Amanor said, "Bismark and Gideon have been with me for years." He looked to his men, both in their forties. "Good luck."

Duff said, "Who's in charge?" He knew a power struggle down there would be the last thing anyone needed, and it would likely get everyone killed.

Amanor said, "You were the last man in this building, the first to be sent in to clear out this room. *You* are in charge. You've earned it."

Mensah gave Duff and the others some quick directions; Larsen pulled a small plastic map of the facility off the wall and handed it over to him.

Then Nichole stepped up, reached out, and put her hand on her husband's face.

She lowered it, and spoke to him.

Though she looked both tender and terrified, the words that came out of her mouth were hardly gentle.

"Kick ass, soldier."

Duff and the three Ghanaians went to the stairs; Bismark led the way down, Duff right behind him, the Kalashnikov rifle at his shoulder.

AS SOON AS THEY WERE GONE, NICHOLE DUFFY WALKED OVER TO the dead man in the RIVCOM uniform who still wore a pistol on his belt. She knelt down to pull it, but behind her, Julian said, "What are you doing?"

"We need all the firepower in this fight we can get."

"You know how to use a gun?"

Nichole pulled the weapon, rose up, and turned to him. "I was an officer in the U.S. Army."

Julian just looked at her, then repeated himself. "You know how to use a gun?"

Nichole sighed, checked the weapon and the magazine, and pulled another magazine from the dead man's utility belt. She said, "My dad had one of these when I was a kid. I prefer Berettas and SIGs, but I've sent enough lead downrange with one of these to know which end the pointy things come out of."

Regional Security Officer Jay Costa called to Julian now. "I know this woman's history. She's proven herself in the past. She can help."

Julian nodded, then looked to the American female Foreign Service Officer. "Just don't point it at me or my people."

Nichole fought an eye roll and jammed the pistol into her waistband.

She knew the man wasn't being sexist, he was being anti-officer. *Must have been an enlisted man,* she told herself, and then she didn't think of it again.

TWENTY-ONE

VRA RIVER COMMAND SERGEANT ISAAC OPOKU RAN OUT THE FRONT door of the police station wearing his sweat-soaked V-neck "Super Dad" T-shirt and carrying a wooden-stocked AK-47 at his shoulder that was probably older than some of the men following behind him. The rest of the RIVCOM men wielded AKs as well, along with small canvas chest harnesses, most of which held three extra thirty-round rifle magazines. Nearly half the men were otherwise bare-chested, but many had undershirts or tank tops on.

Four of their number peeled off and went towards the admin building on the left, while Isaac and eleven others broke right.

The western edge of the dam was three hundred meters distant, and there on the river side of the dam, a small concrete building sat, housing both an elevator shaft and a ladder shaft, essentially an extremely steep metal stairwell. Both shafts went down into the bowels of the facility, thirty-six stories to the subterranean levels.

Just beyond the building and out of Isaac's view from his position, a steep concrete staircase ran down the entire length of the embankment to the river, the power house, and the transformer switchyard.

Most dam employees up here took either golf carts or VRA vehicles down the winding road beyond the dam, but the 735-step descent down the thirty-five-story-tall structure was an option, as well.

But Isaac's plan wasn't for him and his men to head down to the power house just yet. Instead they ran the three hundred meters, made it to the dam wall railing just beyond the elevator building and to the left of the stairs, then fanned out, aiming their new and untested rifles down at the scene below them.

The noise from the water gushing through the spillway below them to their left was incredible, but they could tell there was no more shooting down at the power house at the moment.

The parking lot, the power house, the switchyard, and the churning river were all visible from here. Isaac counted fifteen or so bodies lying around the riser erected for the delegation visit, though he couldn't tell who was friend and who was foe from this distance.

But he also saw clusters of men, very much alive, aiming rifles at the power house, and he was reasonably certain these men were wearing RIVCOM uniforms.

"Anyone have binos?" he called out to those around him. A young corporal scooted closer to him, reached into his pocket, and pulled out his iPhone.

Opoku admonished him. "The phones are dead, man."

The corporal pointed the phone at the scene below. "The camera works, Sergeant." He zoomed in on the clusters of men, and Isaac could see the red berets, the dark camo, and the M4s of his police unit.

"That's them," Isaac said. "They don't have control of the power house, which means someone in there is fighting back. We're going to help them."

"The tunnels?" a man asked. A warren of tunnels several stories below them could be accessed by both the elevator up here and the ladder shaft, then a sequence of internal walkways, stairways, and more ladders.

Isaac shook his head. "That'll take fifteen minutes. Best thing we can do is engage from here. Everyone find a target. Aim half a meter above their heads; these big, slow AK rounds will drop a lot at this distance."

"We can't hit them," one said. "These old guns with their iron sights."

"We can draw their attention, keep up the fire, drop a few of them and give them something to worry about."

Everyone had their weapons resting on the railing, but before Opoku gave the order to fire, he looked up and down the dam.

He said, "Wait. I want the man on the far left and the far right to take a knee and aim to the west and east to provide security. We don't know if there is anyone else around up here."

Just then, several gunshots came out of the admin building. From the disciplined cadence of Kalashnikov fire, he said, "That's our boys. They've found some rebels. Be on the lookout for more."

He turned his attention back to the enemy, some three hundred meters or more away from his position and thirty-five flights down. After sighting on a group standing around a truck with their rifles over the hood pointed at the building, he shouted, "Fire!"

Suddenly twelve AK-47s began pounding; semiautomatic rounds hurled down the steep decline, and lead and steel and copper bullets impacted in and around their targets.

CONRAD TREMAINE, ALONG WITH JUNIOR, KRELIS, AND BAGINSKI, drove onto the eastern side of the dam at speed, heading west, intending to just cross the river so they could head to the south towards Akosombo. The downlink-jamming drones were still in the air, meaning contact with Accra was a no go, so Tremaine knew that he remained de facto leader of this entire operation now, and he wanted to get on the road to the south with the other rebel forces.

He'd report to Kang some of what happened here, he'd lie about other events, but none of his Sentinel boys here would dispute him, and all of the rebels would be dead by the time the smoke cleared in Accra.

They'd only made it a hundred meters across the dam before a huge volley of muted gunfire erupted from somewhere far ahead. Krelis swerved the vehicle, assuming they were under attack, but quickly the men in the truck realized no rounds impacted around them or even passed by close to their truck.

No, somebody was shooting, but they weren't shooting at Tremaine and his team.

The Sentinel leader gave the order. "Get us behind cover, we'll try to raise Belov on the radio."

They pulled behind a row of trucks parked on the northern reservoir side, and then all four men quickly bailed out, assault rifles at their shoulders. Rushing to the bed of the pickup, they each pulled a combat pack, slung it over an arm, and began running for better cover behind a small metal-and-concrete building there.

Tremaine pressed the button on the radio hooked at the shoulder of his body armor as he moved. "Condor, this is Bear. You reading?"

There was no answer. After a moment he jogged across the two-lane road at the top of the dam, heading towards the Volta River side. Water gushed from the spillways just below him, a rumbling roar, but still he could easily hear a massive amount of AK gunfire coming from several hundred meters farther up the dam.

His order to Belov had been that the Dragons would wield the RIVCOM men's M4s so the delegation wouldn't recognize them as infiltrators, so those barking reports of Kalashnikov fire weren't coming from his people.

He thought a moment. There was one platoon made up of four squads of Dragon fighters here, thirty-two men in all, or at least there had been originally. Each squad had a squad leader, and each squad leader had been given a radio to keep in contact with the three Sentinel men assigned to this platoon. He quickly called again. "Any squad leader. This is Condor. Do you read?"

Quickly he heard a squawk, and then a man with a Ghanaian accent spoke. "Delta squad, over."

Just after that he heard another man. "Charlie squad."

Over the transmission he could also hear gunfire. "Delta, report status."

The man was young, Tremaine could tell, and while he couldn't remember anything about the squad members in this platoon—there were four hundred forty-eight rebels in this force, after all—he knew the man would have been deemed by Belov to be the most squared away in his squad of eight, otherwise he wouldn't have been put in charge of the others.

The voice on the other end said, "We have two dead. The rest of us are in the switchyard, hiding behind the transformers. There are shooters above us on the dam, I think RIVCOM escaped, and I can't reach Alpha squad."

Tremaine shut his eyes a moment in frustration. "Okay, Charlie. What's your status?"

"There are three of us, outside on the rocks at the edge of the river. Taking fire from those men on top of the dam. No dead, but we have five men in the power house. They were guarding the VRA employees and assisting the Russians, but the president's security forces are in control of that building, so I don't know if our men are dead."

"Where are the Russians now?"

"I don't know. They went in the building as soon as they got here." He added, "I see three guys from Alpha squad still alive at the base of the staircase up to the dam. Lots of dead, everywhere."

A new voice chimed in. "Condor, this is Bravo squad. We lost three men in the initial assault, but the rest of us are at the front guard post."

Tremaine thought a moment more. It sounded like there were about twelve Dragons accounted for down there in front of the power house, and another five a few hundred meters away at the front post. He looked to Krelis for ideas.

The Dutchman said, "If those RIVCOM guys shooting up here on the dam didn't set up security, then we might be able to slip up on them. Once I have line of sight, I'll use the grenade launcher to thin them out."

Tremaine agreed; they pulled the six-shot 40-millimeter grenade launcher from the truck, along with an extra bandolier of shells, and began running west on the long dam embankment. Ahead on the right was the admin building, and beyond that the police station. Well beyond that and on the river side of the embankment was a squat concrete building, almost all the way at the eastern end of the dam. Behind this would be the police firing down on the rebels.

They were still halfway to the administration building, hundreds of meters from the squat concrete structure and the enemy, when a group of three men carrying AK-47s appeared out of the front door of the admin building, then turned right, running away from them. The men all wore white undershirts.

Krelis stopped and raised the grenade launcher at them, not more than fifty meters away, but Tremaine called out to him.

"Hold fire!"

"Why? Those aren't our guys."

"We'll give away our position to the larger force before we're in cover and before we're ready to fire on the main element."

The four mercenaries turned and retreated back to their pickup, and there Tremaine pulled a pair of binoculars from the dashboard and looked up the length of the dam.

"They've set security, facing this way. We can't get close enough to use the grenade launcher."

Junior spoke up now. "We can pull out the mortar. Nail them from here."

Their 60-millimeter mortar would be able to travel the distance to the RIVCOM men, dropping high-explosive shells right on them.

But Tremaine shook his head. "Too long to range that fucker. We're on high ground, wide open to the south. Might be able to get a signal to Second Platoon, they're out there somewhere."

Junior said, "Too far away, boss."

Tremaine pulled his walkie-talkie off his chest rig. "Peak to valley, these radios have a range of up to twenty klicks." Pushing the button, he said, "Second Platoon, this is Condor, come in."

A faint reply came several seconds later. "First Company, Second Platoon, over."

Tremaine knew the voice. This was Copper, one of the Sentinel officers attached to the Dragon platoon that had been blowing up the radio tower and hitting the police station in Akosombo town. Copper was African, from Liberia, and Tremaine had worked with him in the DRC.

He said, "We're in trouble at the dam. RIVCOM is still in play. Head north to us."

"Roger. We are ten kilometers from you; the road is bad, though. Will take us at least twenty minutes."

"Expedite it."

"Roger, Copper out."

"Wait!" Tremaine shouted, thinking for a few seconds. "Copper, who is just south of you?"

Copper replied, "That would be First Company, Third Platoon. They're on the N2, already heading south towards Accra."

"Try and pick them up on your walkie-talkie, turn them around and get them here. If the delegation got word out somehow, then there might be an attempt to take the dam back before we have the explosives set, and we need to be ready to thwart it."

"Roger that."

Tremaine's original plan didn't have him here at the dam at all, so he hadn't studied this hydroelectric facility like Belov had. But now Belov was somewhere in the bowels of the structure with the other two men who knew the lay of the land here, leaving Tremaine to manage things at surface level with limited information.

After thinking a moment more, Tremaine turned to Krelis. "Krel . . . let's get that sixty out and start dropping shells on those police."

Tremaine hadn't wanted to take the time to set the mortar, but now he didn't see another option.

The Sentinel commander looked to Baginski now. "Help Krel. Fire from cover behind the truck, try to walk the rounds past that concrete building the RIVCOM men are positioned behind."

"Right," the Pole said, and while Junior and Tremaine covered the east and the west, he began helping Krelis remove the mortar tube, the baseplate, and the shells from the bed of the pickup.

DUFF, KAKU, AND THE TWO MEMBERS OF AMANOR'S DETAIL MOVED out of the stairwell and into a dimly lit space that felt to Duff like the cargo hold of a massive tanker ship.

Instead it was an enormous concrete room under the power house, fifty meters deep and two hundred meters wide, and in the low emergency lighting he made out a row of five circular forms, each one the size of an aboveground swimming pool, rising some five meters in the air. Duff knew nothing about hydro dams, but he could put together that these were the generators the deputy plant operator spoke of, under which the turbines would sit.

There was a loud constant rumbling here, and he assumed it was from either the water pumping through the facility or the cascading water gushing through the spillways he'd seen when he was outside.

He looked around the big room; it seemed to be empty, but it would take ten minutes to fully check it. Mensah had clearly said the Russians were heading to the turbines, so Duff decided to press on. "I see no movement in here. We've got to descend again and check there."

Back in the stairwell they hunted for targets, for rebel sentries left here to control the stairs, because it seemed impossible that anyone working down here would fail to post a guard at the stairwell that led to the control room.

But they made it unimpeded to a door twenty meters below, and they formed on it. Duff checked the latch, finding it to be unlocked. After a nod to the others he opened the door a few inches and was immediately met with a burst of gunfire, tearing through the metal door on his right.

A piece of metal shrapnel scraped his scalp in the same place where he'd cut his head during the initial shootout, and he fell back into the stairwell, crouching behind the wall on the left. Looking up, he saw the man called Bismark stumbling back, then falling on the stairs, both hands on his throat, blood pumping through his fingers with the pulse of his heartbeat.

His throat made a sickening gurgling sound that Duff had heard before and always prayed he'd never hear again.

Duff reached his AK around the doorjamb and began firing, although he had no idea what he was shooting at.

Kaku's pistol barked above Duff while the American climbed back to his knees, shooting out the door as he did so. After a dozen rounds from the rifle, he stopped shooting, and Kaku retreated around the wall to reload.

Gideon pulled Bismark to the side, but his partner was dead before he got him up to the wall to check him.

They waited several seconds for the gun smoke to clear, and when it did, Duff saw that they were facing a low and narrow concrete hallway, essentially a tunnel.

And there, in the middle of the narrow space, a man in a RIV-COM uniform lay on his stomach, his rifle wedged under him.

Gideon stepped away from his fallen comrade, walked out into the hall, and fired once into the back of the unmoving form. Then he knelt down and pulled the man's rifle, reloading it with a fresh magazine he found after flipping the bloody body on its back.

The three men moved up the narrow tunnel without a word, then stopped at another metal door. It was locked, but Kaku went back to the body and felt around, finally finding a set of keys.

Duff began going through them, fumbling them more than once because he was trying to hurry. He knew at any moment this entire dam could blow, or someone else from the opposition could burst into this tunnel, responding to the sound of the gunfire.

He found the right key, opened the latch, and pulled the door open, swinging his AK around with one hand at first, scanning for threats.

He faced a large concrete chamber, similar to the generator gallery above. The visibility was equally poor here, but the emergency power did illuminate some spotlights high on the wall that pointed down.

From what he could tell, the turbine gallery looked much the same as the generator gallery, except where the generators only rose about fifteen feet, the turbines went all the way up to the ceiling, where they attached to the generator's housings through the floor. This essentially put five massive column-type structures in a room the length of a football field.

This would be incredibly challenging for only three men to clear, but he had no alternative, because his ambassador, the president of Ghana, the chief diplomat of the European Union, and even his wife were directly above them, surrounded by gunmen and unable to flee out of the blast radius of the bombs somewhere down here.

He stepped out onto the gallery floor, his wooden-stocked weapon swiveling back and forth frantically as he did so.

The noise here from the spillway water crashing into the river just outside was loud, like a jet aircraft's engines at idle. Duff imagined the pressure the world's largest human-made reservoir put on this concrete structure, and he shuddered thinking about bombs going off here and weakening the dam.

As he moved, Kaku and Gideon followed close behind him, and they stuck to the wall as they progressed, because the glow from the spotlights centered on the middle of the gallery and the turbines there.

Duff was looking for three Russians and at least two more of the local rebel force dressed as RIVCOM cops, but with the low light, the equipment running down both walls in huge brown cabinets, and maintenance rooms and offices every dozen meters or so, he knew the task ahead of him was nearly impossible.

And with the combination of both the noise and the ringing in his ears from all the gunfighting, he knew he couldn't rely on his hearing to help him identify threats ahead.

He considered firing a few rounds into the air so that the enemy might come to him, but then he decided against it. He pressed on in the shadows, hoping to get lucky before some Russian assholes blew up the bombs that he knew were somewhere down here.

TWENTY-TWO

AFTER A MINUTE OF NEAR-CONSTANT SHOOTING, RELOADING, AND shooting again, Sergeant Opoku ordered his men to hold fire here at the top of the dam, though there were at least a half dozen and likely more rebels still down in front of the power house. Accurate fire from this distance with the iron sights of their just-acquired AKs was exceedingly difficult, and Opoku wanted to save as much ammo as possible.

He knew he had to close on the enemy to be more effective, and he also knew taking the stairs down the massive embankment would expose him and his force to enemy guns, but he didn't see much alternative. Yes, they could have gone down the elevator or the ladder shaft in the building next to them and eventually ended up in the power house, but Opoku knew that route would require several minutes without any visibility on the enemy, minutes where the now-hunkered-down rebels could collect themselves and hit the building, perhaps kill the president and anyone else who might be inside.

No, he couldn't afford to take the safe route to engage the enemy; he had to do it the hard way. He called out to the men on the railing around him. "Everyone, put a fresh magazine in if you have one. We're going down the stairs; I will lead. Keep three meters separation, and keep your sights on the switchyard and the riverbank and watch for any—"

He stopped talking and turned his head to the east, in the direction of the police station and the admin building. He thought he'd heard a shot or some other noise.

The young corporal he'd ordered to provide security to the east was still aiming in that direction.

"Muntari. You see anything?"

"No, sir. But I heard something."

Opoku pulled his cell phone out, opened the camera, zoomed in as much as possible, and then raised the phone towards the admin building and the road in front of it. He'd just focused in on a single black civilian truck parked there when an explosion rocked the center of the dam, only forty meters away from Corporal Muntari on the eastern side of the RIVCOM men.

Shrapnel, concrete, and asphalt came raining down on them.

Opoku knew what he'd heard, which meant he knew what had just happened, which meant he knew the danger he and his men were in.

"Mortars!" he shouted. "Get down!"

The second explosion came thirty seconds after the first, and twenty-five meters closer, which told Opoku, a former Ghanaian Army special forces captain, that the mortar crew was ranging their weapon, "walking in" the shells. He had his team hidden behind the elevator building, but clearly the enemy knew exactly where they were, so he yelled for the officers around him to follow him.

He rushed down the stairs, keeping his AK up on his shoulder and his eyes on the parking lot below. He was ready to stop and drop to a knee to fire on any enemy who revealed themselves from behind cover, but he was hoping he didn't have to, because his men were still on the dam, trying to get onto the stairs.

The third mortar impact smacked the top of the elevator shaft building only ten meters from the last of Opoku's men, but the shrapnel went up and out, firing over the heads of the cops there. Still, eardrums were pounded and the shock wave and terror of being under accurate indirect fire meant the men began scrambling down the stairs even faster.

Isaac recognized the loss of order above and behind him, so he focused even more intently on the scene below and in front, thinking that his team wouldn't be watching for threats the way they should.

Almost immediately a pair of rebels behind a smoldering pickup in front of the switchyard stepped out and raised their rifles, and Isaac began firing on them.

To his relief he heard shooting from just behind as two of his men clearly saw the same threat that he'd seen. They all kept descending as they fired; the stairs took some hits from more enemy below, but Isaac kept the charge going, knowing what they were fleeing above.

Two mortars slammed down on the top of the stairs, just three seconds apart, killing the last two of the RIVCOM men in line instantly and injuring the man in front of them.

Isaac didn't know this—he was occupied battling the rebels in the switchyard from two hundred meters away and ten stories below him—but the increased cadence of the mortar fire told him the crew knew they had dialed in their target's location, and it also likely meant they would now rain down hell on the area.

MARTIN MENSAH AND HIS TEAM OF TECHNICIANS HAD SPENT THE last five minutes restoring power to the rest of the nation from the hydroelectric dam. It was still coming back up; in a few minutes more, he explained to the members of the joint delegation around him, the dam itself would have juice, and soon after that the lights all the way down in Accra would turn back on.

Benjamin Manu stood on his now-bandaged leg. The wound in

his thigh was killing him, but his immediate focus was not on the pain but rather on the noise outside. Close in there was the sound of undisciplined gunfire but no sound of bullet impacts here in the building. From farther away there was more shooting, and the guns sounded to the well-trained Manu like they were probably AK-47s, with a louder boom and a lower report than the M4s most of the rebels carried.

But it was a third sound that caused him the most concern: the unmistakable thuds of mortar shells impacting somewhere a few hundred meters distant.

Julian Delisle shouldered up to him in the middle of the control room. "Are those RPGs?" he asked.

Before Manu could answer, Chad Larsen spoke up from across the room. "No. Not frag grenades, either. Those sound like mortars. Sixty mil." When Delisle just looked at him, Larsen said, "I was in a Marine infantry battalion for six years. I know a mortar when I hear it."

Delisle looked to Manu. "Who has mortars?"

"The army has mortars, but there's no army around here. That must be the other side."

"But they're not firing at us?"

Jay Costa called out from the doorway to the bathroom. "There's a battle going on out there. Maybe the police showed up."

The man from the EU nodded at this, then turned to Mensah. "We aren't going to wait around to see who wins. Can you get us out of here through those subterranean passages you mentioned?"

Mensah considered this. "If we don't encounter any Russians or rebels on the way, yes."

"Where will that put us on the outside?"

Mensah replied quickly, "We could either take the elevator or ladder to the top of the dam, or we could go all the way to the reservoir side. There's some maintenance and warehouse buildings and the motor pool."

Costa looked to Delisle. "If we can get out of here far enough away from the fighting, we can get those helos to come pick us up."

Nichole Duffy had no authority in the conversation, but she spoke up anyway. "What about Josh and the other three men?"

Costa looked to her. "We'll try to find them on the way. Hopefully they've stopped those bombs from being planted."

"And if we *don't* find them?"

"Look," Costa said, "that fight outside could come in here at any time. And those mortars out there could start dropping on this building. We *can't* just sit here."

Nichole clearly saw the logic. She helped one of the wounded stand, and then the entire group, both the delegation and the dozen power house employees, began moving towards the stairs that Duff and his hastily formed team had taken less than ten minutes earlier.

Mensah said, "I must stay here to make sure the rebels don't turn off the electrical transfer again."

Delisle shook his head. "If the dam blows, you won't stand a chance. You all are coming with us, and as soon as the army comes and routs these rebels, you can come back and go back to work."

"But—"

"Non-negotiable," Delisle said, and Mensah nodded reluctantly.

Forty-six people began descending the stairs, with Chad Larsen and three of the President's Own Guard Regiment leading the way, pistols out in front of them.

FAR BELOW THEM, DUFF, GIDEON, AND KAKU HAD MADE IT ABOUT A quarter of the way down the right-hand wall of the huge turbine gallery when Gideon reached out and put his hand on Duff's shoulder.

Duff looked back and saw him pointing to something above. There, on the left of their position, the turbine shaft rose to the ceiling. A catwalk halfway up went around the circular structure, apparently for maintenance workers to use to access the internal components of the gargantuan machine.

Duff quickly saw what Gideon was pointing at. A meter-wide and meter-tall hatch, just above the catwalk, sat open, the metal covering propped below it on the catwalk railing.

Gideon leaned into Duff's ear; he had to shout to be heard over the sounds of water coming through the walls and the floor. "There's going to be a bomb right inside there."

Duff knew he was right. He'd seen no other hatches open.

Fuck, he thought. He knew there was a computer that could trigger the weapon remotely, but he had no idea if the bomb fifty feet from him was also on a timer that was ticking down to nothing, or if the Russian with the detonation code was somewhere safe with his thumb on the bang switch.

"You want to check it out?"

Gideon nodded, then ran to the circular stairs leading around the turbine shaft. He was exposed on the catwalk, so Duff kept his weapon forward, hunting in the dim light for any movement ahead.

A minute later the Ghanaian returned. "There's a big military-looking satchel down at the bottom of the shaft. They must have lowered someone down with a rope to place it. It's attached somehow to a joint in the turbine housing. No way to get close to it to remove it."

Duff wanted to run for his life, to go back up and grab Nichole and get the hell away from this disaster waiting to happen, but the only way out of this was to move forward and get the trigger from whoever had planted the device.

They did not see an open hatch on the next turbine shaft, so they moved forward to the third in the long room, and here, again, the metal cover was detached and propped open, and the darkened hatch looked ominous to the three men.

They moved forward a little more, found the fourth turbine undisturbed, then headed for the fifth and last turbine shaft to check it for the third satchel.

LEV BELOV WATCHED WHILE GRESHA CLIMBED DOWN THE STAIRS OF the fifth turbine, then ran forward, rejoining Belov, Vadik, and the two Western Togoland Dragons with them. He handed Belov the tablet computer.

"All detonator codes are entered. This is now the firing system; its radio range is about three kilometers."

Vadik handed Gresha his rifle and rucksack back while Belov zipped the tablet back in the administrative pouch on his body armor, right in the center of his chest. Then the five of them stepped into the stairwell at the far end of the turbine gallery, intending to take it up one level so they could walk half the length of the generator gallery to access the ladder shaft to the top of the dam.

The power remained out, of course, so Belov assumed the elevators would be out of commission. The climb up thirty-five flights of a sharply angled ladder with their body armor, packs, weapons, and ammunition was going to be arduous, but they'd known all along that the twenty-minute climb from the depths of the dam was going to be a bitch.

On the generator gallery floor the men broke into a jog, keeping their rifles up at their shoulders, flashing the weapon lights occasionally to check the shadows in case there were dam employees or some other potential threats down here.

They encountered no one, however, and soon arrived at the ladder shaft, right next to the large elevator. Belov led the way into the shaft, but as he did so, he heard a squawk in his walkie-talkie, hooked to the left shoulder strap of his body armor vest.

He ordered the rest of them to stop with a closed fist, and then he pushed the button on the radio. "This is Bear, repeat last."

"Delta squad for Bear."

Delta squad should have been somewhere above him and out of radio range.

"Go for Bear."

"We have entered the power house. We went to the control room; two men are dead, their weapons are gone, and the hostages are missing."

If they were missing, Belov reasoned, then the security forces of the delegation must have been somewhere down here, trying to escape through another exit in the massive hydroelectric facility. Neither of his men spoke English, so he relayed the message quickly to them in Russian, speaking over the sound of rushing water coming from all around.

Then Belov returned his attention to the walkie-talkie. "Do you have comms with Condor?"

"I did a few minutes ago, then someone started shooting at us from the top of the dam, and we raided this building to get out of the line of fire. I can't reach Condor from here, but mortars are exploding out there."

Lev Belov rubbed sweat from his face. "Condor and his team have a sixty. Those mortar shells mean he's here and in the fight. How many of you are left?"

"There are eight of us on our feet, including me, but that's from three squads."

"Okay, I want you and your men to head down the stairs off the control room, follow the signs to the turbine gallery, and protect that room until we come for you."

"Yes, sir," the man replied, and Belov wondered if he'd be detonating the bombs he'd placed down there in just a matter of minutes, killing the man he was now talking to. He wouldn't detonate until Condor gave the order, and Condor would only give that order if the facility was completely retaken by the army and there was no other choice to keep the power off in the nation while the coup was under way.

But Belov's main concern was not the fact that he was about to kill the rebels. The rebels were utterly expendable. No, his main concern was that the assistant plant manager in the control room had known he was going to plant the bombs, so it was possible the delegation was down there looking for them right now.

Quickly he turned to his small team.

"Gresha. Me and Vadik will stay here with one Dragon, guard the ladder, and watch for anyone on this level. You take the other Dragon, go back down to the turbine level, and protect those bombs."

Gresha looked at him like he was an idiot. "Two of us?"

"You just have to hold any enemy off until the other eight Dragons arrive down there. When they do, come back up here. We'll all go together up to the surface."

Just then, lights came on in the big gallery, and the hum of spinning turbines below grew, even over the sound of the water.

"Shit," Belov said. He realized the dam technicians had managed to restart the electricity, and now he was certain he'd be ordered to blow the bombs as soon as he got to the surface.

Gresha stepped over to the freight elevator next to him and pressed the down button, glad for the chance to use an elevator and avoid the ladder well.

DUFF, KAKU, AND GIDEON ALL DROPPED TO THEIR KNEES IN THE turbine gallery, startled as bright lights took away the shadows they'd been moving through, and loud mechanical noises filled the air.

To their left the turbines began spinning, the whine growing by the second.

They'd checked the fifth turbine at the end of the room and found the third device but no Russians, so they'd backtracked towards a stairwell door they'd passed on the south wall of the room, halfway down. Their objective had been to go back upstairs to the control room, then escort the entire force out of here via the warren of tunnels, ladders, or, if the electricity returned, the elevators.

They'd just arrived at the stairwell and the big elevator next to it when the power suddenly came back on, and instantly Kaku rose and hit the call button.

From the multilevel map he'd been given in the control room, Duff thought this elevator might lead to the same level of the power house he'd left the rest of the delegation on, as would the ladder, but this gallery was several stories high, as was the generator gallery above, so the ladder would take much longer.

Over the sound of the turbines and the rushing water, Duff heard the elevator car lowering, and he stood with his shoulder next to the door as he covered to the west, and Gideon covered to the east, his own shoulder against the elevator door, while Kaku stood in the middle, watching over the rest of the gallery, waiting for the door to open.

Duff felt the door begin to slide up; he heard a shout of alarm from Kaku behind him and then a furious exchange of gunfire just yards away. Swiveling into the car, whipping his rifle up, he saw he was not alone.

Two men, one white and in combat gear, and the other Black and in a RIVCOM uniform, stood there just at the door and within striking distance.

Both men held rifles; the Ghanaian's gun was down but the Russian's was up and had just fired, hitting Kaku in the chest and knocking him down to the turbine gallery floor, but both Duff and Gideon had shifted into the car so close to the pair that no one could get their muzzles on another target.

Duff charged closer as he swung around, hoping to get a hand on the Russian's gun. Gideon did the same to the rebel, but a step slower than Duff, and as a rifle shot cracked close, Duff heard the president's bodyguard cry out in pain.

Both men threw their bodies into the two combatants in the elevator, and then they all four fell to the floor, desperately trying to get their rifles in position and keep their opponents from wielding theirs.

TWENTY-THREE

THE RUSSIAN THAT DUFF FOUGHT WITH WAS STRONG AND WELL trained in hand-to-hand, stronger and better trained than Duff, but the American had a lot of fight in him, and he retained the presence of mind to realize the man was trying to get his hand down to the pistol on his hip because Duff now had both hands on the Russian's rifle.

They fell backwards; Duff slammed the man up against the bank of buttons there, and immediately the door began to close.

With Duff's hand around the muzzle, the Russian fired his rifle; the barrel went hot in Duff's hand and he let go briefly, but only to lunge back towards the man to get a hand on the pistol that the Russian had simultaneously pulled from his drop leg holster.

Duff's rifle was pressed between him and the man, pointing to the floor; the Russian's rifle was over Josh's left shoulder at his neck, and he couldn't retract it enough to put the muzzle on Duff's face, so a pistol was the only option for either of the two combatants.

Duff couldn't go for his own weapon, however, because his opponent already had his hand on his gun, and Duff had to try to control it before he was shot dead.

As they pressed together, the Russian fought his way back to his feet, his hand still on his pistol, which was pointed at the floor, with Duff's viselike grip restraining its movement at the wrist.

Behind him, Duff heard the desperate noises of a vicious struggle between Gideon and the young-looking rebel, and it sounded like the president's bodyguard was in a similar predicament as Duff himself was, slamming from wall to wall, both men shouting and crying out.

Duff saw blood smeared on the wall, and he thought it belonged to the man from the President's Own Guard Regiment.

The Russian managed to thumb off the safety of his Beretta and squeeze the trigger; the bullet slammed into the floor of the car and ricocheted up into the wall to Duff's right.

The American tried a head butt that missed; a knee to the groin landed but still didn't seem to have much effect on the incredibly powerful man.

There were no words between the four, all fighting for their lives in a space only three meters wide and four meters deep. But even in the panic of this moment, Duff registered that the elevator was moving.

Duff missed with a punch and was grappled by the Russian around his shoulders, but he pushed back on his prosthesis, pulling the bigger man with him, still holding the man's gun arm with all his might.

LEV BELOV AND VADIK HAD BEEN COVERING THE LADDER JUST A few meters from the freight elevator with the lone Dragon rebel when they all heard the boom of a rifle below them.

They then ran back to the freight elevator and immediately heard the sounds of a vicious struggle, maybe twenty-five meters below.

A pistol cracked now, and the Russians looked at each other.

Vadik said, "Is it coming back up here?"

Belov said, "I don't know. I'll take the ladder down and engage any enemies if it's there; you two stay here in case it comes back up."

The Sentinel deputy commander raced for the ladder, leaving Vadik and the young Dragon behind.

Vadik Tarasov hefted his weapon now and pointed it at the door, and then with a free hand he reached down to the frag grenade hanging from his utility belt.

I'm not taking any chances, he thought. He'd toss the grenade in as soon as the door opened, no matter who was inside.

INSIDE THE FREIGHT ELEVATOR, DUFF HAD THE WIND KNOCKED OUT of him when the larger man slammed into his chest with his body armor, banging him up against the door. To Duff's surprise, the Russian mercenary let go of his pistol and it fell to the floor. Duff saw this as an opportunity to put both hands on his own rifle to try to push the man away from him so he could get a shot off, and he let go of the man's wrist to do just that, but as soon as he did so, he realized he'd been tricked.

The Russian's now-free right hand reached down for something on his hip; he pulled it, and before he even looked down, Duff knew it had to be a knife.

He pulled the man to him and tried another head butt; this one connected, and then both men separated a little from each other.

Neither had his hand on the rifle that hung from his chest; however, they were still too close to get the barrel in front of their target. Instead the Russian swung the knife at Duff's face; he ducked away from it, but a second sweep at his midsection made contact with the nylon sling holding his rifle, cutting it away and dropping Duff's weapon to the floor. The man struck out, stabbing with the shiny blade, and to avoid it Duff fell to the left. The point of the weapon nicked Duff's shoulder, then stuck in the elevator door, embedding it there.

The Russian saw the American on the ground now, so he left the knife in the door and went again for his rifle, but Duff sat up, leaned forward, grabbed the man's boot, and pulled it to him, flipping him onto his back.

Duff grabbed the Russian's gun barrel to control where the weapon was pointed, and both men kicked out at each other, but neither caused any damage. They sat and faced each other, and now the Russian hefted his gun and, as he did so, he kicked again to push the American back into the door.

Duff slammed hard into the freight elevator door again, and as he did so, he knocked the knife loose from where it had been embedded just above him.

The Russian aimed at Duff's chest from three feet away; Duff saw the knife drop into his lap and scooped it up while kicking the gun barrel away with his left. The rifle fired, and Duff rolled up to his knees, then dove forward.

Duff buried the knife in the Russian's neck, just above his body armor, and arterial blood sprayed across the small space. The strong Russian climbed back to his feet, Duff slammed him into the wall, and then the gravely wounded man surged forward, crashing into the American, and Duff fell backwards, pulling the Russian along with him towards the floor of the elevator car.

The American landed on his back; the dying mercenary kept fighting him even though a knife's hilt jutted from his throat and his life's blood pumped away, but still, Duff had no idea whether he himself would be the first to give in to utter exhaustion.

Just then, he heard another handgun round crack off in the enclosed space. He looked back to see that Gideon had managed to wrestle a pistol from the rebel and fire into the boy's stomach. The man in the RIVCOM uniform fell back against the wall of the car, his mouth open in shock, and then he slid down, leaving a blood trail on the wood behind him.

Gideon looked exhausted; he was wounded with a gunshot to the abdomen himself, but he began moving towards Duff to help him up.

As he did so, however, the elevator car lurched to a stop, the doors opened only a foot or so, and a hand grenade came sailing in.

It bounced on the floor, closer to Gideon, and Duffy grabbed the shoulder straps of the dying Russian on top of him and rolled him in the direction of the impending blast.

THE ELEVATOR DOOR STOPPED OPENING WHEN THE GRENADE DETO- nated, leaving about a meter of space for Sentinel contractor Vadik Tarasov to peer through, but the smoke that poured from the car caused both Vadik and the Dragon in the generator gallery to hold their positions to the side of the door.

The Dragon, it was clear to the Russian, was terrified, and not of the men in the elevator car. There had been another rebel in there when Vadik threw the grenade, and for all the Russian knew the two were friends, but he didn't give a fuck about this guy or his buddy, just like he hadn't given a fuck about his own comrade. Vadik was a mercenary who was here to get it done and get paid, and a hand gre- nade had made that happen.

Listening through his audio-enhanced earplugs for the sounds of movement, he heard nothing, so he nodded to the Dragon across from him. Both men swung in, their rifles at their shoulders.

In front of them, through the thick haze of smoke, was a scene of utter carnage. Bodies lay in heaps, blood glistened off every surface, and human tissue and body parts littered the floor, the wall, even the ceiling.

One man, Black and big and wearing a Ghanaian military uni- form, had had almost all his face blown off. Another body, facedown and mostly covered by Gresha's still form, was completely blood-covered and missing a leg.

A Dragon rebel was slumped in a back corner, a smear of crimson showing where a bullet had gone through him and then where he slid down to the floor. His face, too, was shredded with shrapnel wounds. His jaw was clearly broken.

Vadik moved towards Gresha, who was also facedown, assuming that it was his own grenade that killed the man, but as he looked down at the other Russian more carefully, he saw the hilt of a knife protruding from his neck.

He kicked the foot of the white man under Gresha's body and got no response.

Vadik clicked his radio button now to call Belov downstairs. "Bear? This is Shark. Over."

"Bear to Shark, go ahead."

"Gresha's fucked, but all enemy are down."

Belov responded. "Okay. I'm downstairs, I'll take the ladder back up to you."

"Roger," Vadik said, and then he motioned to the Dragon still standing in the doorway to step back so he could get out of the car. He began to lower his weapon and turn away for the ladder, but just as he did so, he registered a sudden movement behind him.

Spinning his head back towards the bodies on the floor, he saw that the white man under Gresha had rolled over onto his side now, still under the bigger Russian. He held a pistol in his right hand, reaching around Gresha's shoulder and back to do so. He was covered in blood, and his left leg was gone below the knee.

Vadik Tarasov didn't understand what was happening, but he instinctively raised his rifle back up as fast as he could.

Next to him, the young Dragon panicked and fumbled for the rifle hanging off his chest.

The bloody man with the missing leg was faster. The first round hit Vadik's chest plate, the second his right cheek, and, just as Vadik fired his rifle once, he caught a 9-millimeter round through the bridge of his nose that expanded on impact and shredded his brain, dropping him dead on his back in the doorway to the elevator shaft.

Only then did the rebel have his weapon up, but he was shot in the chest twice before he fired it, and he fell onto his back in the generator gallery.

JOSH DUFFY SCANNED FOR MORE THREATS, HOLDING THE BERETTA pistol he'd taken from the floor with one hand while feeling over his body with the other, checking to see if he'd been shot. He wasn't searching for blood—he was covered in it, after all—rather, he was searching for fresh holes. When he found no major wounds, he looked down at the dead Russian lying across his waist and legs. The rifle round fired by the other Russian had impacted the center of the man's back, striking his body armor. The back plate did little good for the dead man—four inches of tempered steel knife blade was buried in the side of his neck, after all—but Duff's small intestines had been on the other side of the prone body when the bullet impacted, so he knew the Russian's armor had likely just saved his life, just as it had when the grenade detonated five feet from him and right next to Gideon twenty seconds earlier.

Playing possum had been a gamble, but he was disoriented from the concussion of the grenade, and he didn't know how many enemy would be outside, so he'd smeared more blood from the Russian's neck across his face, yanked off his prosthesis and flung it across the car, then turned his face down, lying on the pistol and waiting for the enemy to expose themselves before he targeted them.

Now he pushed the Russian with the knife embedded in him to the side, then eyeballed the other Russian in the doorway and determined him to be dead, as well. He crawled onto his knees and scooted around the body of Gideon, whose face was a sickening mangled mess from the blast from the grenade, and then he made his way to the wall of the big freight elevator, where he picked up his carbon fiber leg and foot.

He put the device back on the stump below his left knee, climbed back to his feet, and while still disoriented from the hand-to-hand combat, the gunfire, and the grenade blast, he began checking the backpacks of both dead Russians, hoping like hell one of them held the triggering device for the bombs planted one level below him.

When he found nothing, he hefted a rifle and slung it around his own neck. It was a South African Vektor R5 that Duff had only fired once or twice in his life, but a gun far superior to the obviously damaged AKs there lying on the floor in the blood and guts, because both AKs' magazines and lower receivers were heavily cratered with shrapnel scars.

Josh Duffy stepped out into the now well-lit generator gallery, and he headed for the stairwell that would, according to the map he'd left back in the elevator, take him all the way to the top of the dam.

Just before he turned into the open stairwell he heard gunshots behind him, but they were in another room, or maybe the tunnel from the stairs to the control room that he'd traveled down several minutes earlier. He immediately thought of his wife, and he turned towards the sound, raising his new rifle as he did so.

FIVE METERS BEHIND DUFF, LEV BELOV CLIMBED TO THE GENERATOR gallery level on the ladder, but he stopped before stepping out, hearing the sounds of fresh gunfire.

He didn't know if Vadik, Gresha, and the Dragon were still alive, but he wasn't going to stick his head out and check, because protecting them or engaging whoever the fuck was shooting wasn't his mission. His mission was getting the computer with the detonation codes to Condor, and to do that he had to get out of this fucking dam.

The stairs would take him up; he'd studied the blueprints of this place daily for the past month, so he turned for the next ladder and began climbing again.

His leg hurt where he'd been shot over an hour earlier, but he ignored the pain like he ignored the exertion.

With his rifle slipped around to his back, Lev Belov began working his way up the steep ladder, coming to a landing every ten meters and turning, then taking the next ladder up.

It was going to be a long climb, and the wound in his leg wasn't getting any less painful, but at least he'd accomplished what he'd come down here to accomplish.

THE FEW SURVIVING DRAGONS OF WESTERN TOGOLAND WHO HAD been on or around the lot in front of the power house had descended to the turbine level minutes earlier, where they had run into the group from the three helicopters in the hallways between the stairs and the generator gallery, and now the Dragons fired on the security men of the three delegations while the security men fired back up the hall at a distance of thirty meters.

The President's Own Guard Regiment security men were far superior to the rebels, as were the officers from the EU and the group from the U.S. embassy, but the Dragons had good cover.

While Chad, Ben, and Malike joined in the fight, Jay Costa and Julian Delisle moved the ambassador and the high representative into the gallery, positioning them behind the first generator. President Amanor was led there by two of his security men, as well. The unarmed junior diplomats and government functionaries, along with the media members and the hydroelectric dam workers, huddled behind the VIPs for safety, but Nichole Duffy had appointed herself as another bodyguard of Ambassador Dunnigan. She held the Browning pistol in one hand, and she kept her other hand on the ambo's back, as did Jay Costa, while Dunnigan knelt behind the massive generator in the now well-lit room. Nichole listened to the fighting some twenty yards away, and she hoped like hell her side had enough ammo to keep the enemy back so they could continue on towards the exit the deputy plant manager had promised would let them out of this massive facility, picking up Josh and the others along the way.

TWENTY-FOUR

SOME SEVENTY-FIVE YARDS AWAY FROM HIS POSITION JOSH Duffy saw his people, as well as Amanor's people and Aldenburg's people, and he was sure his wife was somewhere in the crowd ahead.

But Duff did not run to them. Instead he stopped his advance, turned, and retreated back to the ladder well, because he realized that running to Nichole, Costa, and the others just to be one more gun in a fight was much less important than stopping the bombs below them all from detonating.

He had to find the last Russian and get the tablet computer.

He told himself there was nothing he could do but ascend, knowing there was at least one more Russian here, and that man must be in possession of the device. The obvious assumption was that he would try to get away from the dam before blowing it, and Duff knew his best course of action was to hurry to the surface and try to find the man before he could do so.

He began climbing, unaware he was just four flights below the person he was after, because there was too much noise in the operational hydroelectric facility to hear his target's footfalls above.

SERGEANT ISAAC OPOKU OF THE VOLTA RIVER AUTHORITY'S RIVER
Command police force gave the order for his men to fall back. They'd
made it into the control room of the power house right as the electricity turned back on, and then, as they began descending the stairs,
they heard the sounds of gunfire below them.

Opoku determined that the security forces were engaging the
rebels, and as much as he wanted to help his president and the others, he was aware of a problem they might not have been aware of,
and it was a problem that needed to be sorted out.

There was a mortar crew with an unknown number of bad actors
somewhere on the eastern side of the dam. The mortars had killed or
wounded four of his men before they made it into the power house,
and Isaac knew that if the joint delegation's helicopters returned, they
could easily be targeted and destroyed as long as that position and
those fighters remained in place.

His men were confused, but when he got all thirteen of his remaining police back in the lobby, he said, "We're going behind the power
house. The VRA maintenance vehicles are there, and we're going to
drive them back up to the top of the dam and try to knock out the enemy
there so the president can be extracted safely, if he's even still alive."

The group began moving, even the walking wounded, and soon
they were back outside, rifles swiveling left and right as they headed
in the direction of the switchyard. Then they turned right, moving
around the side of the power house to a small parking lot where two
pickups and two vans sat.

One of the pickups and one of the vans had the keys in them, so
Isaac took the front passenger seat of the truck; the rest of his men
loaded up into both vehicles, and they raced off to the north up the
winding road that led to the top of the dam and the reservoir beyond.

TWENTY-FIVE

ONCE THE DELEGATION'S SECURITY MEN KILLED THE LAST OF THE Dragons sent down into the dam complex, deputy plant operator Martin Mensah hurried across the generator gallery and entered a set of double doors on the other side. The entire entourage followed him, ARSO Chad Larsen shadowing him closely with his gun up, protecting him like a vigilant bodyguard because he knew that keeping this man alive to direct them was their only ticket out of here.

They spent the following few minutes moving through the depths of the construction, traveling past, under, and over piping, encountering rooms full of monitoring and control systems. The entourage moved on, until finally Mensah stopped at an elevator bank and pressed a button. He turned to the others. "These elevators are large, but it's going to take at least three trips with this many people."

Nichole heard this, then rushed forward to the regional security officer. "What about Josh?"

Costa said, "Josh didn't need us to come down here and rescue him. He'll get himself out of here once he gets the detonator."

"You don't know that—"

"Josh's job," Costa interrupted, "is to protect the ambo. It's my job, too. You just need to let us both do what we're here to do, and trust him to succeed."

Dunnigan was covered in sweat, small blood splatters dotted her face, and her eyes remained slightly dilated. Still, she said, "If he's not up there, then we need to come back and get him."

Costa did not respond to this, but Nichole registered the look on his face. They would *not* be coming back down for him.

President Amanor, however, did speak. "How long until the elevator arrives?"

Mensah said, "It's thirty-five floors, sir. If the car is at the top of the dam, it will be here in about two minutes."

Nichole was certain two minutes would feel like a lifetime.

She looked back up the hall, her gun in her hand. She thought about going it alone, hunting for Josh down here in the bowels of this big and confusing place, but she didn't think about it for long. Her brain quickly reasoned that Josh's chances of getting out of here were better than her chances of finding him and providing more help than hindrance.

No, the only thing she could do was pray that once she got up to the surface she'd find her husband there, mission accomplished and waiting on them.

LEV BELOV WAS IN GOOD CONDITION FOR FORTY-EIGHT YEARS OLD, but the last hour had been one hell of a bitch on his body. He was exhausted, moving slower than he would have liked. The body armor, the rifle, the big battle belt around his waist: everything seemed to be working against him as he climbed ladder after ladder, heading towards the top of the dam. He'd made it over thirty stories, however, and he knew in minutes he'd be outside in the evening and in contact with his Sentinel commander.

He took a moment to catch his breath and, as he did so, heard the unmistakable sound of someone climbing below him, audible even over the rumbling of equipment and water gushing over the spillway outside. Quickly he spun around, aimed his weapon awkwardly, but the steep ladderlike stairs didn't afford him a view of anything more than the landing ten meters down.

The footsteps were slow and careful, a lighter touch than his own, as if the person walking below Belov was aware of his presence up here.

He heard just one individual, and he considered waiting for whomever the hell this was to make it up here so he could shoot him, but instead he decided to continue on, to hurry his pace, and get to the surface. There, in the small concrete structure on top of the dam that housed the elevator and the ladder, he could find real cover and drop his pursuer with ease as whoever it was climbed out of the ladder well.

The Sentinel operator pulled himself onwards with his free hand and both legs, ignoring the fatigue, telling himself he needed to put some distance between him and the man below so he'd have time to find a good position.

One floor below the top, however, Belov realized there was a problem. It was dark above him, whereas the rest of the ladder well had been well lit, and the steep metal ladder had bits of debris on it, masonry that crunched under his boots.

He climbed out of the ladder well, and his heart sank. This concrete shack was partially destroyed, there was a round hole in the roof above him about a meter in diameter, and the metal door to the left, in front of the elevator, was blocked by heavy broken cinder blocks that had come from the roof and upper walls. The hole in the roof could be climbed out of by stacking bricks and stepping on them, but anyone trying this would be exposed to the ladder well, from where Belov knew an enemy approached.

He realized it was likely Tremaine's mortar that had caused this damage, and since he couldn't climb out via the hole in the roof, all he could do now to get out of here was to start the slow and arduous process of moving the debris from the door.

He shattered the one bare lightbulb still working above the elevator shaft door, lowered his rifle, and pulled his pistol, keeping it aimed generally at the exit to the ladder well. Then he got to work with his free hand, tossing masonry and concrete cinder blocks across the room to free the door.

JOSH DUFFY WAS FUCKING WIPED OUT AFTER CLIMBING UP THIRTY-four stories; his face was covered in sweat, and the stump on his left leg hurt because he'd not properly reattached his prosthesis after his stunt in the elevator, but his hearing had cleared enough for him to know he was no more than one floor below a man wearing a lot of gear who was struggling to get up and out of the dam.

This was his target, he was sure of it, so he pulled himself up with his legs and his left hand while his right hand held the Beretta pistol he'd taken from the elevator. Keeping his rifle hanging behind his back now, muzzle down where he could sweep it up quickly, aided him in his climb, and the pistol was his protection in case he heard the man stop.

But if Duff could hear the man above, it was highly likely the man above could hear *him* as well. This was a chase that was going to end in violence, Duff was sure, but all he cared about was the computer with the detonation codes, so he kept his careful but steady pace.

But then, after rounding yet another landing with his gun hand high, he came to an abrupt stop. It was darker at the landing above, and though Duff couldn't see it, he could tell his enemy had reached the exit.

But instead of the man simply walking away, it sounded as if he was hefting stones or bricks and then tossing them onto the floor.

Duff lowered to his knees, holstered the pistol, and raised his rifle. Wiping sweat from his eyes, he began crawling up the ladder slowly now, step by step, trying to be as quiet as possible.

He made it near the landing, then considered rising, stepping the one rung up, and then spinning around to fire above, but he realized he couldn't tell exactly what was going on. Surely the man had a gun aimed down here; Duff knew he hadn't been quiet enough to escape detection.

No, stepping into the line of fire wasn't the right call. It sounded like the man was stuck, at least temporarily, so Duff decided on another tack.

BELOV TOSSED A CONCRETE BLOCK OUT OF THE WAY OF THE DOOR, which he could now see was itself damaged, wedged into the frame and dented with shrapnel. He grabbed another piece of material and threw it, then another.

He had to get a few more big pieces out of the way to even try the door, but before he could do so, he heard a shout from below him.

A man spoke English with an American accent. "Having some trouble up there?"

Belov furrowed his eyebrows and paused from his work for a moment, but then he got back to moving rubble. As he did so he said, "Nothing I cannot handle. *You* are the one in trouble, American."

The voice called back a moment later. "You're Wagner Africa Corps? Working with an indigenous rebel force?"

Belov kept working, and soon he heard the man speak again. "Wait . . . no . . . that's not it, is it? I know who you're working for."

Belov sniffed, grabbed another broken piece of masonry, and tossed it away from the door.

The American below him shouted up. "You're not Wagner. Not anymore. You're Sentinel, aren't you?"

JOSH DUFFY KEPT HIS RIFLE POINTING AT THE CORNER OF THE landing, waiting for a response. He'd remembered what the odd CIA man had told him at the party in the French ambassador's residence about the commander of Sentinel and Duff's old nemesis being seen in nearby Togo. Now it all made sense. He decided to go for broke. "You're with Conrad Tremaine."

Duff heard the movement of the rubble stop above him. The Russian did not call back down, and Duff took the lack of reply as an answer in itself.

He pressed his luck. "You planned on killing the president but failed. You planned on blowing the dam, but you can't get out of here to do it, can you?"

It was quiet for a moment more, and then the man above him fired a shot down the ladder. He didn't have an angle on Duff, however, and the bullet slammed into the wall at the landing.

Duff realized he'd been right not to turn the corner. The Russian above might have his attention divided between protecting himself and working on getting out, but he had enough attention focused on the man below him to be dangerous.

Duff said, "That gunshot sounded like desperation. Your day not going the way you'd planned?" When he heard no response, he said, "Look, man. I know Tremaine. He'll sell you out, one way or the other. You better have that trigger in your possession, because if it's already in *his* hands, then he won't think twice about blowing your ass up along with the rest of us."

Now the man above spoke. "I have the detonation device, and I'm going to blow *you* to hell."

Duff replied. "The way you're slinging those stones, you sound to me like a man who wants to live to spend the money he's making. You aren't going to blow the dam till you're off the dam, and I'm not going to let you out of here."

The Russian laughed loudly. "Stick your head around that wall and try and stop me."

Duff ducked his head around quickly, then looked up at the small building, the hole in the roof.

He retracted himself back to safety just before a gunshot cracked; the bullet ricocheted off the wall within a foot of his face.

ISAAC OPOKU HAD THE FRONT PASSENGER WINDOW OF HIS TOYOTA pickup down, his AK-47 hanging out and pointing forward as the vehicle raced to the east along the top of the dam.

Behind him two of his men stood in the bed with their own weapons trained on the eastern side of the facility, and three more men waited to jump out and take up defensive positions if this force of RIVCOM men encountered the enemy.

The mortar crew had been up here fifteen minutes ago, but since then the mortars had been silent, and Isaac had no idea if the enemy up here had bugged out or not.

But this question was answered when the windshield cracked between him and his driver, and then a second unmistakable bullet hit the screen pillar that went from the hood to the roof, tearing through the metal with a crunching sound.

Isaac's driver was a twenty-eight-year-old named Sergeant Arthur, and Arthur got the message the enemy was sending, loud and clear. He jacked the wheel to the left, then raced across the width of the dam road towards the reservoir side, and Isaac heard and felt more rounds slamming into the truck, both in front of him and below him.

Soon, however, they were out of the line of fire, and Arthur bounced off the road and onto a narrow grass strip that led to the edge of the reservoir side of the dam. He positioned his vehicle behind the police station, hopefully out of the line of fire from what sounded like three or four weapons that had opened up on them, and he turned off the machine.

Isaac saw steam rising from the engine, and oil had splattered the windshield.

He climbed out, his borrowed AK-47 in his hands, and looked back at the other vanload of men. The vehicle was right behind his, out of the line of fire from the east, but it was even more shot up than Isaac's truck.

One RIVCOM man, a corporal who was new to the unit after serving as a police officer in Kumasi, lay on the ground behind the vehicle, two men huddled over him attempting to treat him, though blood gushed from his upper torso. The rest of the men had bailed and now held defensive positions around the side of the police station, their guns sweeping for any targets in that direction.

Arthur shouldered up to Opoku. "Was that the mortar crew using their small arms, or is it a bigger force?"

"I don't know," Isaac admitted. "I'll take five men and try to flank around the rear of the station and the admin building, see if I can come up on them from behind. You hold it down here. There's a couple more vehicles behind the police station. Once we clear the enemy up here, we'll bring them back to you."

"Roger."

Isaac chose the five men closest to him, and they moved over to the reservoir side of the building, then began heading towards the rear of the police station.

CONRAD TREMAINE UNSLUNG HIS RIFLE AND CLIMBED INTO THE passenger seat of the Toyota pickup. Krelis was already behind the wheel, and both Junior and Baginski opened the back doors and got in just after their leader sat up front.

They'd fired on the vehicles approaching up the road after confirming this was not the thirty-two-man Dragon platoon Tremaine
had called in from the south. These VRA vehicles had to have been
the real RIVCOM, so Tremaine had given the order to engage, and
then they'd run both vics off the road behind the police station, some
one hundred twenty meters away.

Now Tremaine gave the order for Krelis to get them the fuck out
of here. He wasn't sure how many police had been in those two vehicles, but he recognized that they had the will to fight, and that was
as important as the sheer number of men and guns they possessed,
if not more so. There were only four Sentinel men up here on the dam,
Tremaine included, and until Second Platoon arrived, wiped these
guys out, and retook the dam, this area wasn't safe for one pickup
truck with only four operators inside.

They raced to the east in the dusky light, heading towards the jungle, and Tremaine hoped to get some high ground on one of the hills
there so he could reestablish coms with Belov, because, more than anything else, he needed that fucking computer.

NICHOLE DUFFY FOUND HERSELF IN THE MIDDLE OF A TIGHT GROUP
of people shuffling out of an elevator car and into a small motor pool
garage building about twenty-five yards from the banks of Lake Volta,
on the other side of the dam from the power house.

When she got to the exit of the building, she searched the small
part of the top of the dam she could see, looking for any evidence of
her husband, but she could only make out the tops of buildings; she
had no view of the road itself.

Mensah had said there were several elevators and ladder wells
that led to different parts of the complex, and Nichole had no idea
which one Josh would take, so she hunted for any signs of life among
the buildings around her.

But there was nothing—this grouping of structures felt like a ghost town.

Everyone in the joint delegation was told to wait inside the garage, while Julian Delisle tried to pick up the helicopter pilots on his hand-held walkie-talkie. He went outside with one of the President's Own Guard Regiment to do this, leaving the three VIPs, the remaining security, the dam workers, and the other members of the delegation, Nichole included, back inside.

But Nichole tried to make herself useful. She held the Browning pistol in her hand, low and pointed down, as she manned a west-facing window of the motor pool garage, knowing she was the only set of eyes looking in this direction.

It was evening; the light had all but faded in the west, and the area appeared to be abandoned. She marveled at the peaceful setting outside the building. It seemed that the horrific firefight at the power house could not have possibly taken place just a few hundred meters away.

RSO Costa was just a few feet from her, and he pulled his satellite phone out, tried to make a call, then slipped the device back into his pocket.

"Nothing?" she asked.

He shook his head. Softly, he said, "In a million years you won't be able to convince me that a rebel force in Ghana was able to jam satellite communications."

Nichole just said, "No way in hell."

Dunnigan spoke up now. "Russia or China. Place your bets."

"No question," Aldenburg said.

Before anyone else chimed in, Julian Delisle walked back inside the building. "I just reached the helo crews on the walkie-talkie. They landed five klicks away to conserve fuel, but they haven't been able to make comms with anyone else. Only these walkie-talkies are working, and only at short distances."

RSO Costa was with the ambo, just a few feet away from Nichole. He said, "What are you thinking, Julian?"

Delisle said, "I don't hear any gunfire, and I don't hear the mortars. I say we bring the helos in, have them sweep by once. If they don't take any fire, we go ahead with the extraction."

Nichole spoke up now. "Have you tried your sat phone?"

Julian nodded. "Still down."

To this, a member of the President's Own Guard Regiment said, "We tried ours. Still jammed somehow."

Nichole looked at the RSO. "Jay, how about I keep trying the phone so you don't have to worry about it?"

He pulled it out of his pocket. "Why not? That jamming has to stop eventually. Let me know if you reach anyone in Accra."

She took the phone and stepped a few feet away back to the window, and she did not try Accra. She tried Josh.

Just as the men said, however, there was no signal.

TWENTY-SIX

AFTER THREE MINUTES OF MOVING RUBBLE WITH ONE HAND, LEV Belov finally accessed the bent and twisted metal door of the elevator shaft building. One look at it told him it would be hard to open, but with his pistol still pointed at the exit to the ladder well, he pulled on the door and found it completely wedged into the metal doorframe around it. The partial collapse of the roof had bent in the metal, and now the door wasn't budging.

The man down the ladder shouted up now. "Sounds like you're going to have to blow that exit open. You try and climb out through that opening in the roof, I'll put more holes in you than God intended."

Belov's frustration showed in his voice. "A stalemate, you are saying?"

The man downstairs gave a little laugh. "Maybe, but the army will be here soon enough, and you and your shitty rebel force will be wiped out."

Now Belov laughed. "The army is hours away, my friend, and they have bigger problems than saving you. I, on the other hand, have people in the area, and they will come for me."

Duff noted what the man said about the army, then replied, "I've killed a lot of those people in the area, including two of your Russian pals, so you'll forgive me if I'm not too impressed by the cavalry you say is coming to your rescue."

Belov stepped quickly to the ladder well, reached his pistol around the side, and fired yet another shot.

After the boom faded, the American said, "Dude, you have a weird way of managing stress."

Belov groaned loudly in frustration, then walked back over to the rubble next to the door, well out of view from down the ladder. Looking at the evening sky showing through the hole in the roof, he got an idea.

He realized he was going to need help getting out of this building, and he wondered if he could somehow reach Tremaine on the radio.

He stepped around towards the elevators, away from the door and out of view of the ladder, then pulled his walkie-talkie from his chest rig. Speaking softly enough so that the American couldn't make out his words, even if he could hear his voice, he said, "Bear for Condor."

To his surprise, the response came quickly, though the signal was scratchy and broken in places. "This is Condor. Report status!"

"I'm in a ladder well in a building at the top of the dam. West side. The building I'm in is blown to shit, the door is wedged shut, and I need help getting out."

"Confirm that you still have the computer in possession."

"Confirmed."

"And the explosives are set?"

"Affirmative."

"All right, I'll send Second Platoon to get you out. You *can't* let that tablet fall into enemy hands." Tremaine thought a moment. "Be aware, there are RIVCOM assets on the top of the dam. We saw two vehicles, and we engaged them, but you can expect significant oppo up there."

"Roger," Belov said, and then, "And . . . and we have another problem."

"What problem?"

"I've got one enemy below me. An American, he must be from the U.S. ambassador's security detail."

"Just hold him back till Second Platoon arrives. They'll deal with him."

"No, it's not that. It's what he told me."

There was a pause. Then, "What did he tell you?"

"That he knows I work for Sentinel, and he knows you are in charge."

A longer pause followed.

"I said, he knows you—"

"How the fuck does he know—"

"No idea, but he mentioned you by name."

ON A TWISTY CLIMBING JUNGLE ROAD THREE KILOMETERS AWAY, Conrad Tremaine ordered Krelis to pull the Toyota to a halt. As soon as the vehicle stopped, Tremaine had Belov repeat his previous transmission.

Again, the Russian claimed the American knew that Tremaine was part of this endeavor.

Tremaine just sat there while his three men looked on. They'd been running the truck with its lights off. It was dark in the jungle; the moonlight illumination just barely made it through the canopy of trees here.

Tremaine sat in silence . . . because he was completely dumbfounded. This operation was an hour old, he'd covered exactly zero meters of ground on his movement to the capital, and already somehow he'd been exposed to the enemy.

For six months he'd been so careful, because if he was uncovered as being involved in this endeavor he would never be able to return to South Africa, he'd never see his family again, and he'd be hunted down for the rest of his days by everyone from the Ghana Armed Forces and intelligence services to the African Union, the International Criminal Court, private concerns who stood to lose billions in mining rights in West Africa, and God knew who else.

Plus, knowledge by the wider public of mercenary involvement in the coup d'état would put a target on all Sentinel men's backs. Kang had to make this look like it was a legit coup attempt from the Western Togoland Restoration Front with help from the Russians. Involvement of a high-dollar Manila-based private military corporation led by a former officer in the South African National Defence Force would make the entire endeavor reek of outside influence.

Tremaine knew that Kang would easily double-cross Sentinel in this to keep his own nation's involvement under wraps.

No . . . whoever the fuck Belov was talking to in that ladder well, Tremaine needed to somehow shut the American up.

He opened the door to the pickup, climbed onto the hood of the stationary vehicle, then stepped up onto the roof, desperate to get the best signal he could get for his radio.

Changing the channel on his walkie-talkie now, he pressed the talk button.

"Condor calling Goose. Condor calling Goose."

The distant reply came several seconds later.

"Goose for Condor. Go."

Goose was the code name for a Serbian Sentinel operator named Hristov. He was the mercenary with the Chinese technical team across the river at a farm outside Akosombo who were working to jam the satellites. He provided security for the five independent contractors from Hong Kong along with a single eight-man squad of rebels from First Company, Third Platoon. Right now they were at the farm, more than ten kilometers away, but their drones circled over the dam, keeping the downlink from the satellite jammed.

Tremaine said, "Tell the techs to turn off all jamming until I tell them to turn it back on again."

The Serbian replied with an uncertain tone. "You are saying you want them to land the drones? Kang said we had to—"

"I don't give a fuck what Kang said! Do it now, Goose!"

"Okay, boss. Will take a minute, stand by."

Both Junior and Baginski had climbed out of the truck and now they held security, one man posted facing each way on the road, while Krelis remained behind the wheel and Tremaine stood on the roof of the Toyota, his walkie-talkie in one hand and his satellite phone in the other.

THE SUN HAD SET OVER THE CITY OF ACCRA, AND FROM HIS VIEW from the office of his three-story modern white mansion on Ankama Close in the Aburi Hills north of town, Kang Shikun could see twinkles in the distance that he took to be gunfire and explosions, and plumes of smoke had begun to rise from various points across the city.

He could hear nothing from his location, of course—he was miles away from the action—but he was pleased to see the flashes near the police stations, the military bases, the airport, and the presidential palace.

The shooting and the killing was not being committed by the rebels; no, Kang's best estimates didn't have the hapless camouflaged fools from Western Togoland here in the capital until midnight, but the Islamic extremists from Nigeria, Benin, and Burkina Faso had already begun sowing disorder in the city.

In the end, Hajj Zahedi was able to supply eighty-eight men, far less than the two hundred he'd originally mentioned. Still, eighty-eight men operating in four-man teams meant twenty-two si-multaneous attacks had kicked off just ninety minutes after Kang called Zahedi and told him the operation was being pushed up a day and a half because of a potential compromise.

The Iranian Quds Force commander wasn't happy about the change, and he had been forced to scramble units that weren't in the correct position this early, sending them to alternative targets.

But the most important thing to Kang Shikun was not the tactical successes of this force but rather the panic they would cause.

And eighty-eight trained fighters with the commitment of these men, the willingness to die for their cause, could sow a great deal of panic, indeed. Of the twenty-two cells, twelve carried an RPG-7 gre-nade launcher in addition to their Kalashnikov battle rifles. Four more teams operated British-made 81-millimeter mortars stolen from the Nigerian army, a potent indirect-fire weapon that sent a 9-pound shell up to a mile.

The mortar teams were set up on the roofs of abandoned build-ings in derelict districts in the east and west of the city, far enough away from businesses and residences to where the sounds of the shells launching out of the tubes wouldn't give away their locations, but close enough to the important parts of the city to be in range.

The other six teams had hand grenades, improvised explosive de-vices, and even suicide vests. There were no heavy machine guns, just the battle rifles, because other than the mortar crews, it was the job of these teams to stay highly mobile and even covert, at times, driving from neighborhood to neighborhood, targeting police and military installations and generally creating mayhem and confusion.

And from the flashes and smoke rising from a dozen parts of the city, Kang saw that the Iranian Zahedi and his African extremists were holding up their end of the bargain, at least so far.

But Kang knew there was not as much mayhem and panic as

there should have been, because he saw one glaring problem, one obvious lapse in the operation. Not by Zahedi and his force but by Tremaine and his. The power had been off for only about thirty minutes before it was restored to the city. Now the gunfire and the rocket and mortar detonations miles away weren't the only illumination. No, the city lights remained bright after the sun set, and this meant something was going wrong at the dam.

The satellite phones were still down in the Akosombo area, and Kang took the fact that he had yet to hear from Tremaine to mean that the Sentinel commander was still under the drone umbrella around the hydroelectric dam.

Just then, however, his sat phone buzzed on the glass table behind him. He rushed away from the window, snatched up the device, and accepted the call.

"Yes?"

"Kang, it's Condor. No time to explain, I need you to get some intelligence for me in a hurry."

Kang wasn't ready to take orders from his hired mercenary. "Why is the power on here in the capital?"

"You get me the information I need, and I'll be able to turn the power back off."

Kang said, "You don't need information to do that. Just blow the turbines if you can't hold the facility. Follow the contingency and you—"

"Listen!" the South African shouted. "Give me what I'm asking for, or this entire operation could fail."

Kang took a breath, noting a flash of light near the airport, and he felt sure the jihadis had just dropped a high-explosive shell on the tiny Ghana Air Force facility there. He sighed. "What do you need?"

"I need you to find out the names of the American security officers protecting the U.S. ambassador."

"Why do you need that? I haven't even looked into—"

"Because they are here."

Kang turned away from the window again. With a furrowed brow, he said, "*Who* . . . who is *where?*"

"The delegation, the *entire* delegation, is at the dam."

Kang slowly lowered down to his chair. "What are you saying?"

"Look, I need to reestablish jamming here, I don't want the enemy to get a signal out. Just get me the names of the U.S. security personnel."

Kang was barely listening, but he had heard, and after a few seconds he snapped out of it. "Jia!" he shouted, and soon the female intelligence technical contractor rushed into the room, in keeping with the urgency of her boss's beckoning.

"Sir?"

"Find out the names of the security officers at the U.S. embassy. The ones who would travel with the ambassador."

She nodded. "Right away, sir."

Now Kang turned his attention back to his call. "Getting you the information, but listen carefully to me. The president, the ambassador, and the EU representative must not be hurt. That would bring more international attention to this—"

Tremaine interrupted. "Those were my orders to the Dragons, but something went wrong. There's been a gun battle for the last forty-five minutes."

Kang could not believe this. "Why did the helicopters come to Akosombo?"

Tremaine didn't answer, he just said, "It's a fluid situation. I have a platoon of rebels coming here in the next fifteen minutes and I—"

"Is the president dead?" Kang asked.

"No." He sounded unequivocal, but then added, "I mean . . . not as far as I know." After an extremely brief pause, the South African said, "Do you *want* him dead?"

Kang answered quickly. "We've discussed this. A successful decapitation operation by poor rebel boys would not be believed. We only need the Dragons to look sophisticated enough to cause havoc until General Boatang routs them, damaging the dam, putting the police and the Southern Command on the back foot. *That* is our plan, and *that* is what needs to happen."

Quickly, Kang said, "What about the French helicopters? Where are they now?"

"I hear rotors in the distance. They're probably about to extract the delegation." Frantically, Tremaine said, "I need those fucking names, Kang!"

Jia came running back into the room. Kang thought she looked nauseated; her skin was pale, and sweat hung from her brow, but he didn't care about her health. "We have it?"

She nodded and handed a single sheet of paper to her boss, and Kang began reading it into the phone.

"Personnel of the U.S. Department of State Diplomatic Security Service at the U.S. embassy, Accra. Regional Security Officer Javier Costa, aged fifty-four. Assistant Regional Security Officer Chad Larsen, aged thirty-five; Assistant Regional Security Officer for Investigations Carla Houston, aged fifty, although our intelligence tells us she is not traveling with the joint delegation, she is back at the embassy overseeing—"

"Who else?" Tremaine demanded with a shout.

Kang ignored the insubordination. "Assistant Regional Security Officer Joshua Duffy, aged thirty-six. That's all the Americans on the security force, but Benjamin Manu is the Foreign Service National Investigator, and the Local Body Guard force consists of Kaku Yeboah, Malike—"

Kang did not finish reading the page, because Conrad Tremaine screamed into the phone again. "Duff! It's motherfucking Duff!"

"I'm sorry?"

ON THE NOW COMPLETELY DARK JUNGLE ROAD IN THE HILLS TO THE east of the Volta River, Conrad Tremaine stomped his foot down on the roof of the Toyota Tacoma, and he thought about those few moments before he pulled the trigger of the Dragunov. He'd seen a white man looking his way, he'd even focused on him with his sixteen-power scope, and he thought the man looked familiar. Now he realized that he *did* know that face.

Tremaine hadn't seen Duff in seven or eight years, and back then the American always had a mustache and a beard, and virtually always wore a ball cap with the logo for United Defense, the private military corporation both men worked for.

Tremaine had seen him on television once, as well, when he became temporarily famous for some contractor disaster down in Mexico. Tremaine had been working in Somalia at the time and hadn't been privy to the whole story, but he'd seen a quick news report about the incident, and he remembered the American who worked under him for a time in Afghanistan.

Tremaine said, "I need to know everything you have about Assistant Regional Security Officer Joshua Duffy. Where he lives, where he shops, if he has family in country . . . everything. And I need that information now!"

Kang snapped back at him. "I don't know what is going on, but if you are still in the satellite downlink jamming zone, I demand to know how you are able to—"

Tremaine hung up on him, dropped his phone into his pocket, and clicked the walkie-talkie on the shoulder strap of his vest. "Condor for Goose."

The response was quick. "Go for Goose."

"Tell the techs to resume jamming."

"Roger. Will take about two minutes to get the birds back up into position."

Tremaine jumped down onto the hood, then down to the ground. Climbing back into the vehicle, Krelis spoke up from behind the wheel.

"Where to, boss?"

"Somewhere on this hill where we have line of sight on the dam."

"Back down?"

"No. Up higher. Get me a little to the south, as well." Tremaine had a plan, but he knew he'd have to haul ass to pull it off.

"Got it." Krelis floored the truck, and it climbed on in the dark.

TWENTY-SEVEN

NICHOLE DUFFY HEARD THE FIRST HELICOPTER SOMEWHERE OFF TO the south, but she didn't look up because she was busy dialing Josh's satellite phone again. She didn't expect to get through, but it was just the busywork that she needed at the moment, because she wasn't in command of anything here, and her only real job was to look out the window in front of her and wait for rescue.

To her utter astonishment, however, the call went through to the other line, meaning the downlink was no longer jammed.

"It's ringing!"

Julian was back outside, signaling the approaching helicopters with a small flashlight along with the one man from the President's Own Guard Regiment who had a satellite phone, but Costa was here and he had heard her exclamation.

Costa immediately reached for the phone and, as much as she wanted to talk to her husband, Nichole handed it off to him, knowing it was the right decision.

"It's Josh's phone," she said.

Costa took it and hit the speaker button as Duff answered. The RSO said, "Duff? Good to hear your voice, man. Been trying to raise you on comms."

"Yeah, lost my radio down in the dam."

"What's your poz and status?"

"I'm in a ladder well, I don't know where it leads out of, but I've got a Russian above me. He's got the detonator, but he's obviously still in the blast radius so he can't use it. He's stuck in the building, some damage to the door, I guess, and I've got coverage on the broken roof, so he can't climb out without getting shot. I heard him talking on a radio but couldn't make out what he was saying. Figure he's trying to get some help to come his way."

"Will do. Can he hear you now?"

"Negative." Duff added, "The three other guys who came with me didn't make it."

"Understood," Costa said. "I've got the plant operator here, describe where you are."

Duff described the ladder well, explained that it sounded like the structure above him was damaged and the man he was in pursuit of was stuck.

Costa looked around but couldn't see the top of the dam from the front of the garage.

Mensah said, "There are three ladder wells with elevators alongside them. One on this side of the dam. One in the center that comes out near the administration building, and one on the far side used for plant maintenance."

Costa said, "Duff, there is no way we can go up there and check all three. That's nearly a half mile of ground to cover, we're low on ammo, have wounded, and the extraction helos are inbound."

"Understood. I'll keep this guy occupied so he can't get away to blow the dam. You just work on getting everyone the fuck out of here, and I'll do my best to make it to the last bird out."

Outside, all three Caracals rocketed over the dam from south to north. Flares fired from the sides of the helicopters, an attempt to spoof any heat-seeking missiles, but none of the aircraft took any ground fire.

Costa said, "Look, man, I've got to call the embassy. You just keep your ass alive, and keep that Russian from detonating the explosives, you got me?"

As a response Duff said, "You need to get in contact with Bob Gorski at CIA. Tell him he was right about everything he said. This whole operation is being run by—"

Duff's voice stopped coming through the speaker. Costa brought the phone up to his ear. "Duff? I lost you. How copy?"

When he didn't get an answer, he looked back down to the phone. "No signal. Shit!" he yelled.

Just then, Julian Delisle and the president's guard ran back into the warehouse. Delisle said, "The helicopters will land in the parking lot one building over. We checked it, no power lines or other obstructions, but there's only room to land one at a time. Mr. President, you and your people, along with the remaining media personnel, will leave in the first helo, EU will take the second with the wounded, and U.S., you take the last bird out to give you more time to recover your man."

Costa told Julian they had a brief sat communication with Duff, who was fighting for the detonator inside the dam, but then the signal had gone away again. Both he and the president's security man checked their phones and saw no hint that the jamming had ever stopped.

"All right," Julian said as he put away his phone. "Everyone get ready to move."

JOSH DUFFY PUT HIS PHONE IN HIS POCKET, THEN CLIMBED BACK UP to where he could see the room above. He knew he was fighting a race against time, so he knew he had to force a mistake by his adversary.

Thinking quickly, he called back upstairs. "What's your name, Ivan?"

He heard a scuffling above. Then, "It's not Ivan."

"How long you been with Sentinel?"

"Why do you care?"

"I used to work as a contractor myself. That's how I know Tremaine."

"I don't know a Tremaine."

"Yeah, you do. I get it, you can't *say* that you do. I respect that." He paused. He stood on the landing now, his eyes up towards the darkened room with the open hole in the roof, the weapon trained on what he could see in the hopes that he'd detect some sort of movement in the darkness he could fire at.

But the Russian was clearly somewhere off to the side of his view.

Duff said, "I met that South African prick in Afghanistan. Worked for him. He actually got fired from my company, and it was a company that was just about impossible to get fired from." Duff added, "And now he's *your* boss."

The man above said nothing.

"He uses people. He's using you. I don't know how, maybe *you* don't know how, but you'll figure it out."

"Shut up," the man said.

"I mean," Duff continued, "it's likely you won't figure it out until you're drawing your last breath. Tremaine will leave you to bleed out in the street if it serves his purpose, I've seen him do it."

"That's the job, isn't it?"

"Is it?" Duff said. "I thought the job was to seek your fortune, then retire young and rich."

Above him, the man laughed. "We Russians don't believe in fairy tales."

"What, you just fight other people's wars till you die?"

There was no response.

"Hey," Duff said, peering through the sight of the rifle, concentrating like he'd never concentrated before. "I guess it beats going home to Russia. Your country is a shit show, isn't it?"

He heard fresh shuffling, and he put his finger on the trigger of the R5.

He didn't see any movement, but a gunshot crashed in the tight confines of the ladder well. The flash came from the left above, and Duff could tell the man wasn't even trying to aim down the ladder; instead he was just firing in frustration.

The boom of the pistol shot caused a little more stone to cave in from the mortar hole in the roof, and as it fell into the room and the crumbling debris tumbled down the ladder around Duff, he quickly moved up several rungs, letting the sounds mask the noise of his movement. Now he was halfway up, pressed to the left wall of the ladder well so he couldn't be seen by the man on the left side of the room.

His rifle remained in his right hand, and he froze so as not to make any noise.

The Russian couldn't have known that he'd ascended, and he told himself if the man fired wildly again that he would ascend even higher, even though he was well aware that a bullet striking a concrete wall could ricochet right back into him from where he stood.

But then, however, he heard the sound of a helicopter again, and this time it was flying over much lower.

The Russian called down. "Your helicopters are landing. Can you hear them? I guess your people are getting out of here, leaving you behind."

Duff said nothing; he'd give his position away if he did so.

The sound grew and grew, as if they were flying low over the dam, and slowing down even more, as if to hover. Duff realized the noise would mask his footfalls if he climbed higher, and he also realized the Russian might figure this out, too.

Still, with the roar of the rotors directly overhead, he flipped his weapon's fire selector switch to full auto, then moved up the ladder, pulling himself with his left hand.

He fell forward on his stomach, out into the room.

It was too dark to see anything without turning on the weapon light, and he didn't have time for aimed fire anyway, so he just pressed down on his trigger, firing to the left, sweeping the rifle back and forth, using the light from the muzzle flashes to hunt for his target. He saw the man there in the corner, and he laid down fire until he'd expended an entire thirty-round magazine.

The flash and the noise were ungodly, and he was temporarily blinded and deafened, and therefore unable to detect if any return fire came his way.

He hadn't been shot, however, so as soon as his mag ran dry he pushed back out of the line of fire, dropped his rifle, and pulled his pistol.

Waiting several seconds for his head to clear, he finally heard the scratchy labored breathing and moans of a wounded man who had clearly been shot through the windpipe.

The scuffing sounds of arms and legs on the rubble indicated a man lying on his back.

Duff climbed back up, brought his head and his pistol around the left wall, and listened for the sounds. Almost immediately he had pinpointed the Russian's location, just a half dozen feet away, and he fired three rounds from the Beretta, silencing the man's labored breathing.

The helicopters had moved off to the north, but not far, and it sounded like one was landing just a couple hundred yards from where he stood.

He thought it doubtful he'd make it onto one of those helicopters, but he told himself he was going to try.

But first he had work here to do.

He moved through the dark, stumbling over broken pieces of the roof and the wall, moving in front of the elevators to where he kicked the boot of the man on his back. He didn't take time to check for a pulse; instead he lifted one of the man's eyelids and thumped the eyeball with a finger from his other hand.

When he felt no involuntary jerking response from the body, he began feeling through the Russian's equipment. He found the man's pack next to his body, dumped out the contents, and rifled through them in the near darkness for a moment, finding nothing of value.

The dead man wore body armor like the other Russians he'd faced off with, so he frantically began unzipping the pouches he could find on the bulky load-bearing vest.

The deputy plant operator had explained that the detonator was a tablet computer, so he checked every pocket large enough to hold one. Finally, in a zippered administrative pouch just behind the dead man's row of rifle magazines, he discovered what he was looking for.

Holding the black tablet up, he saw that it was rubberized, military grade, and he thought it likely that this was the device that was set up to detonate the sophisticated explosives.

He also saw that he'd put two bullet holes through it when he shot the Sentinel man, and the machine was dead.

Just then the radio on the shoulder of the corpse's body armor squawked.

"Condor for Bear. How copy?"

Hearing Tremaine's voice sent a chill up his spine, but he did his best to ignore the radio. He began taking the man's rifle magazines, replacing one in his empty rifle and stuffing a second and a third into the dead man's backpack. Along with the two left from the other Russian he'd killed in the elevator doorway below, he now had one hundred fifty rounds of ammunition.

He put the tablet in the dead Russian's pack, as well, then began rummaging through the man's pockets, and here he found a cell phone, a wallet, and a folding knife.

Condor called for Bear again.

Duff tossed the wallet and the phone—either could be used to track him—but he pocketed the knife.

Another radio transmission crackled in the dark little room. "Condor, Bear, over."

Duff walked over to the door and pulled on it, but it didn't budge an inch. He turned around, looked at the hole in the roof above the ladder shaft, and realized he was going to have to climb out, so he began placing broken bricks and pieces of mortar directly under it in an attempt to build a mound of debris he could use.

The sound of the helicopter to the north diminished some; Duff thought it had landed and was now idling while it loaded up, and he heard other helos circling nearby.

This made him pick up his pace.

The radio squawked once more, and the voice of Conrad Tremaine came over the net yet again. "Well . . . I'm guessing that if I'm not speaking to Bear, then that means I'm speaking to Duff."

Duff stopped what he was doing. Turned and faced the dead man with the radio on his shoulder.

When he again heard nothing, the South African said, "You know I'm here, I know you're there. Let's not play around, kid."

Duff walked over to the body, found the radio, and unhooked it from the man's rig. It had blood on it; Duff had shot the man multiple times, it seemed, and one of his rifle rounds had struck the Russian's neck, just a few inches away from where the device had been attached on his shoulder strap.

He pressed the talk button now. "This isn't a game, Condor."

The South African barked back, "There you are! You slotted my man, did you?"

"If you're in charge of the three Russians I've met in the past hour, then I've slotted them all."

"Respect, brother. Just like old times, you've made quite a show for yourself."

Duff went back to putting bricks on top of each other, trying to build a two-tiered base that he could use to climb out. He clicked the radio. "Flattery will get you nowhere, asshole."

"I suppose my man Belov did not blow himself up with a grenade, then?"

Duff didn't understand why Tremaine said that, but he answered back honestly. "No. I shot him with another Sentinel boy's rifle."

Tremaine said, "I hope you're in the mood to do a little horse trading."

"Meaning?"

"Your life for his possessions."

Duff looked down at the backpack. "You want the tablet so you can blow up this dam. Well . . . you can go fuck yourself." He knew the computer was destroyed, but he didn't bother to tell this to the South African.

He hooked the radio on the sling of his rifle, then turned his concentration to the project he'd been working on. He positioned one more cinder block on the lower stack, then carefully put his weight on his right leg, because balancing on his prosthetic left leg was exponentially harder.

Duff made it up onto the higher of the two structures he'd made, then let go of his rifle, letting it hang on his chest so he could reach up with both hands and check the hole above him. Twisted rebar there felt like it would take his weight, but he realized he'd have to throw the backpack up onto the roof first.

A minute later he rolled onto the roof and looked up at the night sky a moment, catching his breath.

TWENTY-EIGHT

CONRAD TREMAINE STOOD IN THE DARKNESS JUST METERS BACK from the edge of a rocky outcropping high above the eastern bank of the Volta River, just a kilometer south of the dam. He had a decent view of the well-lit facility and could see two of the helicopters circling beyond the structure out over the reservoir to his right, their lights off but their silhouettes easily distinguishable in the night sky.

A third helo had disappeared behind some buildings inside the facility's gates and alongside Lake Volta; he knew that aircraft would be loading up right now, but he had no idea who would be on board.

His dirty black king cab pickup was parked on the gravel road behind him, out of sight, though it was doubtful anyone would have been able to see it up here in the darkness from the dam. Two of his three Sentinel operators had posted security around the truck, and the third man, the fellow South African named Junior, stood by his side.

Tremaine thought about his brief conversation with Duff over the radio. He assumed the American would be getting on one of those three French helicopters, but he didn't think it possible his former colleague could be on the one that now began climbing out of the buildings by the reservoir. No, the American must have just found the radio, because Tremaine had been talking to Belov just before this, and Belov had been stuck in a room at the top of the dam.

So if Duff wasn't on the first helicopter to leave, he would have to be on the second or the third. And if Duff got out of there alive with the knowledge that Sentinel had been involved in this attack, along with the tablet computer that proved it, then he had the ability to ruin everything.

Duff's proclamations that Tremaine and Sentinel were here were bad enough, but the militarized rugged tablet computer was the real problem. If Duff had that, then he had everything, all the information about the operation set in motion, and the plans for the next hours and days of the coup.

It had been foolish to read Belov into the complete operation, but Kang had insisted. The intelligence officer had been worried about Tremaine becoming a casualty, so he demanded that someone in the Sentinel force not connected to Tremaine's direct-action fire team carry a carbon copy of the tablet Tremaine himself carried in case they needed to take over command.

The device found in the hands of the Russian leader would reveal every target and waypoint from here to the capital, every target in the capital, and even the safe houses the Sentinel operators had been told to hole up in while the overthrow was conducted by General Boatang.

The tablet in the possession of Josh Duffy was the smoking gun that would get Tremaine and his men killed, and if Tremaine couldn't get it back, then he told himself he'd have to destroy it.

Tremaine's mission changed in that very moment. Now his secondary objective was regime change in Accra. He'd get it done, but he wouldn't let it get in the way of his primary objective—killing Josh Duffy and destroying that evidence before they both made it back to the capital.

The South African's jaw fixed as he steeled himself for his next actions. He turned to Junior. "Load the RPG and bring it to me."

Junior understood what his commander was planning to do. "Moving target from this distance, boss? In the dark?"

To this, Tremaine just said, "Bring extra rockets. Double time."

Junior ran off and then, after changing channels on his walkie-talkie, Tremaine clicked the talk button and said, "Copper, Condor. You reading me?"

Copper was the Liberian Sentinel contractor embedded within Second Platoon, racing up from the south on their way to support this operation at Akosombo that had turned to shit. Tremaine could only hope he could reach him on the radio.

To his relief, the radio squawked. "I read."

"What's your location?"

"We're on the road along the west side of the river heading north; we've passed the Adomi Bridge. Should have the dam in sight in three minutes."

"How many RPG-7 launchers do you have with you?"

"Four."

"And three Russians with you?"

"Two Russians. Antonio is Chilean. Why?"

"Stop your vehicle, load up all your RPGs as fast as you can. I want all of you on the weapons, and I want you ready for helicopters coming your way. They will probably fly a river heading, but they might bank to the southwest before they get to you. I have eyes on now and will advise you of their flight path when able."

"Helicopters? Whose helicopters?"

"Doesn't matter, the first will be on you in thirty seconds. It's less important, let it pass if you can't get your weps in position in time. But the other two . . . knock them out of the sky!"

"Roger!" Copper said, and with that, Tremaine turned to Junior, took the RPG launcher from him, and hefted it in his arms.

The RPG-7 fired a dumb rocket, meaning it had no homing capabilities. Just like a gun, its accuracy was dependent on the user taking into consideration a myriad of factors: the speed of the projectile, speed of the target, distance to the target, range of the projectile, angle to the target, even wind conditions.

But the optical sight on the weapon had a simple yet effective rangefinder and targeting grid on the glass, and though it took some practice, the weapon was relatively easy to employ in the field.

Tremaine had fired RPGs probably three hundred times in training and in combat, and he knew he was adept, although he imagined that at least one of those Russians on the opposite riverbank and to the south would be better than he was with the device.

He looked back to the reservoir now. The first helo had climbed away from the buildings and turned to the south; the second began its descent to the landing zone, lowering its wheels as it did so, while the third circled a half mile to the north out over the lake.

Tremaine watched the first big Caracal as it began heading south, crossing the top of the dam, maintaining a river heading. As it quickly increased speed, he felt certain his men to the south wouldn't have their weapons ready in time to attack it.

He thought about taking a shot himself but decided to hold his fire. No, if he hit the helicopter, it would crash right there, and then the other two helo crews would be aware that someone was out here targeting them.

If the president was in the first aircraft away from the dam, then that meant the president was going to live tonight, because all Tremaine cared about at this point was killing Josh Duffy and destroying the evidence he'd taken from the Russian mercenary leader.

THE LIBERIAN NICKNAMED COPPER ORDERED THE CHILEAN BEHIND the wheel to slam on the brakes in the middle of the road, and then he climbed out, shouting at the other three men.

Both Copper and Antonio assumed that the two Russians were

better on the RPG than they were—it was a Russian weapon, after all—but all four were adequately trained, so all four men grabbed a launcher, then began pulling rockets from a case in the bed of their pickup. While they did this, several flatbed trucks and pickups pulled to the side of the road around them. These were the rebels in Second Platoon, thirty-two men strong.

The first helicopter raced by over the water while the Sentinel team was still loading the tubes.

"Faster!" Copper shouted to the others. He evaluated the altitude and speed of the aircraft above them, and he hoped the others would pass much the same, because he had no doubt at all that with four rocket launchers, at least one of them would be able to hit the next helo if it flew the same route.

FROM HIS POSITION SITTING ON THE BROKEN ROOF OF THE LITTLE shaft building on the top of the dam, Josh Duffy watched the first helicopter disappear into the night, heading south, back towards the relative safety of Accra.

He then looked back over his shoulder and saw that the second Caracal was already landing, and he hoped like hell Nichole either had been on the first one or would be getting on this one, because if there were still enemy around here in position to attack, the last helicopter would be the most vulnerable.

He looked down at the radio clipped onto his rifle sling, and he wondered why Tremaine had stopped communicating.

He began to stand on the broken roof of the little building, trying to find a way down, but then he heard a noise to the east.

Duff looked up and saw a group of men wearing camo pants and black boots climbing out of a parked RIVCOM pickup on the road just thirty yards away from him. They wielded AK-47s or some variation thereof, and some had bare chests while others wore T-shirts.

Their pants were uniform dark jungle camo, but none of them wore the RIVCOM tunics or berets he'd seen on the rebels.

Who the fuck are these guys?

He'd only just noticed these men; he hadn't been able to hear them approach over the sound of the rushing water of the spillway below him, but it was clear they had seen him first, because their guns were up and they moved carefully towards the building he knelt on.

With the sound of the water he also couldn't hear if they were shouting commands at him, but he was pretty certain he wasn't going to be taking on nearly a dozen men who already had the drop on him while kneeling on the little broken roof of this tiny building.

He put his rifle down in front of him and lifted his hands into the air.

NICHOLE DUFFY WATCHED FROM THE DOORWAY OF THE MOTOR POOL garage while Johanna Aldenburg and her five remaining security officers boarded through the sliding door of the second Caracal to land in the parking lot. The EU diplomatic corps climbed in next, and then came the surviving members of the media. There were injuries in all the groups; three people had to be carried by their arms and legs by others, the crew chief of the helo jumped out to help another injured person on board, and then, after no more than thirty seconds on the deck, Julian Delisle looked across at the garage from where he crouched in the cabin, gave a quick wave, and shut the door.

The aircraft's rotors increased in pitch, and the big helicopter lifted into the air.

As soon as it did so, Jay Costa shouted to the nineteen other people destined for the third and final helicopter. Dunnigan, Nichole, Scott, and Arletta were the diplomats; Ben Manu, Malike, Larsen, and Costa were the remaining security officers; and Martin Mensah and his eleven power house workers made up the rest of the group.

"It's going to be a tight fit," Costa said. "Give the wounded space to lie down."

Costa looked to Nichole now. "Holster that weapon and help Ben, okay?"

"Got it." She didn't have a holster, but she stuck the gun in her waistband, then moved over to the Foreign Service National Investigator, putting his arm over her shoulder and assisting him up to his feet, just as the third and last helicopter landed out front.

THE MEN FROM THE PICKUP SURROUNDED THE DAMAGED CON-crete building on the top of the dam; Duff stood on the roof now, his hands still up, and he spit away a little blood that had drained into his mouth from a cut on his forehead.

The gray belly of the second Caracal passed directly over his head just as one of the men in the street shouted something to him. Only twenty feet away now, Duff still couldn't hear the man under the deafening rotor noise, but he looked at him and cocked his head in confusion when he realized the man's T-shirt had the words "Super Dad" on the chest in red letters.

He thought about the prospect of being gunned down by someone wearing a novelty T, and then he shook his head to clear it from his mind. After waiting for the helo to continue towards the south for a few seconds, he then shouted back. "What?"

The man spoke English, and he was clearly Ghanaian. Even with the helo gone, he still had to yell to be heard over the spillway noise. "I said, who are you?"

"Who are *you*?"

The man shook his head. "No, man. It doesn't work that way. We have the guns."

The American had to agree with the logic. "Duffy. U.S. Diplomatic Security."

The same man who spoke before looked around to his mates, then back at Duff. "How do we know you are telling the truth?"

Duff shrugged. "You don't have to trust me, just don't shoot me." He added, "I'll climb down and show you some credos, but I'm going to kick off the rifle and toss my bag down first."

"You don't need your rifle."

"Have you been paying attention to what's been going on?"

The Ghanaian in the "Super Dad" shirt hesitated, then shrugged. "Do it carefully. The pistol, too."

Duff used his left hand to pull the Beretta from his waistband, and he tossed it down onto the street, then used his boot to scoot the R5 rifle to the edge of the roof until it, too, fell to the ground. He knelt and grabbed the pack, then dropped it over the side, and finally he climbed down from the roof, dropping the last three feet to the ground.

With his hands still up, he walked over to the person in the middle of the entourage to whom he'd been speaking. He noticed that the man had a bandage around his waist, blood seeping from it, and his clean-shaven face was covered in sweat and showed signs of exhaustion.

"I'm going to reach for my wallet," Duff said.

Guns remained trained on him while he pulled out his diplomatic credentials.

The man took them, looked them over, and handed them back.

He lowered his rifle and waved for the others to lower theirs.

"Who the fuck are you guys?" Duff now asked.

"I'm Sergeant Opoku. We're River Command."

"You lose your uniforms?"

"We know the rebels copied our uniforms. Didn't want to start shooting each other."

"Where'd you get those rusty Kalashnikovs?"

"The rebels stole our guns. We stole theirs." Opoku looked up, and Duff followed his gaze. The helicopter that had just passed them climbed as it gained speed, and it headed south over the river.

AS THE EU HELICOPTER DISAPPEARED OVER THE TOP OF THE DAM, Nichole Duffy helped Benjamin Manu up through the hatch of the third helo, then climbed aboard herself. She strapped into a rear-facing bulkhead seat next to Dunnigan and looked over her shoulder into the cockpit, and her eyes immediately went to the fuel gauge. She was pleased to see that the helo had at least partially refueled since landing in Akosombo earlier, and she assumed its crew chief had at least a few small bladders or tanks in the storage compartment along with the luggage, because she knew they hadn't flown to any airport around here during the firefight.

She turned her head to look back out the open starboard-side door. She was hoping to see her husband running towards her in the night, but he was not there.

Costa made sure everyone was on board, and then he strapped in using an eye bolt and a harness, buckling the canvas apparatus around his waist so he could remain in the open door with the M4 rifle he'd been carrying since the power house.

It was a tight fit, but he motioned to the pilots that they were ready to go, and then the helo lifted off into the night.

CONRAD TREMAINE WATCHED THE SECOND HELICOPTER CROSS THE top of the dam and begin heading his way, increasing in altitude as it did so, but he didn't aim at it. Instead he used his radio. "Copper, this is Condor. Over."

"Go for Copper."

"You're in position?"

"In position."

"Second helo passing you in thirty seconds, flying a river heading, two hundred meters and climbing."

"We're lined up and ready."

"Good. Drop it."

"Yeah, boss."

Tremaine did not fire on the second helo as it passed under him, because if he fired then, the pilot of the third aircraft would simply turn and head off to the north. If Tremaine waited for the second helo to make it a couple of kilometers to the south, however, right at the bend in the river, by then the third helicopter should be in the air and flying over the dam.

All his hopes to take out Duffy and his evidence of Sentinel involvement in the operation rested on knocking both of these helicopters out of the sky.

Tremaine watched as the second helo all but disappeared in the dark, and he waited expectantly for the fireworks show to begin.

SERGEANT OPOKU POINTED TO DUFF'S LEFT, TOWARDS THE HELI-copter now lifting off the parking lot by the reservoir some three hundred meters away. "Are those your people down there?"

"They're in one of the helos, don't know which, I don't have comms."

"Well, no matter which one they're in, you missed your flight."

"Not the first time."

The sergeant nodded. "We can arrange for you to get a ride back to Accra, but first we need to clear this entire facility of any enemy."

"I'll help you, Sergeant."

Opoku said, "Our president, do you know if—"

"He was alive the last time I saw him."

The RIVCOM man put his hand on his heart. "Thank God. I'm Isaac."

"Call me Duff." The men shook hands.

"Let's get in the truck."

Duff reached to pick up his bag and his rifle, but as he did he looked to the south, and he saw a small flash of light coming from the western bank down below, nearly a mile away from where he stood.

Isaac followed his look just as a second flash came, and then a third.

A fourth sparkled in the evening.

All four pinpricks of light rose skyward towards the helicopter.

Duff rose back up, terror on his face. "Oh my God."

TWENTY-NINE

JOSH DUFFY DIDN'T KNOW WHO WAS ON BOARD THAT SECOND HELI-copter, but his heart stopped while he stood there, watching along with the group of River Command police.

The first rocket missed; Duff was too far away to know if it went in front of or behind the helo, but either way it appeared to pass by very close before streaking on up into the night sky.

But the second rocket found its target, striking the side of the helicopter, creating a larger flash of light.

Even with the impact, however, the helicopter seemed to continue flying.

The Caracal turned evasively just as the third rocket approached; the projectile sailed below it, and the fourth and last burning projectile looked like it might miss high, but to Duff's horror it slammed straight into the rotors of the machine flying nearly one thousand feet in the air, and this time there could be no doubt that the explosion was catastrophic. Even from a mile away he could see the helicopter spin to the right, 360 degrees, then violently begin tumbling through the air, losing altitude.

Only now did the boom of the first detonation roll over the dam.

By the way the stricken aircraft fell, it was clear it had no main rotor now; it was essentially a school bus in the sky, and it possessed the same flight characteristics as such.

An onboard explosion rocked the French machine as it fell, and the H225 turned from a twenty-five-million-dollar aircraft into a fireball racing towards the earth. As the American watched helplessly from a distance, the flaming form turned end over end, dropping at over one hundred miles per hour as the second boom reached him where he stood.

The second helicopter to leave the hydroelectric facility then slammed into the center of the river, right at the bend to the west.

Duff knew that with those detonations at that altitude, and with the machine falling at that speed, there could be no survivors of the crash.

Isaac spoke animatedly on his radio now in a language Duff did not understand, and someone else answered back, but Duff tuned it out quickly as the whine of rotors behind him turned his head. Duff's dread only grew as he looked back and saw that the third helicopter was already in the air, banking over Lake Volta, turning in an arc towards the south.

The pilots wouldn't have seen the RPG launches, and they likely wouldn't see a smoke trail in the dark, or even the burning wreckage in the water a mile away from them for several seconds more.

Duff furiously waved his arms in the air as the helo passed a couple hundred feet above him; some of the RIVCOM men around him did the same, but the darkened aircraft flew over the dam and climbed out over the river, its flight crew having no idea of the dangers that lay directly ahead.

Duff grabbed the radio off his rifle sling and pressed the button. "Tremaine! Do *not* fucking do this!"

He received no response.

Isaac handed him his walkie-talkie. "You know the channel for the helicopter?"

Duff did not, but he knew the channel for the radios he and the other DS men carried. He quickly dialed into it, well aware that his team's radios were only half a watt and their range wasn't very far.

Pressing the button, he shouted into the microphone. "Jay! RPGs! RPGs on the west side of the river!"

ON THE EAST SIDE OF THE RIVER, CONRAD TREMAINE LEVELED HIS RPG-7 launcher at the helicopter approaching his position, then shifted to his left to lead the machine a little, hoping for an impact with the cockpit or the open port-side door as it passed.

But just as he put his finger on the trigger of the weapon, the aircraft banked sharply to the left, throwing off his aim.

It was clear to him that the French flight crew could now see the burning wreckage over a half mile away and eight hundred feet below, and they were desperate to avoid the same fate.

The Caracal dove now, banking farther left, back in Tremaine's direction, and he tried to follow its path, to anticipate its next move. The Airbus's speed increased as it raced towards the western side of the river.

"Can't . . . get . . . it . . ." he said as he concentrated like mad, desperate to get the rangefinder in the weapon's optic on the target so he could calculate the distance.

"He's speeding up!" Krelis shouted, and Tremaine ignored him because he could see exactly what the pilot was doing.

His rangefinder told him his target was one hundred fifty meters distant, so he then went to work trying to calculate the speed.

IN THE THIRD HELICOPTER TO LEAVE THE DAM, NICHOLE DUFFY HELD on to her seat with both hands, tucked her head down, and leaned into Ambassador Dunnigan in a vain attempt to try to steady the woman.

Nichole was a former helicopter pilot herself, and she knew by the way they were flying that the crew had detected some imminent threat and were responding to it. She hoped like hell someone down below had just squeezed off a couple of rounds from a rifle, because that would be a hell of a lot less dangerous to the aircraft than a shoulder-fired missile.

In the cabin there was nothing for her to do but continue to hope. While others on board screamed and prayed, flares fired out from the side of the big aircraft; it banked violently left and right as it dove for the deck.

She could picture the inputs the pilot was giving his ship: left and right rudder, left and right stick, slamming the collective down to drop altitude.

Nichole thought of her children, and of her husband, and she prayed along with the others.

CONRAD TREMAINE PRESSED THE TRIGGER OF THE RPG-7 WHEN THE French helicopter was only about two hundred meters in front of him and two hundred meters below. The rocket screamed out of the front of the tube; the backblast of smoke and fire sprayed behind him into the jungle, and then he handed the launcher to Junior for a quick reload.

As soon as he fired, however, the French helo reversed its bank, went hard to starboard, and the rocket sailed through the flares eject-ing into the night and impacted with the river below.

Krelis stood nearby now, his walkie-talkie in his hand, and he spoke into the microphone. "Copper, be advised, our first rocket missed. The target is descending and evasive, over."

"Understood."

NICHOLE DIDN'T SEE THE RPG THAT HAD NARROWLY MISSED HER helicopter; the screaming projectile was lost in the shower of bright flares in the air in the split second when it passed. They were banking to starboard now, the helicopter almost on its side as it flew, and she had the sensation they were still in a dive.

Soon they banked back to port, racing towards the west, and flying almost perpendicular to the river. She knew there was a massive hill on this side of the water and more hills to the south, and she prayed the flight crew knew what they were doing, because it felt to her that at this vector they were going to impact terrain in a matter of seconds.

She heard Dunnigan reciting the Lord's Prayer next to her, and Nichole followed the ambassador's lead, praying aloud now herself as the helicopter began to accelerate and climb.

JUNIOR HANDED THE LAUNCHER BACK TO TREMAINE, AND THE Sentinel commander put his eye back in the rubber eyecup of the sight, searching for the helicopter to fire again. The helo was well to his south now, so he ran forward out onto the edge of the rocky outcropping to keep line of sight of it. He aimed through the sight hurriedly, knowing the Caracal would be out of his view in just seconds, probably trying to thread its way through the hills to get out of the line of fire, the crew trusting their flying skills to save them.

As he put his sight in front of the helicopter, it stopped banking suddenly; it needed level flight to pass over a narrow saddle between the hill Tremaine stood on and the next one to the south, and Tremaine knew this was his opportunity. He fired, leading the craft by sixty meters, and the rocket left the tube with a roar, then raced south over the riverbank.

As soon as the flash left his eyes he saw four more rockets fired from the opposite bank, far to the south, and this told him Copper and his men had at least seen the fleeing helicopter, even if they were likely too far away to hit it from their position.

JOSH DUFFY HAD NEVER FELT MORE HELPLESS IN HIS LIFE THAN HE had in the last thirty seconds. The third Caracal had avoided one rocket, and now it flew towards a lower part of the hillside to the west, just skirting the trees and rocks there by a few meters as it tried to get out of the line of fire. Then he saw another rocket streaking from a prominence high on the hill to the helicopter's left.

There was an impact and an explosion, but Duff couldn't tell if the helo itself had been hit or if the ground below it had. Suddenly, however, four more RPGs sailed from the river bend farther to the south. All four hit the hillside, but one of the explosions was close enough to the low-flying Caracal that he couldn't be sure it hadn't been damaged.

As he watched the rear half of the helicopter disappear from his view around a jungled hill, however, his worst fears were realized.

He saw a smoke trail behind a ball of flame as the tail of the big machine burned.

NICHOLE DUFFY HADN'T FELT THE IMPACT OF A MISSILE, BUT SHE'D both heard and felt the shredding of metal below her, and she knew the helicopter had taken some damage.

They'd been low to the ground; it had been too dark to tell how low until an explosion out the open port-side door of the helicopter revealed a jungle canopy just a dozen or so meters below them, and a hillside that climbed high above on that side.

The trees ignited in a ball of fire, and shrapnel tore through the fuselage.

It was too dark in the cabin to see who was hurt, who was alive, who was dead. She reached over and grabbed the ambassador, put her arms around her to check her for injuries, and realized Chad Larsen was doing the same from the other side, so she got out of his way.

The ambo seemed okay, so she returned her attention out the port-side hatch.

The helicopter flew straight, narrow, and fast for several seconds; she felt sure they were now out of the line of fire, she just didn't know how much damage they'd taken from the near miss.

More explosions erupted higher on the hillside to port, and again she heard the terrifying noise of more small pieces of metal or wood or rock biting into the fuselage.

They were moving fast now, probably close to one hundred twenty knots, and just as she began to think they might be okay, she felt a shimmy in the tail rotor that she herself had felt once before, shortly before her own helicopter had crashed in Syria.

The shimmy grew, and she looked back at the pilots behind her, willed them to slow the aircraft down because she realized they were in more danger crashing at speed than they were of getting hit by another rocket.

She knew what was coming next, but knowing made it no less terrifying. The shaking from behind worsened by the second, and then the helo began turning to the left.

The pilot applied the right rudder pedal, but the turn only accelerated.

Nichole realized she was likely the only person on board other than the flight crew who understood that the tail rotor had come off.

The pilots began dramatically slowing down; the nose pitched up, but the spinning continued.

Nichole looked out to port now but saw nothing but black; she didn't know their speed, their altitude, or what obstructions might be in their way, but she knew one thing with absolute clarity.

She knew they were going down.

JOSH DUFFY SAW A GLOW ILLUMINATE ON THE HILLSIDE, AND THIS told him that somewhere in the hills, the third helicopter had crashed. He couldn't see the impact point, but it couldn't have been more than three miles or so away from where he stood.

He grabbed Isaac by the arm. "What's over there?"

"It's jungle, just a valley. There are some dirt roads, that's about it."

"I need a vehicle."

Isaac said, "We've got more rebels on the road to the south of the main gate. Akosombo police have responded to them, I picked it up on the radio. I've got to stay here till the second-shift RIV-COM captain arrives. Should be any minute. You can wait for me or—"

Duff cut him off. "I'm not waiting. This truck?"

He pointed to the pickup parked there.

"Yeah, man. Good luck. Go with God."

CONRAD TREMAINE STOOD ON THE ROCKY OUTCROPPING WITH A freshly loaded rocket launcher, but he was no longer focused on the south where the helicopter had disappeared. Instead he leveled the rocket and pointed it down, across the riverbank. He took several seconds to steady the weapon, and then he aimed the sight on the switchyard, choosing a cluster of massive transformers right in the middle of the location.

"Backblast clear!" he shouted, and then he fired a rocket.

A sparkle of light leading a smoke trail raced from the tube and sailed over the black water of the Volta River a quarter mile south of the dam. A huge explosion, a powerful shower of sparks, and then equipment began tipping and falling, lines bursting with more sparks.

The power went off immediately, enshrouding the area in darkness.

Tremaine instantly handed the RPG to Junior. "Load it up. Gonna hit it again."

DUFF HAD BEEN RUNNING TO THE PICKUP ISAAC TOLD HIM TO TAKE to the crash site, but when he heard the first explosion behind him, he turned back around and raised his weapon. Walking back to the river's southern edge, he looked through his sights, scanning the hillside for a target.

Isaac stepped up to his shoulder, though it was so dark on the top of the dam now Duff could barely see him.

The Ghanaian said, "I think it was another RPG. They wanted to shut off the power."

"Fired from the hill again?"

"I didn't see it."

Just then there was a flash on the hill; flame illuminated the trees and a rocket sailed across the water, slamming into the switchyard, blowing up more equipment and critical infrastructure, and starting a fire.

Duff instantly raised his weapon higher, aimed in on the launch site of the rocket, judged the distance to be about four hundred yards, and put the optical sight of his weapon a quarter inch above a rocky outcropping just visible in the moonlight.

He fired semiautomatic rounds so he could keep control of the weapon, but he squeezed them off in rapid succession.

He heard gunshots next to him, realized Isaac was firing his AK in the same direction, and soon more men on the dam opened up on the same spot of hillside, dumping dozens and dozens of rounds in the general area the RPG had been fired from.

THIRTY

AS SOON AS THE FIRST ROUNDS IMPACTED THE HILLSIDE SOME dozen meters away from him, Conrad Tremaine dropped the RPG launcher, dove hard to the ground, rolled onto his belly, then began crawling on his hands and knees as fast as he could, leaving the weapon behind.

Tree branches snapped and cracked, and leaves and twigs fell all around him; bullets zinged in and then ricocheted off the rocks, sparking in the night and sending debris flying in all directions.

He made it the entire twenty meters back to the potholed dirt road before he realized his enemy didn't have an angle on him here on the road, so all their shots were going high. He stood up, turned around, and found Krelis in the dark.

"Fuck me," he said. "RIVCOM's still in play down there, aren't they?"

"You fired from the same spot four times. What'd you expect, boss?"

Tremaine ignored the admonishment from his underling, and he looked around in the near pitch-black darkness. "Where are the others?"

Junior appeared from the direction of the outcropping. He moved slowly in the dark, and soon Tremaine saw why.

The South African carried two rifles and an extra set of body armor in his arms.

He passed the other two men by, then threw the extra gear into the back of the pickup. While doing this, he said, "Baginski's fucked."

"Bloody hell," Tremaine muttered.

"He ran over to return fire but caught one right in the top of the skull in front of me before he even got his fucking weapon hot."

The shooters at the dam had stopped firing; the zipping rounds over the mercenaries' heads diminished. Tremaine thought a moment, then clicked his radio talk button. "Copper, this is Condor, how read?"

The radio squawked. "Read you, Lima Charlie."

"Do *not* go to the dam. Say again, do *not* attack the dam. There's still significant resistance there, and they're ready for a fight now. I've shut the power off, so our objectives here are met. Turn around, go back to the bridge, and cross to my side of the Volta. I'll meet you there."

"Yes, sir."

"Condor out." To the two men standing on the road with him, he said, "Let's move out."

Neither man moved. Quickly Krelis said, "What about Baginski's body? We gonna strap it on the hood like a bloody deer?"

"He's a Pole, but he looks Russian enough to me. We left three dead Wagner men at the dam. If we do this right, then Moscow's going to be blamed for this, not Sentinel."

Krelis said, "Are we doing this right?" There was a critical tone in his voice. This wasn't a military unit, these were soldiers of fortune, and this was reflected in the order and code of conduct between leaders and followers.

The Sentinel leader spit on the ground. "No plan survives first contact with the enemy. I always knew we'd hit snags, and we've certainly done that. But now our main objective is getting to that second crash site and checking for survivors."

"And if there *are* survivors?" Junior asked.

"Then there won't be when we leave."

The men climbed inside; the pickup rumbled along the hillside, its headlights on now because the deeply rutted and pitted road would be impossible to navigate otherwise.

JOSH DUFFY LOWERED HIS RIFLE, TURNED AROUND, AND ONCE again ran for the truck. Before he got to the driver's door, however, Isaac stepped in front of him, holding a hand up as he spoke hurriedly to someone on his radio. A man replied, and as before, Duff couldn't understand the language.

He didn't want to wait around for the translation, so he tried to push by the police sergeant, but Isaac wouldn't budge.

The conversation lasted another ten seconds; Duff was about to use real force to get behind the wheel of the truck to go to the crash site, but just as he was about to shoulder his way through the RIV-COM sergeant, Isaac put his radio back on his belt.

"I'll drive."

Duff didn't understand why this man was going with him, but he ran around to the passenger side and climbed in.

Isaac fired the engine, then whipped a U-turn in the road on top of the dam and began racing to the east, leaving his other officers behind.

Before Josh could ask what was happening, the Ghanaian said, "The other shift has arrived at the dam. Twenty-four men, including the captain. They captured four rebels at the main gate, then a row of trucks approached from the south, so they got into defensive positions. He just told me the unidentified vehicles were turning around and heading away. I told him I'm going in pursuit of the rebels to the west."

Josh sighed; this wasn't what he wanted to hear. "I'm not looking for rebels, dude, I'm looking for survivors."

"Yeah? Well, my friend, so are the rebels. They went to the trouble to shoot that helicopter down. They must have really wanted to kill those inside. I'll get us there first. I know this area; there is a road we can use that doesn't show on any map, and it will take us over that saddle between the hills to a valley on the other side. If the helicopter crashed, it would have been somewhere around there."

They drove in silence, leaving the now-darkened hydroelectric plant grounds and then taking the twisting road that led up the hill to the east. Finally, Josh said, "My wife was on one of those three aircraft."

Isaac turned to look at him as he drove, his eyes wide. "Your *wife*?"

"Yeah," he said softly.

"Why?"

"She works for the ambassador."

It was silent a moment more save for the squeaking suspension of the truck as it bounced onto a gravel road. Finally Isaac said, "I'm sure she was on the first one. She's fine. On the way back to Accra by now, where it's safe."

The sergeant was just trying to keep Duff positive, and he appreciated the gesture, but Duff had a feeling she had either been on the Caracal that augered into the river at maximum velocity while burning like a campfire, or else she was on the stricken helo that disappeared into the hills, because it made sense to him that the president and his people would be on the first bird out of the kill zone.

Soon they were climbing higher into the hills, the sky blocked out above them by trees as they bobbed over the impossibly bumpy dirt roads below them.

Duff took the time to check his sat phone, finding it still out of commission. Isaac saw him doing this, then took his own cell phone out of his pocket and checked it for a signal. When he put it back into his pocket without making a call, Duff knew he didn't have to ask.

The DS special agent looked over his rifle now, using the interior lighting, making sure it remained in good condition. He realized he only had one spare magazine left, and this caused him to check around in the truck to see what equipment was available. "Any more guns in here?"

Isaac shook his head. "Just mine and yours. I've got a pistol, too."

Duff nodded. He still had the Russian's Beretta stuck in his belt since it didn't fit in his Glock holster. Looking around, he asked, "What about a trauma bag?"

"Yes, all our vehicles have them. You hurt?"

"It's for what we find where we're going." He looked out the window. "How many did you lose?"

Isaac said, "Of my men? At least twelve. Maybe more. How about you?"

"I . . . I don't know. A lot of fine people lost their lives today."

The sergeant asked, "What is this all about? A presidential assassination?"

"Doesn't look like it. They brought bombs to blow up the dam. I think we just happened to come at the wrong time, and someone took a shot at Amanor because he was there." He thought a moment. "Something bigger is going on, but I don't know what. One of the Russians said the army would take a long time to respond to this attack at the dam because they would have 'bigger problems.' I don't know what he meant by that."

"Those rebels," Isaac said. "I think they're Dragons of Western Togoland. It's the only non-Muslim insurgent group anywhere around, but nobody thought the Dragons were real. Just some make-believe group that only existed on the radio and the Internet."

"They seemed pretty real to me."

"Yeah. But . . . I don't know who these Russians are. Wagner Africa Corps is all over West Africa, but we've never seen them in Ghana. This is Chinese territory," he said, somewhat sarcastically. "Or it was until you all showed up."

"They're not Wagner," Duff clarified. "It's a private military corporation called Sentinel. South Africans, too. They're working with the rebels."

This surprised the police sergeant. "Why?"

"Haven't got a clue, man. I just got to your country a week and a half ago."

Isaac chuckled a little, then turned off this bad road and onto an even worse one. Here weeds and brush had grown in between two tire tracks that wound around at a steep incline like a goat trail, but the Toyota was up to the challenge. He said, "This isn't the welcome I would have wished for you."

"Makes two of us." As Duff watched the road, he rested his rifle on the seat between his knees, barrel up, so he could point it out the open window quickly in case they managed to run across the person or persons who'd been operating the RPG launcher up here.

He said, "I actually know the man in charge of the mercenary force. He used to be my boss."

"You were a mercenary?"

Duff thought this question over. "I didn't think so at the time." With a shrug he said, "He's here. Talked to him on the Russian's radio when I was inside the dam."

"You still have that radio?"

"Yeah." Duff unhooked it from the strap of his rifle and stuck it in his backpack.

"Why don't you call him?" Isaac said. "Ask him what his plan is."

Duff just shook his head. "Tremaine probably thinks I'm either dead or else a survivor of the second crash."

"Why wouldn't he think you were in the one that got away?"

"Because I talked to him just before that one took off. No, as far as he knows, I was in the second or third. I don't want him to know I'm still around."

"Well, if you see him, maybe you should use that rifle to let him know you're still around."

"Damn right I will." Duff looked to the man behind the wheel now. "Where'd you learn to shoot?"

"I was in the army, special forces unit, eight years. You? You are former military, for sure."

"For sure," Duff said softly, still looking out through the thick dust.

"An officer?" Isaac asked, but before Duff could respond, a crashing noise outside the vehicle caused him to hoist his gun up and shove the barrel out the window to hunt for targets. Isaac grabbed his arm, stopping him. "Relax, man. Relax. It's just thunder. It's going to rain."

"Rain?" Duff sighed, putting the butt stock of the gun on the seat in front of him again. "Yeah, that's what we need right now."

"It's fine. We'll find the crash site first and get them out of there before the rain gets too heavy. We're on a road now that almost nobody uses."

They slammed down into a pothole and bounced up on the other side. "I never would have guessed."

"The main road has about one hundred switchbacks, but this one goes right over the hill, down into the valley. We'll have a place where we can stop and look out over the valley for any wreckage, smoke, or fire, but we need to get there before the rain." Isaac sped up, and Duff bounced around even more in the front passenger seat of the pickup.

Isaac added, "Where that RPG fire came from, they shouldn't be able to get there before we do, but they won't be far behind, so we'll have to pick up any survivors and go quickly." The sergeant seemed to remember that Duff's wife might have been on board, because quickly he added, "Rescue everyone, I mean."

"Where were you when the attack happened?" Duff asked, desperate to both change the subject and get intelligence on just what was going on.

Isaac said, "Me and three others went to a limestone mine to check on a suspicious vehicle. We were attacked by a Russian and a group of rebels. They had vehicles like ours. Apparently they had uniforms like ours, too.

"All three of my colleagues with me were killed, I was shot, and then I borrowed a motorcycle to get back to the dam."

"You got shot?"

"I'm fine," he said.

Duff tried to check the wound on the right side of the man's torso but found it impossible to do so while crashing over thick brush, rocks, and potholes.

After a moment he gave up and said, "So . . . is it true?"

"Is *what* true?"

"Are you really a super dad?"

Isaac appeared confused as he drove, but only for a moment. He looked down at his shirt, covered in sweat and blood from the bandages above his right hip. "A gift from my wife when my son was born. She bought it before I was a dad, and Kofi is only four months old, so it's a little early to say if I am a good father yet."

Duff nodded. He thought about telling the man about his own children, but he couldn't. Knowing that there was a statistical probability that their mother was dead would make talking about Huck and Mandy more painful than he could deal with at the moment, so they just drove on in silence.

NEARLY TWENTY MINUTES LATER ISAAC PARKED THE PICKUP, AND then Duff followed him down a narrow pathway through some trees. It was impossibly dark here; Isaac's flashlight led the way, but

occasionally lightning flooded the pathway with light. The flashes
came just before the cracks of thunder, telling Duffy there was a
storm cell virtually right on top of them, and the warm, moist, and
windy air indicated the rain could come at any moment.

Eventually Isaac turned off the light, stopped, and grabbed Duff
by the left arm. "We have to wait here. Can't reveal our position in
case any rebels got ahead of us."

The two men just stood there in the pitch black.

"What are we doing?" the American asked after a moment.

"Just wait."

Soon another flash lit up the sky.

Now Duff could see why Isaac had brought him here. As the
thunderclap pounded his already damaged eardrums, he saw that
they were on a hill over a narrow valley, a vast unbroken canopy of
green that stretched from east to west. Duff even caught a glimpse
of the saddle between the two hills he'd seen from the dam back to
the east, where the third helicopter had disappeared about forty minutes earlier.

And in just that instant of light, Duff saw what he needed to see.
A cloud of smoke hung in the air over the trees not more than a thousand meters southeast of their position.

Isaac saw it, too. Both men turned and ran for the truck, and
Isaac flipped his light back on so they didn't snag on any low branches
or vines.

The RIVCOM sergeant jumped back behind the wheel just as the
wind began to pick up in advance of the approaching storm. He said,
"There is a good road down there, but we're going to have to go off
road to get to it. It's going to take a while."

Duff sat down on the passenger side. "We haven't been off road
this whole time?"

Isaac sniffed a laugh, then began driving wildly forward, almost
daring rocks and ruts to flip the vehicle as the rain beat down on the

hood. He said, "There's a stream. It will be impossible to use once the rain comes, but now it should be almost dry. We'll use it as our own road through the jungle."

To Duff this felt like he was back in Mexico, in a damaged armored personnel carrier taking accurate fire from an army of sicarios. He held on and prayed for two things: one, that Nichole was still alive, and two, that Isaac knew where the hell he was going, because Duff could only see dust, foliage, and darkness on the other side of the windshield.

THIRTY-ONE

CONRAD TREMAINE CUSSED LOUDLY IN THE PASSENGER SEAT AS Krelis drove the Toyota over the poorly kept dirt road that wound around the hillside. Tremaine's anger wasn't directed towards the Dutch mercenary's driving but rather the winding road itself. It seemed like every thirty seconds a switchback halted progress towards their destination, sending the truck back the wrong way as they climbed or descended, as if the road itself was trying to keep them from their goal.

Krelis for his part just continued white-knuckling his way behind the taillights of a Ford pickup holding eight rebels, while squinting out the glare from the headlights of an identical rebel vehicle in his rearview mirror.

There were five trucks in all in the convoy; the Sentinel vehicle was sandwiched between the four squads of Second Platoon, two in front of them and two behind. Copper, the Liberian Sentinel mercenary embedded with Second Platoon, was in the lead vehicle, and he stayed in radio contact with Tremaine as they all neared the area where they thought they might find the helicopter crash.

This platoon was working off mission—Kang's plan had them

heading to Accra with their entire company, just behind another company taking the same road. But Condor's updated orders were clear. They were to accompany him to the crash site and search for survivors.

All three of the Sentinel men in the convoy who worked under Tremaine were unhappy about where they found themselves at the moment. Copper, Junior, and Krelis had all been training for months preparing their missions, and none of them had planned on being hours behind the others on the drive to the capital.

They had targets to hit along the N2 highway to make the path easier for the Dragons, and now that they were east of the Volta and nowhere near where they were supposed to be, the three men all silently worried about the prospects of the coup succeeding.

Junior was the first to voice any concerns, from the back seat of the black Toyota pickup. "Boss, we're off schedule, we're out of radio comms with the other units, and we're bloody vulnerable out here. I say we take the safe bet that everyone on board is dead, turn around, and get back on our mission. Send a squad from Second Platoon and let the rest of us just get on with it."

Tremaine shook his head. "Getting our asses out of Ghana alive to enjoy our money *is* our mission, and if we somehow left Duffy in play with Belov's computer, then we have to kill him and take it back, or we're not *ever* leaving this shit hole. Just keep looking out the windows for any signs of a crash."

"I can't see a damn thing," Krelis said.

"The lightning. Use the lightning strikes. There has to be smoke, broken trees, *something*. That helo was going down, one hundred percent. We're high enough on a hill to where we should be able to see out from time to time."

And with that, Tremaine reached down into his backpack on the floorboard of the front passenger seat and pulled out his Iridium satellite phone.

———

KANG SHIKUN STOOD ON HIS BALCONY IN THE NIGHT AS A WARM rain began to fall on him. He wore no raincoat, just his shirtsleeves, but he didn't move a muscle.

The power in the city had shut off again, not long after he last spoke with Tremaine, and at this he was pleased. The fighting continued across the capital; he could see flashes of light, hear the occasional siren or explosion far in the distance, but he wasn't focused on this activity now.

Instead he held his Swarovski binoculars to his eyes and tracked the lone helicopter moving over the capital. Although he couldn't see the aircraft itself, only its lights, he was certain he knew where it was going.

It flew near the airport, but Kang was correct in assuming it would not land there. Instead it continued on to the south for just another minute, then began to descend onto the grounds at Jubilee House, the presidential residence and seat of power.

The unrest in the city would be known to the pilots of the aircraft now, of this Kang was certain, so the decision to fly the president directly to his secure property, surrounded at all times by a company of the President's Own Guard Regiment, was an easy one for Amanor's security to make, and an easy one for Kang to anticipate.

The Chinese spy tracked back to the north now with the binoculars, searching the rainy night sky for the lights of the second and third helicopters.

But he saw nothing else in the air.

His phone buzzed in his pocket; he lowered the binos and put it to his ear. "Yes?"

Tremaine said, "It's Condor. The enemy has taken back the dam."

Only now did Kang turn around and step back inside and out of the warm shower. "How did that happen? Don't they know you can blow the entire thing to—"

"We can't blow it. Our Russian with the triggering device was overrun, and we lost control of it. I disabled the switchyard, shutting off the power to the grid again, and then I told our remaining forces to retreat from the dam and proceed south to Accra."

Though inside the room he'd set up as his office now, Kang had turned back to the open door, his eyes still on the rainy night to the north. *Where were those other helicopters?*

Though distracted, he didn't hide his displeasure and his confusion about what was going on. "This is not ideal."

"Just a complication," Tremaine countered. "I ordered the satellite jamming operations to cease."

Kang let it go. "A helicopter just landed at the president's palace; I assume the other two will go to the airport, but I don't have visual on them yet."

Tremaine said, "The other two *won't* be going to the airport. They both crashed."

The normally unflappable Kang squinted his eyes shut, then took a few breaths before speaking. "They *what?*"

"A rogue squad of Dragons with RPGs attacked the joint delegation as it took off. The first helicopter got away, the second helicopter was destroyed with all aboard, and the third crashed somewhere in the hills. We are trying to locate it now."

Kang took a few more calming breaths now, thought about the peace that his tai chi practice gave him, and wished he could adopt a pose. Already he was thinking about the call he'd have to make to Beijing explaining that the plan he'd sold them on had now turned into an attempted presidential assassination, and the assassination or attempted assassination of an EU diplomatic team and an American ambassador.

"Why is there a 'rogue squad' of rebels? *You* trained them."

"I'll be sure to ask them for their reasons after I wring their fucking necks."

Kang took a long moment to organize his thoughts, then said, "I need to know if there is *any* Sentinel compromise."

"There was. I think it's been taken care of, but I need to check the second crash site to make sure."

"For what?"

"One of the American security men at the dam . . . he knew about my involvement."

"How did he know—"

"I don't have a fucking clue, but he's either already dead or soon will be. We kill him, get the computer he took off of Bear, and then we're golden." When Kang did not immediately reply, he said, "The power is off, all troops are on the move to the capital minus two platoons. Three and a half companies of rebels and some sixty of my operators are doing exactly what they are supposed to be doing. We clean up this one compromise and we are back on track."

Kang, for his part, had his own secrets. He wasn't going to mention to Tremaine anything about the attacks going on around the city by the JNIM terrorists. The South African wouldn't like being involved with Iran or the jihadis, and it wasn't relevant to Sentinel's mission.

Now the calm Asian man adopted a lower, more threatening tone. "We are both professionals, Tremaine. If you are compromised, if you can't . . . *extinguish* this problem before it gets out to the wider world . . . I don't have to tell you what is going to happen."

"I don't need your warnings to give me proper motivation." Tremaine disconnected the call.

Kang put his phone back down on his desk, turned away from the window because he was no longer looking for two helicopters, and headed to the living room to check in with his staff.

RAIN BEGAN TO FALL ON THE HILL SHORTLY BEFORE TEN P.M.; THE showers, though steady from the start, had trouble getting through the jungle canopy at first. But the weather was persistent, and eventually water dripped down through the trees and fronds and vines and then bounced off the aluminum frame of the gray Airbus helicopter that now lay on its starboard side.

The Akwapim-Togo Range was a two-hundred-mile belt of ridges and hills, actually a deciduous forest, between Ghana and the Togo border. The foliage here was impossibly dense, but the crash of the sixteen-thousand-pound helicopter with a fifty-two-foot main rotor had ripped a gaping hole in the forest. The aircraft had hit the treetops at eighty knots, then whipped and spun as it tore through the high limbs of African mahogany and cotton silkwood, propelled from west to east. The rotor had disintegrated along with a half acre of canopy, and then the twisted fiery wreckage slammed into the hillside and rolled end over end, back down to its side as it tumbled along, finally coming to rest partially twisted around a silkwood tree trunk the width of a car.

The helo had been on the ground for over an hour now, and still a small fire burned back where the tail rotor used to be, but as the fresh rain increased in intensity, the fire began to diminish.

The mean annual rainfall here was over forty-five inches, and the jungle floor was moss covered and soaked; the rain that made its way down to the wreckage quickly formed in pools and flowed through the moss and down the saturated hill in growing rivulets.

Soon the rivulets turned red with blood.

There was no movement inside the still aircraft, and outside the sounds of the jungle had returned after the disruption that came along with a helicopter crash into terrain.

But then a new sound emerged in the dark. A tinny, metallic click, a brief squawk, and then a man's voice. "DS? DS, come in, over."

The radio that emitted the voice lay next to the thick roots of the giant silkwood that had stopped the helicopter's forward progression.

The voice spoke again. Urgently, plaintive. "Jay? Chad? Ben? Malike? *Anyone* up on this net, come in. Over?"

The small black walkie-talkie lay alone for a moment; its earpiece cable had been ripped out, its battery slowly draining, the rain saturating it.

"DS? *Anyone*, how copy?"

A hand wrapped around the radio now, lifted it out of the bloody rainwater, and clicked the push-to-talk button.

"Josh?" The woman spoke through sobs, her voice weak. "Josh . . . is that you?"

"It's me! Are you okay, baby?"

Nichole Duffy began crying, but quickly she asked, "Where are you?"

"We're on the road, not sure of your location, but we're close."

Nichole put an unsteady hand against the trunk of the silkwood tree, then leaned against it to pull herself up to a standing position.

"What . . . How do I find you?"

"We're in a technical . . . a pickup truck. We're going to honk the horn, be listening for it."

"Josh . . . it's raining, there are birds, there's so much noise."

"Stand by," he said. Duff's voice was professional and clipped, and it told her she needed to pull her shit together.

Seconds later, the sound of frogs, birds, crickets, all life forms, suddenly stopped. Her husband spoke into the radio. "You hearing us?"

"No," she said. "But the animals do. Keep honking."

For ten seconds she heard nothing but the unceasing rain thumping against the ruined helicopter, pattering on the moss and brush and the leaves above. But then she detected a new noise, a faint car horn in the distance. She clicked the mic. "I hear you. You are off to my right, but I have no idea which way I'm facing."

"That's okay. Just keep listening for the horn. Is it getting louder or softer?"

The horn made short bleats, and in seconds she could tell it was nearing her position. "Okay, you're coming the right way. I don't see a road. I don't see anything, really, except for jungle. You are downhill from me, I can tell that much."

"Okay, that helps. You're on our left. Tell me when the horn starts to pass."

It took another minute, but then she clicked again. "Too far. Back up, maybe one hundred yards, you should be right below us."

"Okay."

"Josh," she said. "We have dead, and nearly everybody alive is injured."

"I understand. We'll have to scoop the survivors somehow and run; we figure we're not the only ones looking for the crash."

Nichole looked down at her hand; it was wrapped around the grip of the Browning pistol that had somehow managed to stay in her waistband through the impossibly violent crash. "I was thinking the same thing."

ISAAC OPOKU HAD JUST DRIVEN OVER A TINY WOODEN BRIDGE ONLY a couple of car lengths in size when he slammed on the brakes of his pickup, sliding on the wet moss underneath the wheels. He shoved the transmission into reverse, but before he could hit the gas, Duff put a hand on his arm.

"If we go back there in the truck we're going to give the exact position of the crash away."

Isaac said, "There's nothing but this road all the way to the N2 highway, no place to hide the truck that I know of. We'll have to leave it here."

Duff nodded. "That might buy us some time, anyway. Let's carry as much out of the vic as we can in case it falls into enemy hands."

Duff leapt out of the passenger seat with a flashlight in his hand that he'd found in the glove compartment. He slung his rifle around his neck, put his pack on his back, and turned on the light. While Isaac went to the tailgate to grab the trauma bag and more gear, Duff began moving as quickly as possible in the rain, stumbling over ruts in the muddy road.

Running across the bridge, he heard the sound of rushing water below, but it was too dark to see what was down there.

The two men ran about one hundred yards, then left the road, heading uphill. Duff was in the lead at first, picking his way through the dense jungle while he shined the light forward.

He struggled for over a minute; the foliage was so thick, the hillside so slippery, and he had to pull his way up through branches with one hand. The prosthesis was a hindrance on ground this unstable, and he knew he was only slowing Isaac down. Soon, though, he heard Isaac coming up behind; he had a light, as well, and two more things that Duff did not: a machete, and the skill to use it to slice a path through the jungle.

Isaac passed Duff the trauma bag so the Ghanaian would be able to blaze the trail more quickly, and soon they'd gone thirty or forty yards up the hill.

Duff understood now what his wife meant when she said how loud it was. The animals were quiet at the moment, but the incessant rhythm of the heavy rainfall drowned out any other sounds. Still, Duff took a chance, left his team radio on his belt, and shouted, "Nikki? Nikki?"

He heard no response, so they went a minute more, and he called out again.

He heard his wife's voice over the rain. "Up here!" They still had some ground to cover, but both Isaac and Duff could tell they were heading in the right direction.

Five minutes later, and some ten minutes after leaving the truck, Isaac slashed through a cluster of thick liana vines, revealing an open space in the jungle just in front of him. He shined his light to the left, saw broken tree limbs and the rain pouring down where the canopy had been disrupted, and then shifted the beam to his right.

Josh shouldered up to Isaac just as the light revealed Nichole Duffy, standing alone by the twisted remains of the Caracal. She wore a gray top that was torn and blood smeared, and mud-covered and ripped off-white linen pants, and her right eye was almost swollen shut.

Josh climbed up to her through the broken and torn foliage. "You're hurt!"

"It's not bad." They embraced, and she winced with pain.

"What is it?"

"Left shoulder. Just banged up, not broken . . . I don't think." She embraced him again. "Thought I lost you."

"I thought you went down with the other helicopter."

"Aldenburg?" she asked.

"Was she in the second one to leave the dam?"

Nichole nodded.

"They're all dead."

She shut her eyes now. "What about Amanor? He was on the first helo."

"He made it out, as far as I know."

Isaac scanned around the wreckage with his light. Josh didn't bother with introductions, not yet, because he had a very obvious question. "Where is—"

"Those of us who could moved the other survivors away from the crash site in case the bad guys came. We had to drag most of them on cargo nets, plus a couple of tarps from the emergency kit. I just came back down here to try and scavenge more equipment and I heard you on Chad's radio." She looked back over her shoulder. "Everyone else is higher on the hill behind a big tree . . . I don't know . . . twenty-five yards that way."

"Good thinking."

Isaac's light flashed through the front windshield of the helicopter; it faced in the same direction as the tail because the machine had wrapped around a tree trunk. Blood glistened on the inside of the broken glass, and inside, both French pilots remained strapped in their seats.

Nichole said, "No pulse on either of them. Dunnigan is alive, though. She might have a broken ankle, foot, leg . . . I don't know, it's swollen. Chad has a broken kneecap and some lacerations; his back is sliced open bad. We got the bleeding stopped, more or less. Benjamin wasn't badly hurt . . . Well . . . he was shot earlier, but he wasn't badly hurt in the crash, thank God. He's back on his feet, guarding the ambo now."

"Jay?"

Nichole bit her lip, then motioned to the helicopter.

"Jay's gone, Josh. He was in the door when we hit; I think the impact broke his neck. He's under the helicopter, but I was able to check his pulse at his ankle. Scott's dead, too; he's still in there, strapped in. Malike was knocked out, but he's up and walking around now."

"And the crew chief?"

"The crew chief fell out of the hatch when we were still airborne; I don't see how he could have survived, but I can't say for sure."

Duff didn't think there was a chance in hell anyone could have lived after falling out of a crashing helicopter at the speed it was obviously going to cause all this destruction.

"Shit," he said. "Okay. Take us to the others. We've got to haul ass."

Nichole looked past him now. "Where are the rest of you?"

Duff realized she had expected him to come with a much larger search party. "Sorry, babe. It's just me and my friend Isaac here, from the real River Command police. We've got a truck."

"A truck?" she said, a sound of disappointment in her voice, but Duff was already moving up the hill, nervous because he knew every second they spent here was another second Tremaine and his rebels had to look for them.

THIRTY-TWO

DUFF USED THE FLASHLIGHT TO PICK HIS WAY UP, BUT FROM BEHIND him he heard his wife shout. "It's Nichole! I've got Josh and a policeman. We're coming in."

He knew that those people above who were armed would be looking at the approaching lights with concern, so he was glad his wife had thought to warn them.

A minute later he found Jennifer Dunnigan lying in the wet moss, her right leg elevated on a tree stump, wrapped in cargo netting torn from the helicopter, her head up. She had a cell phone in her hand and it looked like she was checking it for a signal as the rain fell on her, but she put it back down again and gave a little wave to Josh.

Nichole said, "I administered morphine."

Ben Manu sat next to Dunnigan, an M4 in his arms. The gunshot wound to his leg was wrapped, but the bandages looked like they had loosened to where they weren't doing him much good. Malike was on her other side; he looked past Duffy with a thousand-yard stare.

Arletta James, the forty-year-old Foreign Service Officer, sat with her back against a tree, holding a compress to her bloody forehead.

ARSO Chad Larsen lay flat on his back, his right leg wrapped. Blood dripped down his face from an open cut above his eyes, and bandages were wrapped around his bare chest, but he appeared awake and alert.

Now Nichole said, "Chad refused anything for pain."

The other ARSO looked at Duff and said, "Just you two?"

"This is Sergeant Opoku from RIVCOM. He got me here, but the rest of his force is protecting the dam." Duff shrugged as water drained off his short hair. "What's left of the dam, anyway. We have a truck down on the road, but it's a hike."

Larsen said, "Yeah, afraid I'm gonna have to pass on a hike right now. Take the ambo."

Before Duff could respond to this, Isaac shined his light around more, and a little farther up the hill he saw a group of people, all Black, either standing or sitting around. Some were clearly hurt; makeshift bandages were wrapped around a man's head, and a woman used her shirt as a sling to immobilize her arm.

Josh recognized one of the civilians. It was the deputy plant operator.

Softly, he said, "You've got ten more people?"

"Yes," Chad said, "two from the plant died in the crash, but this is everyone else."

Nichole added, "We wouldn't have been able to get the injured out of the wreckage and up here to cover without their help." Josh nodded. He was glad these people were alive, but he was also painfully aware now that he and Isaac weren't going to be able to get everyone out of here.

Duff was in the process of trying to figure out a game plan, but while doing so, Martin Mensah pushed through the foliage and stepped up to Isaac. He spoke English, likely, Duff decided, for the benefit of the Americans. "Sergeant. What is the status of the dam?"

"When I left there were thirty-five or more RIVCOM, including the captain. We knew of no enemy inside the dam complex, but they were beginning a search."

Mensah nodded. "And the bombs?"

Duff said, "The bombs are still there, but I have the computer with the detonation codes. The power is off at the facility, though."

To this Mensah cocked his head. "*Off?* Why?"

"A pair of RPG blasts to the switchyard. The lights went out immediately."

Mensah put his hand on his head. Softly, he said, "I have to get back there."

Chad said, "Duff, you and Isaac pick the three strongest here, and get the ambo back to Accra."

"I'm not leaving you."

The man on his side waved his hand in the air. "We've got five people who absolutely can't walk, myself included."

Duff said, "We'll fit as many as we can in the truck; I'll have to come back for the others."

Chad shook his head now. "You have to leave all the incapacitated here except for the ambo. Take her, Ben, Malike, and Nichole, and get out of here."

Duff shook his head. "We can get more wounded out."

"No. Everyone is stable enough. Leave me one long gun."

Chad had been in DS for five years longer than Duff, and he was the senior of the two men. With Jay dead, Chad was in charge.

"Look," Duff pressed, "I don't know how long—"

Isaac spoke now. "There are big cats out here. Hippo by the river. Snakes. Other dangers."

Larsen waved a hand and put his other hand on the pistol resting on his chest. "I'm not worried about a fucking snake."

Dunnigan spoke up now, her voice a little slurred by the opioid coursing through her. "Do I get a vote here?"

Duff knew that the actual answer to this question was no. Diplomatic Security could, in some cases, pull rank on an ambassador in matters pertaining to their security. But he also knew Chad wasn't about to do that.

Larsen said, "Ma'am, I think we need—"

"Let's take as many as we possibly can. Once we get to safety, we'll send others back here to pick up the rest."

A female hydroelectric plant worker called out to them from higher on the hill. "Lights in the trees, that way."

Duff shut off his flashlight; Isaac did the same. They looked down the hill and saw an unmistakable flickering.

Isaac said, "Those are headlights on the road. Looks like at least four vehicles, maybe five. Worst-case scenario is forty opposition, but maybe they will drive past."

Duff shook his head. "They'll see our truck, they'll stop, and they'll eventually find the trail we cut."

He said, "Isaac. How do we get out of here?"

The sergeant just shrugged and said, "I have no idea. I've never been off the road here."

"I thought you lived here."

"I didn't grow up in the jungle, man. I grew up in a town on the other side of the river. The N2 highway is to the east. I'm not sure how far, but it can't be more than a couple of kilometers. If we can find it and get some vehicles, we can take that south, over the Adomi Bridge, and then all the way to the capital."

Chad spoke up now. "We're not moving this bunch a couple of kilometers."

"Okay . . ." Duff said, and he looked to Mensah. "Can you and your people build us five stretchers?"

Martin looked around. "Yes, of course, but I will need more material from the crash site."

Ben and Malike volunteered to take him back down to the wreckage.

Chad looked to Duff now. "What are you thinking?"

"We have to be ready to move."

Chad nodded. "Let's get off the X."

CONRAD TREMAINE SAT IN HIS TRUCK WITH HIS TWO SENTINEL MEN while eight rebels from Second Platoon's Bravo squad entered the jungle and disappeared into the darkness.

A security team from Charlie squad stood in the rain on the road around the mercenaries' vehicle.

Junior spoke up over the sound of the storm beating on the roof of the Toyota. "We placing bets?"

"Even money," Tremaine said.

When they came across the RIVCOM truck on the bridge ten minutes earlier, they knew the crash site must be close, but Krelis had suggested that whoever was here probably would not park right alongside the crash. The lack of tracks in front of the truck meant the vehicle hadn't turned around and come back, so they all took that to mean it had passed the helicopter and then whoever was inside the pickup had debussed and gone back on foot.

They immediately radioed the Dragons' vehicles, and then the entire five-vehicle convoy backed up, powerful flashlight beams sweeping across both sides of the road, looking for fresh-cut jungle brush that would indicate someone had burrowed their way in.

It took time, but the rear vehicle eventually spotted just such a disturbance on the northern side, and the Delta squad leader called into the radio for the trucks to halt.

Now the search squad disappeared from the Sentinel men's view; the four who carried flashlights were still visible for a moment, but soon even their lights no longer penetrated the trees.

The Liberian with the call sign of Copper stepped up to Krelis's side of the truck, and the Dutchman lowered his window. "Who did you send?"

"Eight men. Bravo." Copper shrugged. "You want me to go with them?"

Tremaine shook his head in the front passenger seat. "Not in the first wave. If they can manage to suppress any threats, we'll follow them up. For now, just stand by. We need to find out if Duffy was on board, and we need to recover the tablet." He sniffed. "Can't trust the Dragons to do that right."

"Who's Duffy?"

"He's the one who could fuck this all up. Keep security on this road."

Copper nodded and headed back to his truck, shouting at rebels along the route and ordering them to stand guard in the dark rainy night.

Behind Tremaine, Junior said, "How do you suppose that RIV-COM truck found the helicopter?"

"Got to figure they just drove around till they got into radio range."

"That means someone's alive at the crash site."

"Exactly."

They listened to the radio comms of the men heading up; the squad leader reported that the small trail blazed by the arrivals from the RIVCOM truck was narrow and steep in places.

Tremaine said, "I see this going one of two ways. Either those eight Dragons heading up there are going to overrun the survivors, and this'll be over quick, or else we're gonna hear a real fucking fight. And if the fight is real enough, that tells me that Josh Duffy is up there."

Krelis said, "This Duffy . . . he's a warrior?"

Tremaine chuckled. "He's one of those men who's as cool as a cucumber until the fight starts."

"And when it starts?"

"Then he's a fucking maniac."

From the back seat Junior said, "So . . . touched in the head, you mean."

"A complete head case," Tremaine confirmed.

MARTIN MENSAH AND SEVERAL OTHERS WORKED IN THE HEAVY rain fabricating stretchers for the wounded. They wrapped cordage around small tree limbs and tied netting to it, and although Duff wished they'd hurry up, he was damn sure they were working faster and making better stretchers than he'd be able to.

Larsen spoke from where he lay on his side on the ground now. "Duff, have you tried your sat phone?"

Dunnigan clarified. "We can't get to either of our two units. They're both apparently somewhere under the helo."

Duff pulled out his Iridium phone. He assumed comms were still being jammed, but he hadn't checked since leaving the dam.

He started to dial the ARSO back at the embassy, but then he decided to call someone else. He was doubtful he'd make any connection; all his previous attempts in the truck had been failures, but to his utter astonishment, the phone began to ring. He put his finger in his left ear to drown out the rain and pushed the phone up to his right, and he walked away from the rest of the group.

After a few rings he heard a click on the line. "Gorski."

"Bob, it's ARSO Duffy."

"Jesus Christ, Duffy. Are you guys safe?"

"We are so fucking *not* safe I can't even tell you . . . We've got dead and injured, and we're still on the X."

"Who's dead?"

"Aldenburg. All her people. I mean, check the river, but there's no fucking way anybody survived that crash."

"Son of a bitch! Crash?"

"The president's flight made it away from the dam, but the other two helos weren't that lucky. The EU group fell a thousand feet into the Volta. I'm with the wreckage of the aircraft the Americans were in. Dunnigan is hurt but alive; Costa's dead. Larsen looks pretty fucked up to me, but I guess he'll pull through."

"My God. What is happening?"

Duff's emotions got the best of him now. "I wouldn't know, to be honest, because I'm hiding in the fucking jungle in the middle of a thunderstorm."

Gorski said, "What you guys are in? It's part of some larger-scale coordinated attack. The power's out in the city, and some force is attacking police and military targets. They've got RPGs, mortars, assault rifles. My people in the street tell me they think they are JNIM, likely from Nigeria."

Duff said, "Well, up here it's rebels from Togoland we're dealing with . . . we think. Plus, you were right about Tremaine. I talked to him over the radio. He's running all this."

Gorski whistled. "I fucking knew it. What's their play?"

"Unknown, but one of the mercs said the army wouldn't respond to the dam because they'd soon have more to deal with than they could handle."

"Meaning the attacks around here?"

"I don't think so. Accra is a couple hours away; the military down there wouldn't be the first responders to a crisis at the dam."

"You have a way of reaching out to Tremaine still?"

"Affirmative, but I don't want him to know anyone survived the crash. It's a long shot—he doesn't strike me as the type to just give up searching for us—but at the moment we don't have a better strategy."

"Good thinking." Gorski hesitated, then said, "There's another player in this."

"What do you mean?"

"Tremaine isn't the strategic brains of something this big. He's a merc leader; he's not going to bring in jihadists, recruit rebels on his own. There's a Chinese intelligence officer I've been tracking across the continent for years. I think he's involved, but I can't get anyone here or at Langley to listen to me about China."

"Where is he?"

"He fell off the map in Sierra Leone some time back, haven't picked him up since. When Tremaine was seen in Togo last month, I came here on a hunch that something was brewing, and this Chinese guy was somehow involved. As soon as the shooting started tonight, I thought this might have been the opening play in a coup, so I sent a group from Accra station over to the Chinese embassy to look for any special activity. It looks like it's buttoned down tightly, so I'm thinking my guy has some other operations center.

"Believe me," Gorski said, "what's going on has all the fingerprints of an operation by this guy and his people."

"How so?"

"The social media stuff pumping up Professor Addo and the Togoland rebels. The hacking of the Internet providers and national cell carrier. I'd bet my life it's him, and I'd bet my life that he's here."

"Here, in Ghana?"

"Here, in Accra. That's how he did it in the Central African Republic and Sierra Leone. He likes to be close to the action to oversee it all, like he's a conductor on a stage."

Isaac appeared in the rain next to Duff, a worried look on his face. "More lights. Coming this way."

Duff said, "Bob, we might be a few minutes away from a firefight. If I come out on the other side, I'll call you back when I can."

"You just worry about yourself and your people. I'll let DS know about your situation."

"Last thing, Bob. Do you know the status of all the dependents?"

"Yeah, everything is fine on that front. One of the Accra station analysts was just telling me that all the residences are secure, everybody is accounted for in the city."

"What about Iris Gardens?"

"I've been staying at the Movenpick hotel, using radios to communicate, and I haven't been to any of the residences myself. I'm just telling you what I heard."

He added, "Don't worry about your kids, they're safe and sound."

"Any chance of getting military assets into the region?"

"So far, nothing. Sigonella air base can have planes here in five hours, plus the time it takes to muster assets there, but the comms are so bad right now and the picture so opaque in the city, that order hasn't come through. There have been no direct threats to the embassy or personnel, so everyone's waiting to see if this is going to blow over."

Duff said, "Fucking stupid."

"Agreed. But no one has sounded the alarm about the ambo yet. I'll do that the second I get off the phone with you, and hopefully that will get aircraft en route."

"It's a no-brainer, Bob. They've got to bring in the Marines."

"Yeah, well, Benghazi was a no-brainer, too, and look what happened. Good luck, kid, you're on your own for now."

Duff hung up, secured the sat phone in his backpack, then headed back to the group to find Chad sitting up somehow and looking down the hill. "Those aren't headlights," he said. "They're flashlights. Troops are searching the jungle."

Duff agreed with Chad's assessment. "We're going to have to make a stand."

"Shit," Dunnigan said, her voice still slurred.

Nichole moved closer to her husband. "Josh. Those lights . . . you don't know those are enemy. It could be a rescue."

Duff realized she was right. He immediately opened his pack again, pulled out the radio he'd taken from the dead Russian, then turned it on. After several seconds of hearing nothing, a voice crackled, speaking English with a Ghanaian accent. "We're close, I can smell burned plastic, probably the electrical wires."

A reply came soon after, "Understood, continue."

It was the voice of Conrad Tremaine.

Duff turned the volume of the radio down and dropped it back into the pack reluctantly; he wanted the intelligence he could glean from listening to the enemy's comms, but he didn't have an earpiece for the unit, and he didn't want the speaker to give their position away.

Larsen looked to him now. "All right." He turned to Dunnigan. "Duffy is now the agent in charge of your detail."

Duff looked to Nichole, concern on both of their faces, but she nodded to him.

He said, "It's going to take them a few minutes to get to the heli-copter. I'll take Isaac, Ben, and Malike and head down there, give them a reception. Everybody else stay up here, no lights, no noise."

To Nichole, he said, "Take Isaac's trauma pack and do whatever you can to stabilize the injuries for a move through the jungle."

She nodded. "I'll splint the broken bones, get everyone taped up, at least." But before she moved away to begin, she said, "But you don't know how many enemy there are. How can you—"

Duff said, "It doesn't matter. We'll deal with it. Once we get some stretchers made we can start moving the wounded, but that's going to take some more time. We need vehicles and gear. There's only one place around here where we're going to get vehicles and gear."

Dunnigan was a little slower than the others because of the med-icine. "Where?"

Duff said, "At some point we'll have to figure out how to go down there and take a couple of those trucks."

Nichole cocked her head. "How do you know they're trucks?"

"You haven't seen that road."

THIRTY-THREE

DUFF, BEN, MALIKE, AND ISAAC MADE IT TO THE CLEARING CUT BY the helo crash, and they spread out at the northern edge of it, each finding a tree to hide behind. Duff looked around the side of the meter-wide trunk and down the hill in the pouring rain.

The approaching flashlight beams danced through the trees, glistened off wide palm fronds, sparkled the water that had pooled here and there on the green jungle floor. Duff could tell the enemy was close, just ten yards or so from making it into the clearing. In seconds the rebels would see the helo, and then all hell would break loose.

He counted four distinct beams, and he hoped that meant there were only four shooters here to investigate the crash, although he knew he couldn't count on that.

The four defenders had no way to communicate with one another other than by gunfire; the rain made whispering impossible, but Duff knew there wasn't really anything left to coordinate. He'd established himself and Isaac as one fire team, responsible for covering for one another during reloads, and Malike and Ben constituted the other fire team. Everyone was separated with five yards or so between them, and Duff thought this was just about as good an ambush as anyone could form in these conditions and with this amount of time.

At the last moment before the lights made it into the clearing, Duff tucked back around his tree. He assumed the other men would do the same, and they would wait for his first shot to begin their attack.

He heard voices; they weren't speaking English or Russian, that much he knew, and he focused on them, waiting for them to get as close as possible.

A flashlight beam shone right on the opposite side of the tree he was using for cover, its flood sending long shadows deeper into the jungle behind him. He stayed frozen in place until the beam moved on, sweeping over towards the downed aircraft.

Finally, Duff shouldered his rifle, stepped out from behind the tree just far enough to get his weapon up, and dropped to a knee. Aiming at the closest light, he thumbed off his safety and opened fire.

Almost simultaneously the other three men did the same. The reports rocked the jungle hillside, return fire sparked, and Josh just tucked tighter behind the tree while still revealing the right side of his body so that he could fight effectively.

Isaac's AK's lower report told him his new friend was using disciplined fire, and the two M4s held by Ben and Malike spit out three-round bursts.

He saw one flashlight beam spin in the air and then extinguish, and then a second beam and a third fell to the ground and remained on, but the man with the fourth light turned his off as he got behind the helo.

He was invisible now, and Duff knew he'd have to turn on his own weapon light to find him, but before he could do so, more shooting erupted.

Quickly Duff realized there were more than four men down there. Several muzzle flashes came out of the dark, away from the light beams.

Isaac called, "Cover!" indicating to Duff that he needed to reload, but Duff's weapon ran dry at the same instant, so he dropped the weapon, pulled the Beretta, and kept shooting into the clearing below him.

He'd expended almost an entire magazine when Isaac opened up with his AK again, giving Duff the opportunity to reload.

He spun behind the tree to do so, then shifted to the opposite side, dropping to his left knee now and leaning out around the trunk.

He saw one muzzle flash behind the helicopter, detected movement through a broken window, and realized the shooter there hadn't positioned himself behind the big engine of the machine for cover.

Duff flipped his selector switch to fully automatic fire and sent a spray of rounds into the soft skin of the aircraft. After he stopped, he detected no more return fire coming his way.

Duff flipped on his weapon light, swept it over the clearing, and counted five dead. There had been more than five shooters, of this he was certain, so he ducked back behind the tree, knowing if anyone still alive had remaining ammunition they would fire at his new light source.

But no one shot back.

In under sixty seconds it was over. Duff turned his light back on and took in the entire scene. He didn't see any more bodies but imagined the others might be tucked into the opposite tree line, dead or incapacitated, and he didn't want to go looking for them.

He pulled the Russian's radio from his belt and turned it on with the volume low, then held it close to his ear.

Tremaine's voice sent a chill down his spine. "Bravo squad, report." When no response came, he transmitted again. "Alpha squad. You're up."

Ben and Malike rejoined Duff and Isaac, and together the four men headed into the clearing to collect as many of the enemy's guns and ammunition as they could grab before hurrying back to the others. Duff stepped up to the first body and used the barrel of the rifle to jab the man in the solar plexus to check for movement.

Once he'd confirmed the man was dead, he knelt over him and took his AK off his neck and the two full magazines from his rack. He was about to stand back up when he realized the man had a high-explosive frag grenade attached to his vest.

Duff took it off, then went around to the others, collected ammo and frags, and soon the men were leaving the scene of the carnage, heading back up the hill.

CONRAD TREMAINE HAD JUST ORDERED COPPER TO SEND EIGHT more men up to the crash site, but then a thought occurred to him. He turned to Junior in the back seat. "I want you to go find Copper on the road here, tell him to turn to channel forty-four. Tell all the squad leaders left.

"Fucking Duff is up there," Tremaine explained, "and he's still got Belov's radio."

"Right," Junior said. Tremaine himself got out and stood in the rain a moment, seething with rage.

He should have been on the way to Accra by now, coordinating with his other forces, doing his best to keep the Dragons intact until they got to the capital.

But instead he was here, standing in the mud, looking up at a black hill and wondering how the hell he had the misfortune of running into Josh Duffy tonight of all nights.

Tremaine was angry, but he wasn't overly concerned. Belov losing the computer had been a fuckup brought on by a series of unfortunate events, but there were twenty-four rebels and four mercs here, and no matter who Duff had with him at that crash site, no matter if a couple of RIVCOM guys made it up there to support them, no matter what—Tremaine knew he'd be standing over Duff's dead body soon enough, holding the computer in his hands.

Junior returned a minute later. "Copper, Charlie, and Delta have all changed channels. Alpha is on the hill, still using the old frequency."

Tremaine clicked the mic. "Charlie, this is Condor. Follow Alpha up the hill, double time. Move through their trails, and you'll catch up to them. When you do, tell them to change to forty-four."

"Charlie understands."

Then Tremaine clicked the talk button again. "Copper, I want everyone else pulling security on this road. Whoever is left up there might try to make it back down to score a vehicle."

When Copper confirmed the order, Tremaine looked to his two men standing by the truck with him. "You guys keep monitoring forty-four for updates, I'm going to stay on twenty-four and talk to Duff."

"Talk to him?" Junior asked, but Tremaine turned away and began walking up the road towards the RIVCOM car on the other side of the bridge.

ALL FIVE SURVIVORS OF THE HELICOPTER CRASH WHO WEREN'T AMbulatory had been placed on makeshift stretchers made from limbs and vines from the forest floor and cordage and netting and tarps pulled from the helicopter. There were a few ropes, nets, hand tools, and other items left over, and Duff told Martin they couldn't leave anything behind that might make it easier for the enemy to track them. The deputy plant operator and several of his employees hung equipment over their shoulders, crammed tools into their pockets, and stuffed more into Duff's backpack, and even blood-soaked discarded bandages were scooped up and stowed, and soon everyone was ready to move.

Normally there would be one person on each of the four ends to lift and carry each stretcher, but Duff didn't have twenty people, he had thirteen, so he put four women on a litter carrying a wounded plant worker, Ben and Malike took the ambassador, two dam workers carried Chad Larsen, and Nichole and Duff carried Foreign Service Officer Arletta James. Another plant worker was carried by the remaining three of his colleagues.

All the badly injured except for Larsen had been given morphine, and now most of them were unconscious.

They took off to the east, moving parallel to the highway, and Isaac led the way, with the flashlight in one hand and his machete in the other. Duff trudged along just behind him at the front of the litter.

He'd heard the transmission between the rebels and the mercenary commander down at the road, and this had told him he had about ten minutes before the second wave of attackers would make it up to the crash site. He knew his entourage wouldn't be able to move fast at all, but he hoped ten minutes covering as much ground as possible would put them fifty yards away or so, and if the attacking rebels had trouble finding their trail in the darkness, it might just buy them some time.

In front of him, Isaac swung the blade as hard as he could, chopping his way through vines and leaves. Duff himself stamped down on more brush to clear the way at least a little so that everyone carrying wounded would be able to pass without stumbling.

After five minutes Duff decided to check the Russian's radio to see if he could tell how far away the enemy were, so he put down the litter, pulled the walkie-talkie from his pack, and turned the volume up.

Almost immediately, he heard a familiar voice. "Condor for Duff, over. Condor for Duff."

Fuck, he thought. Tremaine knew, or at least suspected, that he was here.

"Condor for Duff, over."

He began moving again, but faster, hooking the radio back on his sling by his face so he could keep the volume low.

Tremaine said, "I know you are out here and in transmission range." When Duff did not respond, the man said, "You've been listening to us, haven't you? Bloody good job."

Duff told himself not to respond, though he felt the urge to press the talk button and scream at the South African.

"Crazy day, eh?" Tremaine said. "You're racking up one hell of a body count tonight, brother. Must feel like the Middle East. Or Mexico."

Still, Duff did not respond, he just followed Isaac and led the others.

"You always were an odd one. A nice bloke, a people pleaser, but a killer, as well. And kid, from what I just heard up there, you haven't changed a bit."

He was trying to bait Duff into a conversation for some reason, and Duff told himself he wasn't going to oblige him.

Behind Duff, Nichole said, "Just ignore him, Josh."

But Tremaine's words were as unrelenting as the rain. "Don't go quiet on me, mate. We had ourselves a good chat earlier.

"Hey, do you know how I *know* you can hear me? What just happened up there on that hill . . . that wasn't the work of diplomatic security, presidential troops, or EU bodyguards. No, mate. That was a full-on ambush planned by and carried out by a cutthroat killer. An old-school merc. Maybe you had help, but your devil brain is running this. And if you're up there, you are *definitely* listening to our radio comms."

The Americans and Ghanaians kept trudging along. A howler monkey cried higher on the hill; Isaac moved a huge spiderweb covered with raindrops out of the others' path with the tip of his machete.

Tremaine continued. "There was that time in J-Bad . . . you, me, Gordon, Caruth. Remember? The Tali had us cornered, a technical with a mounted PK taking shots at the wall we hid behind. Chewing it into nothing. We were about to be overrun, I was about to put my fucking pistol in my mouth, we were done for. You, alone, made it across open ground to another PK. You turned those motherfuckers to paste like it was no big deal.

"You wasted half the lot. We lost Caruth . . . a tough break, but you got us out of there."

Duff did not respond. He remembered that hot afternoon in Afghanistan; variations of it still showed up in his dreams from time to time.

"And still," Tremaine continued. "Duff . . . that evening, after we got back to the compound . . . you were like it never even happened. You acted like the easiest-going bloke back in the team room. No thousand-yard stare, no fifth of Jack, no crying into your pillow. You were mad at me, we'd had ourselves a row back at the sight of the firefight, but later on? I watched you pig out on red beans and rice and enjoy a sitcom on the telly, just another day.

"Everything you did . . . that day and a dozen others just like it. You bottled that shit up, compartmentalized it, forced it down, deep in your belly, so people would think you weren't the sick fuck that you are. But I saw it. I *know* what you are."

Duff was painfully aware that Nichole was just a couple of yards behind him and she could hear every word.

"Tell me, mate," Tremaine continued. "You over the night sweats from what happened in Afghanistan? In Syria? In Lebanon? Maybe that shit that went down in the Sierra Madres has replaced the Middle East in your nightmares, eh? Maybe what happened tonight will cover up Mexico?"

Isaac kept chopping, and Duff kept tamping down limbs and vines and brush as he carried the stretcher. The work focused Duff, pulled at least a part of his conscious brain away from the man on the other end of the radio.

"I know guys like you," Tremaine continued. "Good at their jobs, but not cut out for this work. You're kicking some ass in some African backwater, and if you walk out of here, which you won't, you'll have a lot of people buying your beers and slapping your back.

"But what comes after, mate? Blokes like me . . . we like the memories. We *live* for the memories. But you, Duff? You aren't cut out to handle the repercussions of all your bloody killing. You're not an assassin. You're just a man in over his head."

Duff kept walking; he winced thinking about the decision he was making, but then he stopped. "Isaac. Switch with me."

Behind him, Nichole just said, "Josh. No."

Isaac took the litter; Duff took the machete with one hand and pressed down on the mic button with the other. "Thanks for the therapy, Tremaine. Why don't you come up here and I'll give *you* some treatment?"

Nichole called to him. "Josh. Stop talking to him. It's what he wants."

A flashlight's beam danced through the trees from somewhere far behind them, breaking Duff out of his momentary lapse of reason. He continued moving forward.

Tremaine said, "There's a way out of this for you and anyone with you. I want that bloody computer. You find a way to give it to me and I'll leave."

Duff kept trudging through the brush in the rain. He said, "I've got bad news, Condor. Your Russian was carrying the tablet in his admin pouch on his chest. When I put a dozen rounds in him I shot right through it, destroyed it."

"That's too bad. Come show me and we'll have a laugh about it."

The light moving behind them seemed to increase, as if the enemy had found their trail and were pursuing faster now.

"Going to have to pass. Look, man, the CIA knows about your Chinese friend, your jihadists attacking in Accra. They know you are here. If I were you, I would worry less about this computer and more about getting the fuck out of Ghana."

The pause was longer this time, and through it Duff thought he heard a new sound ahead. Water, but not just the rain. Flowing water, like a river.

Finally Tremaine spoke again. "I don't know what you're talking about, Duff. There's no Chinese, no jihadis. It's just you and me here."

Duff stopped the ragtag column, and they all put down their stretchers. He pulled out his flashlight, put his hand over the lens, and turned it on. Via the glow through his fingers he could see a powerful stream running downhill. It was maybe forty feet wide, swiftly moving, as if it were an existing creek carrying extra runoff from the storm from higher on the hill.

"Duff?" Tremaine said. "You receiving? Listen up, I need you to write a phone number down."

Duff clicked the mic. "Gotta be honest, man. I don't have a pencil."

"Cute. Well, then, scratch it on your arm with Belov's blood."

"Why? What number?"

"A number you are going to want to have in your possession come tomorrow, just in case you make it off that hill."

Duff pulled out his phone and jotted the number down in his note app. He didn't want to give the man any ammunition, didn't want to indicate a vulnerability, so he made no more threats. He just said, "Does this mean you're going to stop chasing us tonight?"

"No, it does not. You know what I want. If you somehow get clear of the men I have after you here, if you get away, you might want to call that number."

"Why?"

"So you and I can have a private conversation, and you and I can come to an agreement."

"What agreement?"

"You give me what I need, and you never hear from me again."

"There's no way I'm giving you the detonation codes back."

"You will if the price is right."

"No amount of money will ever—"

"I'm not talking about money. Condor out."

An icy chill went up the back of Duff's neck. He didn't know what Tremaine knew, but if the Chinese were involved, he was certain they would be able to find out he had children living here in Ghana.

Duff thought about his kids, and he looked back to Nichole. It was obvious she was thinking the same thing.

Gravely, she said, "We've got to get home, Josh."

He stowed the radio, went back to Chad, knelt down next to him, and saw the lights from behind getting closer still. He said, "There's a stream running down the hill, a strong current, but maybe not too strong. Those rebels are going to overrun us in less than five minutes unless we do something crazy."

"Like what?"

"I want to try to use this water to get us out of here."

"Do we know where this stream goes?"

"We left the truck next to a little bridge. I'm hoping this takes us there. If not . . . well . . . at least it will take us away from here."

Martin Mensah had overheard. "It could kill us all."

Nichole said, "Even if it does take us to the road, there will be rebels down there. Mercenaries, too."

Duff nodded. "That's true, we're going to have to fight to get out of here, but I'd rather fight down there."

Lightning flashed and Nichole saw the stream for the first time now. Softly, she said, "You make it sound so easy."

He whispered to her, "That's because I don't fucking know what I'm doing."

Nichole put her arm around him as they both looked at the rushing water. "You've got this."

To her alone, he shook his head and whispered, "I really *don't* know what the fuck I am doing, Nik. I just can't think of anything else."

"I believe in you."

Everyone else gathered around closely now, with Ben and Malike each holding their rifles up to their shoulders, pointing them back in the direction of the flickering lights. Duff said, "We're going to have to get in the water and take the current down the hill. It doesn't look too rough . . . not here, anyway. I'll go alone first, try to put a line up just on the other side of the bridge, maybe two hundred yards or so down the hill. As close to the surface as I can. Once you pass the bridge, grab the line and get out of the water."

Duff sighed and looked at the lights coming his way. It seemed as if they were spreading apart, like the approaching shooters were now finding different routes through the jungle so they could attack on a wider front than just the tiny broken trail this group of thirteen had created.

To the others he said, "This is going to suck, but it beats the alternative. Everybody hold on to the injured on the litters, or hold on to each other. I'm going to go first, along with the flashlight."

The ambassador seemed to wake up a little, and she looked up at Duff. "What if I can't see the bridge?"

Duff smiled a little. "When the rain stops for about two seconds, that means you just went under it."

Dunnigan nodded. "Got it."

"But ma'am, you got some medicine for the pain, and that's going to make you sluggish. Ben and Malike will be with you; let one of them worry about the line, you just try to stay on that stretcher."

To the group he said, "Once we get down there, everyone needs to remain quiet. There will be rebels on the road. We can deal with them, but not if we don't have surprise working for us."

He looked to Martin. "I need some rope." The deputy plant manager pulled a coil of nylon cordage from the duffel bag and handed it over.

Nichole said, "Josh, what about your leg?"

He took out his knife and cut about six feet from the end of the cord. This he wrapped tightly around his left leg, just below the knee. Tying it off, he looked back up to her. "That should hold. Not much else I can do for now."

To the group he said, "Give me about a thirty-second head start so I'll have time to secure the line down there." He looked to his wife. "Good luck."

The sound of shouting came from the west; the lights were bright now, the enemy was closing, not more than a couple minutes away.

Nichole mouthed, *I love you*, and then he stepped in. He had to work to find his balance; this was made all the more difficult because of his prosthesis.

He got about a third of the way across the stream; the water was to his waist there, then he turned around. He could see the silhouettes of the group through the approaching flashlights through the trees. He tried to hold his ground a moment more, to make it to the center of the stream, but just as the others began pulling the litters made of netting in, a heavier gush of rainwater from higher on the hill knocked both his legs out from under him and he began drifting quickly to the south.

THIRTY-FOUR

KANG SHIKUN SIPPED A HIGHLAND SINGLE MALT SCOTCH AS HE SAT at his desk looking out the open balcony door, his eyes on the city to the south. The darkness was profound; a light rain continued to fall, and the clouds blocked out the moonlight.

Hajj Zahedi's people had been fighting across Accra for over three hours, and Kang could see fires burning in various parts of the city. He'd received reports from his people that the police were fighting defensively, not offensively, that the streets were all but empty, and that the extremists had inflicted damage on troops from Southern Command, as well.

In contrast to nearly everything that seemed to be going wrong for Kang's plan at the hydroelectric dam, everything seemed to be going right on the road to Accra. Kang had just received a series of short-wave messages from his Chinese operatives in the field, reporting that Sentinel and the Dragons of Western Togoland were moving south in two columns on two highways and meeting little resistance, owing principally to the lack of effective communications throughout the nation.

He took another sip of the single malt, and Chen Jia came into the office and brought him a report that he'd asked for earlier. It was just a single sheet of paper, but he did not take the time to read it, he just put it on his desk.

She turned to return to her workstation, but he called out to her. "Miss?"

"Xiansheng?"

"Are you ill?"

She turned back to him, avoiding eye contact. "No, sir. I am fine."

He looked at her a moment more. She appeared drawn, pale. "Are you taking your malaria pills?"

She nodded nervously, her eyes still averted from his. "Every morning, sir."

"And your yellow fever vaccination?"

"Received in Beijing two weeks before I flew here, sir."

He continued evaluating her for a moment more.

"Is . . . is there something else?" she asked.

The satellite phone rang on his desk. "No. Thank you," he said, looking down at the number on the screen.

Jia left the room as Kang answered the phone with a statement. "I want to hear that you have taken care of your problem, and you are now back on course, moving towards Accra."

Conrad Tremaine, however, had his own demand. "I need you to tell me about the attacks going on in the city."

Kang furrowed his brow. He wondered how Tremaine knew and, more importantly, just *what* Tremaine knew. He said, "I am hearing the same reports. Some sort of a violent demonstration, obviously brought on by the power outages."

"A violent demonstration? Those are jihadists."

"Where did you hear that?"

"From the CIA."

Kang took a slow sip of his scotch. "So . . . now you are in communication with the CIA?"

"Of course not. But I talked to Duffy. He says the Agency knows about Sentinel, about China's involvement, and about the Nigerian extremists in the city now wreaking havoc."

Kang said, "If the Agency knows about Sentinel, then it knows, or will eventually know, that your force is made up primarily of former Wagnerites. Russians attached to the Ministry of Defense. Everything that points them towards China, the social media campaigns, the jamming, the hacking . . . we've left Russian forensic fingerprints. Moscow will take the fall, not China.

"Now," Kang continued, "if they know *your* name . . . then that is a problem for you. So if there is anyone who can prove you are here, then you might want to make sure they don't live to tell."

Tremaine did not respond to Kang's advice. Instead he said, "Don't bullshit me, mate. You . . . you knew about these attacks in the capital. No . . . you *planned* this."

Kang replied coolly. "General Boatang will be here in the morning. If Southern Command hasn't completely routed these fighters by then, Central Command will do so when they take the streets."

"Why didn't you bloody tell me there was another front to this coup?"

"I needed you to focus on your job. Apparently, even without the knowledge of the additional activity down here, you are having trouble with your mission."

Tremaine said, "You're using jihadi savages? Indiscriminately killing?"

"I'm not using them."

"Bullshit. You control my force, you control Addo's force, there is absolutely no way you can convince me that the other force that just happens to be attacking at the same time isn't under your control."

Kang shrugged, bored with the conversation. "I can't convince you, fine. Perhaps they saw the opportunity arise once they found out about the assassinations of the EU personnel." With a little smile, Kang said, "So maybe it was you who brought this on."

"Bullshit. Ghana doesn't have an armed extremist force in their Muslim population. Those motherfuckers came from Burkina or Nigeria."

"Well . . . if you run into one of them on the street, why don't you ask him for his passport?"

"You knew I wouldn't agree to work with you if I knew we were in bed with the jihadis."

Kang remained unfazed. "We are both committed to this now, Mr. Tremaine. I suggest we work together to see this through."

The South African sighed into the phone, then said, "Did you get me the information I asked for?"

Kang reached to his desk, picked up the single sheet of paper Jia had just left, and lowered his reading glasses down over his eyes. Looking it over a moment, he said, "The State Department employee you referenced. Duffy, Joshua. He has been here in Accra just two weeks. Previously, he worked in the Washington, D.C., area. His wife, Nichole Duffy, is a Foreign Service Officer at the embassy, as well."

"What else?"

Reading down, Kang said, "He has a prosthetic limb. His left leg below the knee was amputated six years ago."

"That doesn't help me."

Kang did not know exactly what Tremaine was looking for, but as he kept scanning, he found the part of this file on the new assistant regional security officer the Sentinel mercenary would be most interested in.

"I have his home address in the Cantonments neighborhood. And I see that he has two dependents."

One word came over the satellite connection. "Kids?"

"Yes. A girl, aged nine. Name, Amanda. And a boy, aged six. Name, Harold." After a pause, Kang said, "But if you have any illusions about—"

Tremaine interrupted. "I will get back on mission, Kang. Right now. I'll leave this platoon up here to finish the job, and I'll be on my way to the capital."

Kang made a face of annoyance, a rare show of emotion from the man. "I do not need any more setbacks."

Tremaine ended the call; Kang sat there with his scotch and stared out at the black night. Flickering sparkles of light three kilometers to the southwest hinted at a furious gun battle between Zahedi's proxies and some police or military unit near Burma Camp, the main installation of Southern Command, but Kang looked away and turned his head to the north, waiting for his rebels to arrive.

And then for Boatang's soldiers from Kumasi to come down and slay them.

FOR THE FIRST TIME IN THE PAST SEVERAL HOURS JOSH DUFFY REalized he wasn't worried about getting shot.

Drowning, breaking his neck, getting lost in the jungle till he starved, leading a group of individuals, including the wife he loved, to their doom . . . these were all his concerns now.

A bullet to the brain seemed almost inconsequential to him.

He lay on his back as he floated down the swift stream, the pack he took from the dead Russian in the dam providing him some measure of buoyancy, aiding him as he tried to hold the flashlight with the same hand that covered the lens.

He slowed a moment following the course of the water, but soon his legs brushed rock, and he heard the sound of crashing farther down. He realized he was heading for some rapids, so he just tucked tighter and prayed.

A flash of lightning showed him he was surrounded on both sides by thick jungle, but he couldn't see around a bend in the stream just below him.

His body followed the flow, then went over a small ledge, dropped no more than five feet, and at the bottom of it Duff went under.

The rifle on his back slammed into rock below him, and his left forearm got snagged by a branch, slicing a three-inch gash.

He screamed in pain and inhaled a gulp of the cool water, then began tumbling down another set of rapids, only his waterproof backpack keeping him up near the surface.

As scary as all this was, it was all the more terrifying because he knew eighteen people would be coming this way in moments, and many of them had horrible injuries.

He rolled himself onto his back again, clutching the pack on his chest, his rifle now dragging on the bottom of the stream, held to Duff only by the end of a broken sling that had gotten caught in the buckles of the pack.

Rain poured on his face, and he squinted into it as he continued to sail downstream.

And then he saw a light.

He'd been in the water no more than three minutes when the bridge appeared; the headlights of a vehicle somewhere on the road off to his right illuminated the top of it, but he saw no one standing there, nor could he even see Isaac's truck.

He began trying to position himself so he would float nearer the eastern bank on his left; he went under the bridge and, just on the other side, he flipped onto his stomach and began kicking furiously for the shore, trying to find something to hang on to.

Twenty yards south of the bridge he made it to slower water near the bank, and here he pulled himself ashore. He found his footing on his good leg, then picked his way quickly out of the current, pulling out the nylon cable as he did so. He found a sturdy branch by feeling around in the darkness, then put the end of the rope around it, just above where it emerged from the rocks and mud. Softly he spoke to himself as he tied the bowline knot. "Rabbit comes up out of the hole, runs around the tree, back down in its hole."

The end secure, he went back into the water and lost his footing quickly; his right knee jabbed a sharp stone, and then he tumbled. Swimming as hard as he could, he still floated over twenty yards downstream before he reached the other side, but here he grabbed onto a boulder, pulled himself out, and found another strong limb to tie around.

When he was finished, he had a diagonal line just inches above the water; anyone passing would be able to grab it, and even if they didn't, they likely could not avoid getting stuck on it.

Then he put his hand over the lens of his light, turned it on, and pointed it upstream.

Stepping back out into the water he waved it back and forth, and in seconds he saw the first two people come under the bridge and grab hold. They were both plant workers, and they appeared frazzled and waterlogged but otherwise uninjured. He held the line as he walked out into the center of the stream to guide the pair to shore. This done, he remained in the heavy current, ready to grab anyone who somehow slipped past.

In under a minute he had everyone, although there were new injuries to deal with. Cuts and bruises were evident; Mensah told Duff he thought he'd sprained his ankle when it was momentarily caught between some rocks in the rapids. Further, everyone who'd been on a stretcher had fallen out of it, but all five non-ambulatory survivors were held on to by the able-bodied as their empty ersatz litters floated past. Isaac went off after the litters, thinking they would be useful for getting the wounded up to the road, and he managed to retrieve two of them just before they spilled down a waterfall and into a cluster of shallow rocks.

Nichole did a head count and confirmed to Duff that they had all of the entourage on the western bank, some twenty-five yards south of the bridge that loomed above them.

CONRAD TREMAINE WALKED OVER TO COPPER'S VEHICLE, THE RAIN pouring off his bush hat. The Liberian stood at the hood, a raincoat on now although he was certainly soaked to the bone. He held his walkie-talkie in his hand as he waited for an update from the men on the hill.

The eight men of Delta squad remained on the road pulling security around the five vehicles, and Tremaine thought Copper was doing a good job keeping his rebels organized, especially considering one fourth of their number had apparently just been killed.

To Copper, Tremaine said, "Change of plans. Me and the boys are leaving. Heading to the N2, then south to Accra. You mop up here with Second Platoon and then get on the road."

"Understood."

"You're looking for a white male, thirty-six years old. He's missing his left leg below the knee, I assume he has a prosthesis. He should be in possession of a Getac tablet computer. I need a photograph of his dead face and that physical device, both brought to the safe house in Accra by dawn."

Copper said, "I'll go up there personally as soon as they have bodies for me to check."

"Good."

A radio transmission came over both men's walkie-talkies.

"Alpha squad to Copper, over?"

The Liberian clicked his mic. "Copper to Alpha, go ahead."

"We've lost them at a stream."

"Did they go to the other side?"

"Maybe. We'll have to cross to find out."

Copper barked back into his radio. "Well? What are you wait-ing for?"

"Yes, sir. Stand by."

Looking back to Tremaine, the Liberian saw his team leader al-ready heading back to his Toyota pickup in the rain.

DUFF HELPED ALL THE NONCOMBATANTS BEHIND A CLUSTER OF boulders that hid them from the road. The wounded were moved as carefully as possible, but the conditions were difficult and Duff's prosthetic foot slipped on a mossy rock while he was carrying Chad Larsen and fell into the water, dropping Chad's bad leg in the process and forcing the injured ARSO to stifle a bloodcurdling scream.

As an apology Duff offered him a shot of morphine, but the ARSO again declined.

Just seconds after finding cover, everyone down by the stream heard an engine rev, and soon the lights on the bridge increased.

A pickup with its headlights shining rolled into view; it moved slowly around the parked RIVCOM truck just on the other side, but once it did, it raced off with a throaty howl from its V8 engine.

Malike and Ben held their rifles up towards the bridge, but no other vehicles passed. Still, light to the west told them all that there were more vehicles, and likely more people here.

Duff crawled up the bank, pushing through mud, clinging to rocks with his free hand, always keeping his rifle up and at the ready.

When he made it to the southwest corner of the bridge, he looked back and saw Isaac's truck on the right, its taillights illuminated by the headlights of a vehicle to the left. Duff knew that if he tried to make it to the truck, he'd be in full view of anyone providing security on the road.

He chanced a look to the west and saw headlights some thirty or forty yards away, but he didn't know if there were other vehicles behind this one that he could not see.

He crawled back down the bank and made it back to the others.

Nichole knelt next to Ben and Isaac, an AK-47 pointed up towards the road.

"Listen up," Duff said. "We know there are at least eight up on the hill looking for us, but I don't know the strength on the road. It could be another eight, or multiples of that. No matter how many, we're going to have to go through these guys if we're going to take their vics to get out of here, and we have to do it before the enemy on the hill comes back down."

Ben said, "How do you want to do this?"

"L-shaped ambush. Ben and Malike, go through the trees on this side. One of you go ten meters, the other fifteen. Find an angle on the road. Initiate on my fire."

The two Ghanaians were both injured, but they hefted their AKs and began pushing into the thick trees, disappearing in an instant.

Now Duff looked to Isaac. "You stay on this side, fire down the road towards the lights. I'll go back under the bridge and do the same from the north side."

Nichole said, "What about me?"

Duff wiped rainwater from his face, and with an expression of pain, he said, "Okay." Reaching into his pack, he handed Nichole two extra AK magazines and a hand grenade. "You come with me, we'll both go under the bridge and fire from there."

He gave a pair of grenades to Isaac, and he kept two for himself, and they all moved out.

COPPER STOOD IN THE DARKENED ROAD CONFERRING WITH THE squad leader from Delta when his walkie-talkie came alive.

"Copper, this is Alpha. We aren't finding any trail here on the east side of the water. I think they might have gone downstream. What do you want us to do?"

And with that, the Liberian looked up in front of him. Fifty meters away he saw the bridge and the RIVCOM truck just beyond it. He raised his rifle quickly in that direction, then shouted over the sound of the jungle rain to the men maintaining security around him.

"Charlie squad! Get lights down in the water off that bridge! Everybody!"

Rebels began running past him, their guns up as they closed on the bridge using the headlights of the lead vehicle.

THIRTY-FIVE

DUFF MADE IT INTO HIS POSITION ON THE FAR SIDE OF THE BRIDGE, finding a rock that jutted up enough for him to prop the magazine of his weapon on so that he could have a steady base to fire from while lying prone. Nichole knelt behind a tree just to his right, her weapon pointed out the right side.

He took aim on the headlights in front of him because he couldn't see anything behind them, and he prepared to fire, but then he registered movement.

Shadows bouncing, men approaching at a run.

"Hold fire," he said to his wife, but Isaac, Ben, and Malike were out of earshot, so he could only hope the men stuck to the plan and waited for him to fire before opening up themselves.

His intention was to draw this group of rebels into the middle of the L-shaped ambush he'd set up, but if anyone opened fire too early, they'd lose the opportunity to catch these men at their most vulnerable.

He aimed at a target, the lead shadow, just a silhouette of a man running forward, and then the man turned on a flashlight. Duff didn't know if he was the squad leader, but he decided this man would be the first to die.

When they were only fifty feet or so from the bridge, Duff assumed they would be right in line with Malike and Ben over in the trees, so he flipped off his safety and put his finger on the trigger of his rifle.

COPPER SHOUTED INTO THE RADIO. "BOTH SQUADS ON THE HILL, double-time it back down here. Enemy is trying to flank us with the stream."

His two squad leaders in the jungle confirmed they'd received the order and were now on the way back, and then Copper began moving to the bed of his truck so he could grab an RPK light machine gun to provide extra support to the men closing on the bridge.

He'd just put his hand on the weapon when a crack of gunfire on the road made him look up.

Instantly several weapons began firing in semiautomatic mode. He could see the flashes, both at the bridge and in the trees to the right of the road, and he dove behind the truck, pulling the big weapon behind him.

He readied the machine gun, opening its bipod so he could rest it on the ground to fire more steadily, and he rolled out behind the left rear of his truck. To the east the gunfire was unrelenting, and he recognized the sounds of AK-47s, some fired haphazardly, and others fired with obvious skill.

DUFF EMPTIED THE MAGAZINE OF HIS KALASHNIKOV, SEATED another mag, then reached under and around the rifle to rack the bolt with his left hand. His wife fired at a cadence measured to conserve ammo, and when Duff again began shooting up the road, Nichole called for cover so she could herself reload.

Duff saw bodies down in the middle of the road just fifty feet or so away from him, but fresh muzzle flashes erupted farther away now, and at least some of the men in the road had dived into the trees on his right.

Duff took out a grenade, pulled the tape off the spoon, then pulled the pin. He let it cook off a couple of seconds in his hand, then side-armed it as hard as he could.

The frag grenade detonated shortly after disappearing into the trees.

Suddenly a fully automatic machine gun, fired from at least fifty yards away, began spraying short bursts in the direction of the bridge, so much so that Duff rolled to his right to seek shelter next to Nichole behind the tree. He saw Isaac still firing across the bridge; the RIV-COM officer had good cover, and even Chad Larsen, whose wounds looked devastating to Duff, had managed to crawl up the bank to the road with an AK, and he provided covering fire for Isaac.

The machine gun—Duff was certain it was a Russian-made RPK—barked, tearing up the trees all around him, but it seemed the man might have been firing from around the left side of a vehicle and therefore he didn't have the right angle on Isaac and Chad.

Duff grabbed his wife by the shoulder and yanked her back behind the tree, then leaned into her ear to shout over the gunfire and the rain.

"Prep a grenade for me, but stay in cover."

He knew the only way he could hit that machine gun with a frag grenade from this distance would be to just throw it as far as possible and hope for a skidding bounce that sent it the rest of the way before detonating.

He shouted across the bridge to Isaac. "Hey! Dump a magazine in that first vehicle!"

Isaac was almost invisible in the shadow behind the rock he used for cover, but Duff detected a nod of his head.

The Ghanaian's AK began firing over and over. The headlights were quickly shot out, and shortly after that the RPK up the road fell silent.

Duff used the moment to step out from behind the tree, and he slung Nichole's grenade as far as he possibly could, ducking back quickly. He heard a detonation, then looked back out, determining that the grenade had bounced off the road and into the trees thirty yards away.

Fresh rounds from the machine gun impacted the tree he knelt behind, but he didn't move, he just began prepping another frag, but while doing so he saw Isaac stand up and heave his grenade, also towards the first vehicle.

Isaac had better luck than Duff. The detonation seemed to take place right in front of the headlights, and both of them immediately extinguished.

No more fire came from either the road or the trees.

Duff tucked back around the trunk, and he put a hand on Nichole's shoulder. "Are you okay?"

"Yes," she said. "Josh . . . we've got to get back to Accra."

She was thinking about Mandy and Huck and whatever it was that was going on in the city. He said, "I know, babe."

All was quiet on the road save for the rain now, but Duff knew he didn't have the luxury of taking his time to make sure the area was cleared of enemy.

The men on the hill could be back down here in minutes, and he needed to find vehicles that weren't too shot up so that they could get out of here.

He rose and ran across the road just as Malike and Ben stepped out of the trees, their weapons still pointed to the west in case anyone remained there and was still in the mood to fight.

He shouted to Isaac, "Get everyone you can in your truck. I'm going up the road to score us another vehicle." To Ben and Malike he said, "Can you guys cover me?"

"We'll come with you," Ben said, and he limped along with Duff as they headed up the pitch-black road in the rain.

Duff ran up the now completely darkened road, his rifle in the crook of his arm. If there were still combatants here, he and the other men with him were likely about to die, but he knew the clock was ticking to get out of here.

The first vehicle they came to was a powerful-looking Toyota pickup, but Duff didn't even try to start it. The hood was up, the engine and front tires were riddled with holes, and the glass was shattered.

Behind it he saw a man on his back lying next to an RPK machine gun on its side. Duff shot him in lieu of checking him for a pulse, giving no thought to the action at all.

A Vektor rifle also lay there next to the truck and the dead man, and by looking over the body, Duff determined quickly that this was another Sentinel mercenary. The weapon, the man's body armor, and even the radio on his shoulder were just like those of the Russian Sentinel operators Duff had killed at the dam.

He ran on, with Malike and Ben trailing, and quickly he found more bodies and two more pickups behind the first one. A man lay slumped behind the wheel of the second truck; Duff thought he was dead but fired two rounds into him anyway, then pulled his body out and let it fall into the mud.

This truck looked to Duff like it was still in good shape, but he knew it would be almost impossible to fit everyone into just this and Isaac's Toyota.

Looking farther west, he saw that a small four-wheel-drive box truck sat parked in the rear of the convoy. He approached it cautiously but found no one there, alive or dead. Soon he climbed behind the wheel. The keys were in the ignition, so he fired it up, ground the gears, and began rolling forward to pick up Ben and Malike, then drive it through the heavy mud to the bridge.

BOB GORSKI WALKED ACROSS HIS HOTEL SUITE, THEN FLIPPED OFF the switch on the shortwave transmitter sitting on the desk. He then turned off the portable power station that had been giving the short-wave its electricity, and by doing so he also turned off the two lamps that had been plugged into the power station, blanketing the room in darkness.

A loud boom in the distance turned his head towards the window, and he looked out into the rainy, misty night. No other explosions followed; it seemed clear to him that the action in the streets was dying down. Two hours earlier he'd stood up here on his tenth-floor balcony and both watched and listened to gunfights around the city, heard the low booms of high-explosive mortar rounds exploding, and watched fires burn at the airport and somewhere far to the east.

But this detonation was the first he'd heard in several minutes, and it wasn't immediately followed by other sounds of combat.

Gorski grabbed his wallet and left the room, heading for the stairs.

The CIA officer had spent many years in Africa, and he'd been in the middle of multiple coups d'état. Some of them had been vio-lent, but Ghana was a bigger and ostensibly more stable country, and he feared that things were going to get worse before they got better.

He'd spent the evening on his shortwave and his sat phone, his only real ways to communicate with senior leaders in Ghana's Bureau of National Intelligence, the nation's spy shop. While CIA station Accra had been reluctant to give credence to any of Gorski's con-cerns, BNI had been more receptive, and now that it appeared Gorski had been right about potential unrest, the local intelligence agency was actively helping Gorski, giving him access to their agents out in the city and in other parts of the nation.

Comms were difficult with the Internet down, the power down, and the cell network down, but a few BNI agents had shortwave transmitters, and Gorski had also been speaking with a BNI officer with a sat phone who'd been driving his motorcycle across the city to meet personally with his agents.

The man had stopped communicating an hour earlier, however, and Gorski didn't know what to make of that.

With his sat phone in his pocket he descended the stairwell, lit with emergency lighting, and when he finally stepped out into the lobby, a pair of armed security men standing by the door turned to him in surprise.

A hotel guest services representative stepped from behind her desk. "Sir . . . may I help you?"

"Don't worry," he said with a smile. "Just heading to the bar."

The woman smiled back, but he could see the strain on her face that this day had put there. "You will not be alone, sir."

Gorski entered the bar, saw that it was illuminated by candlelight, and sat on a barstool that was positioned in front of a candle on the marble top. A couple dozen people sat around the space, foreigners who'd come to Ghana for tourism or to do business but found themselves in the middle of chaos.

The bartender stepped up to him.

"The usual, Mr. Bob?"

Gorski said, "Evening, JoJo. You guys still have ice?"

"For a few hours more, sir."

"Good. Yeah, the usual, thanks."

"Vodka soda on the way, boss."

Gorski's phone rang in his pocket, and he hurriedly pulled it out. "Yeah?"

"Well, Bob, let me be the first to offer you an apology." Gorski recognized the voice of Richard Mace, the CIA chief of station here in Accra.

He leaned forward and put an elbow on the bar. "What do you mean?"

"You come into town, feed us all this talk about trouble in the bush . . . we blew you off. You were right, we were wrong."

"Something else has happened, hasn't it?"

"Damn right. Reports we're getting from Ghanaian intelligence is that two columns of rebels are moving on the city. Southern Command has had their hands full with the extremist cells they've been fighting all evening, and Central Command is forming up in Kumasi to come down and support."

"What's the ETA on the rebels hitting the city?"

"Within the hour. General Boatang and his troops are probably eight hours away, realistically. They won't get here before dawn."

"We have any idea of the number of rebels?"

"Professor Addo, the commander of the Dragons of Western Togoland, has claimed in the past that he has four thousand armed troops."

Gorski waved that away as his drink was placed next to the candle in front of him. "In his dreams."

"Agreed. We're thinking the number will be under one K, but we *are* concerned about the idea that the rebels might have help from soldiers of fortune."

"Yeah, that makes two of us."

"Anyway, I also didn't believe you when you told me Tremaine was here cooking something up, so . . . if you want to drop by the embassy and kick me in the ass, be my guest. I have it coming."

Gorski laughed a little. "No worries, Mace. I don't know if I'd have believed me, either. What about U.S. military assets?"

"Washington wants President Amanor to request them, and so far, that hasn't happened. Understandable, it would be politically sketchy for him to do. It could make him look like a vassal of America."

"Jesus Christ, Mace. The ambassador was attacked, and she's out of the city and injured. That should bring out some sort of response from the military, right?"

"It's up to the White House, as always."

Mace then said, "Just got a call from the ARSO with the ambo."

"Duffy?"

"The other one. Larsen. He says they're on the N2 heading to the city."

"*He's* hurt, from what I heard."

"Sounded like it. He says he's passed off AIC duties to Duffy. We're sending a team of local agents to meet them halfway and bring them back to the embassy. That's all Washington wants to do for now."

Gorski let it go, drank a sip of his vodka soda. "I'd like to debrief Duffy when he gets there."

"Absolutely. But . . . don't go out on the streets. I can have someone pick you up, bring you to the embassy. Get you out of your hotel so you can be closer to the action."

"I'd appreciate that."

"What else do you need from me?"

Gorski had been waiting for this question. "I want to find Kang. To do that I need locals in a private vehicle, maybe SDA personnel or someone else we trust. We fit the vehicle with radio frequency scanners, thermal cameras, electromagnetic emissions detectors, whatever you have."

"And then what?"

"Then they go out into the city looking for signals."

"Bob . . . Accra is eighty-one square miles. It could take days to—"

"We don't have days. We only have till the power comes back on."

Dryly, Mace said, "That could be days."

"Once the city has power, it will be exponentially harder to detect a strong electronic footprint." Gorski sipped his drink, then said, "But your people won't have to go all over the city. You send your crew to me here, and I bet we can narrow down the search zone considerably."

"You really think this MSS guy you're after is in Accra?"

"I *know* he's in Accra."

There was a pause, then Mace said, "Today is not the day for me to doubt you, Bob. I'll get assets on the way to you, ASAP."

THIRTY-SIX

TWO VEHICLES, A PICKUP AND A FOUR-WHEEL-DRIVE BOX TRUCK, pulled up on the narrow residential street in the town of Atimpoku, ten miles south of the Akosombo Dam. The streetlights were out, so when both vehicles stopped in front of a small house with a carport and turned off their headlights, the entire street was again shrouded in darkness.

Deputy plant operator Martin Mensah stepped down from the rear vehicle and began limping his way forward towards the pickup in front of him on the street.

The rain had moved on by eleven forty-five, but a thick mist covered the road, and Josh Duffy stepped out into it when he climbed out of the front passenger seat of the truck. Mensah was limping, Duff saw, and it was obvious the man approaching him was in considerable pain but equally obvious that he wanted to get back to his dam and begin the repairs needed to bring the power grid back up, because he hobbled forward quickly.

Mensah shook the American's hand. "Thank you, sir, but I must return to the facility."

"Of course. Take that truck. But be careful."

"You be careful, as well. It might take us several hours to restore power."

They shook hands again, and then the older man began limping back to the box truck.

Duff turned and met Isaac and Nichole in the driveway. The RIVCOM officer shined his flashlight on a small white four-door under the carport roof. He said, "Like I said, it will only carry four, maybe five people."

"It only needs to carry Nichole and me. The ambo and the others will stay in the pickup. We'll go ahead to scout the area so they don't drive into anything unexpected. We'll return it to you when this is over."

Isaac nodded, somewhat distractedly, and then said, "Oh yes, the radios. Follow me."

Duff, Nichole, and Isaac walked up to the carport door, and Isaac opened it with a key. Cracking the door to reveal the smell of candle wax and a dim view of his kitchen, he called out, speaking Twi. "Abina? It's me."

"Isaac!" his wife cried out from the darkness deeper in the little house.

He stepped into his home, shined his flashlight, and looked through the kitchen into the den, where he saw his wife cradling her son in her left hand and holding a kitchen knife in her right.

"What's happening?" she asked as she moved closer, both relief and panic in her voice. "I heard explosions earlier, police sirens."

"Rebels attacked the dam. Tried to kill the president."

She gasped. "The helicopters, earlier. I heard them."

"The delegation came today, not tomorrow, and the rebels were there to meet them."

"Oh my God." She took Isaac's light and shined it on his T-shirt, seeing the blood. "You're hurt."

"It's not bleeding anymore. Mrs. Duffy here treated my injury during the drive."

Abina Opoku looked past her husband now, shined the light by the door, and saw the white couple standing behind her husband. They were drenched; the man had cuts to his forehead and arms, and the woman had a black eye.

Both carried rifles on slings hung over their shoulders.

"Hello," she said, then looked back to her husband.

Isaac said, "Duff and Nichole, may I present my wife, Abina. My son, Kofi."

Abina shook their hands, a wary look on her face, and then she went to the freezer, pulled out a bag of frozen mangoes, and handed it to Nichole. "This will help the swelling in your eye."

Nichole took it and put it on her right eye, then let out a sigh of relief. "Thank you, ma'am."

Duff said, "Isaac said we could borrow your car. I promise the U.S. government will compensate for any damage or—"

Isaac spoke up, addressing his wife. "I can't stay. I just came to get the car."

"What?" Duff said, cocking his head. "No."

But the Ghanaian nodded forcefully. "I am going to see this to the end with my friends."

"Where are you going?" she asked.

"Accra. The danger has passed here. You will be fine. I just have to get the ambassador back to her embassy, and then I will come straight back here. I promise." He turned to Duff. "Let me change my shirt and I'll be ready."

"You don't have to do this, man," Duff said.

Nichole echoed the sentiment. "You've done so much already. We'll be fine."

But the Ghanaian remained steadfast. "You'll be better with me."

And with that, Duff and Nichole went back outside while Isaac took a moment to change and talk to his wife.

As they headed back down the little driveway, Duff said, "Isaac and I will go in the lead vehicle. We'll stay in walkie-talkie range."

Nichole said, "I want to go with you."

Duff thought it over a moment. Said, "It's going to be dangerous. We're like the counterassault truck for this convoy, except we don't have any armor to protect us."

"That's why you need me." She held up the AK.

After a moment he nodded. "All right, you come with us. It will be fine. It's not like we're in D.C."

Duff stepped up to the truck now. Ben was behind the wheel, with Malike riding shotgun. Ambassador Dunnigan lay in the back seat, and she seemed to be asleep, likely from the effects of the opiate, Duff reasoned.

In the bed, Chad Larsen and Arletta James lay flat, and Chad cradled an AK-47 in his arms.

To Ben, Duff said, "Isaac, Nik and I are going to be in the lead vehicle. We'll try to stay half a kilometer in front of you; Isaac has radios we can use to communicate on the drive back."

Chad called him to the back of the truck now. When Duff looked at him, even in the darkness, he could see that the man was in agony. He said, "Hey, man. Remember how I said I didn't need anything for pain?"

"Stand by," Duff said, and then he reached into the back seat of the truck and unzipped the trauma bag on the floorboard below Ambassador Dunnigan. From it he pulled a syringe of hydromorphone.

He walked around to the other side of the truck bed and said, "You've got five of us with rifles ready to protect the ambo. You just rest, man."

Chad shook his head, "Just a half dose, and you're not taking my AK."

"Wouldn't dream of it." Duff injected him with half a dose from the syringe, then squirted the rest into the street and broke off the needle.

He walked back up the drive as Isaac came out of the house dressed in a fresh RIVCOM tunic; it was untucked because of the thick bandage around his waist. He carried the AK rifle taken from one of the bodies in the jungle over his shoulder, a backpack slung over the other shoulder, and a pair of black walkie-talkies in his hands. He put one in his car and took the other to Malike in the truck.

Isaac then returned and climbed behind the wheel of his 2010 Toyota Yaris four-door; Duff took shotgun and Nichole sat in the back seat, her bag of frozen mangoes pressed to her face with one hand, while she held the AK in her lap with the other.

In minutes the Toyota had led the truck back onto the highway, passing signs of fighting every kilometer or two: burned buildings, bullet-ridden walls, wrecked-out cars.

The one thing not on the road tonight was traffic. People remained locked up in their homes to keep themselves and their property safe, staying away from the combat that had passed here hours earlier in addition to the evening of bad weather and the power outage.

As they drove, Nichole leaned up from the front seat, the frozen fruit still comforting her swollen eye. "Here's something I don't understand. Why does Tremaine want the detonation codes back? He knows you know where the bombs are, and his rebels don't control the dam, so he can assume they've been defused or removed anyway."

"No idea," Duff admitted.

"Show me what it looks like."

He reached down to the backpack between his boots and pulled it out.

She took it, looked it over with curiosity. "What is it?"

"It's a tablet computer, but some military-grade shit. Getac. We used to use these in the PMCs to store our codes, frequencies, routes, op orders, stuff like that. This one looks pretty fancy."

"It also looks like somebody shot it."

He raised a hand. "Guilty."

"Does Tremaine know it's damaged?"

"I tried to tell him, but I don't think he believed me."

She took it in her hands. "But . . . why would you use this to detonate the bombs? Why do you need something this sophisticated?"

He shrugged now. "You don't. I've seen a lot of triggering devices, and none of them are computers. Cell phones, little radio transmitters, stuff like that."

"And," Nichole said, "there's no cell phone service. How was he supposed to use this once he left the area?"

Duff just shrugged in the front seat.

After a time, she looked back up to him, her eyes wide. "Don't you get it? He doesn't want the computer back to detonate the bombs that he has to assume have been disarmed; he wants it because there's something else on here that he needs, or something that will implicate him or others involved with this."

Duff took it back and looked at the two small round holes through the glass. "Whatever was on here, though, we can't access it."

"*We* can't, but forensics can. It might have to go to CIA, it might have to go all the way back to the States, but I'd bet money somebody can get intel off that device. And whatever intel is on that device is what Tremaine is trying to keep out of our hands."

Duff thought a moment. "We could give it back to him, and he could leave us alone."

They looked at each other while Isaac drove in silence. Simultaneously, they expressed excitement, then doubt, then resignation.

Nichole said it first. "We can't do that, Josh."

"I know," he said with a shrug. "He might not come after us, specifically, but if we give this back to him, it will leave him out here in play. We need to bring down whoever is doing all this."

Nichole said, "When are you going to call him?"

"Once the ambo is safe, once we're with the kids and we know they're safe. Then I'll meet up with Gorski, and we'll call Tremaine and see what he has to say for himself."

They passed the burned-out shells of police vehicles; the rain had extinguished any fires, but the smell of burnt rubber was pervasive in the air.

It became quickly clear from their travel south that the rebels weren't interested in holding any territory. There were no roadblocks, no obvious continued fighting in the towns the two vehicles drove past, or any other hint that the rebels intended to do more than just blitzkrieg their way to the capital.

With the help of Sentinel.

MINUTES BEFORE MIDNIGHT, A TEAM OF NINE RUSSIAN SENTINEL operators stepped out of the chemical factory on Fertilizer Road, where they had been hiding out for the past several hours, and they made their way into the forecourt where their vehicles were parked. The group walked past the vehicles, through the darkness, confident in their movements.

They'd come to this place several hours ago, shortly after getting the emergency message from Belov that the operation was to begin immediately, knowing the place was abandoned, knowing also that the forecourt would suit their purposes for their task tonight.

These nine men were the only Sentinel operators inside the capital—all the others had been tasked to hit targets either on the roads to Akosombo ahead of the rebel columns or at the dam itself, and those men had all been engaged for hours already.

But these nine had been ordered to wait until midnight to act.

The men had been surprised by fighting in the city earlier in the afternoon and evening; they hadn't been briefed on any other attacks, but they'd just hunkered down in their shuttered chemical factory, waiting for their time.

And their time was now.

The three 82-millimeter mortars had been erected in the forecourt near their three trucks, and the weapons were ranged for a target three kilometers to the west of their location.

The men used headlamps to see their way around, and in the dancing lights the three spotters went to three ladders propped up by the front wall; a man knelt next to a crate of shells positioned by each weapon, and a man stood with a shell over each mortar tube, ready to drop it in and duck.

The cell phone of one of the men chirped, telling him it was time to begin.

At exactly midnight, three men dropped three high-explosive fragmentation mortar bombs into the tubes; they crouched quickly, and with a single concussive thud the 6-pound explosives launched into the air.

The trio on the ladders had their binoculars out, aimed west, and thirty-five seconds after the first rounds were fired, all three hit Burma Camp, the headquarters of the Ghana Armed Forces Southern Command.

One shell slammed into the closed officers' mess on the north side of the base, causing damage but no casualties. The other two rounds struck in and around the Block 6 barracks.

Most of the troops were out of the barracks, hastily assembling at Parade Square to go out to the north to meet a rebel force of undetermined size that Ghanaian intelligence had informed them of just a half hour earlier.

The Russian spotters registered the impact points of the mortars, then called for fire adjustments on all three weapons.

The second salvo of shells impacted a minute after the first. The motor pool was hit, a shell landed close enough behind the front gate to kill several sentries there, and the officers in Parade Square desperately trying to get their troops together in an organized fashion had to instead get everyone moving away as fast as possible.

The forward observers called to the mortarmen to fire for effect, and then shells began launching every five to ten seconds for the next three minutes.

This massive base had been hit by the extremists five hours earlier; a few were killed at the front gate by an RPG, and a half dozen mortars had impacted around the camp and set some equipment alight, but when over fifty shells detonated in a five-minute period across the length and width of the massive base, pandemonium ensued at Burma Camp. Entire companies of troops hunkered down in bomb shelters; other units rushed out the front gate with no orders, their chain of command disrupted.

The objective of the Sentinel operators was not to defeat Southern Command; it was to suppress any reaction the battalion of infantry there at Burma Camp could make to the rebels approaching the city.

And then, after five minutes of furious work, all nine men began to disassemble all three mortars, then they put them back in a covered-bed truck.

The Russians left the area a minute before a pair of police cars raced into view.

Their orders were to stop at one more location, a sprawling outdoor market two kilometers to the north, and here they would fire another thirty to fifty shells at Burma from another angle, and then the men would return to their safe house in the city to await extraction.

THIRTY-SEVEN

A FEW MINUTES PAST MIDNIGHT, BOB GORSKI STOOD IN THE PARK-
ing lot of the Movenpick Ambassador Hotel with a backpack on his
shoulder and a hard-shell suitcase next to him, and he listened to the
sounds of fresh fighting, wondering what the fuck was going on.

Five minutes earlier he'd heard a massive barrage of what he took
to be either mortars or missiles hitting over at Burma Camp, a kilometer to the east, but now the shooting was coming from the north.
It was small-arms fire exclusively, but there were a lot of guns in the
mix, and Gorski took this to be one of the two rebel columns the station chief had warned him about.

Soon the headlights of a vehicle approached the front gate, fifty
yards away from where he stood at the entrance to the hotel, and a
twelve-passenger van pulled into the drive. The vehicle stopped at the
security booth and was checked over by the hotel's understandably
jumpy security team.

After looking under the hood and under the chassis, and after
having the four passengers step out and produce their identification,
the van was allowed to proceed up to the hotel itself.

The van pulled to a stop in front of the CIA officer, and the sliding side door opened. Gorski climbed in and found a seat in the dark.

All four of the other occupants were Black, and they wore local clothing: colorful dashiki shirts on the men, a bright purple and teal headwrap on the woman.

The van stayed where it was idling near the front of the hotel.

A man in his thirties in the front passenger seat spoke first, extending a hand. When he spoke, Gorski was surprised to hear that his accent was not Ghana, it was Georgia. "Travis Young, S&T."

Science and Technology was the CIA directorate responsible for developing and employing technical systems, and while Gorski had asked for locals to help him with this electronic surveillance, it was nice to see a CIA officer along with them.

He looked to the other three. "Are you all from around here?"

One of the men spoke up in a Ghanaian accent. "We've all lived here our entire lives."

These three Ghanaians worked for the U.S. embassy as surveillance detection assets, locals who lived and worked in the neighborhood of the embassy who were strictly vetted and tasked with keeping an eye out for anything in the area that might threaten U.S. interests.

"Good." He turned his attention back to Travis. "It sounds pretty hairy out there."

"It was only a seven-minute drive from the embassy; we didn't run into any problems. There's some burned-out police cars and an army jeep, all from the fighting earlier. But the attacks happening right now are at the Central Command HQ and in the northern half of the city."

"You feel okay about driving around at night?"

"The government hasn't posted a curfew because the power's down and there's no way to announce it. My diplomatic credos should get me through any government roadblocks. If we run into rebels, then we'll just turn around and try to go the other way."

Gorski had never thought of S&T employees as particularly brave, but this man seemed to have balls of steel.

He looked around inside the van; several electronic gadgets sat in cases on the empty seats. "You have everything you need?"

Young said, "I think so. We'll use radio frequency scanners, thermal cameras, and old-fashioned pavement canvassing. If we're within a couple city blocks of the target location, then we should be able to pick up electronic signals that can take us right there, but if the power should come back on, we'll lose our advantage."

"Where do you want us to go first?" the lone woman asked.

Gorski had been thinking about this. He didn't know Accra well and was counting on the locals to help him pinpoint his target's location. "The man I'm looking for is Asian, from China. He will have a piece of property in or near the city, somewhere he can oversee those working for him. It will be a location where he feels safe, controlled access, a walled compound of some kind, and there will be a lot of electricity flowing there, even with the power outage."

"A generator, you mean?" one of the Ghanaian men asked.

"Exactly. He would have prepped for the blackout. And he won't be alone. I expect he'll have a security and a technical team on site with him, so we are looking for a place where a dozen or more people can live and work. Maybe two dozen."

Travis Young looked to the Ghanaians. "Any ideas on where to start?"

All four nodded, and the woman said, "There's only one neighborhood that matches that description. You're talking about Aburi Hills. Big walled mansions, a perfect view over the city. Lots of places up there will be on generator power, though."

To this, Travis said, "I'll be able to monitor the types of electronic emissions out of the various locations with power. I'll be able to rule out anyone using their satellite TV."

The van took off, heading towards the embassy to drop Gorski off before these four spent the nighttime hours hunting the mastermind of the chaos that was happening in the country.

The sounds of fighting in the north continued, and the veteran CIA officer said, "Travis . . . you guys, please be careful. Kang Shikun isn't stupid. He could have his own surveillance detection assets working his neighborhood. You'll really have to fit in to make this work."

Travis said, "I'll call you every hour with updates."

They drove on; part of Bob Gorski wished he were going with the four on this mission, but the other part of him was glad he'd be at the embassy, behind gates and guns and behind the Marines.

THOUGH THE HOME ON ANKAMA CLOSE IN THE ABURI HILLS RAN under robust generator power, the exterior was kept completely dark and the interior dimly lit at one fifteen a.m. Kang had ordered the lights dimmed or extinguished throughout the night so that the neighbors wouldn't see the activity of two dozen people inside the fence and walls. Security patrolling, technicians at their desks, Kang Shikun himself standing in his office and looking out at the city.

A group of Russian Sentinel men had just arrived at the property. They'd operated mortars in the city, and now they were tasked with keeping the location secure.

Kang hadn't spoken to the men—he didn't even know if they spoke English—and they remained out front, behind the guard shack in their trucks.

Kang leaned back against his desk and took in the impeccable view of his coup d'état in progress through the open balcony door. And Kang's view of his manufactured uprising was outstanding. He left his binoculars on his desk behind him while he watched fires burn over Burma Camp and the airport, and then he looked on as furious small-arms fire sparkled to the northeast, where two companies of Dragons—over two hundred troops—were just now entering the city.

Another column of similar size was also engaging forces to Kang's

east, leaving the N2 and taking the N1 along the coast. He couldn't
see the flashes from where his home sat on the hill, but he'd heard
from his agents that all was proceeding to plan.

He was satisfied with where he found himself at one fifteen a.m.
The rebels were a touch behind schedule, but not far out of range
from where Kang had estimated. And though some portion of Southern Command was definitely in the street and battling the Dragons,
the chaos of the mortar attacks at the base had certainly slowed the
army's response.

Even before the newest attacks, Southern Command had already
suffered through a long evening. Twenty-two groups of extremist terrorists all over the city had been taxing for both the police and the
military to deal with, and even though there were now only a couple
of cells left alive in the capital, the police were all but ineffective and
the military had been fully engaged in combating them, and they'd
not been ready for this next wave of Kang's plan.

Hajj Zahedi's men had not been as numerous or as successful as
Kang would have liked, but the Iranian commander had done his part
to sow chaos in the city, an act necessary to ensure that the Dragons
of Western Togoland were not all cut down before they could reach
the center of the capital.

Professor Addo was in the rear of the second column, still on the
N2, an hour behind the main thrust. He'd contacted Kang a half
hour earlier asking for an update about the force in front of his troops,
and as before, Kang had promised him they'd experience combat,
but they would meet only a token resistance from Southern Command. Kang was certain the professor was still under the impression
that all was proceeding according to the plan Kang had laid out for
him more than half a year earlier, and he assumed the rebel leader
expected to spend Friday night in Jubilee House.

Kang didn't think the fool would live till noon.

He'd spoken by satellite phone to Boatang just as he and his force left Kumasi, and the general told the Chinese intelligence officer that he expected to arrive on the outskirts of Accra by seven a.m.

Kang knew what was happening, thought he knew *exactly* what would happen over the next several hours, but still . . . he could not stop watching the fighting in the city.

His phone rang; he forced himself to turn away to go back to his desk to scoop it up. "Yes?"

Tremaine's voice came over the line. "I'm on the N2, heading to the capital. I should arrive around three a.m."

"Then you, Mr. Tremaine, are out of the fight. The rebels are already at the outskirts of the city. Once they enter, you and your men will stand down and get out of the way."

"Yeah, well, I'm not finished yet."

"Ah, yes. The compromise you mentioned earlier. Well, whatever you're planning on doing to remove it, you had better hurry. Boatang is on his way down the N6 with twenty-five hundred troops; he is due to arrive not long after dawn."

"I'll stay away from the N6 highway. I'm going to Cantonments."

Kang cocked his head a little. "Cantonments? That's next to Burma Camp."

"Don't worry, I'll steer well clear of whatever's left of Southern Command."

Kang thought a moment. "Wait . . . Cantonments. You're going to the U.S. embassy?"

"Near there, yes."

"For what reason?"

"To kidnap a couple of kids."

Kang slowly sat down. "The American bodyguard's children."

"That's right. Duff is a smart man. He can be the hero, or he can get his kids back. He can't do both. I know what choice he'll make."

Kang thought this over for several seconds. Finally, he said, "This computer that Sentinel somehow let fall into the American's hands . . . the material on there is a compromise for Sentinel, but not for me. Not for my nation."

"Yeah, well, if you don't help me get it back, *I* will be your compromise."

"Don't threaten me."

"How's this for a threat? If you try to sell me out, I'll go on Sky News, my face blacked out, my voice altered, and I'll tell the world that the People's Republic of China staged a coup in West Africa. Wonder what the politicians in Beijing will think about that news spreading around the continent."

Kang took a few measured breaths now. As calmly as possible, he said, "That won't be necessary. I have no plans to sell you out. I will assist you with your objective."

"What do you mean?"

"We have assets inside the American embassy. Foreign employees who work for us. I will talk to some people and see if I can arrange something."

Tremaine seemed pleasantly surprised. "Good. You *have* to come through on this, you understand?"

"I am not going to let the incompetence of one of your Russian contractors threaten my entire operation. I will call you back when I know more."

Kang disconnected the call, then picked a sheet of paper off his desk and strolled into the main part of the house. His technicians and intelligence personnel were hard at work at their stations, talking on phones or radios, tapping on laptops, monitoring the various systems they'd shut down in the country the afternoon before to make certain nothing came back online before the right time.

Chen Jia, the female senior technical contractor, faced away from him as she sat at the kitchen island, apparently looking at her computer screen.

He stepped up to her, and when he got close enough, he realized she was asleep at her workstation.

He cleared his throat, and the woman opened her eyes and then lurched back in surprise. "I'm sorry, sir."

Kang let it go. "I need information about our assets in the United States embassy."

Her hands shot to her laptop keyboard. "Of course, sir. What do you need to know?"

Kang looked down at the sheet of paper in his hand. "I need to know if we have someone who has access to . . . the Iris Gardens. It's an apartment complex that the Americans use."

She nodded as she typed, then scrolled through page after page of information.

Finally, she said, "We run a police officer who serves part time as a guard for the Americans. He works at several of the housing compounds, including Iris Gardens." She looked at the man's file a moment, then said, "He's just an informant, he doesn't have any real operational training."

"I assume he doesn't have a satellite phone, either."

"No mention of one in his dossier. I do have his home address."

"What about his work schedule?"

"No, sir, I do not have that."

Kang thought a moment, then called out to a man on the other side of the room.

Seconds later he was back in his office with the door closed. With him was a thirty-year-old operative from the Ministry of State Security who had formerly worked here in Ghana and knew the city. Kang told him what he needed, and a few minutes later the man went outside, climbed into a beat-up Ford Escort, and left the front gates of the mansion.

Kang watched the taillights of the Ford as they wound down the hill in front of him, in the direction of the city. His operative was out to find an asset and to give the asset a job.

He knew he'd have to call Tremaine back. Kang's people weren't going to do the kidnapping themselves; they'd need Sentinel to pull it off. But before he picked up the phone again he looked to the west and saw the fighting dying down. Looking as far as he could to the east now, he saw flashes in the distance, announcing the arrival of the second column of rebels, this one traveling down the N2 highway from the direction of the Volta River.

It was a beautiful sight, and exactly the reason he'd chosen this home as his safe house and base of operations.

THIRTY-EIGHT

THE WHITE TOYOTA FOUR-DOOR PULLED SLOWLY INTO THE TRUCK stop at four fifteen a.m., its headlights off. The power was out here, of course, so the huge lot in front of the gas pumps was pitch black, the truck stop closed and locked, the patrons and workers having fled to their homes for safety.

The Toyota rolled to a stop on the northern side of the lot, its engine idling.

Isaac Opoku sat behind the wheel, wiping the sweat of stress from his brow. He'd been on the road for four hours, though much of the time had been spent pulled in behind buildings along the roadside. Every time headlights approached them, Duff had told Isaac to get off the road, and then Duff radioed Malike half a klick behind them to do the same.

The closer they got to the capital, the more vehicles they'd seen, and this made for slow going.

Duff held his AK at his shoulder now in the front passenger seat, the muzzle resting on the dashboard in front of him and his finger hovering near the trigger.

And directly behind Isaac, Nichole Duffy's rifle was pointed out the open rear door at the darkened building.

They were still several hours' drive from the capital at this pace, and they had no idea what they'd find when they got there, but for now they just sat in the car, waiting for something to happen.

Suddenly, three sets of headlights turned on in the mist, just fifty yards in front of them on the other side of the lot. The lights were blinding to the trio in the car that had been driving dark for hours, but after a moment to acclimate, Isaac Opoku flipped on his own lights and began driving slowly forward.

One of the three sets of headlights pulled forward as well, and both Isaac's and the other vehicle finally stopped in the center of the lot, about fifteen yards apart. Headlights were again extinguished, and Duff climbed out of the vehicle, put his AK on the seat, and walked alone through the mist to a large black SUV with his hands away from his body.

Six men, all Black and formidable looking, all carrying short-barreled rifles, stood outside the vehicle. Five of them seemed to be posting security, while the sixth man stood by the driver's-side door of the SUV and gave Duff a little nod when he approached.

He spoke with an American accent. "You're Josh Duffy?"

"That's me."

"I'm John."

Sure you are, Duff said to himself. Out loud, he said, "We appreciate the help." He took Isaac's walkie-talkie off his belt and spoke into it. "Ben, all good here. Come to us."

The Ghanaian responded immediately. "Two minutes away."

John said, "We've got three vehicles; one is an armored van that's decked out on the inside as an ambulance. Four litters in there if you need them. We've got a nurse and trauma supplies to treat the wounded during the trek back to the embassy."

"Our wounded are in the other vic, they'll be pulling up in a minute."

The man gave a little smile. "*You're* not wounded? No offense, but you look like you lost a fight with a mountain lion."

"Been a long day, a longer night."

"I can see that." John continued, "This vic and the other Yukon we brought are armored, as well. I have ten Local Guard Force guys with me in all."

The other Yukon idled twenty-five yards back next to the van, and Duff imagined that men from that vehicle were watching the south for any threats.

Duff turned around and waved to Isaac's car, and soon both Isaac and Nichole got out and began walking over. As they did so, Duff asked, "What's the road like between here and the capital?"

"It's great if you like gunfights," John said.

"What if you don't?" Nichole asked as she approached.

John looked at her a moment, then took a step closer. "Nichole?"

"John? Thanks for coming." She looked to her husband now. "You met John Sunday briefly at the cookout."

Josh had met a lot of people in the past two weeks, but even though he didn't remember this guy, he said, "Oh, yeah."

The African American nodded. "You make a hell of a good smash burger." To Nichole he said, "We ran into a column of probably three dozen vehicles heading south about twenty klicks from the city. We hid out on a dirt driveway while the column passed, continued north, and then a few minutes later we heard gunfire behind us."

"So the fighting is in the city now?"

"Yeah. I just talked to my COS and he told me two columns of rebels have hit, one from the N4 and the other from the N1. Unknown how many enemy we're talking about, but we're getting reports of mortar attacks in the city, far away from the approaching columns. With the power off it's tough to get good intel, but it's safe to say we're going to have a dicey time getting back to the embassy."

Isaac stepped into the conversation. "We passed probably fifty shot-up or burned-out wrecks, many of them police cars on the way down here from Akosombo."

"There's another fifty behind us," John said, then added, "Plus anything that happened after we passed by."

THE PICKUP DRIVEN BY BENJAMIN MANU AND CONTAINING THE IN-jured pulled into the lot, its own headlights turned off. The truck pulled up next to Duff, but he quickly waved Ben on towards the van, telling him they would help with the wounded.

John told Duff they'd all leave in the armored vics in five minutes, so Duff and Nichole walked over to Isaac, who had gone back to stand near his car.

Duff said, "Look, man. You are more than welcome to turn around and go home, but if you come with us in the van, the nurse will be able to check your gunshot wound. She'll do a better job than you're going to find up in Atimpoku. No offense."

Isaac laughed. "None taken." Isaac stood there thinking in the darkness for a moment while the others loaded up. "Okay. I'll leave my car here." He shrugged. "It will be stolen, probably."

Nichole said, "Buddy, America will buy you a new car. I can promise you that."

Duff overheard. "I'll give you ours."

Isaac laughed a little, then walked towards the van. "See you in the capital."

Nichole and Duff climbed into the Yukon driven by John, and soon they all began heading south again, towards Accra.

THREE HOURS LATER, A DAWN MIST REDUCED VISIBILITY ON THE N6 highway between Kumasi and Accra, but anyone on the road could tell that something was coming this way.

The two-lane highway was lined with little shops, stores, facto-ries, wooden-stalled markets, and other businesses, and even with the unrest in the city and the power outage in the nation, a few people had already begun their daily toil.

Until just before seven a.m., when a rumbling from the north turned heads, pausing everyone from their tasks.

As a fresh crackle of gunfire came from the city behind them, General Kwame Boatang's force from Kumasi appeared out of the ether to the north, heading south in a massive convoy. The Central Command column stretched a mile and a half, and it was composed of three motorized mechanized infantry battalions, totaling over twenty-five hundred troops and one hundred twelve combat vehicles.

In the front, a pair of Navistar Defense Husky tactical support vehicles with Belgium-made machine guns in their top turrets rolled side by side, using both the southbound and northbound lanes, causing the light morning traffic to disperse into parking lots and driveways to avoid being crushed.

The Huskys were closely followed by eight BTR-70 eight-wheeled armored personnel vehicles, each loaded with ten troops and also fitted with mounted guns on the roof. Behind them, the first dozen up-armored Toyota pickups rolled past, with gunmen in the beds, rifles sticking out of the windows.

More Huskys followed, more BTRs followed the Huskys, and more pickups followed the BTRs.

Rows of Ural off-road 6×6 covered troop transport trucks carried more infantry behind all the armor, thirty to a vehicle, and behind them came the support trucks. Tow trucks, gas trucks, water and food trucks, extra ammunition, and two mobile field hospitals lumbered past.

And finally, at the rear of the column and protected by another half dozen Huskys and four BTR troop carriers, were three BTR-50 command vehicles.

General Boatang wore his combat fatigues, his body armor, and a helmet, and he rode in the second command vehicle along with four of his captains, who were constantly on their radios trying to pinpoint enemy strongpoints in the city ahead of them.

Boatang's satellite phone rang and he answered it, conferred quietly a moment, and then hung up. Looking to his officers, he told them to proceed to Black Star Square, on Accra's coastline with the Gulf of Guinea, and to expect resistance along the route.

None of his staff knew where he was getting his intelligence, but all of them knew to trust it, and to trust their leader.

They entered the city itself at seven fifteen a.m.; the lead trucks reported the sounds of gunfire ahead, and ten minutes later they radioed that they'd had a brief engagement with a pickup truck full of rebels in front of a timber market.

The enemy vehicle was destroyed, four confirmed KIA, and Boatang told his captain to inform the lead trucks to keep going.

More gunfire was reported in minutes, a skirmish by a city park, but the rebels weren't set up to defend themselves from behind, and they were summarily routed by the first armored vehicles of Central Command.

The captain reported another success ahead, and Boatang suppressed a smile. All was just as Kang had promised, and he imagined Professor Addo was just about now realizing he'd been set up.

"XIANSHENG? XIANSHENG? I AM SORRY, SIR. I'M VERY SORRY."

Kang Shikun opened his eyes and looked up at Chen Jia as she knelt over him. "What is it?"

"Professor Addo is on the satellite phone. I am sorry to wake you."

Kang lay on the bed in his makeshift office, wearing his shirt and pants and shoes. Looking at his watch, he realized he'd dozed a couple of hours.

He felt rested and energized.

Taking the satellite phone from the young woman's hands, he

waved her out of the room, then stood and headed towards the balcony for his first good look at the city in the morning light.

"Good morning, Professor. What news do you have?"

Addo was angry, perhaps panicky. "What news? You tell me! My men are being slaughtered. Central Command is here!"

"Preposterous. I just confirmed Boatang and his troops remain in garrison."

"Then who has attacked my N4 column from behind? They have armor, and a lot of it! We still have another two kilometers until we arrive in Black Star Square. We don't stand a chance."

"Calm down, Professor. I'm certain the situation is not as dire as you make it out to be."

"Southern Command put up more resistance than you assured us of. And now Central Command is attacking our flanks!"

Kang imagined that Addo had only learned the military usage of the term "flank" in the past few months while being trained by Sentinel operators. Central Command was *not* attacking the flanks, it was attacking the *rear*, but Kang did not correct the rebel leader.

He said, "Professor. Right now over sixty Sentinel operators are in the capital in a dozen squads, and they are making war on government troops."

"I don't see them anywhere."

"Possibly because you aren't at the front lines." Before Addo could respond to the thinly veiled recrimination, Kang said, "Let me reassure you. We have everything under control. You are needed alive for my plan to be successful."

Addo screamed, "Tell it to Boatang!"

After taking a moment to smile, the Chinese intelligence officer said, "Continue on to Black Star Square. Once there, make a short video. As we've discussed, claim the city is already in your hands."

"But it's not."

"Not yet." Kang continued, "Once you've done that, I want you and a few bodyguards to break away from your main attack and to come to my location, bring me the video, and we will use satellite Internet to broadcast it to the world."

"I should remain with my men. Fighting."

Addo, Kang realized, was putting up token resistance to the idea of him leaving the battle lines. He wanted a way out, but he wanted to look like a military leader. Kang said, "You will still be in command of your troops. Plus, we are very secure here. While your main force continues fighting, with Sentinel's help, of course, we will keep you personally out of the line of fire. When the smoke clears, you and your remaining Dragons can proceed directly to the presidential palace."

Kang knew Addo would jump at the chance to leave the fighting, to leave his boys behind, to get somewhere safe to wait out the rough stuff before he was installed as president.

The thirty-five-year-old Ghanaian said, "Yes. After my speech I'll travel with a few men, take a civilian car, and come to you. Where are you?"

"Head north from Black Star Square. I am in the hills overlooking the city. I won't give you an address, just call back when you reach Aburi, and I will direct you to us."

Addo said, "We are fighting for our lives here, Kang. Talk to Condor, get us more Sentinel help, especially down at the square."

"I will see what I can do, Professor."

Kang hung up the phone. And then he just sat there at his desk wondering how long he'd be able to convince Addo that things were going just the way he had promised.

Not much longer, was his conclusion. He just needed Addo to make that speech and bring it here, and he needed his people in the next room to circulate that speech around the world, and then he needed General Boatang to rout the hapless Western Togoland rebels.

Addo would die, of course. Likely right here in this office, at the hands of Tremaine, Kang told himself.

The thought gave him no pause at all.

But a new thought entered his mind, and it *did* fill him with concern. He called out to Jia, and she came into the room. Her oversized sweatshirt looked like she'd been sleeping in it for a week, and her eyes were red.

"Yes, sir?"

"Where is Tremaine?"

"He's in the city, sir. He is working on his operation by the U.S. embassy. I expect to hear more soon."

"Very well," Kang said. No, killing Addo did not stress him in the slightest. But what did stress him was the fact that Conrad Tremaine's missing Sentinel computer threatened to derail the entire operation.

He shook his head, dispelling the thought. No, Tremaine had a good plan to get the device back, and all would soon be well.

He headed for the bathroom to wash his face with cold water and to prepare for the greatest day in his life.

THIRTY-NINE

THREE ARMORED VEHICLES CONTAINING THE U.S. AMBASSADOR TO Ghana as well as the others rolled through the Front Gate Access Control Port of the U.S. embassy after a quick inspection by the Local Guard Force there, and then all three vehicles pulled up in front of the chancery at seven thirty a.m.

Multiple times along the way the small caravan had been forced to hide behind buildings or in quiet residential neighborhoods while military and rebel forces passed or fought nearby.

The CIA operations officer named John who was in charge of the convoy had seen it as his main mission to avoid detection by the enemy, and with three large newer-looking armored vehicles traveling together, this had been hard to do without a lot of detours, a lot of waiting, and some measure of luck.

Still, twice they'd rolled into intersections and were met with small-arms fire, peppering both Yukons with bullet strikes but causing no major damage.

Fighting in the city and the motorcade's attempts to steer clear of it had caused the drive from the Volta River area to take three times longer than it should have, but now, seven and a half hours after leaving Isaac Opoku's driveway, Duff stepped out of the lead SUV and onto the pavement in front of the chancery building.

The sun shone bright; it was already warm.

John had called ahead, and now four young Marine Security Guards stood out in front of the chancery in their pixelated camouflaged combat utility uniforms, carrying two aluminum and nylon litters. Other staffers had come out to assist the wounded, and the embassy doctor was out here, ready to examine the injuries to see who needed the fastest treatment in his clinic.

For his part, Duff was in a lot of pain from cuts, bruises, exhausted muscles, and the intense mental strain of a dozen hours of either combat or the threat of combat. He was also stiff and sore from the combination of all the action and then all the sitting around in the SUV.

He helped Nichole out of the Yukon, and then they both walked over to the van and saw that Isaac was the first out the back door. He'd been rebandaged, his wound had been well cleaned, and some mild painkillers had reduced some of the stiffness he'd developed after his tumble down a wall of limestone rock the day before.

The men shook hands, and then Nichole hugged him.

"They take good care of you?" Duff asked.

With a smile, he said, "They did. The nurse wants the doctor to look at my wound before I go home."

Nichole said, "You're not leaving till the fighting stops. You're staying with us."

Isaac said, "Thank you."

Ambassador Jennifer Dunnigan was placed on a stretcher, and the Marines brought her into the chancery. While Nichole helped with the other wounded, Duff and Isaac followed the ambo inside.

Dunnigan looked over her shoulder at Duff as the Marines carried her towards the embassy clinic. "Good job, Josh. Thank you."

Duff didn't feel like he deserved praise, but he said, "Thank you," anyway.

She then looked to Isaac. "And thank you, sir. God bless you."

"God bless you, Madam Ambassador."

Duff had had time in the SUV to think about it, wondering about how his nightmares in the coming years would involve helicopters crashing, his wife in mortal danger right next to him, and rain-soaked African jungles.

He didn't feel like a hero. Somehow, he just felt more damaged.

But he pushed this out of his mind because all he wanted to do right now was get home and see the kids.

Duff was about to go back outside to help his wife with the others, but the man behind the thick bulletproof glass in Marine Post One on the far side of the small lobby used his PA system to call out to him.

"ARSO Duffy? Can I speak with you?"

Duff walked up to the glass and saw the gunnery sergeant manning the post. "What's up, Gunny?"

"Welcome home. I'm sorry, sir, but I was told to bring you right in to Mace's office."

Mace was the CIA chief of station, and Duff realized he should have expected this.

He said, "Look, I have to get home and check on the kids. I'll be back as soon as I can."

Nichole entered with Arletta James; she was being carried on a stretcher by two more Marines. She saw her husband talking to the guard, so she walked over to see what was going on.

Gunny was twenty-seven, by far the oldest of the seven Marines here at the embassy. To Duff he said, "Your kids are fine, sir. We live two doors down from you guys at Iris Gardens, and I just walked over from there thirty minutes ago. Everything's quiet, the guard force at the gate's been beefed up, a police car is out front. No activity has been reported in Cantonments at all."

Duff sighed. "How insistent was Mace?"

"I would say *very* insistent, sir. He said that if you and your wife were on your feet, then he'd have my ass if I didn't send you both right up the second you walked through that door."

Duff looked to Nichole, she nodded reluctantly, and then the two of them entered the chancery, heading for the offices of the CIA station.

NINE-YEAR-OLD MANDY DUFFY LOOKED OUT THROUGH THE CLOSED and barred window overlooking the second-story balcony of the family apartment, out past the green grass of the courtyard and beyond to the front gate.

Everything was quiet for now, but the occasional crackle of gunfire or loud low booms of explosions told her something was indeed wrong.

Late yesterday afternoon she'd been shocked to hear what she thought to be fireworks, and she'd wondered at the time if there was a holiday here that she didn't know about.

But then the gunfire began. It was distant, as well, but near constant, and it seemed to come from multiple directions. She'd never heard gunfire in real life, but she watched enough TV to know what it was.

Mandy was a curious girl, all the time, and in addition to the sounds she heard, she'd also been very dialed in to the demeanor of the adults around her.

Especially Portia Djangba, her nanny for the past three months.

The evening before, Portia had seemed different; there was a concern on her face, and she kept leaving the apartment and walking across the courtyard to the front gate of the complex, where she talked with the guards.

Portia's father, Henry Djangba, was the lead guard here at Iris Gardens, and Mandy knew that since the phones and the power were down, Portia had no other way to get information other than through her father, because he had a walkie-talkie that he could use to talk to the police, the embassy, or any of the other residences around.

This morning they'd learned there was no school today, but no one had told them why.

Now, while Huck played with his toy truck behind her, Mandy stood at the window, looking out at the view in front of her.

There were usually two guards at the front gate house. This morning there were five. A police car was parked out front, as well, and it had been for most of the past day.

As Mandy watched, another policeman appeared, walking along the sidewalk from the parking lot outside the apartment's outer wall. He strolled up to the front gate and waved to the men in the small guard shack just inside the bars.

Mandy squinted, thought she recognized the officer as one of the guards who often patrolled the complex. Apparently she was right, because the other guards on duty let him in through the pedestrian gate, where they all continued talking.

While Mandy had been focused on this activity, Portia stepped up behind her here in the living room. "You ready for breakfast? Your brother says he wants pancakes again."

Mandy kept her eyes outside. She'd asked Portia what was happening the night before but was just told not to worry because everything was fine. She'd asked again this morning when the nanny informed her there was no school, and again she'd not received a direct answer. Since then, Mandy had kept her concerns to herself, not wanting to either scare her brother or have Portia lie to her again, but now, she couldn't take it anymore. "Miss Portia, can you please tell me what is going on?"

"Everything is fine, Mandy."

"I'm not a little kid," she answered back. "You can tell me."

The twenty-four-year-old nanny put her hands on the girl's shoulders and rubbed them gently, and they both looked outside. The policeman who'd just entered was now walking in this direction, past the swimming pool, apparently on his way to this row of apartment buildings.

After a long sigh, Portia said, "Okay, little one. The army and the police are out in the streets trying to stop some bad people from taking over our government. But I do not want you to worry. It is in another part of town, we are safe, no one is coming here."

Mandy didn't feel particularly safe if bad people were here trying to take over the government, but she didn't say this. Instead she said, "Are my mom and dad coming home?"

"Yes. I checked with my father a little while ago; he has a radio to talk to the embassy. Your parents and the ambassador are on the way to the embassy now. They will go there first, then I'm sure they will come here to be with you."

Mandy heard a knock at the door downstairs, and the nanny stopped rubbing her shoulders to go see who it was.

JOSH AND NICHOLE DUFFY STEPPED INTO A CONFERENCE ROOM right next to the office of the CIA's chief of station.

Bob Gorski was there, sitting at a table with COS Richard Mace.

Both men stood when the couple entered. Gorski said, "Damn good to see you both. Jesus . . . Duffy, you look like you've been wrestling in razor wire."

"You should see the other guy," Duff said dryly.

"Yeah, I'll bet." Gorski looked to Nichole now, focusing on her badly bruised face. He said, "I can't imagine what all you've both been through."

Duff introduced his wife to Gorski; she already knew Mace, though not well.

"What's the latest?" she asked the COS.

Mace said, "Estimates of six to eight hundred rebels, hitting on two fronts. So far there's no sign of mercenary support."

Duff said, "They definitely had the support of mercenaries outside the city. If we don't see them here, that's either because we're not looking in the right place or—"

Gorski interrupted, "Or Sentinel's mission did not include an attack on the capital."

Duff nodded, thinking. "Right. But . . . why wouldn't it?"

Mace said, "Maybe the Chinese who hired Sentinel want this to look like an organic grassroots revolution, as opposed to . . . as opposed to whatever the hell this is." He added, "At the dam we're getting reports of dead whites with Slavic features, Cyrillic text in their phones and on their person."

Duff said, "I could have told you there were Russians at the dam."

Mace nodded. "You *did*, or you told Bob, anyhow. We just like to confirm."

"Understood."

Gorski said, "My guess is the Chinese used Sentinel to prop up the rebels, probably train them, and give them support on the way to the capital. Once here, Sentinel was probably told to slip away. The fact that the dead bodies left behind all appear to be Russian is interesting. My guess is Kang Shikun hired Russian mercs so that if they turned up dead Moscow would be implicated, not China. Once we get pictures of the dead and are able to, we'll run their faces. Bet you a dollar to a donut all those guys are Wagner Africa Corps, or else they used to be before Tremaine contracted them for this."

Mace said, "What do you think is on that tablet?"

Duff pulled it from the dead Russian's backpack and handed it over the table. "Proof of Sentinel involvement, probably. Maybe even something on there implicating the Chinese, if your theory about this Kang guy is right."

Mace looked over the ruined device. "Did you really have to shoot it?"

"I shot the guy carrying it. The computer was collateral damage."

Mace put it down on the table. "We'll have to have it couriered to Langley. They'll pull any intel off it that they can."

Now Nichole asked, "What about U.S. military assets in the area?"

"President Amanor is refusing help from the West. He sees it like this: Central Command is attacking from the north. Southern Command is keeping the rebels out of the airport and Jubilee House. The president thinks his army has this under control."

"So . . . we're still on our own?"

Gorski said, "Your State Department is sending an aircraft to pick up the injured and deliver them to Sigonella, but we're not getting any fighter jets, aircraft carriers, or Navy SEALs." He looked to Duff, then said, "Nichole, your husband is officially the baddest hombre in this country."

Duff shook his head. "The other side has some pretty formidable motherfuckers themselves."

"That is true," Gorski allowed.

Nichole said, "What about the Marines here? Can't they help us?"

Mace shook his head. "The average American thinks there's a company of Marines at every embassy, maybe with a couple of Ospreys sitting on the roof, ready to respond to any issue that may come up. The truth is, we're a big embassy, and we have seven Marines in total; usually one is on leave, so six, really. The average age of these men is about twenty-three. And they have absolutely no role outside the fence line. They aren't a QRF, they don't go out and help Americans in need. Their number one job is to destroy classified material in the case of an attack on the embassy. Their number two job, and it's a distant second, is to protect people inside the chancery."

Now Mace looked out the window. "A coup. Here. Who would have believed it?"

To Duff's surprise, Nichole let out a little snicker. Mace turned to her. "What's that?"

"Nothing. It's just . . ."

"Just what?"

"It's just that I seem to remember that the CIA attempted a coup here once. Unsuccessfully, I might add."

The COS nodded. "Yeah. Not exactly our finest hour."

"What went wrong?" Duff asked.

Gorski answered Duff's question. "It was eighty-five, even before my time. The short answer as to why it didn't work was this: Godfrey Osei, the guy we were trying to put in power, was an idiot."

"What was the problem with Godfrey?"

"Well, for starters, he began strutting around with a walking stick and a Nazi SS emblem on his arm. The American mercs delivering weapons into Ghana thought that was a bad sign."

"Shit," Nichole said, shaking her head.

"And the mercs had their own issues. One of them was a drug dealer who had worked for the Agency."

Duff rubbed his tired eyes. "Christ."

"Yeah. As Richard said, not the Agency's brightest moment."

Now Mace said, "Okay, Duff. Bob is going to debrief you. Everything you saw and did over the past twenty-four hours, your thoughts about it all."

Nichole said, "If you don't need me, I'd like to get home to check on the kids."

Mace nodded. "We're not letting anyone out in the street in a thin-skinned vehicle till this is all over, so get one of the LGF drivers to take you in one of the armored vics."

"Thanks," she said, and then she kissed her husband and headed for the door.

"Tell them I'll be home as quick as I can," Duff said, before turning back to Gorski, who now had his phone recording their conversation in advance of the debrief.

A QUARTER MILE AWAY AT IRIS GARDENS, MANDY AND HUCK DUFFY, along with their nanny Portia Djangba, walked across the grassy courtyard towards the front gate of the apartment complex, following Botwe Brima, a Ghana city police officer and part-time Local Guard Force employee that Portia had known for over two years.

Five minutes earlier, Officer Brima had rung the Duffys' doorbell and told Portia he'd been ordered to drive the kids over to the embassy because their parents wouldn't be able to leave. He spoke in Twi so that the kids couldn't understand, telling Portia that both parents had been injured and would likely spend most of the day and perhaps even overnight in the chancery clinic.

Portia had insisted on going with the kids; she wasn't going to let them out of her sight, not even to go with a policeman in a police car, with the ongoing sounds of distant fighting in the city, and Brima finally agreed to her demand with a shrug.

As they walked towards the front gate of the apartment complex, Portia stepped up next to the officer and spoke to him, again in Twi. "Are the roads safe?"

The policeman said, "In Cantonments, they are. There's fighting around Black Star Square, more fighting somewhere to the east, I'm hearing, but it's totally quiet here."

At the gate Portia left the officer's side and stepped into the guard shack where her fifty-six-year-old father worked. With the kids at her side she asked him in Twi, "Do you know if Nichole and Josh made it back to the embassy?"

She'd known Brima for as long as he'd been part-timing for the Americans, and she had no reason to doubt him, but the children were her responsibility and she wanted to be certain.

Her father said, "They got back twenty minutes ago."

A police cruiser was parked right outside the gate, and Portia had assumed it to be Brima's car, but the officer just waved to the cops in the front seat, then began walking up the sidewalk.

Brima continued on, the kids and their nanny following him.

Quickly Henry Djangba stepped outside the gate. "Hey? Brima? Where's your car, man?"

The officer looked back over his shoulder. "I parked in the lot over here."

"You should have just pulled up to the gate."

"It's fine, boss. No one is around."

The four walked up the road, and the sound of a low boom in the distance turned everyone's head.

Everyone except for Officer Brima.

They reached the intersection with the parking lot; it was only twenty meters from the front gate. Portia looked for the police car but didn't see it.

As if he could anticipate her question, Officer Brima said, "Actually, it's in the next lot. Just this way."

Portia found this odd, and she looked him over. Sweat had formed on his brow; his eyes were wide and searching, his fists balled, the fingers of his right hand squeezing hard against his car keys.

Behind them, Henry Djangba had stepped out into the street, still watching his daughter go with the others, his hands on his hips. Once they passed the first parking lot, he motioned for another guard to come out of the shack and onto the road, and then they began walking after the group.

A string of gunfire to the south continued for several seconds; Portia held the kids' hands, and she began to slow.

Behind, her father shouted out. "Brima! Where are you going? Get them back here, and go get the car yourself!"

Brima did not turn around. He just walked towards the next intersection. Turning to Portia, she noticed he did not look into her eyes as he spoke. "We're almost there."

Just as the words left his mouth a black van raced up the road from the west. It slammed on its brakes and a man in a mask leapt from the front passenger seat.

Brima raised his hands at the man. "No!"

Portia moved herself in front of the kids to shield them.

Mandy grabbed her brother, turned, and began running back towards the apartments, but another man in a black mask leapt from the rear of the van, came around, and cut off their escape. Mandy began to turn away from him, but he was too fast, too strong, and he scooped both her and her brother up. Their feet left the pavement, and they were hauled into the back of the van.

Mandy and Huck both screamed.

Outside the van, Portia Djangba was slammed to the ground by the big man from the passenger seat; she saw he had a pistol in his right hand and, as she began to get up to rush to the vehicle and pull out the kids, the masked man raised the weapon.

Behind her, Portia heard Officer Brima. "No! Don't shoot!"

She looked back to see that Brima had pulled his own weapon; he lifted it up towards the attackers, but a gunshot rang out and Brima's head snapped back. He fell into the street just a few meters from Portia.

She screamed now, then climbed back to her feet, but the man in the mask had already jumped back into the van.

Gunshots rang out behind her; either her father or the other guard was shooting back at the attacker, and she saw the man buckle slightly, as if he'd been hit.

But he did not fall; he lifted his arm, aimed his pistol from his seat, and pointed it out the open door.

She thought he was aiming right at her, and he fired twice in quick succession.

Portia dropped down into a crouch and covered her head in a vain attempt to protect herself.

The van sped off; she rose back up and began running for it.

The back door was closed by a masked man, but not before she caught a glimpse of the two kids held by yet another masked man. In the melee Mandy had pulled on the man's long-sleeve shirt, breaking buttons and opening it at the neck, and Portia could see that the man holding the children was white.

She kept running after the speeding vehicle, as panic like she'd never felt in her life coursed through her.

Behind her, Officer Botwe Brima lay dead in the street. Henry Djangba, Portia's father, a senior employee of the U.S. embassy Local Guard Force, was in the street as well, sitting down, with blood pouring from his left leg. He held his pistol up with both hands unsteadily and pointed it at the fleeing van, but he wasn't going to fire again and threaten the kids.

Portia Djangba did not see that her father had been injured; she was too focused on the children. She ran after the van as fast as she could, but still it pulled farther and farther away with every step she took.

The squad car that had been in front of the apartment complex fired up behind her, then did a U-turn before driving around Henry Djangba and racing off in pursuit of the van. It passed Portia by, but she continued running, because she did not know what else to do.

FORTY

NICHOLE DUFFY WALKED PAST MARINE POST ONE WITH A WAVE AT the gunnery sergeant, then exited the front door of the chancery and headed towards the CAC, the compound access control point, the guarded entrance and exit of the U.S. embassy. She'd had the guard radio for an armored car to take her on the three-minute drive back to her apartment, and when she stepped out of the front gate she found her driver, an LGF man, waiting for her in a beige Mercedes idling in the driveway off Fourth Circular Road.

She waved to the man and had taken only a single step towards his car when a woman rounded the corner into the driveway in front of her in a frantic sprint.

Nichole hurried back towards the door to the guardhouse, thinking an emotionally distressed person intended to do her harm, but when she focused on the woman, she realized she was looking at the kids' nanny.

Portia was hysterical, crying. A panic overtook Nichole; her knees weakened and she froze in horror.

Guards inside saw the rushing woman; they ran from around the desk towards the door, ready to tackle her before she got inside or harmed the embassy employee at the door.

But the young woman collapsed in Nichole Duffy's arms.

"What's wrong? What's happened?"

"They . . . took them! They took Huck and Mandy!"

"Who? *Who* took them?"

"A . . . a van." She sobbed, then said, "Four men."

Nichole took her in her arms and rushed her back inside.

BY THE TIME NICHOLE LEFT PORTIA AT THE CAFETERIA TABLES ON the ground floor of the chancery and ran up the stairs to the offices of the CIA station, Duff was still in the conference room, standing there, white as a sheet, on the phone with Henry Djangba. The wounded lead guard had radioed Richard Mace immediately, informing him of the kidnapping, and Mace had run here from his office.

Husband and wife made eye contact, and Nichole saw both a panic and a vulnerability in her husband like she'd never seen in her life. She ran to him and clutched him tightly, afraid that he would fall to pieces now, but when she looked back into his eyes, she noticed a marked change.

A look of fixed determination blanketed his face. He'd gone, in seconds, from terrified to resolute. He had a mission now, the most important mission of his life.

Djangba was still talking on the radio. Nichole heard him say that his daughter was missing, as well, so she grabbed the radio from her husband's hand. "Henry, it's Nichole Duffy. Portia ran here after chasing the kidnappers. She's inside the embassy and safe."

Henry groaned a little into the phone; he was obviously in pain, and he said, "Thank you, Mrs. Duffy. A police car went after the van. I don't know if they are still in pursuit. One of our LGF men was killed . . . but he might have been in on the kidnapping."

Mace leaned in. "In on the kidnapping? What do you mean by that?"

"He showed up fifteen minutes ago, said he'd been instructed to pick up the children and bring them to the embassy to see their parents."

Duff said, "We didn't ask anyone to do that."

Henry said, "I was afraid of that. Well, if he was working with the kidnappers, he'll never tell." After a moment he said, "I think I hit one of the men in the stomach. Didn't kill him, not immediately, anyway."

"How do you know?" Nichole asked.

"He shot me after I shot him."

Duff looked to Mace and Gorski, and then he just looked at Gorski. In a grave tone he said, "You and me, Bob. We need to talk, *now*."

Mace stood and said, "I'll be in my office talking to the ARSO and trying to get the local police on the radio."

When Mace left with the radio, Nichole said, "It was Tremaine."

"Did someone specifically identify Tremaine?" Gorski asked.

"Portia said at least one of the four masked men was white. They were all wearing masks."

To this Duff said, "Just like most of the Sentinel men I've run into."

Gorski looked like he was going to push back on the conclusion Nichole had drawn, but after staring down both of the Duffys' hard glares for a moment, Gorski just nodded. "Yeah, okay, good enough for me."

He said, "I have agents out in the field. I'll get everyone looking for that van."

"Where are your agents?" Duff asked.

Gorski made a face as if he was considering the question. Then he said, "We've got people in the streets. We've got feelers out. That's all I am prepared to say. If we get any information about—"

"No," Nichole said forcefully.

Gorski cocked his head. *"No?"*

"No," she repeated. "You know where they took the kids." When

Gorski said nothing, she looked to Josh. "He hesitated when you asked him where his agents were. He doesn't want to tell you."

Gorski said, "We are pursuing leads. That's all I can say until we—"

Duff advanced on the smaller man. "Bob. If you know something, you need to fucking tell me right now."

Gorski looked back and forth between Duff and Nichole, then let out a long sigh. "We think we've fixed the Chinese intelligence operation to a location in the city. That does not mean we think Tremaine is there. In fact, I'd be very surprised if that's where he went."

"He's got an injured man. Where else are they going to take him? The hospital?"

Gorski thought a moment more. "I'm not going to give you the address. There is an ongoing intelligence operation there, and we can't compromise it by having you go—"

"We're talking about my kids!" Duff shouted, his fists balled.

"Not yet, we're not! I have people watching the location, and they haven't reported anyone coming or going."

"How did you find it?"

He sighed. "I sent a team of locals and an Accra station S&T tech out into the city with some signals intelligence equipment, thinking that wherever Kang is working out of would probably have one of the largest electronic signatures in the city considering the fact that power is off. Satellite Internet, high-power radios, shortwave. Kang always has a technical team supporting him, and I figure they must put out a lot of wattage."

"It's a big city, Bob," Nichole said.

"Yeah, but the locals started in the Aburi Hills, north of town. Big estates up there, good line of sight for radios and good visibility over the entire city. Kang sees himself as a general looking out over his battlefield.

"It's the same thing he did in the Central African Republic a couple years ago, but we never busted him, so he doesn't know that finding a hill to overwatch the scene is a compromise to his operation."

"And you found something in the hills?"

"About an hour ago, yes."

Duff said, "Other than strong radio signals, do you have anything else tying him to the location?"

"There's a security presence at the villa."

"It's West Africa, Bob. There's a security presence at every rich person's house."

"Our people saw Asian security when they got there, and a group of masked men in pickups arrived shortly after."

Duff raised an eyebrow. "Okay."

"We looked into the property. It was rented four and a half months ago. The renter's agreement doesn't tell me anything, but you'd expect the Chicoms to hide their attachment to a covert safe house. I wanted to fly a mini drone over it, but Mace denied the request. Still, our team on the ground nearby is reporting massive amounts of data still moving into and out of the house."

"You have people with eyes on the place right now?"

"My surveillance detection team is still nearby in a house. As soon as John gets something to eat downstairs I'm going to send him up there, as well. My instructions are for them to see who comes and goes, but not to try to get eyes on the interior. Kang will have his own surveillance detection out in the neighborhood; that's how he burned me once in Sierra Leone."

Duff said, "They took the kids because they want that tablet back."

Gorski and Duff just looked at each other for a long moment. Finally, Gorski said, "Look, Josh. I'm sorry. I can't give it back to you."

Josh nodded. "I'm not asking you for that computer."

Nichole said, "But we can give him another tablet. You told him last night that you shot it and it was broken."

Duff nodded. "We'll go by IRM when we leave here. See if they have any Getac tablets we can have."

Gorski said, "Josh . . . he's not just going to take a broken computer and hand you your kids back. You know that, right?"

"Yeah, I know that. I just need it to get close enough to him to get to the kids."

"To do what?"

Josh looked at Nichole, then back at the CIA officer. He said, "Bob, just tell your people to be on the lookout for Tremaine, the black van, the kids . . . anything. I won't step on the toes of your operation to bring down the Chinese, but you've *got* to help me here."

"I will," Gorski said.

Duff looked to his wife again, because he trusted her intuition. "Is he lying?"

She looked at Gorski hard. After a moment she said, "I believe he understands what we're going through right now, and I believe he will do the right thing when the time comes."

Duff didn't know if that was real intuition or if she was just trying to guilt Gorski into helping them, but he didn't care either way. The only thing that mattered was that Gorski give him the info he needed.

Finally, Duff said, "Who else knows about this location?"

"So far, no one but us. But Mace will probably tell Ghanaian intelligence pretty soon so that they can get troops up there to raid the place."

"I need an address, Bob."

Gorski said, "You are white. You *will* stand out in that neighborhood, and if you were thinking about just going in there with guns blazing, you'll die before you get through the front gate. You go there and you *will* endanger everything."

Nichole put her hand on her husband's shoulder. "He's right. We have to think of something else."

DUFF AND NICHOLE LEFT BOB GORSKI AND HEADED TO IRM, THE INformation Resource Management department. In just a couple of minutes they had their hands on a Getac tablet computer. It was a newer model than the one he'd gotten off the Russian, but it was the same size and had the same black rubberized skin.

The tech who passed it over to the Duffys then pulled a sign-out sheet for him to sign. Duff just looked at the young man like he was going to smash his head into a wall, so Nichole pushed by him and signed with a flash of a smile.

Walking out of the room, the tech said, "Y'all take care of that, okay?"

"I'm going to fucking shoot it," Duff muttered.

"What?"

Nichole looked back at the man as the door closed behind her. "He's just kidding."

In the atrium of the chancery, she asked, "What is your plan, Josh? Are you going to call Tremaine and set up an exchange? You know that's not going to work."

Duff said, "Right now, I'm going to the Aburi Hills."

Nichole said, "We don't even know for sure that's where he's going."

"I think he will. And even if he doesn't, the Chinese operation is our only connection to Tremaine."

Nichole said, "How are you going to put bullet holes in that thing?"

"Just like I told that guy. I'm gonna shoot it."

They went down to the ground floor of the chancery and found Portia walking alongside her father, who was being carried into the clinic on another stretcher, a white bandage wrapped around his left thigh.

Nichole ran after them to check on both Portia and Henry, and Duff continued walking towards the front of the chancery.

But passing the café on the ground floor, he stopped abruptly.

Isaac Opoku stood there in his RIVCOM uniform.

In the last half hour, Duff had forgotten Isaac was even here.

The Ghanaian stepped up to him. "More wounded are being brought in, security is running around, the Marines are at the front gate. What is happening?"

"Tremaine kidnapped our children."

Isaac put his hand on his heart. "My God. Do you know where he took them?"

Duff said, "We think the Chinese intelligence officer in charge of this entire coup is at a house up in Aburi Hills. Do you know where that is?"

"Of course. When I was in the army I was with Southern Command for a couple of years before I was stationed in the north. I know Accra very well." Without hesitating, he said, "I can take you there."

Duff put his hand on the man's shoulder. "Thank you, my friend. But we don't have an address yet, and we don't have any official backing. Our intelligence agency found the place, and they're going to tell the Ghanaians about it shortly."

Isaac's eyes widened. "That is very bad. When I was in SF we were a very good combat force, but we weren't trained on hostage rescue."

"That's what I was afraid of."

"What do you want to do?"

Duff thought a moment. "I want to go up into those hills, get as close as I can, and then, when the Ghanaians come to raid the place, I'm going to slip in and get my kids."

Nichole came back to the atrium, and she'd heard her husband's words. "Not without me, you won't."

Duff shook his head. "You need to stay behind to—"

"No. I don't have anything to stay behind for. Everything I love is going to be at that location, and I'm not going to just sit here while you and the kids are in danger."

Isaac said, "Duff . . . I will go with you, too. These people attacked my dam. Killed my friends, tried to kill my president. I mean, I didn't vote for him, but that doesn't matter."

Duff nodded. "Okay, we need a car. Can't take armor, we have to stay low profile."

Isaac cocked his head. "I'm sorry to tell you, but you and your wife are not going to be low profile in the Aburi Hills."

"Okay, that's a fair point." He thought a moment. "Unless . . . I've come across four Sentinel contractors since yesterday afternoon. Three Russians and an African. They've all been kitted up pretty much the same."

Nichole said, "You want to dress up like contractors? To wear masks?"

He shrugged. "It's our best option. We need to find a Toyota pickup, too."

Nichole said, "Henry has a Tacoma. I can go to the clinic and ask for his keys. But . . . where are you going to find clothes that look like what the contractors are wearing?"

Duff said, "Both of you, follow me."

FORTY-ONE

AFTER A THIRTY-MINUTE DRIVE THROUGH MOSTLY EMPTY STREETS, the black van carrying three Russian Sentinel contractors, the South African contractor called Junior, and the two Duffy children rolled through the front gates of the home at 1 Ankama Close in the Aburi Hills.

One of the men had been hurt; Mandy heard him cussing in English in the front passenger seat throughout the entire drive, using words she'd learned from her dad, while he took off his equipment and his shirt and wrapped bandages around his waist.

As the van they rode in pulled in front of the front doors, Mandy held her brother's hand. The two men in back with her and her brother opened the rear and side doors, and the kids were led out the side and into the house.

Mandy had been fighting tears the entire time; she was scared, but she didn't want to freak her brother out. For his part, he looked to his sister for guidance on the drive, and since she'd remained reasonably calm, Huck had, too.

She'd spent the time trying to do exactly what her father had always told her to do if she found herself in trouble. Breathe slowly, relax, take in as much information as she could, and plan her next move.

Looking at the four men during the drive, she realized only two of the men spoke any English at all. One of the men in back with a very strong accent had to translate for both the driver and the other man holding her and her brother, while the man in the front passenger seat, the one who shot his gun during the kidnapping and was hurt himself, spoke English with some sort of a foreign accent that was much easier to understand.

Now the foreign man who'd been translating and the other man from the back of the van walked on each side of her and Huck as they passed through a high entry hall, then stepped into a living room with floor-to-ceiling windows with a view of the city wrapped around the curved back wall. A large open kitchen was connected to it. Mandy saw fifteen or so people standing and sitting around the large space; most of them were Asian and working at computer stations, but a tall white man with a mustache stood there in the kitchen, and he walked up to the two kids as they came into the room.

The man knelt down and spoke to her. He had a foreign accent, as well. "Your father has something I need. You're going to stay here and be good little children, and when he brings it to me, we'll send you back home."

He smiled an insincere smile. He reeked of body odor, and she saw perspiration on his shirt in the outline of a vest. She'd seen pictures of her father working security when she was little, and she recognized the imprint of the body armor on the white man's shirt.

An older Asian man came out of a side room in the back of the large space, looked at the kids for a moment, then turned around and walked back through the door, but as he did so he said, "Jia?"

A young woman in a sweatshirt with her hair in a ponytail lurched to her feet from where she'd been sitting at the kitchen island, and she scurried into the room behind the older man.

The two men standing next to Mandy and Huck took them by the shoulders and roughly walked them to a staircase, and they all began climbing up.

KANG SHIKUN DID NOT HAVE TIME FOR THIS DISTRACTION. RIGHT now Addo's Dragons were fighting at the coast, and they were about to meet the full force of General Boatang's armored vehicles, and then Boatang would disperse his troops across the city to "restore order." Once this was done, Kang was certain, it would just be a matter of time before President Amanor resigned or was thrown out, especially once Kang's social media machine went into a full-on attack of the government's leadership during the crisis.

Kang had a million things to do today, but it was clear that he had to take care of the Sentinel compromise, and the only way he could do this was to allow Tremaine to trade the children for the missing computer.

Chen Jia entered the room with a little bow and closed the door behind her. Kang, to her obvious surprise, addressed her in English. "Your file says you speak English."

"I do, sir."

With a distracted nod, he said, "You will see to those children while they are here."

"See to them, sir?"

"One of the Russian mercenaries will guard their door, but you are responsible for their treatment. If they need food, if they start making noise. It is your job to control them. And they are not to leave that bedroom. Can you do that?"

Jia was not one to say no, and Kang was not one to say no *to*. She nodded and left the room with a bow.

THE TWENTY-EIGHT-YEAR-OLD WOMAN WALKED ACROSS THE LIVING room heading directly to the stairs, and once on the second floor she started up a long hall, at the end of which an armed man in a mask and a baseball cap stood outside a door, facing her direction.

Jia thought the man might have been Russian. He had a dangerous air about him; she'd noticed this the second he and the other man arrived, and she wondered what those two kids, whoever they were, thought of being held here by a masked man with a rifle hanging from his neck.

The two American children were prisoners here, and that was all she knew. Neither Kang, nor the big white mercenary soldier, nor the Russian guarding the kids had told her any more about what they were doing there or what was going to happen to them, and this terrified Jia.

All she knew was that she'd been ordered to take care of them. The guard would keep them here; she would keep them alive. Food, keeping them calm, watching over them, anything a Russian who only knew how to kill people could not do, Jia imagined.

But this wasn't her main concern at the moment.

No, her main concern was that she was going to be sick.

She made it halfway up the hall to the Russian when she noticed an open bathroom door on her right. She ducked in quickly, shut the door behind her, and, ten seconds later, vomited into the toilet.

It was a full three minutes later when she stood in front of the Russian.

"Are they in there?" she asked in English.

The man just stared at her.

"Do you . . . do you speak—"

"Chto?" was the only reply.

She could only see his steel blue eyes as he watched her open the door, and then she entered the little guest bedroom.

The two children sat on the end of the bed; the TV was off in front of them. It appeared the girl was in the process of comforting her younger brother, but she stopped talking immediately as Jia entered.

"Hello," she said, fighting down another wave of nausea.

"Hello," the girl said.

Jia looked at the television. "Do you want to watch some cartoons? Maybe I can find some on TV for you."

Mandy looked at her with suspicion. After a moment she said, "I want to see my mom."

"Your mom is not here. But I can bring you food, something to drink."

"Why are we here?"

Jia raised an eyebrow. "I do not know." After a moment she said, "I will go down and get some water and some food and bring it to you. She started for the door, then turned back. "Do not try to escape. There is a man on the other side of this door, and I worry about what he might do."

Huck said, "Who is he?"

Jia knew the man was a Russian, a mercenary, a killer. But she just said, "It is his job to make sure you stay in this room. If you do so, you won't have to worry about him."

The Chinese woman turned for the door, but the little girl called out to her. "You are being nice. When my daddy comes to get us, I will tell him not to hurt you."

Chen Jia turned and looked back, an expression of shock in her eyes. Did this kid just insinuate that her father would come and hurt people here? She pushed the thought away and opened the door without another word.

Heading out into the hall, she saw the Russian reach to close the door, but before he did, he walked back through the bedroom and on into the bathroom. As Jia watched, the man tried the window latch. From where she stood, Jia could see that not only did the lock not budge, but it was also way too high for the children to reach.

The mercenary apparently came to the same conclusion, because soon he turned away from the bathroom and began to leave the room behind Jia, but as he exited, he eyed the two American kids with absolute malevolence, and Jia thought she just might vomit again.

AT JUST TWENTY-ONE YEARS OLD, CORPORAL ALBERT SANDOVAL OF Joplin, Missouri, had been a member of the Marine Corps Embassy Security Group for six months, all of it here in Accra. He liked the work, and especially the freedom it afforded, because he spent his time away from his post here working on an online college degree with American Military University, and with it he planned on getting a job at the State Department when he left the Corps.

Sandoval was the only one of the six Marines here at the embassy presently in the Marine house, the freestanding barracks on a small hill in the trees behind the chancery. The gunny was at Post One, and the four other Marines were positioned in full combat gear throughout embassy grounds, while Sandoval was here, for now. He was due to relieve one of the other Marines in a half hour, so he'd already stepped into the Marine Ready Room to kit up in his armor when he heard someone call out from another room. Before he could answer, the new ARSO Duffy walked in, along with an FSO Sandoval had seen but not met, and a Black man in an unfamiliar-looking police uniform.

To Duffy, Sandoval said, "Good morning, sir."

"Hey, Albert. This is my wife, Nichole."

He looked back and forth at the couple. The ARSO had cuts on his head and a bandage on his forearm, and she had a black eye that had spread gray to the entire right side of her face.

Duffy said, "And this is my friend Isaac. He saved my life, saved the ambassador."

The young Marine shook the man's hand. "Thank you, sir."

"No problem."

Duff said, "We need to borrow some of your gear."

"Our . . . gear? You mean you want uniforms?"

Duff shook his head. "Nope. We need three sets of civilian clothing. The kind of stuff you guys wear. Jeans or cargo pants, T-shirts, running shoes or boots." He seemed to hesitate a moment, then said, "Body armor, too."

"Oh . . . you've got to go out into the city?"

"We do."

"Uh . . . don't you have your own body armor, sir?"

"I do, but I'm looking for something with no insignia on it. Your load-bearing vests have removable patches. Mine says 'Diplomatic Security.'"

Sandoval just nodded slowly. "Right."

"Hey," Duff said. "Do you guys have balaclavas?"

Sandoval nodded, even more confused. "Yes, sir. They're still in their packaging. Nobody wants to wear a face mask in eighty-five-degree weather."

Nichole shrugged. "We do. Long story. Would you have any clothes that might fit me?"

The corporal gave her a quick look up and down. "You're about the same height as Sergeant Conti. He's on leave, we can raid his locker."

"Good."

Sandoval just stood there a moment.

Duff asked, "Is there a problem, Corporal?"

To Duff he said, "I'm sorry, sir. I can't let you take guns or electronics. Or night vision."

"Don't need any of that. You have batons? OC?"

Sandoval let out a sigh of relief. It was obvious to Duff the kid was terrified of the prospect of having to tell his ARSO that he couldn't have the guns. That resolved, he was more than willing to help. "Collapsible batons and OC spray, yes, sir. We have plenty of both."

The corporal took them to the team room, where they found the clothes and shoes they were looking for, and then they went back into a storeroom behind the ready room. Here the Marines kept extra load-outs, and the four of them took all insignia off the load-bearing vests.

Once everyone had changed clothes, their armor and new backpacks filled with various nonlethal gear still in their arms, they headed for the door.

Sandoval called from behind. "Sir, wherever you're going, I wish I could go with you."

"I wish you could, too, Albert. You stay here and keep the ambo safe. She's had one hell of a rough day."

"Yes, sir. I will. Good luck."

ISAAC, DUFF, AND NICHOLE EMERGED FROM THE MARINE HOUSE carrying duffel bags with their borrowed clothing: jeans, brown long-sleeve fireproof tunics, boots, socks, and utility gloves. They carried their packs and vests in their arms and headed for the chancery.

Nichole went into the building to check on Henry and Portia, and she came back ten minutes later with Henry's truck key and his permission to use the vehicle. The truck was parked in a monitored lot just outside the main gate, and Isaac went to bring it to the entrance while Duff walked over to the garage where they had brought the three vehicles that they'd taken into the city.

As he expected, several LGF men were here, and they had removed the AK-47s Duff, Nichole, Isaac, Chad, Ben, and Malike had been carrying, unloaded them, and had them stacked on a table next to one of the Yukons.

Duff began walking over to the guns and extra magazines, ready for a confrontation from the men.

But it was a voice behind him who stopped him. "Duffy? What are you doing?"

Duff turned around to find John, the CIA officer who'd led the caravan to retrieve them from up north, standing there.

"Did you hear what happened?"

"I'm sorry, man. I know everyone is going to move mountains to get them back safe."

Duff just looked at John, then turned to the two Local Guard Force men who'd been cleaning out the vehicles. "Can you guys excuse us for a minute?"

Both Ghanaians left the garage, and as soon as they did so, John said, "What's your plan?"

"Gorski and Mace found the enemy safe house."

John nodded. "In Aburi Hills. I'm on my way there now to pick up surveillance, just came over to grab a low-profile vic."

Duff said, "Yeah, well, I guess I'll see you there."

"What's your plan?" John repeated.

"Me, Nik, and Isaac are going to go get my kids."

"Dressed like contractors?"

"Yeah." Quickly, he added, "We've got balaclavas."

"You think that will get you through the gate?"

"No, I think that will get me *to* the gate."

He shook his head. "Dude, that's a suicide mission."

"What other choice do I have? Let the Ghanaian army slam through the front gate in an APC and pulverize the place with a heavy MG? I've got to go and try to do this quietly."

John looked at the AKs on the table next to where Duff was standing. "That's your idea of quiet?"

He shrugged. "It's my backup plan, for when my brilliant idea crashes and burns."

"Right. Look, Duffy, I'm not your superior, I can't tell you what you can and can't do, but I do have to let Mace and the ambo know that you just scooped up a bunch of guns and mags and left the embassy."

Duff looked to the floor of the garage, then slowly back up to John. "Do you have kids?"

"My daughter Shyla is friends with Mandy. They played in the pool at the cookout Sunday."

Josh had met two hundred people in the past two weeks, and he couldn't remember all of them. "Right," he said. "What would you do if someone kidnapped Shyla, you knew where they took her, and nobody had a good way of getting her back?"

John stood there looking at Duff a long time. Finally, he gave a little nod, then said, "I was never here." He backed out of the small garage and walked away.

Duff scooped up a dozen loaded magazines and three of the AKs, then left the garage.

FORTY-TWO

PROFESSOR MAMADOU ADDO ARRIVED AT ANKAMA CLOSE JUST AF-
ter nine thirty a.m. in a caravan of three civilian sedans and protected by a total of nine of his rebels. They were checked over by a
pair of Chinese intelligence officers working as sentries at the front
gate, then directed to leave their weapons before proceeding.

Reluctantly the ten men disarmed, then drove on through the
hilly property and parked in the circle in front of the main entrance
to the home.

Combat in the city was centered on Black Star Square on the
coast and at the airport in the center of town; the sounds of the fighting didn't reach this far to the north, but Addo had been on his satellite phone to the two commanders of his force who were still alive,
and the reports he'd been getting during the half-hour drive up here
to the hills had been nothing less than disastrous.

Addo and his men stepped up to the front door and were eyed by
a pair of Sentinel men in masks standing there; then they were led
through an entry hall by a female Chinese intelligence officer, and
then down a corridor that emptied into a huge den with a kitchen
attached to it.

The nine rebels the professor had with him were young, not one older than twenty-five. They were also from the Lake Volta region, not the capital, and they'd all lived their entire lives in various degrees of poverty. This multimillion-dollar property was like no place they'd ever seen, and they looked around with wide-eyed stares.

The professor himself was astounded by the opulence around him, but that did not divert his focus from his mission. He looked around the space at all the people here, saw the Chinese at their laptops and on their phones, saw the curved window looking out over the city, and then he saw the white men.

Three mercenaries, Condor included, sat around a dining table near the window, seemingly deep in conversation. Their masks were off, their weapons, body armor, and packs lay on the floor around them.

As soon as Addo saw the Sentinel leader, he stormed across the room, his men with him.

The two other mercenaries launched to their feet as the rebel leader and his entourage approached, but Tremaine just leaned back in the chair.

The much smaller professor stood over the South African, pointing a finger in his face. "Why are you here? Why aren't you down at Black Star Square fighting with my troops?"

"Why aren't *you* down at Black Star Square fighting with your troops?"

"Because Kang told me to come here."

"Same," Tremaine said.

"My force is being destroyed by Central Command. You and Kang both promised me Boatang would stay out of this fight."

Before Tremaine could respond, Kang Shikun stepped out of his office. "Professor, Condor. Please join me in here." He looked towards Jia's workstation and remembered he'd sent her upstairs to watch over the American children, so he called to another woman working at her laptop. "Bai, make sure the professor's men have something to eat and drink."

The woman dutifully rose and headed to the kitchen, with the wide-eyed boys following eagerly behind.

Tremaine, Addo, and Kang entered the bedroom turned into Kang's office and, as soon as they did so, Addo said, "Kang, your agents *must* be telling you that Boatang is here in the city with his tanks, and Sentinel is not even engaging them."

Before Kang could say anything, Tremaine spoke up. "There isn't a tank in this country, Professor. Boatang has light armored trucks. That's all."

Addo said, "That is a distinction without a difference, Condor. And what about the fact you aren't helping us?"

"I seem to remember you saying something about you not understanding why my people were even here."

"Well, you *are* here, and my force is being defeated by Central Command."

Kang said, "Did you bring me the video of you in the square?"

Thrown off balance by the question, Addo recovered and pulled his phone out of his pocket, opened his camera roll, and began playing Kang a four-minute speech he'd recorded.

He said, "I had to cut off the last two minutes of it because the army showed up. My men were doing what they could to battle them back, but now more than half the Dragons have been killed or injured."

Kang sent the video to his computer via Bluetooth, then handed the phone back.

Addo began berating both Kang and Tremaine, demanding they do something to support his troops, but quickly Kang held a hand up.

"Professor, you have done your part. Sentinel has done its part. And now it is time for me to do my part. I will send the video to

Beijing via satellite Internet connection, and within thirty minutes the world will know you are in control of the city."

"But I'm *not* in control of the city."

"That does not matter. Professor, stay here, relax, and in just a few hours you will see our plan come to fruition."

"Has the president left the capital yet?" Addo asked.

Kang held his gaze for several seconds, then said, "In good time, Professor."

TREMAINE WANTED TO SMASH HIS FIST INTO THE LITTLE MAN'S face. The last eighteen hours had been a disaster for him, and Addo here, bitching in his face as if he actually were the president of his nation, angered him to his core.

Junior had managed to get himself shot while kidnapping Josh Duffy's kids; he was in a bedroom now being treated by another merc. The wound looked little more than superficial to Tremaine; his countryman should be back on his feet in short order, which was good, because Tremaine needed help with his inevitable showdown with Duffy.

Tremaine's sat phone buzzed on his belt, and he unhooked it. "Yes?"

A familiar voice spoke in a very dark and unfamiliar tone. "You didn't have to take them, Tremaine. They're just kids, they have no part in any of this."

"Good morning, Duff. You must be tired. More than twenty-four hours with no sleep, is it?"

"I have your computer. I am willing to trade, but I need to know that my kids have not been harmed."

"They are fine."

"An assurance from you isn't going to get it."

The South African sighed. "All right. Give me a minute."

He walked alone through the big house, climbed the stairs, and headed down the hall. On the way he passed the open door of a bedroom. Junior was standing, and a mercenary from Austria everyone called Graz was wrapping fresh bandages around his waist, leaving bloody dressings on the carpeted floor.

Tremaine just kept walking down to the end of the hall where Yuri, one of the Russian contractors, stood in front of a door.

Yuri didn't speak English, this Tremaine knew from the months of training the rebels, so he didn't bother speaking to him.

Tremaine opened the door and stepped into the bedroom; he saw the woman who was watching over the kids sitting in a chair against the wall, her head in her hands, while both of Duffy's children sat on the bed silently staring at the television. A cartoon in French played, and it didn't look like the Americans spoke French.

Tremaine walked over and handed the phone to the little girl. "Be very careful about what you say."

She took the phone and held it to her ear while her brother looked on. "Hello?"

Duff said, "Hey, squirt. Your mommy and I both miss you."

"I miss you, Daddy."

"Are you okay?"

"I'm . . . I'm scared."

"I know, sugar. Is your brother with you?"

"Yes."

"Huck?"

The little boy took the phone now. "Hi."

"I love you, son."

"I love you."

"Everything's going to be fine. Hand the phone back to the man who gave it to you so I can talk to him, but I'll see you both very soon."

"Okay." Huck passed the phone back, and then Tremaine turned to leave the room.

The Chinese intelligence technician stared at him. Her face was white, and she looked distressed about what was going on.

The South African left the room without another word.

Walking back up the hall toward the stairs, he said, "We need a time and a place to meet. I'll bring the kids, you bring the tablet."

"The tablet is damaged, like I told you. My children better not be."

"I have people who can evaluate that computer to make sure you haven't pulled a bait and switch."

"Good. Have them with you when we meet."

"Do you know where the Aburi Hills are?"

"Yes."

"Good. Call me back when you're heading up into those hills."

Duff hesitated, then said, "Tremaine. I'll give you what you want. Just give me what I want."

"See you soon, troublemaker."

Tremaine hung up the phone just as he made it back to Kang's office.

The Chinese intelligence officer said, "You have a plan for the Dragons?"

He nodded. "I'll get the laptop back, kill Duffy and whoever he brings with him. Then me and my boys kill Addo, the kids, and the Dragons. You need to make sure your people are in line, though."

"Meaning?"

"Meaning that bitch up there with the kids. She looks like she's about to puke from the stress of all this."

"She's looked like that since I met her. I think she has malaria." Before Tremaine could respond, Kang waved a hand in the air and went back to his original subject. "There are ten Dragons here, including Addo. How are you going to—"

"Ten *unarmed* Dragons," Tremaine said.

"Who aren't going to just stand there while you're slitting their throats. You have, what, nine, ten mercenaries here? You need to bring some more men. This needs to be done quietly."

Tremaine nodded and pulled out his phone again. "I'll get a couple more trucks of guys here in fifteen minutes, so when we kill Addo and his boys, we can do it quickly and cleanly."

ISAAC OPOKU PULLED THE TOYOTA INTO THE PARKING LOT OF LEGON Botanical Gardens in the northern part of the city. No one was around; the fighting was well south of here, but some of the extremist attacks of the previous day had happened nearby, and the citizens were staying indoors out of an abundance of caution.

Isaac came to a stop in the center of the lot, and then Duff climbed out of the front passenger seat, pulled out the tablet computer he'd taken from the embassy's information resources department, and placed it on the ground.

Retrieving his AK from the truck, he aimed in on the tablet from fifteen feet and fired a round. The device flipped up into the air and then came back down again. Once it stopped moving, Duff shot it again.

Looking over the device, he made sure that it would not turn on, and then he carried it back to the car and they drove on towards the hills.

Duff's sat phone rang almost as soon as they got back on the road.
"Yeah?"

"It's Gorski."

"If you don't have an address for me, then I don't want to talk to you."

The man on the other end of the connection hesitated, then said, "One Ankama Close. Agents in the neighborhood confirm the black van entered about thirty minutes ago. They weren't close enough to see any occupants of the van."

Duff looked to Isaac behind the wheel. The man just nodded, indicating he had heard the address, and he continued driving north.

"Opposition?"

"Unknown. I'm keeping my people back as far as possible so we don't spook Kang and cause him to flee. I've got John heading up there; he's got a drone and a house he can use a few blocks away. We should get more of a picture soon."

"Who else knows?"

"About twenty minutes ago we informed the Ghanaian Bureau of National Investigations about the place."

"Shit!" Duff exclaimed. The national spy shop knew the location of the HQ of the coup attempt. They'd send the military, and the military would kill everything there that moved.

Gorski understood what Duff was thinking. "Look, it will take them some time to set something up."

Duff looked at the phone, then brought it back to his ear. "I'm not a fool, Gorski. Tremaine isn't looking to trade, he's looking to fix me and the tablet in the same place at the same time, so he can deal with us both. After that . . . there's only one thing he can do with the kids, isn't there? They've probably seen his face."

After a time, Gorski said, "I wish I controlled some group of snake eaters I could send in."

"Me, too." Duff thought a moment. "I just spoke with Tremaine; he told me about the hills, but not the address. I'm supposed to call him back when I get to the area."

"Looks like his plan is to bring you straight to their safe house."

Duff had been wondering about this. He said, "All the more reason to assume this is a double cross. He wouldn't give me that intel and then just let me leave."

From the back seat Nichole said, "We roll up on the property, find a way to make access, and then call him. As he's getting ready for us, we hit the house from behind."

Duff thought the plan was thin, but he had nothing else. They drove on, each mentally preparing as best as possible, though there were nothing but unknowns ahead.

CHEN JIA STOOD IN THE KITCHEN HEATING HOT CHOCOLATE IN THE microwave. The American children—she didn't know their names— had told her they weren't hungry, and they'd turned down her offer of soft drinks. But when she remembered there were some packages of hot chocolate in the kitchen, the little girl looked at her younger brother and they both nodded.

Jia leaned against the counter, taking her weight off her legs a bit, and it felt good to do so. Her roiling nausea had abated—for now, anyway—and she actually thought she'd come back down here and find something to eat once she had seen to the kids.

But what would she eat?

She didn't want chicken, didn't want meat of any kind; the thought of it nauseated her anew.

It wasn't that Jia was a vegetarian. No, the problem was, Jia was pregnant.

She'd told no one here. No one *anywhere*. She'd received the news from her doctor ten days after agreeing to this two-month contract in Africa, and just four days before leaving Beijing to head to Ghana. She'd almost revealed her secret to her employer before she got on the plane, but her mission had been described as one of vital national security importance, and she was certain she would be relieved of her duties the second she mentioned that she was pregnant.

There were others out there who could do her job, and they could do it better without morning sickness.

Jia wasn't married. She'd left her boyfriend over a month earlier after an argument, and she'd almost immediately begun looking for a contract job with the Ministry of State Security. This top-secret operation in Ghana had been pitched to her as a cyber influence op, and that was really all the big picture she knew about it to this day, but it was clear to her that her nation was orchestrating either a real coup or some sort of faux coup for the purpose of strengthening the military here in Ghana.

Her job was almost over, she knew this much, and it couldn't end soon enough. The morning sickness seemed to be getting worse. She could feel her body changing, and she knew she wouldn't be able to hide her pregnancy for much longer.

The microwave dinged; she took out the two cups of cocoa and began stirring them to cool them.

She thought about everything going on. She was a contracted intelligence technical specialist, with advanced degrees in information technology and computer science and a top-secret security clearance with the Chinese government, and she was spending her morning catering to a couple of children who had apparently been kidnapped by the mercenaries wandering around the safe house.

It was a job that would have infuriated her if she'd been assigned it a few weeks ago, but now that she knew she was six months away from motherhood, the idea of caring for these kids had interested her from the start.

Two of the mercenaries entered the kitchen, took bottled water out of the refrigerator, then stood next to her at the island.

One of the men was wounded, with bandages around his waist and no shirt. He was covered in tattoos, and when he spoke he sounded South African. She'd heard him called Junior by the leader of the mercenary force when he'd entered with the children earlier.

The other man had an accent she couldn't place, but she thought it to be European of some kind.

She tried to dial in on the man's origins. She'd spent eight years in college, most of it in Singapore, and she'd had classmates from all over the world. She'd gotten good at discerning accents, and it was something of a pastime for her.

As she picked up the two mugs and passed by the men, she listened to a short snippet of their conversation.

The man whose accent she hadn't been able to determine said, "We just have to kill the dad; Tremaine will do the kids himself."

Jia wasn't certain she understood; she didn't understand the idiomatic expression "do the kids," but still she felt an unmistakable pang of dread, and her queasiness instantly returned.

FORTY-THREE

JOSH DUFFY'S PHONE BUZZED IN THE CENTER CONSOLE OF THE TA-
coma just as they entered the hills on the N4 highway. While Isaac
navigated and Nichole watched their six to make certain there were
no rebels or mercenaries on their tail, Duff answered.

"Yeah?"

"Duff? It's John."

He hadn't expected to hear from the CIA man again after last
seeing him in the embassy garage.

"What's up?"

"I'm three blocks away from the target. I've got a drone up, eyes
on the front gate of One Ankama Close, and two technicals are approaching now."

"Toyota pickups?"

"One is, the other's a Ford. I can see in the front vic, they've got
their windows down. Masked men, body armor."

"Sentinel guys," Duff said.

"That would be my guess. I wanted to let you know that they
passed a vehicle about a block south of the property, slowed down,
spoke to someone inside. My guess is the Chinese running this op

have their own surveillance detection assets out in the neighborhood, and they were clearing them to go up."

Duff said, "Gorski said Kang would do that. I'm hoping we'll be able to fool that first layer of protection by making them think we're Sentinel."

John told Duff to stand by a minute, and then he said, "They just rolled up to the front gate, talked to a pair of Asian-looking guards there. Then they drove on through. Looking at the grounds, I see a third pickup plus three civilian cars, an SUV and two sedans, all parked in the circle at the front. Got a couple more guys in masks by the door."

"Okay. Good information. What's your mission?"

"Just observe and report. Nobody told me I couldn't report to you, too."

"Thank you."

"Something else you need to be aware of. CIA has a field team up here, the group that found this location through electronic signal intercepts. It's four locals and one of our techs."

"What about them?"

"I just gave our guy a drone, told him to watch the area to the south and report anybody else coming up here who looks interesting."

"Good. What does the wall around the property look like?"

"Probably three meters high. No razor or anything on top of it. Big lawn both front and back. I see a couple of patrolling sentries, plus the pair at the front. I can't rule out sentries in the building looking out, but this isn't a fortified military complex by any stretch."

"Okay."

"Stand by," John said again, and then, "Okay. Six people dismounted from the technicals. They are all armed with long guns. A guard at the front isn't impeding them, they're walking right in."

Duff said, "Okay. We'll be there in—" He looked to Isaac.

Isaac said, "Fifteen minutes if we don't run into any problems."

Duff relayed Isaac's words; John acknowledged, then said, "From looking at the property with the drone, there's some good cover on the hillside on the south side, trees and big rocks. If you could get close enough to dismount and go through the trees, you could get right to the back fence. Inside the fence, there's landscaping . . . palm trees mostly. You could get some cover there."

"That's what we'll do, then."

John said, "Let me know before you do anything, I'll support you with overwatch as best I can."

"Thanks," Duff said, and then he hung up the phone and clipped it onto his chest rig.

To the other two in the truck, he said, "Let's put the masks on. The hills have eyes."

MANDY DUFFY SIPPED HER COCOA AND LOOKED AT THE CLOSED bathroom door. She could hear the woman inside throwing up, and it sounded as if she were crying.

Huck looked at his sister. "Is she okay?"

Mandy nodded and took another sip.

Finally the toilet flushed, the water ran for nearly a minute, and then the door opened. The woman had clearly been crying; Mandy could see her puffy eyes now.

She sat back in her chair and didn't look at the kids. She just stared off to the wall beyond them.

Mandy cleared her throat. "Your English is very good."

The woman looked at her but said nothing.

"Did you learn in school?"

She gave a slight nod, and Mandy took that as an opening. "Are you Chinese?"

After a hesitation, she looked away. Said, "Yes."

"We were studying Chinese at my last school. Ni hao."

She saw surprise on the woman's face as she looked back. "Ni hao ma," she replied softly.

"Wo hen hao, xie xie," Mandy said, and both she and the woman smiled a little.

When the woman did not immediately look away again, Mandy said, "Can I ask you a question?"

The woman shook her head. "I don't have any idea how long they are going to keep you here. I just work for them, they don't tell me their plans."

"I was going to ask you something else."

"Oh . . . okay. What is it?"

"Are you going to have a baby?"

The lady just stared at her. Three seconds, five seconds, ten seconds. At fifteen seconds Mandy could see tears fill the woman's eyes. She blinked, they dripped.

Self-consciously she wiped her eyes. Only then did she nod.

Mandy asked, "Are you going to have a boy or a girl?"

"I . . . I don't know yet."

Mandy smiled now. "It's going to be a girl."

Jia cocked her head. "Really?"

The young American nodded. "My mom said when she had me she was a lot sicker than when she had Huck." She shrugged. Matter of factly, she said, "You seem pretty sick."

"I am pretty sick," she said now, and tears continued to flow.

After a long time, Mandy said, "Are you trying to keep it a secret from everyone? If you are, I won't tell." She turned to her brother. "Huck, don't say anything."

Huck nodded.

The woman said nothing.

Mandy changed the subject. "The men who brought us here. They shot somebody when they captured us."

The Chinese woman looked away from them. After a moment she rose from the chair. "I will bring you lunch in a little while."

As she headed towards the door, Mandy called out to her. "Ma'am. Can you do something to help us?"

Jia stopped, but she didn't turn back around. After several seconds she said, "I can't do anything. I'm sorry."

She opened the door; the Russian guard turned around and took the opportunity to give the children the evil eye once again.

Jia walked past him without a word and headed for the stairs.

KANG SHIKUN SAT IN HIS DIM OFFICE LOOKING OUT THE WINDOW AT the bright Friday morning. He'd just taken a call from one of his agents in the city telling him Boatang's forces had routed virtually all of the rebels in bloody street-to-street fighting along the coast.

Kang was pleased. Central Command would take over down here in an attempt to "restore order," at least until the power came back online, and in that time Boatang's profile would skyrocket at the expense of President Amanor.

Kang wondered if the president would even last for the rest of the month before he was forced out of power by a grateful congress and a grateful nation.

Just as he stood up to go out to his support staff and see what news they had, he was startled by a sudden bright light. He turned back towards the room, and he saw that the power was back on.

Lights that weren't being run by the generator flipped on; the TV across the room glowed as it started up.

Kang sat back down. This was *not* ideal. He needed a couple more days of confusion and chaos around the capital city for General Boatang to become President Boatang.

Somehow the people at the hydraulic dam had managed to fix what Tremaine had described as "catastrophic damage" to the switchyard there.

Tremaine appeared at the door from the den. He'd put his body armor back on, and his rifle hung from his shoulder. "Hey. The power is—"

Kang said, "Not catastrophic enough, was it?"

The South African said, "This is Duff's fault. He stopped us from doing the damage we wanted to do to the structure, and by killing my Sentinel operatives, he sowed the seeds for the dam to fall out of our control."

Kang was not pleased, but he said no more about it. Instead he said, "My people are telling me the fighting at the square has died down to nothing. The professor and his nine unarmed men here are now apparently the last Western Togoland rebels still standing."

Tremaine said, "They won't be standing for long. I have the men here I need to do the job. We'll take them down into the basement, sell it like some sort of after-action conference, and we'll kill them all." He put his hand on the knife attached to the body armor in the center of his chest. "We'll be quiet about it."

Kang's desk phone rang now, and he snatched it up. At the same time, Tremaine's satellite phone buzzed on his chest rig, and he stepped out of the office to answer it.

Kang said, "Yes?"

"It's Boatang. We have a problem."

"Tell me."

"I just heard from an officer I used to know who is now with Southern Command. He tells me there is a platoon of special forces en route to raid a property up in the Aburi Hills. If that happens to be where you are, or where any of your people are, then you need to get out of there."

Kang rose from his desk slowly. He said, "Listen very carefully, General. You need to stop that raid."

"I *can't* stop it! General Nkrumuh is in command down here, and he has been talking to BNI. Nkrumuh isn't going to listen to me, and BNI isn't going to listen to me. They've been investigating me, as I'm sure you remember."

Kang called out for Tremaine; he only had a handful of armed Chinese here, but there were over a dozen of the Sentinel men throughout the house that he knew of.

But Tremaine didn't answer.

JOSH DUFFY HELD THE PHONE TO HIS EAR AS HE WALKED THROUGH the woods on the hillside a couple of hundred yards away from the target location.

He heard the phone answered on the other end, and then a voice. "Yeah?"

"Okay, Tremaine," Duff said. "I'm in my car on the N4, and we just got into the hills. I have my wife with me. I also have the computer. Please, let's just end this without any more violence."

"Yeah, that sounds like a plan, my friend."

The truth was Duff and his two cohorts had abandoned the truck just a minute earlier, three minutes after being stopped by a vehicle with two Chinese men in civilian attire. The men didn't speak English very well, apparently, but they did manage to say the word "Sentinel," in a questioning manner.

Isaac said they were, in fact, Sentinel, so the men waved them on up the hill, and Isaac drove on.

Tremaine didn't say anything further, so Duff pressed. "Condor? What's the plan?"

There was no response to his question, but he heard mumbled voices, as if someone had their hand over the phone while they talked.

Finally, the South African came back on the line. "I'm going to have to call you back."

"What? No! Do you want this computer or not?"

There was another pause, and then, "One Ankama Close. Put that in your GPS and get here as quickly as you can. Trust me, Duff, you don't want to dally."

Tremaine hung up the phone.

Isaac looked at Duff now. "Why does he want you to go directly to their safe house?"

Nichole answered the question. "Because he's not able to leave the property for some reason."

Just then Duff's phone rang again. Answering it, he heard Gorski's voice. "Look, BNI isn't telling me what they're doing, but my tech Travis has a drone over the approach up into the hills, and he reports that a platoon-sized element of Ghanaian military are staging there."

"Where?"

"To the north. They're in marked army trucks, so they aren't looking to do subtle. Travis thinks they're going to just crash through the neighborhood and attack at the front gate, but they're still preparing in a parking lot a kilometer away."

Duff began running now, and Nichole and Isaac did the same. They were all aware that they had to have the kids out of that property before the army arrived.

PROFESSOR ADDO STORMED INTO KANG'S OFFICE NOW TO FIND THE Chinese intelligence officer standing by the window and conferring with Conrad Tremaine.

"It's on the radio! My forces at the square are all destroyed, and there is no more fighting at the airport!" Addo shouted. "You should have let me stay with my men and fight to the end!"

"So happy to hear you say that, Professor," Kang replied. He touched an intercom button on his desk. In English he said, "Bring the rebels their weapons immediately."

Addo said, "What is going on?"

"Professor," Kang said, "you and your men will get one more glorious taste of combat today."

"*What?* What combat?"

"The army is coming here. You will fight them back."

Tremaine walked over to Addo, took him by the arm, and pulled him out of the office. "Let's get you kitted up for battle, Professor."

CHEN JIA WATCHED WHILE THE REBEL LEADER WAS MANHANDLED through the den by the much larger mercenary leader. The other Dragons sitting around the room leapt to their feet, but more mercenaries hefted their rifles and pointed them at the unarmed men in camouflaged uniforms.

Tremaine shouted to the Dragons now. "Everyone out front! You'll get your guns back and you'll get a chance to fight for your cause."

The group disappeared up the corridor to the front door of the massive home, and Jia looked at the other employees here. Everyone was trying to figure out what the hell was going on.

Kang stepped out of his office and marched into the center of the living room.

When he spoke, Jia could hear stress in the voice of the normally unflappable man.

In Mandarin, he said, "There is a platoon of soldiers preparing to attack this property. We have maybe fifteen, twenty minutes before they arrive. Our security forces along with the rebels will hold them back for the time we need to get out of here. Everyone break down your workstations, now, and go downstairs to the parking garage!"

The analysts, techs, and computer contractors began hurriedly closing and boxing laptops, unplugging phones and radios, and otherwise disassembling the war room.

But Jia only closed her machine, and then she looked at the stairs.

A MINUTE LATER SHE WALKED AS NONCHALANTLY AS SHE COULD towards the Russian protecting the door at the end of the hall. The man stepped out of her way, his hand on the grip of his rifle as he eyed her up and down. She opened the door and found the kids still sitting on the bed staring blankly at the television.

She could tell the little boy had been crying.

She shut the door behind her, then walked up to the kids, kneeling down in front of them.

Mandy said, "Hello."

Jia looked at her a long moment, then said, "When I leave this room, I want you to wait one minute, and then I want you to climb out of the window."

"We can't," Mandy said. "I already checked. It's locked at the top."

"I can unlock it."

Jia rose, entered the bathroom, climbed up on the counter, and then reached out, as far and as high as she could. Her fingertips grasped the latch holding the window shut. She flipped it, then put her hand on the main latch and turned it.

The window swung open, but she shut it again immediately.

Mandy and Huck were already standing. "Where do we go?"

Jia climbed back down. "Outside is a terrace. If you climb down the trees next to it into the bushes, the guards won't see you. Stay in the bushes until you get to the wall. At the wall you'll have to find a way to climb over it. Maybe you can find a tree or something." She said, "I'm sorry, it's all I can do for you."

Mandy said, "Thank you."

"There will be fighting here soon, you need to run. Good luck."

She rose and left the room, and the kids looked at each other.

Huck began counting down from sixty.

When he'd reached fifty-five, his sister said, "That's enough. Let's get out of here."

They rose and rushed to the bathroom.

FORTY-FOUR

THE SIX SENTINEL MEN WHO'D JUST ARRIVED HERE ON THE PROP-
erty had been positioned out at the front gate, their weapons at the
ready, pointed down the hilly residential road.

All nine of the Dragons had been re-armed, and they took positions on the lawn, down behind fountains, behind massive planters,
even up at the guard shack, replacing the two Chinese security men
who had just gone back inside.

Tremaine shouted to everyone at the front of the property. "I'm
expecting company, an American and his wife. They should be here
before the military. They have something I need with them. When
they get to the front gate, kill them both, and then I will come out
and find what I'm looking for."

He turned to Junior now. "Those kids are just a compromise now.
We don't need them."

Junior just looked at his boss. Finally, he said, "I'm not gonna kill
those kids for you, Condor."

Tremaine eyed him a moment. "Okay. Fair enough. I'll go do it.
You can stay here with the others and fight the fucking army."

He stormed back into the house, leaving the wounded contractor behind to face off against a military attack.

CHEN JIA HAD FINISHED BOXING AND STACKING ALL HER EQUIPMENT to take down to the covered lot below the house where all the passenger vans had been parked since they'd arrived here in country, and she looked around to see who else needed help, but she also stole a glance out a back window. She wouldn't be able to see where the children climbed down from upstairs, but she could see the bushes farther away from the house, and she wondered if the Americans were hiding in there already.

Just as she brought her attention back inside the building, Kang stormed into the den carrying his laptop bag and a backpack. He shouted to the room. "We need to be in the vehicles in five minutes!"

She knelt down to pick up as much of her gear as she could carry in one haul, and then she saw the mercenary leader storming his way across the den. He arrived at the stairs and began marching up, and as he did so, she saw him reach for the big knife secured in the webbing on his chest above his body armor.

She let out a little gasp, and her hands shook.

JOSH DUFFY PUT HIS BOOT ON THE THIGH OF ISAAC OPOKU. THE Ghanaian police officer had his back to the southern wall of the property, and he braced himself for Duff's climb.

Duff kicked his other foot up, put it on Isaac's shoulder and rose over the edge of the fence.

There were trees just inside the fence line here, and they covered his view of the home, but they also covered the home's view of him.

Quickly he reached back behind him, Nichole handed him his

rifle, and he climbed onto the top of the wall and scooted over. Hanging down behind the trees, he dropped and lifted his gun.

He couldn't see the house from here, but his objective at the moment was to simply help his wife and Isaac as they came over.

Nichole dropped down next to him a second later. In her hand she carried a length of rope, and she handed it off to her husband.

Duff wrapped it around his back, then lay down, facing up and holding the end of the rope in front of his body.

Immediately he felt the hard tug of a man using the rope he held to climb with.

Isaac dropped down next to the Duffys, and when he did so, he winced in pain.

Nichole whispered to him. "Are you okay?"

"Yes. It's the wound. It's nothing."

Duff rolled onto his stomach and crawled forward a few feet through the trees so he could see the house.

CONRAD TREMAINE PASSED THE RUSSIAN SENTINEL OFFICER NAMED Yuri, and he reached for the door to the bedroom where the kids were being held. Yuri didn't speak English, but Tremaine didn't need to tell him anything, because he was already holding the big knife in his right hand.

Yuri eyed the weapon, then gave a little smile, visible even under the balaclava, as his boss opened the door.

Tremaine didn't see the kids, so he walked over to the closed bathroom door. He started to knock, but instead he just tried the handle.

The door was locked.

Without hesitation, Tremaine brought his big boot up and kicked in the door.

Seconds later he was running back into the hall, passing Yuri.

MANDY AND HUCK DUFFY CRAWLED ON THEIR HANDS AND KNEES
between a row of palm trees and the outer wall around the property
grounds. They were trying to find a gate to go through, but so far they
weren't having any luck, so Mandy told her brother to stay silent, and
then she crawled out from the palms and looked around at the huge
backyard.

Almost instantly, a hand appeared from nowhere and grabbed her
by the arm, lifting her up into the air.

She screamed.

Her brother shot out of the trees to help her, and he himself was
grabbed by another man.

The two Chinese security officers began dragging the kids back
towards the house.

DUFF HEARD THE BLOODCURDLING SCREAM OF HIS DAUGHTER JUST
as he moved through some papaya trees. He scooted forward a few
more inches, and then he saw the back of the home. Mandy and
Huck were being carried by two men in white polos who wore pistols
on their hips, taking them towards a sliding door on the ground level.

Duff raised his weapon. He was just thirty yards away or so, an
easy shot, but he didn't have a plan for how to get the kids once he
shot the two people holding them, so he kept his finger off the trigger
of his AK.

The sliding door opened, and Duff watched as a big man with a
thick mustache stormed out. He was a Sentinel man, Duff could tell
from the equipment he wore, and he grasped a long-haired Asian
woman wearing a sweatshirt by the back of her head, clamping down
on her hair at the scalp and pushing her forward.

Duff felt movement next to him, and Nichole crawled into a prone position, her own rifle forward. She took one look at the scene in front of her and said, "Oh God, no."

Duff climbed to his knees, and she did the same. Behind them, Isaac was already up.

CONRAD TREMAINE STOOD ON THE BACK PATIO HOLDING THE FE-
male Chinese contractor by the hair as he approached the kids. The two Chinese security men put the children down, and then Krelis and Yuri stepped out from the house and moved behind the Americans, shooing away the Chinese. They put hands on their shoulders so they could not move.

Tremaine said, "First things first, little ones. Who helped you two get out of the house?"

Mandy reached out and covered Huck's mouth. "We aren't going to tell you anything."

"Was it this bitch?" He shook the woman he held back and forth. When the kids said nothing, Tremaine said, "I don't have time for this shit."

He nodded his head at Krelis, and the South African moved forward, pulling the little boy closer to Tremaine, but before Krelis had taken him more than a few feet from his sister, Mandy raised her finger and pointed.

At Yuri, the Russian Sentinel man.

"It was him," she said.

She grabbed Huck and pulled him away from the mercenary; Krelis was so stunned he let her do so, and then she put her arms around her brother's neck and leaned into his ear. "It's okay, Huck. Don't worry." Then she leaned closer and whispered much more lightly now, "Don't say anything."

Tremaine cocked his head in surprise, then looked to the Russian. The man didn't seem to understand what was going on, and

Tremaine was about to question the little girl further, but the sound of men shouting from the front of the property took his attention for a moment. His radio came alive, Junior relaying that the army trucks were approaching.

Tremaine looked back to the Russian mercenary, then drew his pistol and raised it, pointed it at the man. Yuri looked confused, but quickly Tremaine pulled his knife again and handed it over to the man.

Yuri took it, and Tremaine motioned towards the two kids, both now held by Krelis again.

The Russian understood. He moved towards the kids, raising the knife as he did so.

A gunshot rang out from the rear of the property, not the front, and Yuri went flying back; blood splattered the window behind where his body fell onto the patio concrete.

Another shot boomed, and Tremaine felt his vest catch a rifle round. It knocked him backwards, off balance but not all the way down.

He spun away and ran back into the house, and the Chinese security men raced in, as well.

Instantly the sound of machine guns rocking fully automatic at the front gate filled the air.

Krelis was left alone with the Chinese woman and the two kids. He spun away from the three of them and then lifted his gun towards the tree line.

He squeezed off just a couple of rounds before he was hit in the thigh, then the shoulder. He fell to his knees and flipped the selector switch on his Vektor to fully automatic, but before he could lay down on the trigger, another round caught him in the mouth, blowing out the back of his head.

The Chinese woman took the kids by their hands and ran with them back inside.

DUFF LEFT THE TREE LINE AT A SPRINT, HIS AK UP ON HIS SHOUL-
der. Nichole was behind him on his right, Isaac on his left, and all
three of their weapons swept back and forth, looking for targets. The
fight raged in front of the house, however, and no one else seemed to
be back here.

Duff was mad at himself for his shot on Tremaine. He knew he'd
smacked the man dead center in his chest, several inches below
where he was aiming and right in the middle of his armor plate,
but the round had been fired under unimaginable stress, so he'd
pushed the shot low.

They approached the two bodies by the back door; Duff fought
the urge to shoot them again because he didn't want to give their location away. Passing them by, Duff entered the home first, finding a
large den with boxes stacked all around but no people.

Behind him, Nichole said, "The stairs."

Duff nodded and covered for his wife while she headed to the
staircase up to the second floor. She was halfway there when Duff
registered movement on the mezzanine overlooking the den.

An Asian man held a submachine gun and pointed it down at
Nichole.

Duff fired twice, hitting the man in the chest with both shots,
and he fell out of view.

Two Chinese men with pistols came out of the corridor and raised
their weapons towards Duff and Nichole. Nichole was covering up the
stairs as she ascended and Duff still had his gun up on the mezzanine,
so the Chinese men had an insurmountable tactical advantage.

Duff realized they were both about to be shot.

A long burst of AK fire from behind reminded Duff that Isaac was
with them, too. Both Chinese gunmen spun back into the corridor,
each hit multiple times.

———

CHEN JIA RAN DOWN THE STAIRS WITH THE TWO CHILDREN, HEADING for the parking garage under the house. She knew the only way out of here was to make it into one of the vans that would exit out a side gate, to the west and not the north where the army was attacking.

She sprinted into the garage, saw Kang in the back of a van loaded with people and equipment, and took one step towards it, but then the van raced off on squealing tires, shot across the driveway, and headed for the side exit—where it rammed the metal gate and turned onto the road, speeding to the left, away from the heavy fighting.

Another twelve-passenger van was there, but no one was behind the wheel. She ran to it and checked for keys but found none. Looking around the garage now, she saw a table with several sets of keys on it, and she ran to grab them all to try to fire up the van.

NICHOLE REACHED THE SECOND-FLOOR MEZZANINE, KEEPING HER big rifle shouldered as she walked past the man her husband had just shot. As she passed, she kicked the subgun away from the obviously dead man's hand. She swiveled into an open bathroom, saw no threats, and was just about to move back into the hall when her husband and Isaac both passed her position, continuing on towards the other doors on this floor.

Nichole had never trained in close quarters battle. She'd used a rifle once in anger, in Syria after her Apache was shot down and she was attacked by insurgents, and she hadn't fired one again before last night.

But while this felt very foreign to her, she could tell that her husband was fully in his element. He led the way confidently, his weapon an extension of his body.

Intense, close-in gunfire rocked somewhere ahead of them on this floor, and this sounded like a response to all the shooting outside. Nichole wondered if there were gunmen up here firing out the windows at the approaching army. If there were, and the children had come this way with the Asian woman holding them, then she knew she had to get them away from the windows immediately.

In front of her, Josh put his hand on a door latch, looked back to Isaac and her, and then opened it.

He moved into the room quickly to the left, making space for Isaac to flood in behind him to the right, and Nichole took this as her cue to advance straight ahead.

She swung her rifle into the room, saw a masked mercenary at the window spinning around towards the movement behind him, and squeezed her trigger.

A second man was at a window on the left, and simultaneous to his wife's gunfire, Duff opened up on the man.

Both overwatch shooters went down in a hail of bullets, but then return fire from outside ripped into the room, shredding the ceiling just in front of the three of them.

Duff dove onto his wife, Isaac collapsed to the floor to get out of the line of fire, and then they all three crawled out of the room and back into the hall.

Duff shouted to the others. "That was the army out front. We have to stay away from the windows or they'll mow us down."

"We have to get the kids!" Nichole shouted.

Quickly they checked the other doors on this floor, they found no threats, but when they entered a bedroom at the end of the hall, they saw that the TV was on and cartoons were playing. Duff rolled into the bathroom with his gun up and saw the open window.

Isaac said, "The rest of the upstairs is clear. The children must be downstairs somewhere."

Duff said, "Let's go this way."

Duff climbed out and dropped down onto a terrace on the west side of the house. He saw that the landscaping reached almost to the house here, and he quickly kicked a leg over the railing and leaned out to put his hand on the trunk of a mahogany tree.

Isaac and Nichole followed him down, the sounds of bullets snapping overhead as soldiers trying to fight their way into the property battled the safe house's security contingent.

FORTY-FIVE

CHEN JIA TRIED THE LAST OF THE FIVE SETS OF KEYS IN THE VAN, but it still would not start. Unsure what to do, she rushed to the open garage door and looked out. The side gate to the property led to a narrow winding dirt road that went both left and right, and since all the shooting she heard was either in the house behind her or on her right at the front of the property, she thought about taking the kids and running for the gate.

But just as she thought this, bullets whizzed by in front of her, making a snapping sound as they pierced the air.

She fled back inside. To the kids she said, "We can't go this way. We have to go back in the house."

The little girl said, "My daddy is here."

Jia shook her head. "What? No, that's the army."

"He's here," she said again. "He shot the man who was about to kill us. Only my daddy would do that. He will help you."

Jia didn't think anyone was going to help her, especially not the father of the man whose children she'd been complicit in the kidnapping of. She wanted to be sick yet again but knew the dry heaves wouldn't help her out of her predicament.

She began to panic.

The young American girl walked up to her in the garage and took her hand. "What is your name?"

"Jia," she said distractedly. "It's Jia."

"I'm Mandy and this is my brother, Huck."

Jia just looked at her, her panic momentarily abating.

"What are you going to name your daughter?"

Gunfire tore through the air outside.

"I . . . I don't know."

Mandy thought a moment and said, "When we get out of here, I'll help you think of a name."

Jia's eyes filled with tears. She didn't think she was going to get out of here. The gunfire was so intense outside, and it seemed to be getting closer and closer every second.

Finally, Jia said, "Let's go look for your father."

They began climbing the stairs, but just as they did so, a door opened above them. To her horror, the mercenary leader that Kang referred to as Condor spun into the stairwell and pointed his gun at all three of them.

Mandy, Huck, and Jia froze as a second armed mercenary appeared.

Condor shouted to the woman now. "Where's Kang?"

"He, he left with the others."

"Any cars down there?"

"One," she said. "But I can't find the keys."

"Shit." He seemed to think a moment. "Okay, it will take too long to hot-wire it. We're all going out the back, over the wall, and down the hill on foot."

The kids began walking up the stairs, but Jia stood where she was.

Tremaine aimed his rifle at her forehead from five meters away. "You are my hostage, too, bitch."

She began climbing the stairs, her hands raised.

JOSH DUFFY KNELT OVER THE BODY OF THE DEAD CONTRACTOR with the knife that he had shot minutes earlier, as Nichole and Isaac provided security. He was looking for a radio, and he quickly found it.

Pressing the talk button as he and the others went back inside the home, he said, "Condor. It's Duff, over."

Seconds later he heard a response.

"Was that you out back before the army came?"

"That was me."

"Nice shot. Right in my solar plexus."

"Just saying 'hi.'"

Tremaine laughed into the radio. He said, "Hell of a way to communicate. I've got your kids. You have my computer?"

"I do, but I watched as you ordered a guy to kill the kids. If they're still alive, I want to hear from them."

There was a slight pause, and then Mandy's voice came over the radio. "We're on the stairs coming up."

Tremaine seemed to pull the radio away from the precocious girl. Angrily he said, "I can fucking end them right now, Duff! I'm coming up. I have my man Junior here with me, and we will conduct our transaction with you and be on our way."

"Where do you think you're going to go?"

"I've got another hostage. One of the Chinese. Kang isn't going to get out of this clean as long as I have her. He'll have to come back and get us, or I'll put her in front of a TV camera."

Duff said, "I'm already in the house. From the sound of the fighting out there, I'm guessing the army will be in the building in a couple minutes, tops."

A door opened on the left side of the den; Duff and Nichole crouched down behind the kitchen island, pointing their gun towards the movement. Isaac went flat on the floor, then began crawling down the length of the island, remaining hidden.

No one appeared at first, and then Duff heard, "We're coming out, Duff."

Huck appeared first, his eyes wide and filled with tears, then Mandy. She looked around the room, and Duff saw that she had managed to keep her cool, even in the midst of all this madness.

A contractor Duff had not seen before came out—this must have been Junior—and he held a pistol at his daughter's head. Similar to Isaac, the man had bloody dressing wrapped around his midsection.

Following them was the Chinese woman Duff had seen on the back patio, and directly behind her Conrad Tremaine emerged with a hand on the woman's neck, and his handgun pointed at Huck in front of him.

A heavy machine gun opened up out front for the first time, and this made Duff think the army had already received reinforcements, because the weapon hadn't been firing the last several minutes.

Duff pulled the tablet computer out of his backpack and held it up, his gun still on Tremaine. "Here it is. Like I told you, I shot it when I killed your Russian."

"I'll take it just the same, Duff. Throw it over here and I'll give you your kids back. Me and her are going to go out back, you're going to wait right here while we go, and then you—"

A sound in the corridor on Tremaine's left turned his head, but he kept his gun pointed at Huck.

Junior turned to look as well, but like his boss, he knew the Americans would shoot them if they didn't keep their guns on the hostages.

Suddenly, Professor Addo came running into the room with his rifle down at his waist, and he pointed it towards the group that just came out of the stairwell.

Duff shifted aim to fire on the man in the rebel attire; he had no idea who he was, but the man looked as if he was about to fire in the direction of his kids.

But before he could aim in on this new threat, a single shot rang out.

The man in a rebel uniform slammed back against the wall on his right and then tumbled to the ground, shot by Isaac Opoku from behind the kitchen island.

Duff looked back to his kids just as Mandy reached up and grabbed the wrist of the hand Tremaine held his gun with, and she pushed it up and away. Tremaine ducked behind the girl as he wrestled it free, giving Duff no shot on him, so Duff instead charged forward, intent on tackling Tremaine and leaving the other contractor to Nichole and Isaac.

Tremaine got the pistol back, began to raise it at Duff, but was unable to do so before Duff crashed into him, knocking him away from his daughter, then back through the door behind him and into the stairwell.

The two men tumbled down the entire flight of stairs towards the garage.

BACK UPSTAIRS, JUNIOR FIRED ONCE AT ISAAC, THEN SPUN AWAY from the kids to go to the aid of his boss, but then Nichole Duffy rose from the near side of the island and shot the man in the side of the head, killing him instantly.

The Chinese woman raced across the big den and ducked down behind a table; Nichole ran to Mandy and Huck, grabbed them both tightly as if she were lifting them for a hug, but instead she whipped around with them and began running for the sliding door to the patio. Halfway there, though, she saw an armed man in a camouflage rebel uniform running around the side of the property, heading her way.

She turned back into the room and yelled to Isaac.

"We have to make a stand right here!"

She put the kids behind the kitchen island. "Get down!"

"You have to help Jia!" Mandy said.

Nichole looked down at her as she raised her rifle. "Who?"

"The Chinese lady. She's our friend!"

Isaac fired at the rebel coming through the back door, hitting the man in the stomach and the pelvis, dropping him dead.

Once the shooting stopped, Nichole yelled to the woman hidden under a table. "Jia! Come to me with your hands up!"

The Chinese woman rose and, with hands raised, began moving towards Nichole.

AT THE BOTTOM OF THE STAIRS, TREMAINE PULLED HIS BACKUP knife as he sat up on the floor, still dazed from the violent fall. Duff sat up next to him, and Tremaine swung out. The American fell back, and then Tremaine stabbed down at him.

Duff rolled out of the way just as the blade slammed into the concrete, and then the American tried to quickly get up and out of the way.

Tremaine was on his knees. When Duff rose to his feet, the South African swung his massive blade at the closest part of the man to him, his left leg.

The knife smacked into a carbon fiber and steel prosthesis, doing no damage, and then Duff used his good leg to kick Tremaine in the face.

UPSTAIRS, ISAAC FIRED UP THE CORRIDOR AT A GROUP OF MERCE-naries who'd escaped into the house to flee the withering fire at the front gate. He ducked out of the line of fire as the men there responded to his shooting, and then he dropped to his knees, swung back out into the corridor, and dumped half a magazine at the men in the entryway.

Nichole hugged her children quickly, then said, "I have to go help Daddy. I want you to run out that back door and hide in the trees, can you do that?"

"Jia is going to come with us. She's pregnant."

Nichole looked to the Asian woman. She said, "You're MSS?"

She shook her head. "Just a contractor."

Nichole frisked her quickly, then looked down to Mandy and Huck. She grabbed Jia by the arm, pulled her close, leaned into her ear, and whispered. "Listen, bitch. You charmed my kids, but I'd just as soon shoot you right here. You try *anything* and I will cut your fucking head off, you understand?"

The Chinese woman looked like she was about to vomit, but she nodded.

"Take them out to the trees," Nichole ordered. "I'm right behind you."

Jia took Mandy's hand, and Mandy grabbed her brother by the hand, and then all three began running. Nichole covered for them until they disappeared, and then she ran to Isaac. He had to reload, so she began firing up the corridor towards the front of the house.

His reload complete, they realized they couldn't cross to the stairway Duff had just fallen down, because the shooting from the entry hall was too heavy.

Nichole knew that—for now, at least—her husband was on his own.

DUFF PULLED A WRENCH OFF THE TABLE NEXT TO THE DOOR TO THE stairs and swung it at Tremaine, hitting his big knife. With his backhand swing Duff caught the bigger man on the chin, snapping his head back, but the Sentinel leader recovered quickly.

Both the men's rifles were somewhere on the stairs, Duff had no pistol, and Tremaine seemed to have lost his somewhere.

They separated a few feet now, and their eyes met. Tremaine said, "You fecked up everything, you piece of shit!"

"I'm about to fuck you up."

"Come on, then!"

Duff closed on Tremaine, swung his wrench but missed.

Tremaine jabbed out with the knife as the American tried to duck away from it, but the blade tip stabbed Duff in the neck, slicing open a shallow cut below his Adam's apple. A second swing of the wrench hit the man in the shoulder, and they broke away from each other again in the garage.

Duff put his hand to his throat, felt blood running down onto his chest.

He took a breath to make sure his windpipe hadn't been sliced open. He found he was able to breathe, but a sharp pain told him his injury was serious.

Tremaine closed on him with a wild smile. "You're gonna want to get that looked at, friend."

Duff said nothing.

"Where's the fecking computer? Give it to me and you can go. Take your fecking kids, I don't care."

Duff shook his head now. It hurt to speak, but he did it anyway. "I'm not leaving here till you're dead. The second you brought my kids into this, it was only going to end one way."

Tremaine smiled, wiped sweat off his forehead with the back of his arm. Holding the knife up in front of him, he said, "Fine with me, bro. Charge me with that wrench again and see how that works out for you."

Duff did so. He swung the wrench, hit the knife and knocked it to the side, then leapt forward and caught Tremaine by the torso, getting his arms under both of Tremaine's arms so that he couldn't use them to stab down.

Duff used all his might to generate force on his legs. His prosthesis pushed off on the concrete, then his right leg, and soon Tremaine was backpedaling, still ensnared in the American's strong grip.

Tremaine slammed into the side of the van parked in the middle of the garage, shattering a window with the back of his head, and Duff lurched up, knocking the South African's arm up higher and causing him to drop his knife.

Duff took the man in a wrist lock and sent him back down onto the ground. He fell with him, their body armor slamming together as Tremaine impacted the concrete and Duff impacted Tremaine.

Once on the ground Duff reached out, put his hand on the blade of the knife, and spun it around, wrapping his fingers around the hilt.

As Tremaine frantically tried to control Duff's hand, Duff positioned the knife over Tremaine's throat.

The South African held the blade back, using all his strength to prevent being stabbed, and he wrapped his hands around Duff's, fighting for control of the weapon.

Duff rose to his knees, still struggling to keep the knife over the South African's body. Tremaine kept the blade a few inches away from his own neck. He said, "You're weak, Duff."

Duff felt himself losing the battle, but as sweat and blood dripped on the man below him, he managed a little smile. "Yeah . . . but I'm smart."

He launched his body into the air. With all his body weight, he threw himself onto the knife pointed down at Tremaine's neck, and the weight and momentum forced the blade in deep, right above the man's clavicle.

Duff rolled off quickly and kept rolling as Tremaine flailed, the knife stuck in him and blood gushing wildly, spurting on the floor of the garage.

The wound was fatal, this Duff knew, so he didn't wait around to watch the man's death throes, because his own wound very well could be fatal if he didn't get it treated. Instead he climbed back to his feet on exhausted legs, then began racing back up the stairs, grabbing Tremaine's rifle as he passed it, leaving the South African to his fate.

NICHOLE AND ISAAC HAD KEPT THE ENEMY IN THE FRONT ENTRY hall, thinning their numbers, but then a group of four more mercenaries entered from the front door and began pouring fire towards the den area.

Nichole's rifle ran empty. She spun out of the way to reload as Isaac kept up the fire, and then the door across from them opened again, and she saw her husband there. He was on his feet, but blood ran from his throat. She looked at him in horror; instantly she realized she had to stop his bleeding or he'd lose consciousness in minutes, but she had no way to get to him across the fatal funnel of the corridor.

She dropped to the floor, fell out into the line of fire, and began firing fully automatic bursts to cover for Josh.

Behind and above, her husband began firing in the same direction, and he took the opportunity to cross over into the kitchen.

Soon all three of them were running through the backyard. They found Mandy and Huck with the Chinese woman in the trees, then they all made their way to where the rope still hung over the wall.

Isaac climbed over first while Nichole used a dressing from the med pouch on her body armor to wrap tightly over her husband's neck wound, only somewhat stanching the blood for now.

It took two full minutes to get all six over the wall and into the rocks and trees beyond; Jia needed a lot of help from Isaac and Nichole, but she made it over, and then they all ran for the Toyota pickup Duff had left a quarter mile away.

Nichole held her husband up, Mandy held her father's hand, and Isaac carried Huck.

Jia dropped to her knees at one point and heaved, but Nichole grabbed her by the arm and yanked her back up, and in seconds they were moving again.

No one spoke, out of fear and the adrenaline and exhaustion and pain on the adults' bodies, and bewilderment and disbelief in the minds of the kids.

Behind them, the last of the gunfire drifted off down the hill and over the city.

EPILOGUE

NINETY MINUTES AFTER LEAVING THE PROPERTY AT 1 ANKAMA Close, Josh Duffy was stretchered into the clinic of the U.S. embassy in Accra by four Marines. Nichole had redressed his neck wound on the drive from the hills, and the bleeding had almost stopped, but his face was pale and he was barely conscious, and this indicated to her that he needed a transfusion as soon as possible.

About halfway through the drive Isaac realized he'd been shot again, this time on his right thigh just above his knee, and he bled like a stuck pig, but Nichole managed to tie a compression dressing onto his leg as he drove.

Mandy and Huck were silent for the first ten minutes of the drive, and then they began talking, relaying every single thing that had happened to them as the adults listened.

Here in the clinic, the Marines put Josh down on a table, while Nichole helped Isaac into the room and lowered him onto a chair. While a doctor brought in to help the ambassador treated Duff, the same nurse who'd accompanied them into the city the night before began treating Isaac's new wound.

The Chinese woman, Chen Jia, had been put in a conference room with Bob Gorski and COS Richard Mace, and Nichole didn't think she'd be coming out of there until she'd given a complete accounting of everything she knew.

As the doctor began working on her husband, Nichole left his bedside and walked back into the atrium of the chancery to check on her kids. When she got to the café tables, she found Portia on her knees hugging Mandy and Huck. The young woman looked up and saw Nichole, and Nichole saw that Portia was crying with joy.

Nichole did not interrupt the moment, she just smiled, and when she caught Portia's eye, she mouthed the words *Thank you*, then headed back to check on Josh.

FIVE DAYS LATER, ALL FOUR DUFFYS WERE BACK IN THEIR APART-ment at Iris Gardens, and Mandy stepped out of the little kitchen with a tray of cupcakes that she had personally decorated.

Huck snagged the first one right at the door to the kitchen, much to his sister's disapproval, but she made it into the living room with the rest, and she took them over to the Ghanaian couple, their guests.

Abina Opoku shifted her baby from her left hip to her right so she could take a cupcake from the little girl, and then Isaac picked one as well, took a bite, and pronounced it the best thing he'd ever tasted in his life, to Mandy's pleasure.

Isaac had a cane near his chair, a temporary accoutrement and a reminder of all he'd been through. Across from him, however, Duff's injury was more readily apparent.

A thick white bandage was wrapped around his throat like a turtleneck. He looked ridiculous, but everyone had declared it a small price to pay for walking away from a knife fight with his life.

Nichole poured more coffee for both of the Opokus, and then more for herself, and just as she began to sit down, a knock at the door came.

She left, then returned with Bob Gorski.

The older man wore an open-collar white dress shirt, black slacks, and a dusty blue sport coat, and he moved into the living room with an apology. "Sorry to intrude, I just thought I should drop in and tell you the latest." He saw Isaac, walked over, and shook his hand. "America owes you a debt of gratitude, sir."

"Thank you."

He was introduced to Abina and Kofi, and then Duff had him sit down.

Mandy brought him a cupcake, and he took it with a smile.

After Mandy and Huck wandered out of the room, Gorski said, "Kang Shikun was arrested at the border with Togo last night."

Duff put his hand on his throat to talk; putting some pressure on the wound kept it from hurting as much when he spoke. "I thought the border with Togo didn't exist," he said, parroting something he'd said to Gorski the first time they met.

"Yeah, that's what *Kang* thought, too. John and Travis were able to follow him with the drones the day of the battle in the hills, at least long enough for us to get a team of agents on his ass. For the past three days we've tracked his movements to the east, and we had BNI officers at the border there to pick him up when he tried to cross.

"We have Chen Jia at the embassy still; she's been very helpful explaining everything she knew about the operation here. We're going to give her a visa to come to the U.S. to have her baby there." He looked to Nichole. "She'll never go back to China; they will hold her responsible for everything that's happened after the failed coup."

Duff cocked his head. "What's happened?"

"Well, President Amanor is still in power, and General Kwame Boatang is in the stockade. From what we've pieced together from Ms. Chen and other physical evidence left at the home in the hills, the Chinese set up the rebel coup d'état, as well as an extremist terror attack, as a ploy for the leader of Central Command to come down to the capital and take over the streets. Boatang had promised the Chinese they'd kick out the West and give them a couple of diamond mines in the process."

"Is Kang talking?" Isaac asked, and Gorski just shook his head.

"He claims he's a political prisoner, unjustly detained." The man shrugged. "All the usual claptrap from a senior intelligence officer."

Gorski said, "The tablet computer was able to show us all the names of all the Sentinel operatives; looks like about twenty-one of them died over the course of the operation, but that means there's another fifty out there, mostly Russian. We've got their names; they'll turn up down the road."

Mandy and Huck came back into the room; both of them were eating cupcakes, and they sat on the couch with their mom and dad.

Nichole hugged them both, then turned her attention to Isaac. "I know I've said it already, but I want to thank you again, not for what you did for the U.S., for the ambassador, but what you did for my family." She clutched Huck tight now while he played with his toy truck on the floor in front of her. She said, "I can *never* repay you."

Isaac smiled. "I did it for Duff . . . because Duff would have done it for me."

Nichole looked to her husband. He couldn't really turn his head in her direction without shifting his hips, so he just moved his eyes to hers, and they smiled at each other.

"You're right," Nichole said. "He would have."

Duff shifted back to Gorski now. "Did you hear we're being recalled?"

Gorski nodded. "I did. It sucks, but it's the right move."

"I know it is," Duff said. "But we really don't want to leave Ghana."

"Why would you?" Gorski asked. "It's the most stable nation in West Africa."

Everyone laughed, the Opokus included. Isaac said, "It was . . . it will be again. Hopefully long before Kofi here grows up."

Gorski looked at Isaac. "With less international meddling and more good people like you, I'd bet on this nation to turn out just fine."

Mandy said, "I don't want to leave, either."

Nichole wrapped her arms around her daughter now. "They will send us someplace nice, I promise."

Duff said, "They're sending us back to Washington. Not so nice, but at least it's familiar."

"Just until you're one hundred percent," Nichole said. "Then . . . who knows?"

Gorski said, "That's the life."

"What about you, Bob?" Duff asked. "You caught Kang. What will you do now?"

He shrugged, as if he'd never asked himself this question. "I don't know. Is it too late for me to pick up golf?"

Duff laughed. "No . . . but I don't see it."

"Me either." He shrugged. "I'll stick around Africa awhile. This is a job where you never actually finish your work, you just move on to the next problem. There are other Kangs out there. Other Tremaines. Other Boatangs. Other Addos."

Duff said, "Well, one thing's for sure. There's only one Gorski."

THE CONVERSATION WENT ON A WHILE LONGER, AND THEN NICHOLE tried her hand at grilling smash burgers for everyone out in the courtyard while Duff sat convalescing at the picnic table, talking to Isaac, Abina, and Bob, while Mandy and Huck played with Kofi.

It was a good day, Duff told himself as he looked at his beautiful wife at the grill. He only hoped his dreams would start chronicling the good days and not the bad.

He hadn't had a nightmare in the past three nights, and he wondered if that meant something other than the fact that he'd been on heavy painkillers.

Nichole wiped sweat from her brow and took a sip of wine from a plastic cup, then caught her husband watching her. She stepped over to him with the tongs and the wine in her hands, and she sat in his lap and kissed him.

"How are you feeling, sergeant?"

"Never better, captain."

"That's what I like to hear, soldier," she said, and they kissed again.

ACKNOWLEDGMENTS

I would like to thank Josh Hood (JoshuaHoodBooks), Ryan Geho, Chuck Diamond, Ethan Abrams, Michael Hagen, Allison Greaney, Trey and Kristin Greaney, Jon Griffin, Jon Harvey, Mike Cowan, Nichole Deaner, Christopher Gunning, and Isaac Kwabena.

I'd also like to thank Ambassador Virginia Palmer and everyone at the United States embassy in Accra, Ghana.

Much gratitude goes to my literary agent, Scott Miller of Trident Media Group, and my film agent, Jon Casir of CAA. As always, a special thanks to my editor, Tom Colgan, and all the incredible staff at Berkley, including Carly James, Jin Yu, Loren Jaggers, Bridget O'Toole, Elise Tecco, Tina Joelle, Jeanne-Marie Hudson, Craig Burke, Christine Ball, Claire Zion, and Ivan Held.

Humble appreciation goes to my amazing copyeditors and proofreaders, as well as the incredible art department at Penguin Random House, and all the editors and staff who publish the foreign editions of my books.